THE EMPEROR OF ICE-CREAM

THE EMPEROR OF ICE-CREAM

Dan Gunn

Seagull
BOOKS

LONDON NEW YORK CALCUTTA

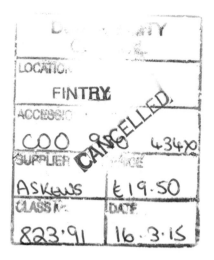
Seagull Books, 2014

© Dan Gunn, 2014

ISBN 978 0 8574 2 223 1

British Library Cataloguing-in-Publication Data
A catalogue record for this book is available from the British Library

Typeset by Seagull Books, Calcutta, India
Printed and bound by Maple Press, York, Pennsylvania, USA

For Kristina

PROLOGUE

Churchill's exclamation—'Collar the lot!'—was beetling round my head as I parked myself creakily at a table in my preferred of the recently sprouted Italian cafés on Broughton Street that specialize in serving what I believe are now called the *gay crowd*. I was counting the ironies. Of the books I was aware I would need, I had brought only one, and I laid it, yellowing and tattered, carefully on the table before me. Just two days previously, I had returned from Emilio's memorial service at which I had made a spectacle of myself reciting the most explicit of his poems about the sinking of *The Arandora Star*.

The young sociologist François Lafitte, who describes himself on his inside-front cover as *a young man of no importance who tries to be a good European*, must have worked day and night to compile within three short months his withering condemnation of government policy that became the Penguin Special, published in September 1940, entitled *The Internment of Enemy Aliens*. The grainy photograph above the brief biography of the author reveals him looking like an apprentice Orwell. It was years since I had taken my copy—one of fifty thousand that sold in the month of its publication—from its shelf; had forgotten that Lafitte was *the adopted son of the late Dr Havelock Ellis*. The explanation for his devotion to his subject is compelling, though not (I could not help remarking to myself) as compelling as my own: *His interest in the Government's treatment of refugees derives partly from the fact that a number of his own refugee friends who had struggled illegally against tyranny in Germany and Austria and had suffered at the hands of the Gestapo, were later locked up in France and Britain as 'enemy aliens'*.

The froth on my cappuccino subsided as I read again the statement printed opposite the photograph of the youthful Lafitte, under the book's title and above the dancing penguin, pronounced as it was

in the House of Commons on 22 August 1940, by one Major Caza-
let: *No ordinary excuse, such as that there is a war on and that officials are
overworked, is sufficient to explain what has happened. Horrible tragedies,
unnecessary and undeserved, lie at the door of somebody.* Those three words,
unnecessary and undeserved, had me chewing my inner lip again, though
I had sworn to myself after my performance at Emilio's memorial to
be more measured and circumspect. *Frankly*, Major Cazalet continues
in François Lafitte's epigraph, *I shall not feel happy, either as an Englishman or as a supporter of this Government, until this bespattered page of our
history has been cleaned up and rewritten.* Now, as never before, the
Major's words felt like a challenge. I tried unsuccessfully to ignore
what I had scrawled indignantly in pencil a long time ago, at the foot
of the page, copied from a footnote in Churchill's *Britain at War*: *Now
in the full light of the after-time it is easy to see where we were ignorant or
too much alarmed, where we were careless or clumsy.*

My coffee went cold, the rain began to beat on the café windows.
I thought again of the moment when I was seated alongside Emilio in
the Royal Box at the Albert Hall: a little more than one year ago, just
weeks before he learnt of his cancer (the seats offered to us because,
by then a famous poet and professor, he was the author of the libretto).
'I've something important to tell you, Lucia,' said my brother, over
the noise of the orchestra tuning up for rehearsal of *The Arandora Star*
Commemorative Concert. 'I want you to write about it.'

I shook my head, not that it budged the awful grey helmet the
hairdresser had clamped to my scalp that morning. I said, 'You're the
writer of the family, Emilio. I've been at best a lowly secretary, good
for making reports. Giulio was always the brainy one, you were the
wordsmith, and Dario—Dario was the disaster.'

The requiem's bearded Estonian composer, seated to my left in the
Royal Box, threw me a sympathetic glance. The orchestra went silent.

'This will be Giulio's story,' whispered Emilio. 'And it will be
our story. To which my poems, my pages about the ship, and this
libretto also, are nothing but a prelude.' He smiled knowingly at me.
'So go on, make your report!'

With his baton, the conductor tapped the lectern.

It was an evening of the sort that blesses only northern cities: winter had abruptly lifted, windows were thrown open, housewives were singing and exchanging the knowing nods of survivors. Even the horses pulling their carts up Broughton Street were snuffling and twitching their tails more like thoroughbreds than Clydesdales. Emilio tried not to limp as he approached the hopscotch patch. 'All wanted indoors,' he announced, 'for a family *chiacchierata*.' The kitchen window was closed in our top-floor tenement flat, and Papà had ceded his leather armchair—he sat in it so much that it had taken his shape—to Mamma, which was unusual.

'We're all here, then,' he started, needlessly counting the four of us. 'Uno, due, tre, quattro.'

'Cinque, sei,' added Dario, with all the scorn of his sixteen years. He'd left school already but had turned up his nose at the one job he'd been offered. He hung around Calton Hill with his pals, smoking cigarettes and bantering with girls.

'You're going to have to be brave,' Papà said, before he subsided into silence, his own bravery momentarily mislaid. 'Mamma, will you explain?' Mamma's hair was shining in the evening light as she shook her head. I wondered again why I had failed to inherit it. All the customers at McVitie's Tearoom, where she managed the till, would admire it, men and women alike. 'This summer your Mamma will be going home. Her sister in Chicago, Zia Sabrina, has sent the money, enough for three.'

'Be glad to go,' said Dario. 'Back to the homeland. Why not us three boys—I can look after the other two.'

'This may be your mother's last visit,' Papà said, his voice faltering. 'Because . . .'

'Because I'm not well,' Mamma explained. 'Which is why you must obey your Papà and grow up quickly and go regularly to confession and be good to one another and look after little Lucia.'

Emilio fiddled with his calliper while Giulio rocked back and forth on his feet. 'It can't be anything too serious,' he said.

'I want you to be prepared, just in case.'

'And what about Jesus?' Coming from Giulio, this was less a question than a barb; he had told us of his *doubts*. 'What about the Archbishop?'

'The Lord giveth and the Lord taketh away.'

'It has to be the oldest then, *evidentemente*.' For Dario, it was decided.

'I don't see why,' said Emilio. 'You were born in Italy, so at least you've seen it.'

'I was two months old when we left, you dunce.'

'It's not our fault you have a poor memory.'

'We thought,' said Papà, 'you would draw straws.'

'Why not ask us first?' Giulio suggested. 'Maybe we don't all specially want to go to Italy.'

Before the question could be put, four arms reached rigid into the air; then eight, when Dario boosted his claim by raising both. From behind the mantelpiece clock, Mamma removed three wax tapers used for lighting the fire—two long, one short. 'I only see two,' said Giulio.

'This is a chance for you boys. Lucia's still wee and will have her day later.'

'Still a baby,' echoed Dario. 'And her birth a mistake in the first place, straggling along after us three boys.' Normally, when he would say this, Mamma would go after him with her biggest wooden spoon. Not tonight, however.

'I don't think that's fair. I don't think I want to play.'

'That's decided then, me and Emilio. *Perfetto!*'

'Are you sure, Giulio? Your sister will survive without you for a month. You'll be able to write her letters, think of that.'

'It doesn't seem fair.' Everything wrong with Mamma was crammed into Giulio's judgement.

'Go on, Giulio,' I urged him. 'Don't miss your chance.' It felt both disastrous and beautiful to be saying it.

Giulio closed his eyes, raised his palm resignedly.

It was less at school that I learnt to read and write than in copying my brother. Mamma was ever determined we hold our own in language, 'speak proper', unlike Nonno with his four or five essential words, unlike Papà his son who'd be silent whenever he could. With her dictionaries and directives, Mamma ensured that words mattered to all four of us. Dario was the talker, even as a teenager. Emilio liked to rhyme and joke, through his interest in poetry, then his own first ventures in verse. I did well enough at school, even came top of my class, until Mr Blister (as we nicknamed our pockmarked master Mr Lister) went so far as to say—and this of a Catholic girl too—that I 'showed promise'. But all I was ever doing was to imitate what I thought my brother might have said. For Giulio, as long as I could remember, not only read to me, he *spoke* to me—spoke to *me*

And now not only did he speak to me, he *wrote to me too*:

Dover, 2 June 1920

Carissima Lucia mia,

The train to London was noisy and dirty and so busy that Dario and me had to stand all the way from Newcastle. He wanted to visit Soho with its famous Italian restaurants and Mamma wanted to see Westminster Abbey. But we couldn't afford to go anywhere. Now the ship to France from where I'll write again soon.

Baci and love,

Your Giulio

'It was best, the way it worked out,' Papà concluded as he watched me read. 'That the two eldest boys should go.'

I was almost ready to agree, for here I'd received a picture post-card, addressed to me—my first. The neighbours were amazed, at the thought of such a journey. Already we were the lucky ones on our stairway, with a bedroom for the parents and another for the boys (with me in the recess), and rumour was that Mamma descended from nobility (I sometimes liked to believe it myself, though her father had been the most minor Maclodio gentry). Now, with the ten-year-old receiving mail from abroad, even the Scots folk on our close would nod respectfully.

Paris, 3 June 1920

Cara,

Everywhere from the train the effects of the War with the land grey and pitted and stations still in ruins. When I speak Italian they understand a little. Mamma uses rouge but still looks tired and her cough keeps us awake. Dario disappeared to stand outside a place called Folies Bergère—dancing girls! I'd have liked to go to Versailles where the treaty was signed, but no time for that.

We all miss you, especially your brother
Giulio

In the local haberdashery, with a farthing Auntie Lena from across the landing gave me for the purpose, I purchased a metre of pink silk ribbon with which to gather my letters. I read them so often that soon the ribbon was grubby, until I washed and ironed it myself.

Napoli, 5 June

Cara Lucia,

It's even hotter here than you can imagine, though it's beside the sea like Edinburgh. Vesuvius makes Arthur's Seat look like a dwarf! We stay with Auntie Teresa. She lives in a flat even smaller than the smallest on our close, and now there's 8 of us in it. Children everywhere very sad to see with protruding tummies and yellow eyes; the smell in the air very strong of you-know-what.

I'm writing this letter on a table on the street where we also eat our pasta. Cousin Federico is amazed as he's two years older than me but can barely sign his own name. A neighbour asked me to write a letter to his landlord but Auntie T scuttled out and said he'd have to pay—a pity as I'd have done it for free.

The War seems more distant here but people are still angry and say Italy has been betrayed, which I don't really understand . . . yet.

Tomatoes! Lemons! So many shapes of pasta! But you know what I'm after . . .

Love from your brother

Giulio

I had to show the stamps and read out passages, not just to Papà and Emilio but to the other children on the stairway.

Amalfi, 6 June

Dearest Child,

This picture post-card shows the cathedral where rest the bones of our beloved Sant' Andrea whose shoulder blade lies in St Mary's. It gladdens my heart to touch his relics. I hope you are being kind to Papà. Your loving Mamma

Feels like I never saw colours before—all so bright and gay! A presto, your Giulio

Ragazze bellissime, cheap ciggies, si mangia benissimo, caffè stra ordinario, sole sole sole. Baci, Dario

Giulio had often told me about the creature, the one pal of Dario's he'd warned me to avoid. I don't know how he knew, but he knew, and sometimes when I was practising with the catapult that my grandpa—my Nonno—had given me before he left for Italy months before, he would mutter his name.

'See you,' said McEwen, whose approach I hadn't seen. 'Lucy on the wall?'

I thrust my letters back into my satchel. 'The name's Lucia.' I knew I shouldn't answer him but get up from the wall on which I was seated and beat a retreat. 'And I bet you can't even say it right.' (Scottish folk spoke my name with a *c* as in *Lucy*.)

'What you doin there? You're tae young for love letters.' As he came closer, squatting right in front of me just two yards away, I slipped my catapult out of my satchel. 'What ye got there? Bet you couldn't hit that tabby on the branch over there.'

I sensed it was a trap, walked straight into it. 'I can think of things I'd rather hit.'

Sometimes on Fridays, when Mamma was tired from working the McVities till, we'd be given a penny each and sent down to buy chips, ordered to keep away from 'that disgusting vinegar' the boys so loved. Ewan McEwen would be helping his father with the frying, carrying that look of under-nourishment that came from some hunger unassuaged by quantities of batter or black pudding: thin, drawn lips tending to blue even in summer, ginger hair, runtish growth, close-together eyes that never stopped roving.

'Go on, I dare you.'

The trap was round my ankles, so why not to the knees. I knew if I looked down, a missile would present itself, as it always did. The world would turn flat as I loaded and took aim, then rediscover depth just as I released. And here on the wall was a shard of brick, right enough; I loaded it into the soft leather pad.

'You dinna dare, cos you're a lassie.'

'Lassies can do naughty things too, you know.'

'Nae chance you'd dare.'

I clenched the missile between finger and thumb, pulled on the pad so the rubber stretched. I still knew I would not let go, only wanted him to disappear and let me get back to my letters. But he wasn't looking at my aim, rather straight up my skirt. 'You ken your brother Giulio what's gone to Italy?'

I was right, he wouldn't have come near me but for Giulio's absence. I refused to close my legs just for him, even if I did wish I'd put on pants in the morning like Mamma said I always should even in summer.

'Well, he's down our chippy full of daft ideas about custard pies and frozen sweeties. You think that's normal for a boy his age?' I pulled the band back another inch, to full. 'So next time you see him you can tell him from me that he can take his grand ideas and shove them you ken where.'

'I'm only ten,' I breathed. 'I'm not supposed to know where's where.'

'I'll show you then.'

And that's when I released it.

I expected his father to be round in the evening with complaints and the doctor's bill for sewing up his son's forehead. I grew even more concerned when nothing happened: no angry parent, no minister or priest, no policeman to lead me away to gaol. If he had failed to clipe, it meant I'd slid further into his trap—up to the waist.

The words roared round my head: 'I could see yer fanny! I could see yer fanny!' through the blood streaming down his face. 'And I'll see more than that before I'm finished wi you bunch of fuckin wops!'

Maclodio, 8 June

Dear Lucia,

A whole day to reach Maclodio, first by train then by cart and finally on foot. Not what I expected home to be. But until I can judge better let me tell you about the big event in Naples.

Mamma dragged me to San Domenico Church where there's a giant painting of a Christ about to be whipped, stripped to the waist, very beautiful and upsetting. Then I left her so as to drift down via Roma which is like the city's Princes Street only filled with poor folk and animals, fishes like I've never seen—more like sea monsters. It was noisy and hot as if Vesuvius was breathing on us.

Then I saw it! The name, La Scimmia, means The Monkey. Even from a distance I could feel the cool air. Flavours I've only read of in story-books! Stracciatella creamy with little flakes of dark chocolate. Walnut with lumps like tiny shrunken brains. Hazelnut so very smooth. Peach which as you remember is a fruit with a furry skin. Cinnamon ice which is dark dark brown. Lemon granita which looks like slush. Amarena which is a sort of cherry. Pistachio that kind of nut that makes an amazing bright green colour . . .

I was smiling like a simpleton. Then I said I was from Scotland and the manager said that since I'd come so far I could have a tub of any two flavours of my choice. (They use little waxed boxes like at home, though all else is different.) I chose a scoop of green Pistachio and one of Cinnamon. All I could think to say was 'Questa è la vita!' The other customers found this odd but clapped and cheered the 'ragazzo scozzese'.

More soon and meantime lots of love from
Your Giulio

The handwriting was strong and deliberate with only occasional crossings-out. I longed to reply, to confide in him about the catapult and how his letters were the remedy for my nightmares. At school I had my pals, but I couldn't share this with them; Emilio wouldn't listen, busy pretending he didn't mind that his bad leg meant he was for ever being left behind. By the time a letter reached Giulio, he'd be home: I concentrated on that certainty in the dead of night.

Maclodio, 12 June

Cara,

I've not written for days as there is not much to tell. Maclodio is a tiny hilltop village not far from a larger one called Picinisco, and it looks as if it wants to slide off its hill. Stray dogs and goats pass by houses as tiny as they are dark and smelly. Given there are no proper toilets, it's fortunate there is the hill as most runs down to the swamp below. Lots of giant mosquitoes and scorpions, so I'm up scratching half the night. Scotland is a mystery to folks here. Sheep and family and sheep are what everyone talks about. On what they call the piazza, just an empty space between church and town hall, we chatted to a man who fought at Caporetto. He couldn't remember if he'd fought the Germans or the Austrians or the French.

We went up to visit Nonno in his cave and at first it almost seemed as if he had forgotten how to speak, as if he was turning into a tree. He talked about the stars and asked for news of you.

I'll write again when I'm happier.

Love, your Giulio

He was fourteen years old, but to me he was ageless, his style irreproachable. Mr Blister, between declensions, spoke of Cicero and Caesar. To me they might have been Giulio in peplum.

Maclodio, 17 June

Cara,

The photographs we've seen are flattering! I barely recognized a single one of Mamma's sisters! Zia Lalla is fat and hairy. Zia Antonella wept the whole time while she crossed herself and prodded Mamma with her crucifix. Zia Flavia is younger and prettier and we could see that Dario agreed, so we shortened our visit. Despite what Nonno said, we also visited his rival's son Roberto (Papà's half-brother, if I've got that right) whose wife Zia Paola is less than half his age and also beautiful. She wanted me to sit on her lap!

Love from your

Giulio

Though his figurines were ornate and he could blacken the range in an hour, Papà had never mastered the art of boiling macaroni. Life at home was dull, and the endless fish suppers were giving me spots. Emilio had to fetch them as I refused to enter the McEwen shop, and this meant a drenching of salt and vinegar—'Because they're for free.'

'So is the rain,' I'd say, 'but you don't stand under it.'

The next and final letter arrived on the same day as its author, exhausted, at Waverley Station—Mamma looking like a ghost. When he saw me clutching it, he put his forefinger to his lips.

Paris, 25 June

Dear Little Lucia,

I'm almost sure Dario managed a private meeting with Zia Paola whom he ended up preferring even to Zia Flavia. At least she's not a blood relation!

Everyone was in tears and me too when Mamma had to say good-bye. She wanted us to sit still in Naples Station but when she went for coffee I snuck off to you know where. I was so excited that I told the manager my ambition. He let me try some sorbetti whose tang I still feel on my tongue.

Mamma was furious, which made Dario happy. Brothers!

A presto, cara, with love from

your very own Giulio

Mamma's tomb, when it was built, looked nothing like as grand as the Italian ones Giulio had described for me. A photograph from before the illness became an eternal enamel cameo staring out reproachfully, reminding her children to change the flowers; until Dario found some silk ones—pinched, probably—which he said would do the job.

Dario didn't change much as he left his teenage years behind: still big-boned and sturdy, his natural athleticism as yet unimpaired by cigarettes and booze. He rarely rushed, yet arrived before the crowd; not exactly elegant, but his every gesture, even the discourteous ones with which he plagued me worse than ever now Mamma and her wooden spoon were gone, contained something of the inevitable, some unpremeditated thoroughness—dark, primitive, yet in step with the times. I rarely saw him read, yet he loved to quote from big-sounding authorities. Compared with him, Emilio became a fully fledged angel. No one could resist running a hand through his incongruously fair curls, and though he lost his dimples, his face retained its heart shape. He cracked jokes about how poor we were now Mamma was gone, complained about potatoes every night and the undeviating porridge made with water; he said he studied hard, but never came top of his class. While Giulio, he shone so bright at school that the masters were sure he was bound for the varsity, despite the time he spent on his paper round. He didn't seem interested in the things that absorbed his peers, but I told myself that this was because he was Italian . . . because he was grieving . . . because he was so brainy . . . most of all because he was my brother.

I may have been the lucky one, always welcome at McVities where the waitresses were all 'aunties', who'd smuggle me into the kitchen where they'd feed me toasted tea-cakes with butter, and where Auntie Rebecca the Lithuanian (she replaced Mamma at the till, and she looked like the Madonna) stocked shortbread just for me; and where, just as we were preparing for the second anniversary of Mamma's death, Auntie Sandy (a great one for the boys, said the others) showed me what to do when I started to bleed. 'Your Ma would have telt you,' she said in the toilet stall. 'But here, hen, let me get you what you'll be needing.'

Perhaps it was the confidence gained by Auntie Sandy's calling me 'a woman now' (or rather 'a woman now, hen') that made me, on that very day, deploy my secret weapon. McVities was on Hanover Street, and on the way home from it I stopped off at St Mary's for confession, where Padre Clemente the Sicilian was panting as ever. I didn't know if my first period was something to confess or not, so I fed him the usual run of petty insubordinations and how hard I was finding it to concentrate on my grief. I was almost home when Dario emerged from a nearby close, drink on his breath.

'A thousand rats' tails your hair looks like, after they've dragged themselves from the sewer.' I knew I wasn't beautiful, that my hair didn't shine like Mamma's, but I refused to start sobbing—which only provoked him further. 'I don't know how Mamma, with her *bei capelli*, could have spawned a *bambina* with such lank lengths of twine. Unless you're not really Mamma's at all and the midwife swapped you for a foundling nobody else wanted.'

'Zia Paola.'

He jerked his chin up in question.

'Zia Paola,' I repeated, following Giulio's instruction to the letter.

He lifted his hand instinctively, but I was already out of range. 'What do you ken about Zia Paola?'

I was uncertain what the word meant, and even Giulio was unsure if it applied to a step-nephew with a step-aunt-by-marriage. 'Incest, then?'

The face he pulled made it clear he was no wiser than us. But my triumph was short-lasting. 'I'll kill that bastard Giulio when I lay my hands on him!'

'It wasn't him who told me.' He'd be upstairs waiting for the rest of us, so the melancholy rites could begin.

'Who was it then?'

This was a tight spot. Giulio was nothing like Dario's size, and Dario would batter him if he knew he'd been telling tales. We were half-way up the stairs already. 'Zia Lalla,' I tried, little knowing if this name would serve.

'How's that? Zia Lalla? She wrote to *you*?'

This was too improbable as I had never met her, only dusted her photograph. 'She wrote to Papà, and I secretly read the letter.'

'So Papà knows and all?'

I was so amazed by the success of my lie that I wondered if I should drop the idea of becoming a nun and try rather for a spy.

'You'd better not mention this again,' he said, 'I'm warning you.'

In our flat at the head of the stairs, Auntie Lena from across the landing was seated by the kitchen fire. Papà, all in black, was seated beside her, heedlessly eating the scones she had baked for us. Emilio was lying on the boys' big bed trying to suppress his giggles at whatever it was he was reading. No one knew what we were supposed to do, Papà least of all who complained of the lack of a piazza where people could mourn in public. 'It's not like Giulio to be late,' he remarked, as if, when all were assembled, Mamma might miraculously reappear, a genie from the family lamp.

Until, finally, here he was, bearing something to disturb the ceremonial imagining of grief. 'Have yous all heard the news?'

No one but me heard the question, let alone the news. Emilio was avoiding Dario's rant about how Jimmy Something should never have been replaced by Ronnie Something-Else as Hibernian centre-forward. Auntie Lena was brushing crumbs from the kitchen floor, while Papà attempted to convince her that Mamma was smiling in

Heaven (papist Heaven, that is, which she presumed to be closer to the fires of Hell).

'Did you see the news?' He was clutching the newspaper as if its headline announced Mamma's beatification.

'Ronnie may work a little magic in mid-field but up front you've got to turn on a sixpence, and with his two left feet . . .'

'The news!'

Papà pointed to a chair by the fire. 'We can't all see it at once, Giulio. Read it out to us, if you must.'

'Yeh,' Dario sneered, 'let the wee swot read to us!'

'The Italian Ice-Cream Association is taking over the Houses of Parliament.' Emilio found himself hilarious.

Seated, Giulio shook his *Scotsman* importantly. 'Pipe down. The column's headed *Triumphant March on Rome*.'

'The colossal Stone of Scone.' Rhyme and alliteration had become Emilio's chief resource when other quips failed him.

'*Yesterday, accompanied by some two thousand of his most loyal supporters, the Italian sometime revolutionary Mr Benito Mussolini marched upon the capital to claim power. The move comes at the conclusion of crippling strikes, governmental inertia and months of national unrest.*'

Dario was agog; his hands turned white, so tightly were they clutching the kitchen table. With that instinct for what would serve him, he sensed something momentous walking into the room—and not Mamma's sacred spirit. It was surely the first time he'd heard the name *Mussolini*, but it reached him with a special sound, or a special scent more like, the kind he sought in pubs, in cigarettes, or in women's unkempt armpits in the close after dark.

'Are you sure this is the moment?' Papà asked. 'It's your Mamma, not the politics, we're thinking of this evening—of all evenings.'

'Aw, spare us, will you! We're no living in a bloody mausoleum. Go on, Giulio!'

'You should no be talking to your father like that.' Auntie Lena waved her broom.

'*They carried,* it says, *only light arms and the bundles of sticks, or fasces, from which they derive their name.* Then in brackets it explains, *their symbol derives from the rods with an axe which Roman magistrates carried to display authority.*'

Only a well-aimed kick from Dario put a stop to Emilio's foraging around the hearth for twigs.

'*It is expected that King Victor Emmanuel III will name Mussolini as his country's Head of State.*'

Politics was boys' stuff, and as of today I was a woman, determined to hit back. 'I wonder what our *zias* will make of that? Especially Zia Paola . . .?'

Dario gave me a furious stare and attempted a dig with his elbow. Papà shook his head. 'What you havering about, Lucia? Rome's even more obscure to them in Maclodio than it is to us here. Why should they care?'

Dario remarked, 'It might bring down the price of your local obsession, the sheep and billy-goat gruff.'

'That only shows you've not grasped Mussolini's economics.' The name might be new to the rest of us, but not, apparently, to Giulio. 'He takes a real interest in the peasants, comes from peasant stock himself. Says regeneration has to start with the land, the force drawn from nature.'

'I know that,' Dario drawled. 'Everyone knows that.'

'Read on then if you must, son, get it over with.'

'I'll be leaving,' said Auntie Lena, continuing to sweep.

'*The Roman populace cheered, bunting festooned the boulevards. This great country, ally in the recent War, which suffered at Caporetto and had meagre pickings at Versailles, is once again a nation with a worthy leader.*' Giulio lowered his *Scotsman.*

'And you know this Mussolini?' Papà asked.

'Fettucini?'

Dario struck again with his foot, catching Emilio on his bad leg. Normally, Giulio would have comforted his brother who retreated, whining, to the corner. Not tonight. 'I've read about him of course.

Big war hero, socialist, now turned against them. Loyal friend of D'Annunzio. Even Lucia's heard of D'Annunzio.'

I shook my head as I tried not to picture the poet's face with those extravagant Ottoman whiskers. The proper names were buzzing round the room like flies, out of season in late October. Mamma was buried here in cold Scottish soil; thought of her inspired me. 'Mamma never talked of them.'

'That's normal. When D'Annunzio captured Fiume, Mamma was too ill to realize the importance. Our greatest living poet, on horseback, at the head of a trusty band of followers, flying the flag over one of our own territories.'

'You'll no be wanting any more scones, then?' Still Auntie Lena hesitated to leave. It had started to rain, maybe even sleet. The door finally closed behind her, and no one had thanked her.

'I don't see why you're suddenly so patriotic,' said Papà, 'just because of some jumped-up Garibaldi.'

'*Remember, readers, how new is this nation of Italy, forged only sixty years ago and bedevilled by one weak government after another. Then you will understand why flowers were cascading as the country's new leader, in a procession which lasted six hours, made his way through the streets on his charger.*'

At the word *charger*, Dario twitched. 'Does it say what he was wearing?'

Papà had somehow cranked himself out of his armchair. Through the open door to his bedroom, he could be seen by the bed clutching Mamma's wedding dress.

'*The festa in the streets lasted longer than that. Only time will tell if this blacksmith's son from the town of Predappio in the Romagna province—*'

'I thought you said he was a peasant,' sniped Dario.

'Peasants work the soil,' snarled Emilio. 'Blacksmiths work in smithies using anvils.' He surprised with his vocabulary. 'And we're neither, children of an exiled figurine-maker.'

'The point,' said Giulio, 'is that he's one of us, not a nob. And if things were not so bad back home, if folks were not so poor, then they wouldn't have gone into exile like Nonno did, would they. That's what politics is about.'

'So politics,' I tried, 'is what makes you go from being poor at home to poor abroad?'

'He's saying,' added Dario, who for once was agreeing with Giulio, 'that we could be sitting *al sole* surrounded by our fields and olive trees and servants, if they didn't all belong to some overfed landowner who lives in a *palazzo* in Rome . . . not freezing our balls off in this miserable country.'

'And that way,' I said, 'we could see Zia Paola every day.' I knew he would pounce but did not retreat to Papà's room; let him nip my arms till they bruised.

'*Mussolini's stern black shirt, his uniform and his jackboots, purport a more martial future—*'

'I told you!' Dario exclaimed, interrupting the Chinese burn he was applying to my wrist. 'Something stylish. *Camicia nera* and riding boots.'

'Will you let me finish! *But if there is any indication in the war wounds which the leader displayed on his march, then soon this country will turn from the scars of recent times towards a pacific and prosperous future.*'

I had witnessed family squabbles before, but none quite like this, where old alliances were redundant, what the builders of Babel must have felt when the curse of tongues fell upon them. And Mamma ever more frozen in her grave.

'What made you stop?' I sobbed, when Dario finally let go of me. 'I was just starting to enjoy it.'

4

Now there had been a day the previous summer when, by some meteorological freak, the temperature had risen to above eighty degrees, and Papà had feared he might be soldered to his armchair if he sat any longer with the window shut against the soot. He had organized—yes, *organized*—a first-ever family Sunday outing, to North Berwick. We caught the train together from Waverley Station and one hour later we were on the beach. Dario paced the sand in his singlet showing off his muscles, turning swarthier by the minute. I removed my Sunday frock and went paddling in my knickers (I'd made a point of wearing knickers ever since McEwen had discovered me without); no one looked askance at my skinny legs, amid the weans and withered grannies, all stripped to the smalls (but for the lucky ones in trunks who'd been taught how to swim). Even Dario remarked that with a bit more sun my hair might bleach to almost blonde. The sun could do that apparently: make you look, if not beautiful, then healthy and at least presentable. And it was free!

'Come away in, Emilio!' I called from the shallows. But he refused to budge from the sandstone dyke at the rear of the beach, his brace off, a kitchen towel draped over the offending leg.

'See over there,' said Giulio, who had rolled up his trousers. 'That's Treasure Island, the model for Robert Louis.' I tried to picture Ben Gunn's unkempt head, Long John Silver hopping across the rocks. When I turned back, Giulio was making towards an ice-cream trolley on the end of the pier.

When I dipped my finger in the carton he bought for me, and raised it to my mouth, then for the very first time I understood what *ice-cream* could mean, on a *scorcher of a day* . . .

'I'm quitting school, Papà,' Giulio soon announced, 'not going to varsity.'

'No,' Papà had said with equal confidence, from his work-bench, 'that can't be right. Mamma always said that Giulio would become a lawyer or a judge, first of our Italian community to wear the wig. Or a doctor, maybe a surgeon, and find some technique to fix Emilio's leg.'

'There'll be other ways to raise our reputation in the city. Just you wait. I've no wish to spend my days being treated like a pauper by some public school toffs who've never had to work for it. I want to bring pleasure into people's lives.'

Papà was putting the final touches to Melchior, lining up his Marys and Josephs, his stables and asses, for what he always hoped would be a Christmas rush. He shook his head incredulously.

'You'll see, Papà, within a few months. Just be glad we've not got years more of me studying, earning next to nothing. I've been offered an apprenticeship with Signor Cavazzoni who's got the shop down in Stockbridge.' He turned to me. 'And you'll no be sorry, will you Lucia, especially when the weather turns hot?'

Giulio had often taken me down to Signor Cavazzoni's ice-cream parlour, through horizontal rain that penetrated every seam, where the barrel-chested Signor would greet us by declaring that the sun was about to break through; or, if it was already palely glowing, by deeming it a 'lovely day', or a 'grand one', or 'swell', or 'smashing', a '*bellissima giornata*'.

'Ciao, *bella*,' he said to me on my first solo visit. 'A braw worker, that brother of yours, a real eager beaver.' The wind had threatened to saw me in two as I passed St Stephen's Church, the gloomiest half-light though it was only 3 p.m. The shop was large enough for only two customers at a time. And when one of them was Carlo Balestracci, on his way home from early shift at Leith docks, almost as broad as he was tall (as broad as Signor Cavazzoni was round and plump), even two was a squeeze. Not that I cared about that: from Carlo I inhaled nothing like Papà with his turps and enamels, nor like Giulio who these days smelt of sugar and eggs, nor like Dario with his cigarettes and beer; from Carlo wafted sea air laced with sweat. The tattoo on his bicep looked like some sort of scythe, but he didn't flex it as Dario would have done, kept it bashfully covered up most of the time. Other odours too, from the cargo holds, which he'd later explain to me: tea from Ceylon, dried figs from Morocco, currants from Corinth in Greece, tobacco from Odessa.

'The Greeks fought the Persians near Corinth,' I put in, to impress.

'And now they're building a giant canal.' He dropped the currants in my hand, dark as coal and pungent. 'So the ships come faster to port, while the tea-pickers in Ceylon carry ever heavier loads up the plantation steps.'

I didn't see why Carlo should be worrying about folks in Ceylon, nor about carrying weights since he could carry a tea crate on one arm with a tramcar on the other. Story was he'd left Italy in 1918 after winning lots of medals; but he never talked of that, and avoided speaking Italian whenever he could.

'Away through to your brother now,' Signor Cavazzoni urged me. 'Leave some room for customers. A fine day like this, they'll soon be pouring in.'

Not ugly or off-putting but not handsome either, with his protuberant nose and his narrow chin, and awkward when observed; not elegant the way Dario could be when he tried, nor angelic like Emilio. But now, as I pushed open the door into the kitchen, here was Giulio transfigured. Cats with mice I had watched, swallows constructing their nests under the eaves, that scimitar approach to add a fresh daub of mud. But humans hardly ever, focused as they almost invariably were on the next thing or the last. Signor Cavazzoni was mistrustful of electrical refrigeration, preferring the tried-and-tested ice and saltpetre, which Giulio was stirring. He paddled a finger, then tasted. The exact viscosity of the resulting cream, or *custard*, with its rich solution of egg yolks, depended upon the proportion of ice to saltpetre, and in turn determined the temperature at which the mixture would set (that's how I'd remembered it, at least, after repeated explanations). But by no such worldly prognostications did Giulio appear absorbed, nor by the chilblains on his swollen fingers, any more than by the stench of a rotten egg in the bin. He was gazing into the ice like Nature itself, like a father watching his infant's first steps, mindful it not come a cropper yet certain it can manage on its own.

Finally, he looked up, smiled, the precocious seventeen-year-old who two nights before had battled with his brother about the meaning of the word *corporativismo*. 'I'm figuring,' he whispered, 'that if I can go on getting this part right, then sooner or later old Cavazzoni will trust me with his magic formula.'

'Let's hope so,' I said, aware that formulas had little to do with the magic I'd just witnessed.

'It can't be anything very complicated he adds.' Every ice-cream manufacturer, every *gelataio*, he'd explained to me, had his own special something he added to the mix, a gill of rum or a sprig of mint. 'Not that I'm so bothered. After La Scimmia he's not going to impress me with a sprinkle of nutmeg or a pinch of ambergris.' As he cracked the eggs, he caught the yolks in the domes of the half-shells, dropping the whites into a porcelain bowl.

'I was talking to Auntie Sandy.' Ever since she'd called me a *woman*, I'd been wondering how I could return the favour. 'Her at McVities, you mind?' I was feeling my way blindly, as she hadn't told me much about what grown-ups got up to; had added it to my imaginings, to the way McEwen leered at me, to the moaning heard in the street a few nights before, emerging, so said Dario, from 'some lucky *bastardo*'.

'Her the one for the boys?'

'Old wives' tales. She was asking about the ice-cream.' In truth, she had asked me about my 'handsome brother', obliging me to tell her that all he cared about were cigarettes, clothes and football—oh, and now Mussolini . . . unlike the second one, the brainy one, who was not so much of a Catholic and was bound in time to have his own posh establishment.

'You ken the basics. Tell her about the cream, saltpetre and so forth.' He folded sugar into egg-yolks with an even smooth stir, then asked me to taste the blend, grinding a flake of vanilla in a mortar until it turned to dust. Carlo's laughter could be heard through the door.

'Is Carlo a'courting?' I tried.

He stirred the vanilla in. 'You'd need to be asking him yourself. He's not too keen on me, nor on Dario either, not a single kind word for our new *Primo Ministro*. I asked him if he'd help set up a social club, he'd be a useful founder-member, what with his military record. "Away and join the boy scouts," he tells me, "if you're so keen on wearing uniforms."'

'She was asking about Signor Mussolini as well, and the changes in our country.' I neglected to mention that she'd called him 'Mustardini'.

'So what did you tell her?'

'That's the thing . . .' At last! 'I didn't know what to tell her because it went all zigzag in my head.'

'How's that? Not know what to tell her? You've heard us talking, heard me read out the latest.' Stirring had ceased: it was time for Giulio to take over in the front shop while Signor Cavazzoni worked his magic, announcing as he always did, 'The abracadabra will no take a jiffy!'

I had to wait until the walk back home for the remainder. The tone was pedagogic, almost Mr Blister. 'You could have told her about setting the economy back on its feet, getting the wheels of industry turning. About Caporetto and how Signor Mussolini's making Italy proud again, changing the way we feel about ourselves and our fellow-man. Or the Battle for Grain in the South, draining those mosquito swamps. Even Zia Flavia should care about that, though in her latest to Papà, she claims she's only heard dreadful things about the *Usurper from the North*.'

'I could never explain all that technical stuff. Better you do it yourself.'

'Tell her about the photos of him in the lion's cage, not feart in the least, or the one in *The Scotsman* the other day of the balcony on Palazzo Chigi, talking to the thousands, or about how everything's going to be different, freer, truer. Not that he's proved his promises yet, mind.'

'Or the one about his giant *manganello!*' Without our noticing, Dario had fallen in behind us. 'Who's this bird what's needing *edu-ma-cating*, as the local philistines have it? And how come she's still ignorant of the rule of *manganello?*' He made a fist in his trouser pocket and thrust it skyward, laughing.

Giulio ignored the innuendo, though it was the one part that interested me. 'Call it a *bludgeon* or call it *manganello*, I see no need for wooden clubs if the policies are right.'

'How else you intending to drive some sense into the Bolshevik skull? Couple of knocks with *manganello* will work wonders, added to castor oil—faithful *olio di ricino*—down the throat. You won't be hearing another Bolshy complaint about workers' rights or the International . . . Is that no right, Lucia?' he added, before diving into some basement where two ill-clad individuals were waiting for him.

'I suppose it's a good thing,' Giulio mused, walking on, 'that now he's interested in more than Hibernian F. C. and the latest cut of jacket he can't afford.'

It did occur to me I could ask Dario about it all, but I was scared of what he might say: I'd heard it was painful for lassies and had a sneaking feeling that this was partly why he liked it. 'So should I tell Auntie Sandy to come down with me some afternoon?'

'You know there's only two flavours, plain and strawberry, and that strawberry tastes like nothing despite the abracadabra?' We'd reached the entrance to our close, where Auntie Lena was lugging her messages in a string bag. He looked at me knowingly. 'You don't think your brother has enough on his plate between learning the ice-cream trade and launching the Edinburgh branch of our Italian Club?' Despite his smile, an awkwardness, his Adam's apple rising, until somehow he coaxed it down. 'So of course, bring her over, we'll try her out on strawberry.'

As we turned into the close, it appeared to occur to him that he had said something risqué. He pulled a face as if he were swallowing not strawberry but lemon rind. Wearily he mounted the steps as if preparing to do battle.

5

'It was a clubhouse, ken, for the bowls. But comes the Great War and they dug up the lawn, so now it's all turned tae waste.'

In the vacant lot I'd counted two demolished settees, the twisted chassis of a pram, four rusted saucepans, three burnt-out stoves and three and three-quarter stray mongrel dogs.

'Cannae deny it could do with a bit of maintenance.' A wooden porch had turned into stumps protruding from the cement. 'Firewood was in short supply. But as yous can see, inside there's plenty of . . . light . . . and stuff.'

'The *stuff* being dog shit and fag-ends?'

'Don't mind my brother,' said Giulio.

The stench of urine was oppressive, the damp of countless winters, even though the building—or *hut*, since that was what it was—had stood for only twenty according to the page the agent distributed. Daylight had to scale surrounding tenements and break through reinforced glass. 'For the rent yous are offering,' the agent insisted with a minimum of patter, 'you winnae find better in the district—or any other district either.'

It was a part of Leith, between the Links and Dalmeny Street, which had little to recommend it ('Pubs and grime and crime,' was Emilio's verdict when finally he paid a visit).

'How are we meant to inspire noble thoughts in this piss-pot?' Even the proximity to the Hibs stadium at Easter Road was not enough to win Dario over.

'We can do it up,' said Giulio. 'Will sit a good forty folks.'

'What use is forty? Should be talking four hundred!'

The agent consulted his fob-watch. 'You gents planning an Italian branch of the Rotary, or some confectioners' association?'

Dario rounded on the possibility of irony in the agent's voice. 'We don't all make ice-cream, *capisci*?'

'And the lavatories?' Giulio asked.

'Only gents the now.' Reluctantly, the agent moved towards a plywood door through which, when he opened it, a vision of filth was revealed that ensured I never looked at lawn bowlers in the same light again—not just the floor but smeared on walls and ceiling too.

'But we'll need ladies' toilets,' Giulio explained, unperturbed by what he saw. 'In the movement we're starting there'll be an equal place for women.'

'That'll be right,' added Dario, masticating audibly.

'Didnae ken yous Eye-ties—you Eyetalians, I mean—went in for that *suffering-jet* business. But you could make this for the ladies, and the gents, when nature calls, have got the waste-lot outside.'

Dario was disconsolate. 'Can you see me talking about Nietzsche and regeneration in this dump?'

'Peachy,' I muttered, repeating the rhyme that Emilio had struck when it had been revealed that this name belonged to a philosopher, the *Primo Ministro*'s favourite.

'We'll take it,' Giulio concluded, 'but at five bob less than you're asking.'

Out came the handshake and the agent's satisfied smile. 'A noble cause, I gather, so I think we can grant yous the discount.'

One week later, with the lease signed, Dario had convinced some neighbours to join in, claiming it was to be a Hibernian Supporters' Club. Giulio had enlisted two school pals, Ermanno and Beppe. It was a fifteen-minute walk downhill from Broughton Street and there was no need to pass by McEwen's chippy . . . only, Dario was determined.

'Mister Pezzini,' said McEwen after Dario prised him out from behind the deep-fryer. 'Emilio . . . Dinnae often have the privilege. Lost the taste for our black pudding?' Finally, he stopped pretending not to have noticed me. 'And you, Lucia?' His lips had turned invisible. 'Would you no fancy one of oor home-made . . . *saveloys?*' He grinned as he pronounced it. 'On the house like?'

As my whole body quivered, I barely needed to shake my head.

'You'll needs be coming doon the club,' Dario declared, his brogue falling into step with his audience. 'It's no only for the Eyeties. There'll be educating talks, you could do wi some of those, and social evenings, women invited too.'

'So what's it called, this club of yours?'

Dario turned to me who turned to Emilio who turned to Papà who, since Giulio was not there, had for once to propose something. 'The Consul called it the *Edinburgh Fascio.*'

'Edinburgh Fashion Show?'

'You taking the micky?' Dario was swelling out of his overcoat.

'Thanks for offering us a chip,' said Emilio, as Dario crumpled the newspaper poke and wiped his hands on his brother's back.

'And what's a *fascio* when it's at home?'

'It's a bundle of sticks, a symbol. You wouldnae understand. Ancient Rome and the power of the senators. When we were building the Colosseum yous were going round in sheepskins, living in caves.'

I added 'Veni, vidi, vici,' despite my resolution to keep silent. 'What Julius Caesar said when he saw this country. I came, I saw, I conquered.'

Though his cheeks were reddening, he forced a lipless smile. 'I couldnae see your Giulio doing much conquering. Or you, Emilio, on your game leg.'

'Warned you about taking the micky.' Dario had no sooner shrunk than he was looming again.

'So we must be getting on,' said Papà. 'The boys tell me there's a wee bit sorting to be done before the club can open.'

'Be seein you around though.' He was staring at me when he said it.

The force of Papà's understatement sent him reeling into his arm-chair when Dario opened the clubhouse door—only his armchair wasn't there for once so he had to lean against the wall . . . until he saw how grubby the wall was.

'*Ecco!*' offered Ermanno, who was already at work with Giulio. 'Sit yourself on this, Signor Pezzini.' He unfolded a handkerchief.

'But there's no time for sitting around,' said Giulio. 'Not with the place in this state.'

It was our first time all together since the day trip to North Berwick, and on this occasion we were *doing* something, not just pre-tending to relax. Mr Taylor from downstairs, though a Presbyterian, popped by to lend a hand. Beppe started in on a song about bandits who fought the landlords from Rome, and though no one but he knew the words, by the third verse we could join in the chorus, with even Dario lending a baritone, so sonorous that it almost hid the fact that he couldn't hold a tune. After an hour, when I looked up from my mop, I was amazed to see how much progress had been made. *Progress*: it was a word that Giulio had grown fond of, but which I couldn't remember applying to anything in our half-Italian world.

Yet no one approached the lavatory, not until Papà, out of curiosity, opened the door, cloth in hand, and tiptoed inside. Dario must have been expecting it, for with a single bound he was wedging a rickety chair beneath the door handle. Emilio laughed, then thought better of it. 'Let him out, Dario. Grand joke, now let him out.' The door rattled, the handle turned, two loud thumps from inside. 'Come on, Dario,' Emilio insisted.

'Stand back!' Dario stopped his brother in his tracks.

Giulio was sure to resolve it, as he always did. But Giulio had turned away, applying himself obsessively to a lump of petrified gum glued to the floor, hacking it with a blunt knife. 'Do something,' I whispered.

'*Molto buffo!*' cried the hollow voice. 'Dario, I know it's you, but let me out now, be a good boy. Dario! It's reeking in here with no ventilation. Let me out, or I'll be sick.'

'It'll only stink worse,' Dario called back.

Beppe thought it was a lark, but he hadn't seen inside. Mr Taylor approached Dario gingerly. 'I really think, Dario, that enough's enough. Where's your club going to be without some respect for the elders?'

'You'd be the first to admit, Mr Taylor,' said Dario, as if he'd rehearsed it, 'that we've got to be prepared to suffer for our convictions. No exceptions. Papà is an ineffectual lazy-bones who's never taken an initiative in his life. This is his chance. The greater good of the many is at issue here.'

'For a final time, Dario! I'm begging you!'

'*Work*, Papà, dixit our Duce, *is the restorative drink that nourishes the Italian soul.*'

'Do something, Giulio!' I pleaded.

'I am doing something.' He went on hacking at the gum, until I stopped his knife with my shoe. '*Credere, obbedire, combattere!*' he proferred, translating for Mr Taylor's benefit. 'Our Duce's motto, *Believe, obey, fight!* Fortunately there's nobody to fight, but we keep the spirit alive when we all pull together.'

Was it cowardice that immobilized me then? Or fright at being abandoned in favour of some ideal I could not grasp? Yet it was no cowardice that made Papà's whimpers fade from my hearing as I returned to my mop; joy in the heart where pain had just been present—the joy of sacrifice. (The fact that it was not myself I was sacrificing did not so much as occur to me.)

Another hour, and the light had begun to dim. Electricity, Dario promised, would be just one of the attractions of the club—modernity in its every aspect. 'Enough work for today,' he announced, discarding the brush he'd been wielding like a megaphone.

Seeing his brother was not about to stop him, Emilio pulled away the chair. On his feet—where else—Papà was leaning against the one wall he'd dis-encrusted—how remained a mystery as he had no utensil save a rag. With his foot, as the door opened, he made a scraping gesture that corralled a few dried turds and ushered them towards a notional heap. He looked neither angry nor aggrieved, only older, as if two hours had lasted two years.

'Just in time, Papà' Dario announced, 'for the day's main event.'

The hall was rectangular, forty feet by thirty, with a disproportionately high ceiling. Dario took up position at the far end, facing the door. 'In future this will be the dais.' He peered in the darkening window to check his tie was straight. 'I hereby declare the Edinburgh Fascio almost open.' No one applauded or knew what to say. 'And what you do not yet know is that my initiative has already been commended.' It was suddenly apparent why he was not his usual confident self, sniffing out advancement, timing each assault to perfection: he had *rehearsed* this speech until he had it off by heart. 'As far away as London, and even Roma, heart of our great Patria . . . Yous all OK with *Patria*?'

Mr Taylor nodded. Beppe muttered, 'But whoever she is I wish she'd get on with it so we can go and grab a pint.'

'With the consequence that our *Primo Ministro* has called the Great Britain Fascio *il mio primogenito all'estero*, which means . . .' Somehow he'd failed to rehearse the translation 'How d'you say that in English, Giulio?'

'My first-born abroad.'

'*Giusto*. And here's a letter from the Edinburgh Consul himself whom we may never have met but who promises to visit when the club is firmly founded. Since you insist, I'll read it to you.' Only, this was where his script ran out. 'Giulio, you come up and translate it.'

'Up where?' asked Emilio. 'I don't see any *up*.'

'Enough of the smart Alec. We've been imagining a dais here, *vero*?' Dario handed over the letter as if it were holy writ.

Giulio scanned the page. 'It's on consular letterhead and it begins *Egregious Doctor*.'

'That no an insult?' said Mr Taylor. 'Egregious?'

'Who's the doctor?' said Emilio. 'Doctor Doctor, I've a pain in my leg from all this standing.'

'Pipe down, Emilio.' It was Papà, first words he'd uttered since being released. 'Lots of doctors don't have stethoscopes, in Italian.'

'*Egregious Doctor, It is with pleasure and . . .*' Giulio hesitated. '*And praiseful salutations that I greet you in this, Year One in the rebirth of our noble and honourful Italian Fatherland.* Gey formal, this.'

'Of course it's fucking formal. From the Consul, what do you expect!'

'*From our Leader himself I bring congratulations on the something something of the Patriotic spirit that links us Italians . . .*' Giulio found it hard to translate in anything but word-by-word, hopelessly unsuited to the exalted tone required. '*Whether at home or helping to establish our Italian culture with its noble Roman something . . .*'

'*Discendenza*! Jesus, I thought you were supposed to be good at this!'

'*Abroad.*'

Beppe had slipped out to kick a tin can round the vacant lot. Ermanno was about to join him when Giulio promised, 'Not much more, lads. *For too long the Italian government has ignored its subjects who had to choose exile to the colonies because of a . . . disastrous economic something made by . . . decadent liberalism. But from now this changes and we salute your advancement of our historic ties.* Phew! What a mouthful. Then there's the signature and all the consul's titles.'

'Bravo, Giulio!'

'Bravo *Giulio*?' Dario barked. 'Why Giulio?'

'Bravi all my children. Brava even Lucia for standing there shivering.'

6

A subscription to *L'Italia Nostra* became a family necessity, a newspaper which described itself as the *Official Organ of the Italian Fasci in the British Isles*. 'Where would we all be,' Giulio asked one evening after reading the latest issue, 'but for Giulio Cesare?'

'And gladiators,' added Dario. 'Would've liked to know a few of them.'

'Tiberius was emperor from 14 BC to something AD.' I said it to show I could. 'He was a very wicked man.'

'Wicked, she says?' Dario was smirking. 'What would you know of wicked?'

'Did wicked things with boys then threw them off a cliff. We learnt it in class from Mr Blister.'

'With boys!' Dario hooted. 'With boys, she says!' I was glad he didn't ask me to elaborate, as I'd not have known how, especially as everyone was silent, looking in all directions except at one another— like the one time I'd taken the lift in Jenners Department Store. Papà cleared his throat, Emilio adjusted his leg-brace, Giulio stared at the floor, *L'Italia Nostra* saggy in his hands. 'Could you not,' Dario eventually said, 'produce something useful for a change, Papà, instead of more Marys and myrrh?'

Papà looked relieved, despite the barb. 'It's a symbol, not a tool, you know.'

'The sticks and axe for a start. Or you could try the Imperial Eagle. That might sell, once the club gets going.'

Emilio pointed to the drawing of Mussolini's face looming on the back page of *L'Italia Nostra* that had slipped from Giulio's hands to the floor. 'Or do one,' he suggested, 'of the Big Man's jaw? Would fit nicely in the hand, can feel it already.'

Dario moved closer. 'You looking to feel my hand across *your* jaw?' Then, in the sinuous way of his by which one thought led to another—'I canna be doing with these jokers, I'm away down the gym. Who's for chumming me, see what real men are about?'

Giulio surprised me by offering—surprised Dario too, to judge by his raised eyebrows. 'I'll come along,' I tried, chancing my luck.

'It's no place for girls,' Papà protested.

'*Al contrario*, it's the very place for girls,' Dario corrected him, 'for finding them that is. These two should see how we're forging the muscles to fight for the future. *Forza*! Don't worry, Papà, I'll look after her.'

The entrance to the gym was disappointingly unglamorous. On the walls were photographs of earnest-looking men with flattened noses and naked oily torsos. 'That there's Jack Dempsey,' explained a balding overweight Irishman. 'And that's Tommy White, he's a Yid but a fine boxer aw the same in the lightweight division. I'm Joe, by the way, the coach. Dario'll be back in a moment when he's kitted up.'

The odour of liniment and perspiration was overpowering in a way that made me wish it stronger still. 'And does Carlo come here too, Mr Joe?' I asked, ignoring Dario's injunction on questions.

'Carlo Balestracci? The docker? He came here once but nae heart for it. Says it all gin out of him in the War. Any case he's too dangerous, he is, flatten the ugly mugs in here with a single punch.' He peered at Giulio and me. 'Yous Saint Ninian's?'

'St Mary's,' I said, when Giulio pursed his lips.

'And was the Archbishop himself no for blessing our gym just last year. Taking the hoodlums off the street and giving them a purpose?'

And here he was now, our very own *hoodlum*, skin slippery and shining. For an instant I thought he'd taken leave of his senses as he was punching the air as if it were the enemy; then an inoffensive rugby ball suspended from the ceiling, which bounced back as fast as he could whack it. 'D'yous two know O'Donnell here?' asked the coach. 'One of the few of us papists who's made it anywhere in the Force?' He used the word *papist* as if it were no insult at all.

'You maybe no recognize me in civvies, but you're sure to have seen me on the beat. I'm great pals wi your brother, he'll go far, that one. Always trouble wi yous lot though. Too much macaroni in the diet, they says! Still, scarce a single mason among the Eye-talians, that's one thing to be thankful for.'

I knew that wasn't right. 'Mr Celati's a bricklayer and Giulio's school-pal Beppe with the singing voice is a jobber's mate on a site in Gorgie.'

'That's no the sort of mason we're talking aboot here, lassie. It's the sort what runs the police force, keeping us oot the top posts. This lot dinnae build walls. Wear aprons they do, share secret hand-shakes. But your new Prime Minister, the Muzzle Man, Dario tells us he's stamping them out all over Italy. Could do with a bit of that over here, give me a chance of promotion.'

Dario relieved me of the effort of imagining Italian bricklayers with no bricks to lay, dressed in pinnies, being chased by a model of Mussolini's jaw. 'Who's up for it?' he shouted. 'Couple of rounds?' Stepping up to the ring, holding a skipping rope that in any other grown man's hands would have made me laugh, was McEwen, half-naked. As usual, I hadn't seen him coming. Giulio instinctively reached out and held my hand.

'I'll gee you two rounds, Dario,' he hollered, 'wi interest.' Dario patted the challenger on the back like a comic-book bear with big brown mitts. Then they were through the ropes, strapping on padded hoods, shuffling their feet to a dance audible to themselves alone.

'I think we should leave,' whispered Giulio, pulling me gently.

'In a minute,' I protested, just as Joe was stepping in, inspecting their gloves, then pushing them apart. Puppets at first they appeared, revolving round the mat. When the first blow struck, it was on McEwen's chest.

'Here we go,' muttered PC O'Donnell, a line of spittle escaping his mouth.

McEwen continued skipping, then flashed one blow after another. Stomach shoulder chin. 'Nice work, Ewey!' Then Dario struck to the side of the head so that Joe put his arm out to scold him. 'Keep it clean!' And then the PC clanged a bell and the two retreated to opposite corners, dogs held back by imaginary leashes.

'There's nothing for us here,' said Giulio, though this time he didn't pull me, stood grim-faced with nostrils flared as we awaited the sequel.

Again the bell rang. McEwen was skinnier than Dario, shorter too; his forearms were covered in burn scars from where the fat had splattered him. He was wiry, elusive, weaving this way and that, dodging, regrouping, waiting till Dario got puffed and then landing another four blows to his torso. But then, just as the PC was approaching the bell, a step forward to Joe's blind side, and Dario caught McEwen in the kidneys.

'Nice rabbit-punch,' laughed the PC. 'He'll be feeling that next time he's heeding for a piss.' Giulio was transfixed, squeezing my hand so hard that it hurt. As McEwen staggered, Dario moved in for the slaughter. Seven blows to the stomach and two on the nose, which started pouring blood. With McEwen doubled over, he was just about to thump him on the back of the neck, crying, 'This one's for the Duce,' when the bell sounded and Joe intervened.

'Aw come on there, ref, I was just starting to enjoy myself! All right now, Ewan?'

I didn't hear the answer, as Giulio was pulling me so hard, away from the ring then out of the gym, that my shoulder hurt and I almost tripped. 'Too good to be true,' he fumed.

So uncharacteristic was his fury, I didn't dare ask what he meant.

7

Between cleaning and collecting funds for refurbishing, what with the electrics and the paintwork, it took time to make the Fascio ready. Outside, the vacant lot proved intractable. No sooner was a rotten horsehair mattress removed than a rusted bedstead or a sack of broken slates would appear. Dario roamed the perimeter, throwing stones at the strays, but they returned to urinate. He pinched my catapult from my satchel, only to bruise his thumb so badly the nail turned black. 'Matches the shirt,' scoffed Emilio.

Interest among Italians was sluggish, who had, they told us, trouble enough putting bread on the table without worrying about *i politici* in Roma. Giulio explained how changes in Rome would lead to improvements here. He'd present newspaper photographs showing Mussolini alongside Prime Minister Chamberlain in Downing Street, at the gates of Buckingham Palace on his way to an audience with King George. 'But he's atheist, no? Hell-bent on demolishing the true power of Roma which lies by right *al Vaticano*?' It was precisely Giulio's hope—years since he'd set foot inside St Mary's, not even for my Confirmation. But this did not stop him expounding that the Duce's one reservation was when religion meddled in politics—nothing new here, he said, even our Dante had advocated a clearer division between Church and State . . .

As Giulio was persistent, so was I, calculating how best to win an invitation for Auntie Sandy—from him, not from me—to the opening gala. 'We could go down Cavazzoni's tomorrow,' I suggested. 'You'll love his vanilla now the weather's turning warmer.'

'His vanilla!' Auntie Sandy gave a laugh whose throatiness made me wonder if I'd said something dreadful.

Tomorrow, of course, brought wind whipping in from the North Sea. Signor Cavazzoni greeted us through rain-streaked windows. 'Away in out the storm, you *belle ragazze*. I'd offer you an ice but I'm sure you'd rather have it from our young genius in the kitchen. On you go through, so's no be blocking the customers. Weather'll soon be clearing.'

And here he was seated on a milkmaid's stool with a scoop in one hand and a minuscule wooden spatula in the other, very deliberate, almost detached, as if he were watching himself from the ceiling. 'What'll it be?' he asked.

'Strawberry for me,' said Auntie Sandy.

After serving her, he continued with his stirring. 'Must be a job for you,' he said, 'waiting on the genteel McVities patrons all day.' I'm almost sure he glanced at Auntie Sandy's ankles, and surer that she hitched her skirt up an inch.

'Yet it's no so tiring that it stops me goin down the dancing of a Friday night. To the Scala.'

'Look at this.' Giulio held out his mix. 'And with a little cold it will change into something people long for. Not that this is aught more than a pale reflection of what's possible. Think of it, Bitter Cherry and Blood Orange so tart it sets the roof of your mouth on fire. Dark green Pistachio. And orange-flavoured chocolate that we call *Gianduia*. Lemon ice *granita*, with the lemons grown on the Isle of Capri, picked only hours before with rind so sweet you can chew it like it was candied. And—have you ever seen a pomegranate?'

'Is that something naughty?'

'A dull-looking fruit, bit like a turnip. But crack it open and out tumble bright crimson seeds. Crush to remove the juice, lace into the ice like holy blood.' He caught himself, adding almost apologetically, 'Which is not to say I've anything against the Scala.'

I wanted him to shut up, for he surely couldn't complete two steps without tripping over the exotic dances they did down there. I said, 'I'd like to go.'

'You're too young to get in,' Auntie Sandy told me, 'but I'll let you know all about it.' The rain hadn't slackened when we left the kitchen. 'Fair poetic,' said Auntie Sandy, as we defied the wind, 'when he talks about the ices.'

And that evening Emilio was poetic too. 'Will you listen to this?' he asked me. '*The March of Nineteen Twenty-Two.*' He wagged a finger to signify a line-end. '*Our hopes went with him and our fears . . .*' Wag. '*Regeneration would be true . . .*' Wag. '*And wipe away a nation's tears . . .*' He looked up enquiringly. 'It's for the gala. Not that I believe a word of it, mind, but I want a heroic poem to read out, or maybe Beppe can put it to song. What do you think?'

More than by the words I was surprised he should care what I thought; he'd learnt that too from Giulio. 'Splendid,' I ventured.

'I'm stuck over a rhyme for *fascio*, which must be because it's Italian. Can't use *fashion show* because McEwen used it first.'

I squirmed. 'But he won't be at the gala, will he? He's not one of us. I don't think I'll attend if he's going to be present . . .'

Though I did, of course. And he did—of course. At opposite corners we sat, on chairs begged from neighbours or restored from cast-offs on the vacant lot. After our high hopes, that the Ambassador would fly up from London, we were doubly disappointed when the Edinburgh Consul showed up late, accompanied by two large and largely perfumed ladies who wore fur coats though the evening was a mild one, and hairdos to match—one was his wife but it was unclear which. I had persuaded myself not to expect a toga, but this short dumpy man with fat gold rings and fillings, no hint of a hooked nose, a handshake damp and flimsy, his suit a size too small, and (to the barely disguised disgust of Dario) no black shirt—he seemed an insult to the name of *Consul*. When he rose to the dais, which now stood two feet proud, his speech was unprepared in Italian, never mind in English. When he attempted his impromptu summary of the past two years, since the Glorious March on Rome, his accent was so strong that only nouns were comprehensible: moder*nity*, nat*ion*, patriot*ism*—he even tried to stress the final syllable on prosper*ity*.

(There was more, signalled by a tinkle from Dario's glass.) Disci*pline*, cour*age*, em*pire*, viril*ity*, vir*tue*. 'In Italy as in Scot*land*' something something something . . . nouns would soon prevail. Between each phrase he sipped the red wine that the grocer Signor Baldini had provided, so that by the end of his speech, with two-thirds of the bottle drunk, he found his own locutions hilarious, as did both his ladies in the front row—they were looking round the renovated clubhouse, its bunting and balloons, with much the same faces that we had pulled when we inspected it with the agent nine months prior.

Applause was faint from the thirty-odd participants, though questions were muttered about what the nouns meant *in practice*. The Consul looked set for another bottle, but his ladies, finding no one to their taste, led him one by each arm through the door towards the waiting automobile.

Giulio was up next, though by this time people were tiring of speeches. 'Now and for the first time,' he summed up, 'there's a mean-ing to being an Italian abroad. At last we have someone who recog-nizes our existence.'

When Signor Cavazzoni wheeled in his cart, the official cere-mony was effectively over. Dario paced up and down cursing Giulio for upstaging him since he had 'important news to announce'. Emilio clutched his poem which had stretched to forty lines When I asked why he didn't read it out, over the hubbub, he said it was codswallop, that *fascio* didn't rhyme with *Moscow*, and that the only solution, since the heroism was laughable, was to turn it humorous on a rewrite. McEwen kept his distance, with paws if not eyes. Only once did he approach me.

'All this Caesar stuff,' he said, 'but yous've forgotten Hadrian's Wall.' Then he drifted off to drink some more—even if wine, he moaned, was 'a drink fit fae lassies'.

Within minutes of ices being served, conversation had reverted to the usual topics of who was courting whom, whose baby had just been christened, the automatic floor-cleaner recently purchased by Mamma's sister Zia Sabrina in Chicago that worked by means of a vacuum (Papà's contribution), the forty-second cousin back home who had succumbed to malaria but been saved by the Madonna of Pompeii, the deadening monotony of the local Edinburgh fare with not a *peperoncino* in sight, the length of the queue at the *bru*, how Archbishop Smith favoured the Irish over the Italians despite Italians being so much closer to the true Roman church ('cleaner too,' someone added)—and all this gossip notwithstanding the presence of Giulio who was nipping between each group to elevate with news of the elections set to confirm popular support for the Fascist Party's policies . . . The proper length of the veil for a confirmation dress, the summer trip home if the lottery came lucky, which was more flavoursome, Signor Cavazzoni's strawberry or Signor Luca's in Musselburgh . . .

'Neither,' whispered Giulio, as infuriated by this as by his failure to exile chit-chat from the historic occasion.

The evening was anything but rowdy, yet it took hours to clear up. The pubs were out when we trudged back up Leith Walk, and Auntie Sandy, to whom Giulio had hardly spoken a word all evening, kept close within our group, Dario chatting to her flirtatiously.

'See you, hen?' called a drunk from somewhere near the Rob Roy pub. 'What you walkin out wi the Eyeties for? Wi the tarries?'

Dario stopped. 'You got a problem with us, *signore*?'

'Should stick to yer ain kind!'

'Come on,' said Giulio. 'We've heard it all before.'

'You want to repeat that?' said Dario, approaching the drunk.

'Trouble wi yer hearing, pal? I said, whit's the bird doing wi a bunch o yous spics?'

Dario raised his fist, before he broke into a laugh. He said, 'I'll let you off for now. But don't you ever repeat that.'

8

Auntie Sandy was beaming. 'A really marvellous dancer. Not that he kens the steps yet, but he picks them up that quick.' There was a glow more eloquent than her words. 'And he's no feart to lead, unlike most joes who either dinna have the nerve or drag you round the floor like a sack of tatties.'

I closed my gawping mouth. 'And is that all?'

'Don't say *all*, hen. You've nae idea, not knowing what it's better than, but imagine floating in air and your every wish anticipated, all limbs in step, and no fear of getting into trouble, no mess after, no apologies or lies. Anyway, yer brother's a sweet laddie, right enough.'

'And what? Not your kind?'

'I dinna think he'd be interested in me,' she laughed. 'But we'll definitely be dancing again. Dinna look so disappointed, Lucia, you'll be out a'courting yerself before long, then you'll find out what it's all about.'

'But I want to know *now*!'

Auntie Sandy stopped in her tracks, not far from our tenement. Her explanation was rich in metaphors but bluntly Marie Stopes where necessary—'Though what I'm saying is probably blasphemy to yous Catholics.' Pleasure, she explained, wasn't handed to women on a plate. Practice, she said, as in all things, made perfect. And no point in waiting for Mr Right to come along and know the ropes, as Scottish men were a dead loss in that department store, though she'd heard tell that Italian men might be better—'in general I mean, no referring to anyone in particular'.

The front door was always ajar at home, so a knock was unusual, especially at tea-time. Emilio bobbed to the door on his good leg;

he'd left school to become a quantity surveyor's clerk, spending more
and more of his free time in his rhymes (to the disgust of Dario who
wanted him out canvassing for the Fascio). Hearing the woman's
Italian voice, I recollected the cat that got locked in the clubhouse,
and how it eyed the exit when the door was unlocked two days
later—for here was the exact same look on Dario's face, who even
considered the open window, three floors up.

'Let me show you in,' said Emilio, barely repressing a laugh.
'They'll be delighted to see you.' From cat, Dario turned rabbit—in
a hutch, waiting to be skinned. 'Aunt Paola from Maclodio!' Emilio
announced. 'Zia Paola!'

Papà offered to rise from his armchair but then accepted a kiss
on both cheeks. Giulio was next, while to me she offered compli-
ments so exalted that it was obvious how nasty must have been
Dario's depiction of me. Only last did she come to him, the eldest
brother (eldest step-nephew), to whom she extended a formal hand.

It must have been days since she had eaten, as she polished off
the overcooked stovies with barely a grimace. She was certainly
beautiful, with long dark eyelashes and the fullest naturally red lips;
not tall, but limbs strong and brown, her raven-black hair wound
into the most complex of braids. She used her fork like a shovel,
then looked up apologetically. Two leather suitcases were all she was
carrying.

Papà had been working on his questions, for eventually, in Italian,
he asked: 'And how is my dear half-brother Roberto? He has sent
you . . . here?'

Zia Paola was determined to try her English: 'He always violent
old pig. Send me? Never!'

Dario looked disgusted. 'Don't play the innocent, Papà.'

'So you're here just to . . . visit us? It's a very long way. The trains
have improved. You're very welcome. The honour is ours.' Each
semi-detached Papà phrase was more incredulous. 'You're here to
join the boys' Fascio? Something to do with the Ballila parades?'

'Fascio what is?'

'The Duce's personal treasure in the Colonies. And the Ballila is the social education system promoted by our great Duce.' It sounded sarcastic, coming from Emilio. 'You know who the Duce is? Who has drained the swamps of the Maremma and who can tame a lion with a few notes on his violin?'

'*Certo* she knows who the fucking Duce is! You think I'd be courting a cretin?'

'I learn English from the *Americani*, the ones who leave and come back.'

Papà was still puzzling. 'So it's not for the politics. Is there something else I should know?'

'You want us to demonstrate?' growled Dario. 'Here on the kitchen table?'

'Why not?' I muttered under my breath.

'Don't blame me,' Dario objected. 'I wrote to her not to come, that it was ridiculous. How can you elope when you're twenty-six years old? She's old enough to be my *nonna*.'

I couldn't let this pass: 'But you're almost twenty-three.'

'Will you shut your ugly mug!'

'You mean . . . ? You mean you two . . . ?' Papà was almost out of his chair, such his amazement.

'Ring the bells of St Mary's, he's remembered.'

'But it's illegal. It will bring scandal. Nobody will buy holy statues from a family so cursed.'

'Spare us, Papà, since nobody buys them in any case unless I oblige them. And nobody's going to know cos you're all going to keep your mouths shut. *D'accordo*? And it's no going to c-o-n-t-i-n-u-e.' He spelled it out to be sure Zia could not follow. 'So lay offa me, right?'

Emilio was smirking. 'Thus doth the Fascista demonstrate the sanctity of the family.' But Dario was already making for the door— and did not return for nearly two days.

'Monster!' shouted Papà down the stairway.

'Please, Papà,' said Giulio, 'think of Zia Paola.'

'I'm sorry, my dear, I wasn't meaning you. Of course you are welcome to stay. Lucia can share her bed with you, plenty of room here.'

Dario might think of Zia as *nonna*, but her body, as she undressed by the light of the kitchen fire, was taut and shapely. It occurred to me that she might help fill some gaps left in my education by Auntie Sandy.

And I didn't even have to ask, as no sooner were we squeezed together than from her handbag she removed a thin wad of letters. She said, 'This send one year back.' I told her she could speak Italian, but she was determined to learn. In a whisper, from the copy she had made: '*My most Dear Dario, That makes four long year from when we were happy together. I miss you so much. Roberto, he is a hog, eats like a hog . . .*' She looked me in the eyes, nodded grimly. '*Caga hog, talks hog, beats and loves like a hog. Either I leave him or poison him, the choice is your because you are my love. Write me at Lalla house. Your carissima little sporran, Paola.*'

'Sporran?'

'He call me. Not is dirty I hope?' When I explained, she seemed uncertain whether to be flattered or furious. 'And he write in his letter two month back: *Dearest Sporran Mine, I miss you so much too and am forever thinking of our precious hours together. But we must be strong. My destiny is in Scotland where I toil to support the family and devote my energies to building a better future for us Italians here in the Colony. But some day surely we shall meet again, in this world or the next, and my heart is a desert until that happy day. Your most doting Dario.*' Reading was not easy for her, though every word had been pored over a thousand times. 'He not tell me to poison Roberto, thus I know he wish me come. All money the train to pay. Lalla help me.'

'And that wee bit there?' I asked, pointing—Zia had neglected the *PS*.

'When we know better you and me.' At which, sighing, Zia turned her back and fell instantly asleep, breathing lightly.

I could not resist temptation, gently easing open the hand clutching Dario's ungainly scrawl. '*PS*,' I read, '*I think of the time when you held my little bird—not so little in that moment—between your glorious breasts, then it sang its pretty song to you.'*

Three days later, with the household barely absorbing the shock of the spring-cleaning Zia Paola had launched—it was autumn— came the further surprise of a telegram. Papà read it out: '*DARIO*, it says, *SEI MORTO.'*

'*Stronzo!*' cried Zia Paola. 'Is the hog, say you dead. He pay word for word, so only three.' Dario snorted contemptuously but Zia could see he was rattled. 'Not to worry, never he leave his goats.'

Dario looked unconvinced, yet like the rest of us he couldn't help remarking that the flat already looked cleaner than since Mamma died, that there was always coffee on the stove, that his black shirts were perfectly pressed. To Padre Clemente Papà confessed on his son's behalf, and had it confirmed that it was a mortal sin even if Zio Roberto was a hog . . .

Still he remained optimistic that Christmas would be a bumper one for Baby Jesus and Joseph; Emilio's income was added to Giulio's apprenticeship pay, and there was macaroni on the table again every evening. And to top it all, in early December, Dario looked as if the door had finally lifted on the rabbit hutch. 'Great news! Listen to this! From the Ambassador in London. He's inviting me, and for some reason Giulio and Emilio too, to Roma next summer for a big Demonstration of Fascist Solidarity from the Colonies.'

'How you intending to afford that?' said Papà. 'Unless you mean to walk like your Nonno?'

'You would say that, you spoilsport—just because you've never done anything heroic in your entire life. It explains here that every-thing's paid for: train, dormitory, food, plus a new uniform when we get there.'

'Sadly,' said Emilio, with no audible trace of sorrow, 'I couldn't get the time off work.'

Giulio was nodding, though his lips were pursed. 'It's certainly an honour.'

'All we have to do is promote the Ballila ideal, which is your basic glorified social club, and the Dopolavoro, which is little more than night class. Giulio can teach some nonsense about the ideals of *fraternity*'—he chuckled at this—'and I can teach the lassies callisthenics, wave the *manganello* in the air.' Zia Paola was serving seconds, all ears. The next bit came out fast to make it hard for her to follow (the rabbit in black shirt was bounding through the fields): 'Think of it. *Finalmente* I'll be able to take Paola—Zia Paola—home to Zio.'

'Think again, nephew mine.' It was the first time she'd ever called him *nephew*—her English had improved already. 'Never will I return to the hog. *Mai! Capisci?* I tell him you are in Rome, he will kill you for sure with his goat knife.'

'Dario, this is Paola's home now. You cannot send her home like some unwanted gift.' Giulio needed something more persuasive. 'Who's going to cook the way she does, or wash and clean?'

'Idiots!' Dario shouted. 'You think Pio's about to give her an annulment. After years of matrimony?'

Papà was crossing himself. 'You could come to Mass for once and ask forgiveness if that's what's bothering you. The Archbishop might assist.'

'Or go see His Holiness in person,' laughed Emilio. 'When you're down in Rome. If you can survive without the black shirt for an afternoon—I hear Pio's not so keen on them!'

Zia was adamant: 'The Papa will give me an *annullamento*. No one time in nine years the hog has take me *normalmente*, face to face. You call this matrimony?'

'Thank you, Paola!' coughed Papà, for whom this picture of his step-brother was altogether too vivid. 'You've been taking English lessons from Dario, I hear. You can certainly give Padre Clemente the general picture, though best leave things as they are for now. No need to be telling Roberto about Dario visiting Rome. Of course you'll stay on here?'

'And what about me?' I was in nobody's thoughts, not even Giulio's.

Dario made one of his rapid calculations: if Paola was a fixture, then he'd better be in her bedfellow's good books. 'The Ambassador says in his letter that if the event's a success, then the following year could be the girls' turn.'

I even came to believe in his benevolence. He had left for the Fascio, 'in order to oversee Christmas decorations'. Zia was down the steamie where she had already impressed by the speed with which she passed the laundry through the mangle. My homework done, I was at a rare loose end, so set off to lend Dario a hand; I didn't possess a key but used my own sneak entrance through the broken bars on the lavatory window.

So *that* was *normalmente*! They'd laid four cushions in a row. Face to face all right, with Zia on top. He was still in his black shirt, while she rocked back and forth dressed only in her stockings. Though I tried to be quiet, I released an involuntary sigh. Frozen mid-thrust, they seemed, by that same rabbit instinct, to think that if they kept perfectly still then no one would see them.

'Don't stop for me,' I said, all matter of fact. 'Why not let the little bird sing its song?'

'What the fuck? You told her that?'

'So?' said Zia, forgetting she had not. 'She has fifteen years. They made me marry at sixteen.'

'Pair of fucking perverts, yous two are.' He wanted to move, but Zia had not released her grip. 'Clear out of here, Lucia. You tell anyone about this and I'll murder you!'

'The same way,' I asked, 'that Zio Roberto is going to murder you?'

Zia laughed as she dismounted. 'Canny *ragazza* this niece of mine! *Furba!*'

'I'll kill you worse than he'll kill me.' He was searching for his trousers. 'I'll string you up and use you as my punchbag.'

'There's no need for that. I'll be silent as the grave. Just so long as you make sure I'll be in Rome for summer 1927. *Capisci?*'

9

Bologna, 16 July

Carissima Lucia,

I have been visiting the mediaeval centre, including the Torre degli Garisenda which leans so dramatically that Dante mentions it in Inferno. My companions range from professors from London University, shopkeepers keen for new customers, to others like me and Daniele—the one soul-mate I've found—who want some deeper change in society and the church's strictures removed. The moment we crossed the border at Ventimiglia, Dario's pals removed their manganelli from their suitcases and dangled them from their belts. Many bruised knees as a result!

Something hilarious I must tell you. When I made to shake the local Prefect's hand, he darted his right arm in the air and saluted me in what he assured me was the 'Roman manner'. And he insisted on calling me not 'Lei', which as Mamma rightly taught us is the ONLY polite way to address a senior or stranger, but 'Voi'. He informed me it came down from the Duce himself and that no longer do true Italians shake hands—a degenerate and feminine habit. Like the Fascist salute, 'Voi' reminds us of our glorious Imperial past.

I gave it a go. I even practised with Daniele: placed my upper teeth on my lower lip to prove to him I could use this virile Fascist address. Inhaled the necessary air. But all that escaped was a puff, then a snigger . . .

Countless dull speeches, so we made off in search of you know what and eventually found the Gelateria dei Commercianti under the porticoes. Interesting use of cherries from Vignola and an exquisite

Mascarpone which craftily uses up the left-over egg-whites. When I see what even a modest gelatauro achieves here I wonder why I bother!

Next stop the Eternal City. Baccioni

Your Giulio

By summer, it had been decided I should go to the New Town Secretarial College since I had done so well at school, whence I would emerge one year later with shorthand and typing, judged the skills a modern lady needed to secure her family's future. Papà said I should take a *vacanza*, but I had no idea what that would involve and no money beyond the few pennies Emilio could spare. When Zia Paola refused assistance in the kitchen, I felt purposeless and lost, no longer a schoolgirl but not yet anything else, wandering the streets far beyond my narrow zone, past the stretched green playing fields of posh boys' schools, into Ravelston Dykes where bungalows were under construction. I watched how people lived in districts where there was not a single Italian, each family separated from the next by a garden or wall. Through the windows of Newington houses, hundreds of books on neatly stacked shelves; Morningside pubs where men with bowler hats dared to enter; Fettes' College with its turrets and spires as tall as any fairy castle; could almost see the blood dripping from the battle pennants suspended from the pillars in St Giles Cathedral.

Roma! 20 July 1926

Cara,

Prepare yourself for a long letter! For yesterday was our big day, which started with a dress rehearsal of our march in the Colosseum—what a sinister edifice, with its ghosts of the slaughtered lurking in the shadows! The black shirts soak up the sun, so I suggested removing them to hang up and dry: an odd sight we looked, but not without charm. With his acute sense of history, our brother challenged the parade officer to a wrestling match (one hand behind their backs). It took the officer two minutes to pinion our dear brother on his face in the Roman dust—an experience he pretended to enjoy, while the rest of us didn't need to pretend!

Up the Via Appia Antica we duly marched. It might have been atmospheric but for the complaints of a comrade from Soho who worries he is being made to wear the horns while away from home. Finally, feet blistering and shirt droukit, I entered the city shoulder to shoulder with Daniele and aimed for Villa Chigi.

Oh dear, I'm being told to switch out the dormitory light and I'm nowhere near finished. More in my next.

Love, your Giulio

In vain did Zia Paola intercept the postman each morning, who finally confided in me, 'She's that pretty, yer aunt, I'd write to her myself.' God would give her courage, she said, to ask the Archbishop for an annulment; then wedding bells would ring and she'd move into her own home—not too far from us, mind, so visits would be frequent.

Roma, 21 July

Cara,

Where were we? On the road to Piazza on our military manoeuvres designed to impress the Duce . . . We were four men down by the time we got there—missing in action (the action being offered by daytime ladies of the night). With only half an hour's delay our Scottish contingent marshalled before the famous balcony on Villa Chigi.

Forty minutes on and we were three more down brave and true. Two office-types from Glasgow had fainted from the heat, while Arturo from Kilmarnock wandered off, remarking, 'I canna hack this for a lark. Old Muss may be makin the trains run on time but he's no havin much luck wi hisself.'

Dario reminded us: 'You think gladiators complained about a wee bit warmth? Call yourselves Fascisti?'

I chose a moment when our brother wasn't watching and had only to trust my feelers; three minutes from the scalding square, here was a street urchin wearing no shoes yet rich as a lord with a tiny tub of granita. GIOLITTI's is the name of the Roman Val Halla.

Blood-Orange Sorbetto, and a pale green concoction which Signor Giolitti in person told me is called 'Kingdom of the Two Sicilies' and which mixes Pistachios with Almonds, Sultanas and Sponge. That morning our Honourable Treasurer (Dario), unhappy about how the wad of cash interfered with his creases, had passed the day's allowance to Daniele. So here goes for one of those lists you like so well: Reign of the Two Sicilies (1 tub), Melon and Watermelon Sorbetto (1 tub), Torrone (1 tub), Gianduia (2 tubs), Hazelnut (1 tub), Pine Kernel with Cinnamon (1 tub), Stracciatella (with chocolate flakes—2 tubs). And because it was closest to black I could find: Dark Bitter Chocolate (1 tub).

If ever I forget my purpose here on earth, I need only recall the expressions on my countrymen's faces back on the baking parade ground as the tubs glided from hand to hand and as everyone searched for ways to describe how the orange complemented the chocolate or the cinnamon worked with the pine kernels. Faces relaxed, smiles spread.

And then it happened, as somehow it had to happen. I thrust the box of Dark Bitter Chocolate into our brother's hand. For here on the balcony—to what raptures the exhausted and deep-baked audience was capable of producing—here at last was our Duce!

Many things I'd like to tell you about what he taught us. But the loudspeaker near our delegation was faulty, so I heard only every fourth word. Through binoculars I could follow the gestures, as the Duce's chest puffed up big as a courting pigeon, then exhaled like a donkey. Arms akimbo as if to challenge each one of us personally. Then smiling benevolently as if we were his very own bambini . . .

But all pales compared to what I witnessed when first he stepped onto his balcony. For in automated unison up went the arms of our contingent, in ardent Fascist salute. And so it was that I watched our Duce being hailed . . . by tiny wooden spoons containing . . . ice-cream!

Melon and Watermelon Sorbetto! DUCE! Hazelnut! DUCE! Pine Kernel and Cinnamon! DUCE! Reign of the Two Sicilies! DUCE! And in the hand of our most devoted brother—Dark and Bitter Chocolate! DUCE! DUCE!

In the flattening light of late afternoon, the chocolate looked almost as black as his black shirt. As I told Daniele in the dormitory, I shall never view the Fascist salute in the same way again!

Tanti baci, your Giulio

When she tired of pestering the postman, Zia Paola took to pestering me. 'How about the famous fish and chips so loved by the Scottish? A night with no cooking is an idea, no? Each day I pass before McEwen and smell the fry. Now I want to try it.'

'There's plenty other chippies,' I said, 'better ones, cleaner ones.'

I recollected one of the reasons why Zio Roberto was so furious at losing his wife—her stubbornness, put to use in sale of livestock. 'But I don't pass by others each day.'

For nearly two months I hadn't set eyes on him and I'd begun to hope he'd left the neighbourhood . . . joined the army . . . dropped dead. 'Long time nae see, Lucia,' said his father. 'Four fish suppers coming up. And who's this fine-looking lass?'

Nothing in the father appeared to explain the son. 'This is my Zia—my Aunt Paola. She's come to try your finest.'

'Salt'n vinegar? No? Well, Ewan will be sorry to have missed you. Not just yous Italians what has your social clubs. Ewan's gone joined the . . . Canna mind the name but something like Fascist Nationals, so I gave him time off for some big jamboree doon London. I'll be sure to tell him you were here though.'

Back home, Zia Paola inspected the *frittura* with a forensic eye; bisected cod and batter; taste convinced her no more than texture or appearance. 'And you tell me we Italians have fish-and-chip shops? No is possible an Italian make so bad.'

Maclodio

28 July

Dear Lucia,

Rome was already too close to Zio Roberto for our fearless brother, so Daniele accompanied me as he has no family to visit. Transport may have improved on the main lines but in the countryside one shrinks back a century. Not that I care, cara, because I am happy.

In our final days in the capital we were instructed to marvel at: a factory producing ball bearings; a primary school where children really believe we're in Anno 4 as the Fascist calendar dictates; Cinecittà, where the films are made about the Duce's control of every aspect of the country's well-being. Unofficially we were taught to wonder at the Duce's superhuman amorous capacities! I walked the area round Via delle Botteghe Oscure but found no more hostility towards the city's Jews than I'd find in the usual Scottish pub. Statues are being erected on every public building and train station of big muscly men wielding sledgehammers and bounteous-breasted women gathering corn or tending to innumerable bairns.

Zia Lalla considers our Duce an impostor because he is of humble origins and from the North, but admires his reputation as a womanizer. Zia Antonella curses him as an atheist. Zia Flavia has two photographs of the Duce on her wall as ordered by the new mayor (who insists on being called a 'Podestà') but only uses them to scare the illegitimate infants in her care; she tells them he came by his enormous jaw by crunching up baby bones!

The entrance to Nonno's cave has overgrown with briars. Inside, a single table, a chair, a cot-bed, Papà's letters unopened in a heap. He knows nothing of the Duce but does not like what he reads in the stars. He asked Daniele several questions and found the answers amusing. He enquired about your catapult!

Zio Roberto was expecting me: for this visit I went alone. Strained pleasantries, then, 'So what have you to offer me?' I told him I came with sympathy for his solitude. (Everyone knows he has a new 'maid' who shares his bed and whom he controls because of some debt of her brother's.) 'And the slut now works for your Papà? While I must pay a servant and negotiate alone the prices on the sheep and goats.' I agreed that life on this earth is full of suffering (realizing with a nasty start that I was sounding like Padre Clemente!). 'Compensation might halt the affront and for the wealthy foreigner no burden.' I hastened to dispel the wealthy-foreigner myth, showing my chapped hands in evidence. 'A gesture goes far to mending a broken heart.' I hoped his heart would once again be free, adding that Zia Paola has asked our Archbishop for an annulment.

I saw him feel in his pocket for a stiletto I hoped was imaginary. 'She wishes to marry that bastardo thief your brother? May he burn in the fires of Hell! And on what grounds does she hope for this annulment?'

This was the hardest part. 'Lack of children?'

'That afflicts many honestly wedded couples.'

I dared to hint that this might be due to a . . . a certain lack of appropriate . . . marital attention?

However hard I try, I'll never be able to explain what happened next. For somehow Zio Roberto had leapt to the other side of the room and was blocking my exit, coming at me with a knife that was all too real! Desperate straits urge desperate measures, so I reached for his shepherd's crook and slammed it into his chest. Given his speed, this resulted in his flipping comically onto his back. I stood over him like Moses on the Mount. 'Basta!' I cried, magnanimous in victory. 'I'm sure Zia Paola is saving to make some gift of atonement that will ease the pain of your old age—so long as there's no opposition to the annulment.'

Instantly, he was meekness itself. 'The Holy Pontiff who knows all things will decide. Who am I to contradict his will.'

I awoke in the night, sweating at the sight of Zio leaping past me like out of the Olympic Games. Daniele couldn't stop laughing. One more day in Rome, exploring the sights together, then home—though didn't I use 'home' for Maclodio?

Your loving Giulio

PS. Life is so beautiful when one has a special friend to share it!

10

The Pitman shorthand symbols wobbled like drunken spiders across my page. The system I learnt quickly enough, though I had trouble with the diphthongs (Giulio explained that this was connected to their absence in Italian).

For the very first time, pleading that he was too worried about the declining health of his special friend Daniele, Giulio declined to give a speech at the Fascio Christmas party. Emilio showed up for only ten minutes, claiming a head cold. Just as circles were forming for songs, a bang at the door signalled a stranger. There in the chill night air was a taxi-cab, its engine running, the driver, like St Nicholas, lugging towards us an enormous package dressed in ribbons and bright-red paper. Only when the exhaust fumes had vanished did the spell break.

Back inside, Dario scanned the card. 'Go ahead,' he told me, 'you open it.' Under everybody's gaze, I undid the ribbons, slid back the paper.

'*Magnifico!*'

'*Caspita! Une bestia!* For us?'

'Yes,' crowed Dario, 'for us! For the whole Edinburgh Fascist community, for the proud patriots we are, comes this gigantic custom-made *panettone*. And whence does the gift derive?' No one could imagine. 'On the orders of Palazzo Chigi itself, in recognition of our efforts. And . . .' He paused for effect before reading out the card: '*In tribute to Dario Pezzini for boosting Party membership and ensuring last summer's magnificent march in Rome.*' He looked up, almost abashed. 'In this providential act I see the hand of the Duce himself, he who thinks of everything!'

Applause was spontaneous and sustained from the forty-odd assembled. Dario pulled a flick-knife from under his trouser leg and invited me to slice into fifty parts that peculiar mix of eggs and air that makes Italian Christmas cake so unlike the heavy dark Scots variety. After a dozen slices I passed the honour to Ermanno, so I could retrieve for my scrapbook the card from Palazzo Chigi which Dario had screwed up and tossed in the bin. Instinctively I retreated to the toilet to unfold it.

> *To All the Children*
> *Wishing you prosperous times in 1927*
> *as we have known in Chicago*
> *this year*
> *Tanti baci from your Zia Sabrina*

I emerged into the usual dispute, about which village produced the most beautiful songs. Of Beppe, who had a stirring voice, I requested the one about the brigand whose *innamorata*, though wed, sends him a lock of her hair, which he's wearing round his neck when he's thrown down a well shaft, above which her lock floats magically . . .

But instead of this, I heard Dario announce: 'These songs of long-lost love are all very well, but we know where our duty lies this evening and the gratitude to which our hearts must give voice. We know the tune and we surely know the words!'

Next to his brother on the dais, Giulio was the oddest mix of awkwardness and resignation. A hush went round the clubhouse as he raised his hand. 'My own favourite is Beppe's about the boys of the village press-ganged into Ferdinando's army.'

Beppe rose to his feet, but hardly had a single note sounded before Dario broke in with '*Basta*! First our Fascist duty.' Then launched into the anthem which everybody knew but few had learnt to love. '*Giovinezza, giovinezza*,' he sang, going straight for the refrain, '*Primavera di bellezza*.' His cronies joined in, and by the time they reached the lines about 'Per Benito Mussolini, Eja eja, alal,' they were thrusting arms in the air. Beppe had not desisted all the while, and Giulio joined in, as did some of the older folks for whom the Duce's anthem, with its plodding tune and its lauding of youth, valour and beauty, held little charm or promise.

Seats shifted, frowns were exchanged. Dario surely wished to desist, but feared that without his baritone his side of the hall, as it had now become, would be drowned out by the brigands opposite, swelled as these were by several basses and by the less obvious advantage of these voices being seasoned by adversity rather than triumph. In the final verse of Giovinezza, Dario's choir claimed 'Siam pronti alla morte'; but the Lock of Hair minstrels, accustomed as they were to extemporizing, extended their song to include an episode in a dungeon, an encounter with the Devil disguised as a goat, a miracle cure effected by a witch . . .

The evening finished earlier than expected, the clear-up took longer than usual. In nameless, wordless ways, between anthem and ballad, Duce and Brigands, something had got lost. When we finally made it home, no one could miss the glances Dario was casting at his siblings round the kitchen table. It was me he picked on first, who had sliced the panettone so poorly. Next Emilio, who had 'disgraced his family with his lack of respect' (leaning over the grate, Emilio pinched a fingerful of ash which he sprinkled on his head). For the chief denunciation, he unbuttoned, so the hairs showed on his burly chest. 'And as for you . . .'

Giulio did not look up from the book in his hand.

'I'm talking to you, Iscariot. What do you mean by interfering with Giovinezza, it's no a bloody carol competition. You hear me?' When Giulio failed to respond, the book was snatched from his hand. 'And speaking against me in public, me the Treasurer and Founder, your older brother to boot, who's due some respect.'

'Is that to jackboot?'

'What?'

'Is that, older-brother-whom-I-should-respect, to jackboot?'

'You taking the micky? Because I'm warning you, we can always do without your type!'

'What do you mean?' I moaned, '*his type*? Can't you see he's worried about his pal?' But no one was listening. Giulio was reading his empty hands as if they were a book.

'Well? Say that again and there'll be trouble.'

'What? About the jackboot? It was a joke, Dario. To boot, to *jackboot*? The Duce's favourite footwear?'

'Say that word one more time and I'm warning you!'

'Which word? Jackboot?'

'I'm warning you!'

'Dario!' groaned Papà.

'Jackboot.'

The blow caught Giulio on the temple. He reeled to one side then pulled himself upright. Still he refused to look at his brother.

'Stop it!' I screamed. Papà put his face in his hands.

'Jackboot.' He only whispered it, but the fist hit his cheek just as hard, causing a screech of teeth. I sprang at Dario, but he effortlessly held me at arm's length.

'Jackboot.'

The third blow fell vertically on Giulio's nose.

'Jack . . . boot.'

The fourth, which hit the back of his head, was the knockout. The silence which followed, after his body hit the floor, made the noise of smashing plaster all the louder, when Zia Paola, who all the while had been watching from the window, brought one of Papà's unsold Magi, with the full force of her washerwoman's arms, down on the back of Dario's skull.

It must have added to Giulio's injuries when his brother collapsed on top of him.

11

London, 8 July 1927

Carissimo Fratello,

The train runs so fast that here we are in London already! We formed two groups, with some girls wanting to visit St Peter's in Clerkenwell & others recalling how the Duce has declared that priests are black microbes lethal to mankind. But then Assunta from Fife was true to her holy name and reminded us that Pio-Pius declared that when the bullet of the would-be assassin Violet Gibson spared the Duce, this was due to *La Divina Provvidenza*. So most of us girls went to church, while Dario and the men-folk visited Quaglino's which is some fancy restaurant in Soho.

But my first-ever letter & here I'm writing things of scant interest to you! Thank you again for the lovely birthday present of the dress. Can it be one week ago already? I can hardly believe I am 17 years old! My only moment of sadness came when I thought of how I should have been meeting your friend Daniele . . .

At our Embassy, Ambassador Bordonaro gave us a photograph of the Duce walking on a beach by himself. It makes me almost sorry for him, so alone and with so many cares. In an hour, we catch the train for Dover, so I must stop now. Shame you don't read shorthand!

Love & affection from your fondest

Lucia

I wanted my letters to be worthy of those I'd received. I'd do a draft, then a neat copy using a carbon. I used italics whenever I could, to impress him with my hand, and ampersands as marks of my independence; I'd even borrowed a thesaurus from the Central Library in order to surprise my brother with my vocabulary.

Between Florence & Rome, 14 July

Dearest Giulio,

My *ballila* chums are worn out from our visit to the Uffizi Gallery, but not me, so I went out walking. The summer heat was enough to bake a potato. Lots of poor people with no shoes on, huge queues snaking from the shops. What they feed *us* is very scrumptious but many of our girls have upset tummies since, as Dario says, 'Here in civilization, olive oil's not sold in chemists' shops.' Through the window of this train I see vineyards & fruit trees & olive groves, with no sign of Man fighting Nature like in Scotland. Though I admit the carriage does look like our back yard with washing lines everywhere since we girls have to wash our shifts non-stop because of the heat, and lie around half-undressed. Not that after all those naked ladies in the Uffizi we look so remarkable!

Just been told to prepare for arrival. I shall write to you again soon!

Your Lucia

After nine months of dragging my feet to College, dragging my pen along the lines dictated by secretarial protocol, I was free for three whole weeks. I had grinned and borne it, had qualified, would 'never be short of a job again' according to the Principal. Even had it not been so hot, I could hardly have slept much, time was so precious. I was young—the idea surprised me—and I was heading home.

Roma Aeterna, 18 July

Dear Giulio,

Now I see why they call it Eternal! Now I feel what it is to be Italian and have this magnificence as our past.

Our guide is named Valerio Valentino. He is 22 & speaks some English. He has taken us round the Forum, the Pantheon and the Colosseum. He noticed I understand Latin & makes me translate the inscriptions chiselled on the stones. He keeps the beggars at bay & chides the Roman men pinching our bottoms—though he is rather dashing himself.

I don't suppose you'd care to hear about our visit to St Peter's, which is a pity as it is so vast and beautiful. Christ may not have been born in Italy, but Papà's *presepe* nativities are right to show how he *might have been*. Don't scold me for praying that one day these two great pillars of our Italy—Duce & Pio—might one day be friends.

The Party pays for everything, even for ice-creams from your favourite Giolitti! But don't think we've been neglecting our marching drills and callisthenics. Our outfits are black tunics & neckerchiefs & wee-girl gymslips (which Assunta says will make the pinchers go wild). At first we were to carry rifles, but His Holiness was so furious at the idea of girls shouldering arms through His city that even the Duce had to pay heed. Instead, we're to be given little bows & arrows— just like Cupid, says Valerio!

I'm looking forward to meeting the Zie and have Zia Paola's ransom safely stowed. Give my love to Emilio & Papà & save a big scoop for yourself.

Your Lucia

The months had raced by since Christmas, and the incident after the party had left few traces, on the surface at least; Giulio's bruises soon healed, or had been absorbed into the gloom—I could sense him trying to conceal it—he had felt when he learnt of Daniele's death. Dario overflowed with apologies, while Zia Paola treated Dario as if he were lucky she hadn't inflicted a more lasting wound. More surprising still, Dario was not just accepting but enthusiastic. 'The Fascist method,' he crooned. 'Took the nurse at the Infirmary an hour to get all that frankincense out my scalp.'

Roma, 22 July

Dearest Brother,

Arrows can be perilous! Assunta was practising in the dormitory when her hand slipped & she did a Violet Gibson on Valerio, grazing his cheek. 'All heroes need a scar,' said he, returning from the doctor's surgery.

But what, you ask, was he doing in the girls' dormitory in the first place? Taking me aside—only, I'm not sure I should tell you this when you never tell me *anything* of this sort—he says to me, 'One arrow pierced my face, but another from Cupid's bow has pierced my heart.' So put that in your bachelor's pipe and smoke it!

After all the rehearsals, today was our Big Day, parading down Corso Vittorio Emanuele II in our gym slips, with nobody daring to pinch our bottoms. All manner of speeches on Piazza Venezia but so distant that all I heard was something about the importance of empire. Then we pointed our arrows at the sky & Pfoof! Paf! flashed the flash-bulbs as our tribute was captured. We chanted 'Duce! Duce! Duce!' & after fifteen minutes someone appeared & we raised our arms in salute. Then he was walking down the ranks, talking to people as he went. Keeping the arm raised proved tiring, but my determination was rewarded since—can you credit it!—when our Duce came up level he paused & gave us an admiring look. (I hardly even noticed but Dario told me later he was wearing military uniform with an Alpinista's hat.)

You may not believe what I tell you next, but I've been promised the photograph to prove it. Picture this: I'm standing with my right arm aching in salute, trying to look like a Centurion, when the Duce steps up to me—yes *me*!—and, looking at our Union Jack, says, 'Brava!' Adding in English, 'From where do you come?'

I was so surprised that I almost forgot. 'From Scotland,' I get out, before I realize I've no idea how to address him. Should I say 'Sir'? Or 'Your Excellency'? Or 'Your Highness'?—or what? So 'Imperatore!' I blurt out, since that's all that comes to mind.

This makes him smile—yes, *smile*! I forgive Mister Blister all his jibes about us papists since I learnt enough Latin to make our Duce smile. He says to me: 'Home of Robert Burns who was poet of his people & Walter Scott who built a castle.' Then he nods again & repeats, 'Brava!'

Please tell Emilio that our Duce spoke of poetry & of course tell everyone since the honour is not mine alone but for all our Scottish Fascio. As Dario later put it: 'Is there anything he does not know!'

Love,

Lucia

The following day, as I traversed Piazza Navona, the fountains sparkled for me alone. This was what it meant to be alive. And young! Before, being young had only ever meant being left out or offered last choice. And what was more, at the Trevi I had an *appuntamento*, my first. I wondered, when I wrote my next to Giulio, just how much I would tell him.

Rome, 24 July

Dear Giulio,

Now I know the magic of the picture house—yes, I was *invited* to the pictures! Valerio says he finds me *exotic* & that my funny accent *delights* him. First came a short informative film about someone called Marinetti who believes in *Futurismo* and who advises eating *Aerofood* (whatever that is) while rubbing sandpaper on the leg! Then there was the Battle for Babies being won at a maternity clinic. Then closing down a temple in the Battle against Freemasons. Then someone called Italo Balbo flying his plane in Libya in what I believe was the Battle for Empire.

Then came the feature, the talkie called La Vita di Romano Conti. It shows Romano born into a poor family in the South where he falls in love with his neighbour Angela. But then he is lured to Naples where he sells contraband & takes up with a lady of ill-repute & starts drinking, until he becomes a down-and-out as bad as any in the Grassmarket. Then he sees the Blackshirts tearing down a slum & this restores his hope. He returns to his village & marries Angela & has numerous children & works the land. I cried of course even if Angela was rather less beautiful than the lady of ill-repute. Valerio would not accept his handkerchief back, so now I have to hide it from the girls as it bears the VV monogram.

I may not be as good at description as you but I'm not sparing the personal details, as you see. Goodnight now & may God & the Duce bless you (even if you don't want the former),

Your Lucia

The train was slow, scruffy, and seemed to stop for every passing goat. The black-clad women who shared my bench threw suspicious glances when I took pen and paper from my handbag. I could feel the kiss Valerio had given me in Roma Termini station—my first of any but the fraternal sort.

Maclodio, 28 July

Dearest Giulio,

Home for the very first time! Even if home is so small & everyone so poor & there's *such* a pong ...

Let me confess to you, who never confess: my mind's a wee bit spinning with VV who saw me off, insisting he never wished to say *Addio* again. He's very handsome—all the girls agree—with hazel eyes & a long Roman nose. He works in an office which distributes new housing, but since his father is high up in the Party & since he knows English he was given time off to help us harridans. Could it be all the *peperoncino* in the food that makes these Italian boys move so fast? Or the birthday dress you gave me which I wore for the send-off?

The mule cart took me from Frosinone via Picinisco. You know the scene well, but oh the parched barrenness of the land! Zia Lalla & Zia Flavia full of amazement and dread that a young woman could travel unaccompanied. Zia L is so fat and hairy & Zia Antonella so devout that I chose to stay with Zia F. Strange she never married, attractive as she is.

Now I must go see the Podestà who wishes to make a photograph of my photograph of the Duce with his arm on my shoulder for the wall of his office. Who'd have imagined your sister so famous!

Tanti baci,

Lucia

12

I sent my brother *baci* but neglected to tell him of the *bacio*. It may be that Zia Flavia could read my mind, for as she served me chamomile infusion she explained how she had never loved a man enough to marry, though several had proposed on account of her owning a one-room cottage. Once, there had been a priest; but her sister Antonella had denounced them, so the priest was replaced by an ageing lecherous toad of whom Zia Antonella approved. Apart from the orphans whom she tutored, it was animals she loved now, for their blameless hearts, she said, and their furry stomachs.

Maclodio, 28 July

Dearest Giulio,

Zia F was so curious that I told her about my having an *innamorata*. She said to learn from her lonely life & do differently.

If the Battle for Grain is being won, there's little sign of it here. I'm told the Battle for Babies would be more successful if even 50% survived the first six months. I was in piazza with Zia L & Zia A when Priest bumped into Podestà—I mean that literally, as both refused to give way, both in their finest black. Word for word is beyond me as most of the dispute was in dialect and curses, but the crux was who had greater authority—Pio or Duce—with the two claiming their own ruler to be *assoluto* . . .

Of course, everyone wants to know about Zia Paola. I've not yet plucked up courage to visit Zio Roberto. Naturally, I'll need a *cicerone*. Can't even go to the lavatory—if there were a lavatory—without company, being a *dangerous unmarried young woman*.

When I hiked up to Nonno's cave what a shock I received. He really does look like a cave-man. He was full of questions, including some about you. He showed no surprise when he learnt you were not yet married. I wanted to ask him about the past, to quiz him about why he moved to Scotland in the first place, all those years ago. But he said the future is clearer to him than the past. He stared at my palm. 'You'll live long, like me,' he said. 'But unlike me, you'll not forget.' I gave him Papà's present of the tartan scarf & the socks knitted by Zia Paola.

Now I have to stop, as Zia Lalla wants me for the *quattro passi in piazza.*

Your fondest sister

Lucia

For so many years I had longed for Maclodio; now I was there, I longed for Rome, where I'd have only one more day before the train north, far from VV.

First came duty. As *cicerone*, for irreproachability, I chose holier-than-thou Antonella.

Maclodio, 31 July

Dear Giulio,

Mission accomplished—but only just!

Zio Roberto's door was open, rosolio and stale biscuits on his table, no sign of his housekeeper-serf. Taking your advice, I chose the chair nearest the door, though he looked so antique I believed I could easily escape (believed mistakenly, as you will shortly see). The thought of his ancient wrinkly body next to Zia Paola's lovely smoothness I tried to banish from my mind . . . The predictable formalities about my journey, and my enquiries about his goats, every last 34 of which he chose to name, which passed some time.

'And dare I enquire,' he finally started, hunched in his chair like some hobgoblin, 'about my beloved wife who has abandoned me to a miserable & unprotected old age?'

Zia Antonella could not contain herself. The insults she bandied about her late sister's husband's half-brother's wife will give her confessor a sore ear. 'A corrupter of honest souls . . . a bitch in heat with a brazier between her legs . . .' etc., etc., flecks of foam whitening her lips. Zio Roberto enjoyed it at first but was soon indignant to think he was still married to such a shameless hussy. I saw my chance and explained how our dear Zia Paola asked to be fondly remembered in his thoughts & prayers. Reminded him of how she is seeking an annulment from the Archbishop.

'And the grounds?' He coiled in his chair like a spring.

The grounds, I explained, had of course not been revealed to a virgin like myself. But I added how her hands are worn to the bone & how every penny she puts aside for the gift she intends to make to sweeten the years between the annulment & his being welcomed back into the arms of his Maker.

'God's ways are not the ways of man,' said Zio, who had visibly perked up. 'And when should we expect this atonement? Before the Vatican Commission sees my story?' He was goat-herd no longer, more like that Manager of the Royal Bank who interviewed me for the job. It seemed a good moment to withdraw, figuring I could get away without releasing Zia P's ransom (as she said I should if I could). But I'd barely risen to my feet, when he sprung like a jack-in-the-box from his chair to the doorway, which he now blocked. If I were Zia Flavia I'd say it was black magic. 'And in your bag?' he said. 'No tokens of fondness from my still-beloved wife?' Was he just hopeful or had his spies informed him? I wasn't going to test it, so I gave him the bundle of shirts & collars that Zia P. had patched & stitched.

The evening light on the hills helped me ignore the stench of human **** in the street. What a terrible burden to be bound to one you hate; what a glorious chance to be bound to one you love!

Your sister

Lucia

PS. As Zio R. surely has a spy in the postman, I'll send this only when I reach Rome tomorrow for our final day.

Two days later, on the train between Rome and Florence, I told myself to throw caution to the winds. I wrote faster than I ever had, the words pouring out of me.

2 August

Dear Giulio,

What can I tell you? What *should* I tell you? What *dare* I tell you? My pen can't keep pace with my thoughts . . .

VV met me off the train, more handsome than ever. We strolled round Piazza Minerva admiring the marble elephant with the obelisk on its back. Then he wanted to take me to a restaurant—a real *ristorante*! I was well into the *primo*—fried artichokes with leaves & all— when I noticed that many men were sporting saucers on their heads. VV explained we were in the *ghetto* & that this was Jewish-Italian food & these Jewish-Italian folk.

Gulp! Did that mean he was Jewish too? I fear I rather blurted it out. He explained how his deceased Mamma was Jewish, so technically he is, though his Papà is Catholic & he's been raised Catholic. I said I feel mixed too, with Scotland & Italy, and tried not to think of those awful things we read in Dario's National Fascisti newsletter. VV said he'd brought me here to show me more of who he really is.

Soon it was time for VV to take me back to the dormitory. He said he couldn't bear for me to leave tomorrow & that he wanted to see me waking up in the morning & even watch me sleep at night (which seemed rather farfetched to my practical Scottish side). We stopped by the elephant, not a soul around. Then it was *I* who led *him* into a more dimly lit *vicolo*, & I who leant against the wall & I who invited him with my eyes. He didn't take asking twice but kissed me as if it could go on for ever. I hitched up my skirt since it was getting in the way & since it was too hot for stockings I could feel him pressed against my bare legs. It was me who put his hand where (with a little encouragement from Auntie Sandy) I've learnt to put my own. My thighs felt wobbly & I wanted to do it all & would have laid down there on the cobblestones . . . But V shook his head. I could have kicked him, it seemed such an insult when I was offering him all a girl has to offer.

'Not like this,' he said. 'I want to be part of your life & your future & your past.'

It sounded terribly abstract to me, but after a minute I admitted he was right & let him lead me back to the digs. Slept surprisingly well. And today was all about souvenirs and trains. I gave VV my address so he can write to me & maybe some day visit & make me his *promessa sposa*.

I'll post this from Florence where we change trains. I hope you won't judge me too harshly & that it will maybe even inspire you to share some of you own stories.

Your loving sister

Lucia

My hand hovered over the post-box in Florence station, until the announcement that the Milan train was departing. I ought to be confessing to Padre Clemente, not bragging to my brother—of all people! My name was called, my hand withdrew automatically as common sense prevailed. What was I dreaming of, sharing suchlike scandal with my own kith and kin!

When I saw him on the platform in Waverley station, my relief at having been wise outweighed the disappointment at risks untaken. And when we left the station, my sensible Scottishness was polished by the Protestant storm clouds oppressing the capital, all those greys after the reds and turquoises of Italy; then buffed to a shine by the unflattering outfit I purchased for the job I was about to start at the Royal Bank (junior shorthand typist, trial period); and finally put in a showcase almost as baroque as the one containing the relics of St Andrew, by the intricate penances imposed by Padre Clemente when I told him of the kiss at the station—I spared his wheezing lungs the artichokes and the *vicolo*.

13

I did not find it hard to fit in at the Royal Bank. If there was a distance between me and the other junior employees, it was mostly of my making. I put it out that I was Catholic and devout, let myself count out loud in Italian. My life felt so full already, any dullness in the days' routine more than mitigated by the excitement of the Friday pay packet, by the sudden acceleration in our lives as Paola worked for her annulment, most of all by the letters from Rome which arrived almost daily. My only anxiety was that, as the rest of us streamed forward, Giulio seemed rooted to the spot, watching us wistfully. I would listen to Paola's groans of envy when I read her extracts in bed. 'If only Dario, once, would write to me *così*.' She'd turn up her nose only when Valerio digressed into politics—he was unhappy with how the Party cronies received housing perks, he was nervous about rumours of closer ties between the Vatican and the Duce. 'Spare me the politics,' Paola would say. 'Enough of such things from Dario I hear. Wee boy bairns dressing up in costumes. I hope they grow up soon.'

'Girl bairns too,' I reminded her, pointing to the photograph of the Duce smiling down at us from above the bed (I'd used my first pay packet to have it framed and protected with glass). 'Without the Duce and the Party's generosity, there'd have been no trip to Rome, and no letters at all. Do you think,' I added, 'that Giulio has ever received love letters like mine?'

She screwed up her face unaccountably. 'We can't all have your luck, finding the right man so fast.'

And, as if to prove it, days later she did receive a letter, not the one she longed for, from the Vatican or Archbishop, but from her husband who reminded her that he would be perjuring himself to acquiesce in the enquiry into his failure to perform his conjugal duties; his wife should understand this could not be done lightly. Just how heavily was weighed in a currency which itself had a whiff of Inferno: twenty-two goats.

'It means my wedding dress will have no train,' she regretted. And when I asked her how she'd propose to send the goats: 'He will accept the money, a way we shall find.'

By Christmas she was vindicated, in an audience with the Archbishop who explained that the Pope, having considered her case in his infinite wisdom, had decided that, her desire to bring forth children in accordance with God's will having been thwarted, an annulment would be granted.

Giulio was the first to congratulate her, and I was surely the only one to detect some sadness in the corner of his eye. Very different from the misgiving—almost panic—in the eye of Paola's betrothed, as it dawned on him that the family flat where he had lived for twenty-five years would no longer be home.

'Have you no understood,' he moaned, 'that family is the heart of Fascismo? Only with that bond secure can the larger cells of our new society make sense.' He tried to convince his brothers that they could sleep in the kitchen, while the newlyweds took over their room, or that I could share with my brothers while he and Paola occupied my recess. 'In any case,' he added, 'I'll be away a lot with meetings and the like—Zia Sabrina and her Joe have written from Chicago saying that a pilgrimage from yours truly might be required.'

For once, Papà was firm; though he wasn't required to be so for long, since days later, Auntie Lena from across the landing announced that she was moving out—the three flights of stairs were proving too much for her arthritic hip. Within a day, Zia Paola had secured the lease on the two-room flat (kitchen and bedroom). 'It's a rum business,' moaned Dario, 'and a waste of hard-earned cash. But it beats being kicked onto the street as my ain folks appear to want.'

I had to water down VV's romantic profusions—not for Giulio but for Zia, disappointed as she was when she learnt that, because of Dario's involvement in the Fascio, the doors of St Mary's Cathedral were barred to her. A minor church in Leith might be negotiated, wedged between a warehouse and a pub. Whenever she tried to discuss the invitations, the dresses, the cake, the flowers, her intended would take off on some tirade, as if such details risked undermining his Fascist credentials.

'Gardenias or pansies?' She had studied the English names and told me I was bound to catch the bouquet.

'I know some who'd like pansies,' Dario laughed. 'But it's no me. Listen to this, from *The Times*.' He was well armed with newspapers whenever the subject of the wedding arose. Emilio withdrew to the bedroom, as he always did when Dario got going. Giulio, just home from work, sat on the arm of Papà's armchair and held his hand in his. '*I have been able to do no less, like so many others, than to remain fascinated by the simple and kind behaviour of Mussolini and by his calm and distant nature.*'

Zia, used to his tactic, was not so easily deterred. 'Invitation list . . . almond bonbons . . . reception hall . . . musicians.'

'Honeymoon,' added Giulio.

'That's my gift,' said Papà, surprising everyone, maybe even himself. 'First child I give away. Your Mamma would expect it of me. A weekend in North Berwick or the Silver Sands at Aberdour.'

'*Tante grazie*, Papà,' said Zia, kissing the bald spot on the benefactor's head. No one imagined he had the money—the offer the more precious.

Dario frowned over his *Times*. 'Honeymoon?' he repeated, as if the word were new to him. 'You think I've got time for careering round the country? Listen, there's a two-bob prize for whoever guesses who's written this column. *If I were Italian I can guarantee that I would have been wholeheartedly with Mussolini from the beginning against the bestial appetites of Leninism. I must say one thing about fascism: this movement has done a service to the entire world.*'

'It'll be good to invite Beppe,' suggested Giulio, 'for the songs.'

'Who says you're inviting anyone, to my wedding?'

'Zia's told us we can have two guests each,' I put in. 'Since we've not been invited back to Rome this summer, I hoped that Valerio might come, but he's not been given the time off work.'

Papà said, 'I'll invite Auntie Lena, and Mamma's friend Auntie Rebecca from McVities.'

'What!' exclaimed Dario. 'Rebecca the Lithuanian? But she's a Yid!' Of the people in the room, only he was unaware—having failed to hear me out—that Valerio was technically Jewish. 'I thought this was meant to be a Fascist wedding. A Fascist family.'

From the bedroom came Emilio's voice: 'Show us, dear brother, where in the venerable Duce's speeches it says that nobody of the Jewish persuasion can be invited to an Italian—even to a *Fascist* wedding.'

'What's with *persuasion*? It's the Hebrew race we're talking about. And there's more to Fascism than old Muss, you know. Too stuck in your damned poetry to realize it.'

Giulio was interested. 'You talking about the British Fascisti?'

'No balls on that lot. *National* Fascists, more like.'

'I didn't mention my second guest. It's Carlo.'

'Carlo who?'

'Balestracci. If it's all right with you, Zia?'

'You need to stop calling me *Zia*, Giulio. If your *zia* I remain, then I cannot marry your brother.'

'You mean Balestracci the docker? Him I beat to pulp at the gym? You don't even know him!'

'Barely a day goes by that he's not down Cavazzoni's for a scoop of ice-cream. He's as Italian as the rest of us, so no objections there.'

'Not only has he refused to sign up to the Fascio but he's threatened me with violence if I go on insisting. He's also in with that bunch of scabs daring to call themselves the Lega Italiana dei Diritti dell'Uomo. And you intend to invite this Bolshy bastard?'

'I'm not asking you to marry him, however, or the LIDU.'

'You telling me that on top of it he's one of them?'

'His wife died of the flu aged twenty-two.'

'Over my dead body will Carlo Balestracci come to my *matrimonio*.'

Emilio had come to the doorway. '*He held him with his glittering eye . . .*' From his tone, we all knew he was reciting. '*The wedding guest stood still / And listens like a three year's child; / The Mariner hath his will*.'

'Enough of your nursery rhymes! *Credere, Obbedire, Combattere*! Believe, obey, fight! That's all the verses any of us is needing.'

'The priest'll be happy to hear it.'

Dario waved his fist. 'You're laggards, the lot of you. Ganging up against the first-born. But there'll be no fucking riff-raff when Dario walks down the aisle!' On which idea of walking, he walked out.

'That's a shame,' said Papà without irony. 'So nobody won the two bob.'

Hours later, tidying up, I found the article in *The Times*. I would never have guessed the name at the foot of the column, having heard it rarely before: *Winston Churchill*.

14

The priest, in the event, was so nervous that he called Dario 'Davide' and imagined Papà to be Paola's uncle. He couldn't move fast enough through the service, then chased everyone out into the July rain as if we were mice. I failed to catch the bouquet, and Emilio threw the rice so hard that a fight almost broke out on the steps. The reception was like a miniature meet of the Fascio, the hall looking dingier than it had for years. All the family tried to drop the 'Zia' as Paola sold her garter to the highest bidder (with Dario frowning as if already sprouting a cuckold's horns, only family dared bid, leaving Papà with the trophy and a kiss).

I was wrapping the garter round my wrist when a voice whispered, 'Pretty colour, Lucia. Would look smashin on you. Though you might need some help hitchin it up the thigh.' I'd spotted him in a rear pew, then back-slapping Dario on the steps. Now his face had narrowed . . . and these men he was with, were these unfortunate specimens the National Fascisti?

'What you say? I've no got all night.'

I recoiled from the alcohol on his breath. 'I've nothing to say to you, McEwen.'

'But you do have a soft spot for me, go and admit it.'

There was a repulsion so strong I could not claim indifference— and had no words for the rest. 'I have a man already,' I said, breaking all my own rules.

'You're far too young to be walking out wi any man.'

I knew I shouldn't try, but could not resist. 'Not consider yourself a man, then?'

He ducked as if avoiding a blow. 'You think that just cos you're Dario's sister you can get away wi anything. But changes are in the air. He'll no be Chief Extractor for ever. Your Mussolini's a babe at the tit compared to what we've got coming.'

I was still quaking as the accordion played the cue for Signor Cavazzoni to wheel in his cart; Giulio had convinced him to expand on his staples to include Orange Sorbet, Chocolate and Cherry. Emilio mounted the podium to recite a poem he'd written which alternated couplets in English with couplets in Italian. The songs which followed raised the usual rivalries, only this time the struggle was settled by the bride who announced that the next person to mention *Giovinezza* would receive the cake knife rather than its slice of wedding cake.

I slept alone that night for the first time since Zia Paola—no longer *Zia*—had stepped into our lives. Only, I wasn't quite alone with Valerio's letters stacked round my pillow—a year of them now, and not one without some protestation of how much he missed me or how urgently he awaited my response (I wrote to him at lunchtimes, seated on a bench in Princes Street Gardens). I knew I should pay more attention to the passages about how upset he was to witness the marvels of old Rome being torn down to make way for boulevards; how worried he was at the money being spent on military parades, at the new laws persecuting inverts; how determined he was to continue to visit Via delle Botteghe Oscure ... But I sped through these parts in favour of accounts of how he'd give his next month's salary for a photograph of me, regretting how upright he'd once been, how he was pressing flowers to include in his Christmas mail, how he was saving all his money for the time when he could visit ...

I knew I was not beautiful, that I had not inherited Mamma's lustrous hair or shapely ankles. But as my eighteenth birthday passed, and I could marry without Papà's consent (not that he'd ever have dared withhold anything I requested), I finally came to realize that I did have something to offer, some allure that drew men to me. The future was infinite and inviting: only when, the night of Dario's wedding, Giulio asked if I might consider moving to Rome, did I realize that my union with VV did not take place in any worldly space, be it Italy or Scotland, but in a nameless zone of our own invention. Giulio told me he wanted me to be happy; I told him I already was, and that the one way he could make me happier, since he seemed almost as fond of Valerio as I was, was by finding his own route to joy—a joy which, I added, he would then communicate to me. Look, I pointed out, here was Dario off on his honeymoon, here I was in daily correspondence with a man who said he was determined to make me his *fidanzata*. What about himself, who was four years older than me?

'Let's first see how that honeymoon works out,' he sighed.

And was anything but surprised when the newlyweds returned after only one night in North Berwick, Dario claiming he was too busy for more and that the money would be better spent on baby clothes; where Roberto had failed for seven years, he was on a nine-month count-down to the birth of his first son.

I asked Paola if there were any special new husband-and-wife delicacies she wished to report to me.

'Delicacies?' she scoffed. 'More dirty tricks than a *puttana* it needs to make him perform. To see those again he must pay.' She seemed almost reluctant to cross the landing into what was henceforth their home.

Only once did a letter from Valerio divide us, and not along the expected lines, with myself left alone—worse, with Dario my sole ally. We'd all been busy, distracted, so the news had reached us as a rumour. It took Valerio's letter, and the prospect of celebration in the church the next day, to bring it home to us. I had no idea what friction it would cause when I read it out after the Saturday evening meal.

'Go on, Lucia,' Giulio encouraged me, 'read to us.' It was unusual for the whole family to be present, Dario included, and I felt suddenly shy with my paramour's words.

'I'm only going to read you the bit about what he's been doing,' I said, protectively skipping the parts about how much he missed me, how inadequate were the two photographs of myself I had sent him, and correcting his English as I went. 'For once,' I said, 'I really don't see what he's upset about. There's going to be a big celebration tomorrow after Mass.'

'So it's true, then,' Giulio muttered under his breath.

'He writes, *When I left the house, church bells were ringing everywhere. Romans were in the street, cheering with joy. I went as far as Piazza San Pietro but I could not go further as there were two hundred thousand souls, on their knees in the rain, all thanking God for the Patti Laterani.*'

Dario was laughing. 'Too true, and at last the breach has been healed.'

Giulio was fumbling at the newspapers which he'd neglected the past few days, as if by informing himself belatedly he might change the course of history.

'Valerio goes on: *But I am on my feet, fleeing. I suddenly see the world cut in two parts like an apple, with one half the Duce and the other half the Pope. That's not right, rather a peach, with the Pope the stone and the Duce the flesh. Every peach, for ever and ever amen.*'

Giulio was groaning.

'*And I feel my Mamma in myself say, No, there exists more than two. My Papà says that in Italy for everyone there exists a place, and his knees bend. But do the men in black who embrace one another think the same?* I don't understand it,' I added. 'I thought he'd be as pleased as we are.'

Dario was shaking his head. 'I was just saying to Padre Clemente this afternoon—'

'To Padre Clemente?' Giulio could not contain himself. 'You, blackshirt, representative of the Antichrist who dared to challenge the universal authority of the Holy Church?'

'You're behind the times again, little brother. That's the sacred miracle, where God has shown his hand. Pio himself is talking of *the visible intervention of Divine Providence.* They've gone and signed a pact, a *concordat* they're calling it, in the Lateran Palace, with great pomp and show.'

'But he was the only one strong enough to take on the Pope and his band of locusts.'

'Ave Maria, it's all in the past.' I might have said the same myself, had Dario not said it first. It all felt wrong: Valerio and Giulio against Dario and myself. I only wanted everyone to get along together, what was wrong in that? 'Too much time in your ice, it must have frozen your brain. Italy now has her own established church, the Pope has his state in the Vatican but not a lot else. Aye,' he said smugly, who had evidently been studying the question, 'the Pope wins the right to do some educating, bit of cash compensation. The rest goes to the Duce, who's now Head of State with every Pius endorsement and prayer. Church and State perfectly united for the first time since Italy became a proper country back in . . . whenever it was. I'll need to check that before my speech at the Fascio.'

Even Paola was against me. 'I can't believe that Pio, who freed me from the hog Roberto, has united with toy soldiers.' She was impervious to Dario's scowls.

Giulio, for once, was speechless. 'I'm not surprised the cat's got your tongue,' Dario scoffed. 'But you'll have time to see sense before I give my sermon the Sunday after next, at St Mary's.'

'Sermon! You?'

Papà had instinctively reached for his statuettes, as he did whenever there was tension in the kitchen. In his left hand a jackboot, in his right the Carpenter Joseph.

'Of my *speech* then, if you prefer, though the point is there's henceforth a fine line between a political speech and a sermon. It'll be about family, for this is the meeting point between Duce and Pius. How without love and duty between man and woman, without the children this produces, there's no future at all. And without the authority of a father and a leader no hierarchy, just anarchy. Is that no right, Papà?'

The characters in Papà's hands had communicated their truculence to him.

'Figure-*head*, Papà, not figure-*ine*! My point is, and will be, that men and women are made by God to be with one another.'

Emilio clucked quietly from the fireside.

'Shut it, you! Just because you'd fall flat on your face if you even tried to court a bird. What I'll be telling the worthies of St Mary's is that the Duce too has been fighting for family, and not just with his own wife and children . . .'

'And mistresses.'

'Will you shut the fuck up, Giulio! He can hardly help it if lassies keep stripping off and throwing themselves at him—excuse me, ladies, but it's a brutal fact, the Duce's favourite philosopher Niet-zsche says it somewhere, that with power everyone starts to fancy you. But that need not stop you fulfilling your duties as *pater familia*.'

'*Familias*,' I corrected him, glad of any occasion to put a distance between us.

'A bit of Latin's no the point either. It's the Battle for Babies I'll be preaching. What chance do we have against the Krauts with a miserable thirty-eight million? Against the scourge of Marie Stopes and the red-plague Bolsheviks and the suffragette hordes? And then I'll finish off . . .' He stared hard at Giulio. 'I'll finish off with the Duce's famous Bachelor Tax. If ever there was an inducement to do the decent thing, here it is. Any man too feeble to find himself a wife—let him pay! Any man whose blood is so thin that the race'd be better off without him breeding—let him pay! Any man too busy playing around with kiddies' rhymes—let him pay!' He punched his fist in the air with each utterance, his volume rising, until Paola stuck her fingers in her ears. 'Any man so decadent his instinct's got stuck up some fetid blind alley—old Pius agrees with me here, we're talk-ing about the deviants and devious—let him pay and pay double!'

15

The following morning Dario was the first to be dressed for church. And though he hadn't been seen on our family pew for nearly ten years, this didn't stop the priests from shaking his hand to welcome him back into the fold. I tried to forget Valerio's misgivings, to ignore the look of dismay on Giulio's face as the four of us—Paola, Papà, Dario, myself—left for the cathedral that Sunday morning.

Cheers and clapping filled the smoky Fascio clubhouse three days later, following Dario's extended version of his speech on the importance of the Lateran Pacts. I had made a point of wearing the dress that Giulio had given me, while he had asked Paola to press his black shirt a second time, as if the creases had some special significance.

'At such a moment,' Dario droned on, 'when our two great institutions, Church and State, are for ever united after half a century . . . or so . . . of conflict, is it not time for us in the Colonies to make a special effort too?'

His audience of maybe fifty Italians and half a dozen Scotsmen rehearsed the gesture learnt in church when the collection bowl approached.

'No, it's not your coins I'm after. It's *discipline*. You know what I'm talking about, not for the first time. *Lei*, the *Lei* form. Even our Scottish guests understand it.' He pointed to McEwen's group in the corner—their ringleader mercifully absent. 'Our Duce has published his own encyclical against it. When to a single inferior, then *Tu*. But to anyone else it must be *Voi*. For *Voi* is virile, upright, heroic, imperial.' *Lei*, he reminded the guests, meant literally *she*, and when an equal or superior was addressed by saying 'Does *She* want this or that', the entire Italian race was feminized. '*Basta così!*' he shouted. 'Our Italic blood must be purged of this virus. How can we forge our muscles into Fascist formations of which our Duce can be proud if we go around calling each other *She*! Say it with me now! *Voi*! *Voi*! *Voi*!' His smile was solemn as he stepped down, though the chorus was feeble.

No one had noticed that Giulio was making for the dais, where he hadn't been seen for months—no one but me, that is. A grin flashed across his face, as if his jaw had just released the tyranny of an age. 'Friends,' he began—not *Comrades*—'I've been dumb as a mule these past few months, wondering why I'd nothing left to say. This will be the last time I address you from here, and I apologize in advance since I've no notes to read from and only my heart to prompt me.' Everyone was attending, even McEwen's cronies. 'I've known many of you since I was a bairn and there are many things I'd like to say to you . . .'

'Just get on with it,' Dario moaned, loud enough for all to hear.

'I've long since left the church, as you know, convinced it fills our heads with Sin and Hell and Darkness Eternal, and all just for following our natures. I thought our Leader was the one person strong enough to defeat the Curia. Don't be offended, but until the other day the Duce was an atheist who described priests as *black microbes as fatal to mankind as TB*.'

Many of the older Italians were shaking their heads in distaste. 'It's all in the past,' said Dario. 'Let bygones be bygones.'

'They're a cynical sham, these Lateran Pacts, this concordat.' It was one of the first times in the seven years since the Fascio opened that Dario had been publicly, explicitly, contradicted. He watched in frozen fascination to see how far his brother would go; unless he was sensing that his own hold would be complete once his brother had banished himself. 'Yes, both speak of family. But now we're told it's a sin to be a bachelor, that we should be breeding to boost the head count. Are we livestock? I can march for my country, even fight for my country, but I shall not breed for my country. And what of this word *race* my brother keeps using. We Italians are not a race, for we have Greek, Phoenician, Italic, Norman, Etruscan, who knows what else in our veins. Only, nothing of the Nordic or Aryan.'

In the corner, McEwen's boys were restive . . . their leader too, who must have slipped in as Giulio was getting into his stride.

'Thank you all for your patience. When I meet you next, Signor Vanvitelli or you Signora Borsari, shall I address you by the Roman *Voi*? You may be sure you will still be *Lei* to me. What was good enough for our greats of the Renaissance, what was good enough for my dear departed Mamma, will be good enough for Giulio.'

Dario had struck a martyr's pose; unless the pose was of Christ himself, as Judas did his work.

'We must live and laugh and love, not just breed and salute. I understood this on the parade ground in Rome, two summers ago, when my comrades raised their ice-creams.' He was talking almost to himself, words tumbling out of him. 'I've worked hard for Signor Cavazzoni, and he's taught me the trade. Yet I've let my passion smoulder . . . But Vesuvius has only been dormant, smothered by complacency and a crust of black lava.'

He was surely not about to . . . Yes, he *was* about to. And not convulsively, but methodically, almost respectfully, removing his neckerchief first and placing it on the lectern. He had spent so many weeks and months making this place presentable—organizing, leafleting, reassuring the old and mobilizing the young—that the walls themselves seemed to sigh at the sight. He pulled up his sharply pressed shirt tails, undid the buttons, folded his black shirt on top of his neckerchief. Slow, very slow. Through his holes in his string-vest he was almost obscenely pale. 'I took a wrong turn, was never meant to be a politician. I was meant to bring you pleasure with frozen fruits and flavours. Which is where I must go now, showing what ice can bring even to this northern country we have made our home.' He was glowing. 'I'll seek to bring some of the glamour of La Scimmia into our lives, of Giolitti's. It's the only flag I wish to fly, and within the year I intend to wave it above my very own shop.'

Nobody clapped. Nobody booed. Nobody moved so much as a finger.

'I've shared some fine moments with you, even on my misguided path. *Arrivederci* . . . in . . . the Palace of Ice.' He jumped from the dais and into the January night without so much as a scarf to cover his neck.

After the hush, the hubbub, with everyone talking at once, shouting, chuckling, swearing, in what an outsider might have seen as typical Italian chaos. Dario had vanished. Papà was smiling proudly. Emilio was slapping his thighs. A sudden presentiment made me seek out McEwen, but I caught only the back of his head as he corralled his cronies out.

I awoke with a start and tiptoed through to the boys' room, where Emilio was alone in bed. Opened the front door in my shift and felt the cold possess me. Hearing a noise, I lit a candle and ventured onto the landing in my stocking soles. It was rising from the stairwell.

I swept down two flights. The moans were faint, the blood had dripped down the steps. At first I did not panic, but bent down and kissed him.

'Cara,' he whispered.

Then I screamed and screamed until Emilio was by my side.

With Paola under one arm, Emilio under the other, Papà and myself taking a leg each, we carried him up the stairs, trying not to jolt. On the landing, Dario appeared in his pyjamas, rubbing his eyes as if he'd just awoken. 'That's terrible,' he said, not offering assistance.

We laid him out on the kitchen floor to inspect the damage. The skull was badly gashed and there was vomit in his hair. His left hand was swollen and there were bruises all down his back where he must have curled to protect his vital organs. 'Castor oil,' he managed to utter, pointing to his mouth. 'And *manganello*.'

Paola prepared a Maclodio concoction to repair his stomach. With scissors we cut off what remained of his vest, bathed his wounds in iodine solution, wrapped his joints in poultices. When there was nothing more we could do, Papà asked him, 'Who did this to you, son?'

Giulio snorted, winced when he shook his head.

'We'll find them,' Emilio promised, 'and punish them.'

'I didn't see . . .' gasped Giulio through cracked ribs, closing his eyes and smiling. 'But one thing . . . is certain . . . They will never . . . be welcome . . . in the Palace of Ice.'

16

We took turns, sister and sister-in-law, to watch over him through the night of his drubbing. Mopped his brow and applied cold compresses to slow the blood that was coursing into his bruises.

In the morning, Papà wanted the police, despite the victim's protestations. 'I know who did it,' I said, surprising myself. 'It was McEwen and his National Fascisti.'

'Leave it,' Giulio quietly commanded.

No one dared utter what all were thinking: If McEwen, then what of the creature across the landing? The brother . . . husband . . . son?

'Call him, Papà,' said Emilio, tears in his eyes.

Dario was sleepy; a dream had left him tumescent in his pyjama trousers. 'What's the fuss?' he asked, lighting up.

I thought that if I spoke first, I might unearth an escape clause, even an alibi. 'It may be just coincidence but I saw McEwen and his gang race out just after Giulio left the Fascio.'

'That's a lie.'

My heart sank. Could he not at least be subtle? 'They never gave him this working over.'

'*Basta!*' Giulio raised a hand from where he was stretched on a blanket before the fire.

His brother blew cigarette smoke in his direction. 'Someone's seeking to give us Fascisti a bad name. I'll ask my mate PC O'Donnell to look into it. We'll find the *bastardi* who did this to my own wee brother.'

And when I was home from the bank that evening, spooning strawberry through swollen lips and chipped front teeth—Signor

Cavazzoni had brought round a tub—in he strode, jubilant, drunk, uproarious.

'We've cornered the thugs who did it,' he announced. 'Them from the LIDU, so called. They have the nerve to claim they're defending the Rights of Man, but I suspected them from the start. O'Donnell confirms it. Their *capo*, that Carlo Balestracci, the very one you wanted to invite to my wedding—and you see the way he thanks you?'

I begged him inwardly to stop here: didn't he realize we were all our parents' children, that we owed it to Mamma to respect her dying wish to assist one another?

'And the Masons lent a hand, any chance to discredit the Fascio.' I hadn't noticed Emilio, listening from the landing. 'And the Communists, don't forget them, and the Anarcho-Syndicalists, and the Trade Unions and the ranks of the lumpen unemployed down the *bru*—they surely had a hand in it too.'

Dario spat into the fire. 'Makes you realize, eh? Nobody's invulnerable.'

'Shall we prosecute the criminals?' Papà asked. 'With PC O'Donnell's help?'

'It's no so easy, Papà. No witnesses. The police in the pay of the Masons. We'll need to keep an eye out for ourselves.'

Next time I saw McEwen on the street, I inspected his knuckles for bruises, his clothes for bloodstains. He smiled at me complacently, thanked me for admiring.

As he mended, Giulio went on smiling too: at me and my hang-dog expression, at Dario, even at McEwen when, four nights later, a knock at the door revealed him laden with fish-suppers—'From me Pa, for the invalid'—suppers which we women refused to touch, Paola because of the odour and grease, myself because of their courier. And his cheer proved hard to resist, despite the scars, the teeth, the wheezing breath. If something had ended, then something had commenced. Captive in the flat, he drew sketches and made long snaking columns of calculations. One evening when we were alone, he told me there would even be a place for Valerio, if that was my intention. 'You'll see,' he explained, 'most folk don't know why they're here on earth, so they invent reasons, with the help of God or black shirts.' Even as he spoke, his ribs were mending. 'I don't know either, but I do know I can give pleasure.'

'Why not tell that to the bank managers,' I said, 'instead of playing with these lists of figures.'

'If you'll help me?'

'I've been hoping for nothing less,' I said. And I meant it.

'What can I do for you, Miss Pezzini?'

I had never addressed Mr Morton with more than a 'Good morning, sir', and here I was in his manager's office being stared down at by the smoky portraits of dignitaries dating back centuries. 'No indisposition? No professional dissatisfaction, I trust? I hear excellent reports of your work at the bank.'

I tried not to imagine kissing the bushy moustache as I explained in the driest terms possible that my brother intended to 'establish a new business' but lacked 'the necessary wherewithal'. I'd be most grateful if he would receive him to learn of the details.

'Times are hard, Miss Pezzini. And set to turn harder. You've seen the dole queues. What line of business does your brother seek to pursue?'

The founders leant out of their heavy gilt frames to inspect this daughter of an immigrant about to make a fool of herself. 'Ice, Mr Morton sir, ice.'

The upper lip curled as the nostrils flared. 'Ice,' he repeated, finally. 'The supply boats from Norway are losing trade to the new-fangled refrigeration engines. Despite shipment of salmon to the south, a future in ice would appear . . . precarious.'

I had not felt so mistaken since Mister Blister had revealed my ignorance in thinking *puellas* the plural of *puella*. I started to rise from my seat, since it would not be seemly to retreat on hands and knees.

'Now, had you said *ice-cream*, that would have been a different matter.'

Two inches up, I didn't know whether to climb or subside; gravity dictated the latter. 'I believe, sir, he is also intending ice-cream and all such products. He's quite a dab-hand.'

'You should have said so, always best to come straight to the point. Ice-cream, now, as I've been reading, is set to be a developing industry and promises profitability even in times of financial instability. For man—woman too, I dare say!—requires consolation, all the more when life is hard.' Not required to speak, I tried to look intelligent. 'I have scant personal acquaintance with ice-cream, which has always seemed a rather bland sweetmeat. However, in the current climate—and I do not mean the freezing temperatures we are currently experiencing—I would be willing to receive your brother in order to consider his proposition.'

This time I rose fully from the chair.

'And Miss Pezzini?' he enquired as I was retreating from his office, 'I trust you are content here at the Royal Bank? You've been with us, what . . .?'

'Six months, sir. Most content, Mr Morton sir, most content indeed.' In that moment, I certainly meant it.

The interview, as it turned out, was worryingly brief. Giulio hardly had time to repeat his well-rehearsed speech before Mr Morton interrupted, saying that until he had seen the products in question all discussion was academic.

One week later, my legs felt heavy as we trudged up Hanover Street, heading for the bank as if it were a prison. It all seemed too improbable, that Mr Morton, of the abstemious visage and the beady banker's eye, could be interested in what Giulio was carrying in three hermetic containers within his canvas bag: Gianduia, Pistachio Sorbet (it had turned out a paler green than desired), and South and North (with a hint of whisky and abundant sultanas); he had planned for more, but lack of the necessary ingredients had left him sleepless and ragged.

'Please be seated,' said Mr Morton to the two of us. 'You have prototypes for me, I believe?' I had trouble recognizing the manager of the previous week. Still dignified and imposing, but also a ten-year-old at North Berwick on a sweltering hot day. 'I've been eager to sample this concoction of which you spoke so eloquently. As you see, I have brought my own spoon.' Made of silver, with a coat of arms at the end of its stalk.

Giulio opened the insulating boxes one at a time, explaining the names and ingredients. 'Best to start with North and South, then clean the palate with Pistachio Sorbet, finishing with the richest and most powerful, which is Gianduia.'

Mr Morton was struggling to control his grin. 'How intriguing!' The tastes were bombarding him. He tried one, the second, then the third. Finally, he took a deep breath. 'Most unusual . . . An extraordinary colour, this green one, which one would not associate with such a taste . . . As you claim, a rich and—if I dare say—a *sensual* crescendo. I believe Mrs Morton would appreciate these flavours . . . And as you are aware, where feminine tastes have been vanquished, men are sure to follow.'

'It's my hope,' said Giulio, expanding, 'since unlike my older brother, I've never felt much at home in the pubs. I'm hoping, that is, for a place where people can gather, meet, exchange words and thoughts without having to prove a point, sit and read a newspaper in peace, and do so with the senses heightened by some flavour in the mouth . . .'

Half an hour later, the pledge was signed by which the bank would put up six hundred pounds, which we had calculated to be nearly half of what was needed to furbish the shop in the style to which Giulio aspired, buy the latest refrigeration that cut out all that mixing of salt and ice, freeing our maestro to concentrate on what he called *the artistry*. As we left the office, my brother could not resist asking: 'And if the flavours hadn't pleased you, Mr Morton, would you really not have signed?'

The manager was thoroughly manager again, shooting a look to make you tremble if you owed the bank a farthing. 'No question of it.'

'I'm glad to hear that,' said Giulio. 'Now I know what my flavours are worth.'

Spare moments, in the weeks that followed, were for running to abandoned shops, peering through boarded-up windows with an owner or agent, trying to ignore the dead cat, the woodlice, the reek. In the evenings, I did the sums, not with Mamma's alacrity but in uncompromising columns that showed how far we remained from the total required. Activity felt like a way of hiding the implacable fact that despite our rise in fortunes, our family was still far from rich; not *indigent* or *desperate* like the hungry parents begging in the streets—more of them than ever by February '29 as businesses closed and laid off their staff—but with enough just for basics.

The solution, for Dario, was simple: 'Let me put it to the Fascio. Guarantee your cash within the month. Look, if the Masons can have their handshakes, then it's the least we Italians can do, help each other out.' The whole family was crammed into the kitchen, yet Giulio seemed not to have heard. 'Between a contribution from the merchants and what I can make available through the Consul's Discretionary Deposit, it'll be easy.' It was the first anyone had heard of a *Discretionary Deposit*; no one had ever dared enquire about the Fascio Treasury, though managing it was Dario's chief excuse for not seeking a job. 'No strings attached. All you need do is come down the club, give a wee speech on how you've been doing some hard thinking . . . and so on . . . A picture or two of the Duce, for the ice-cream guzzlers to gain their bit of culture?'

'And call everyone *Voi*?'

Dario insisted it was for his brother's own sake, that these days *Lei* was an insult, especially to a joe. 'Either he thinks you're taking him for a lassie or he thinks whoever's saying it is a pansy. You ken what I mean?' Dario's eyebrows were raised. 'Just fix the date, rather sooner than later since—here's what I really wanted to announce . . .'

'I have something I want to announce too,' Emilio interrupted by saying.

'What the fuck . . .?'

I should have noticed there was something new, from the gleam in my youngest brother's eyes, his hair frozen to his head. He had reached some place where 'Peg-leg' and 'Long John Silver'—the usual insults—could not reach him. 'Can you believe that I finally made it to the swimming baths.' He let his words hang for a minute, during which even Dario must have imagined what this had required of him, with the changing room, the limp, the poolside, the flap as he struggled not to drown. Emilio explained that Mr Parker from Accounting had been promising for months to take him to Drumsheugh, the private baths at the West End, saying he had a nephew with a leg like Emilio's and that swimming had been good for it. 'Now I'm saving up to become a member too.'

'But what was it like?' I could not resist asking. 'Could you float? Was it cold? Was it mixed or only men?'

'Water's a bit chilly but only until you start moving. Fluttered round a bit. They've got trapezes and rings that stretch across the pool. I'll take lessons.' He was shaking his head as if to free himself of enchantment. 'Darnedest thing. You landlubbers can't imagine it, you able-bodied folk, what it is to move without pain, forget the fight for a while against the great god Gravity.'

'Fascinating, little brother,' sneered Dario. 'But did nobody teach you it's rude to interrupt. I have some real news to share with yous all.'

Emilio turned to his pasta, an unshakeable smile on his face.

'I was about to tell you I've been invited to Chicago by Zia Sabrina and Zio Joe, where I'll be spreading the gospel of the Fascio.'

Everyone was divining what this really meant. 'And when will you be leaving?' his wife asked, steely.

'There's a ship out of Leith next week. Who knows for how long, but long enough to make some serious lucre.'

'And you wouldn't want to discuss it first?'

'What's to be discussed? The call of duty. *Obbedire*—you got that?'

'*Benissimo*! So I make my announcement too.' With her hands, Paola shaped an imaginary pregnancy. 'The doctor tells me I'm no about to have a son, no daughter either, because I work too hard and so my *regole* I miss. But he also says it's not with me lies the problem.'

Someone would have to suffer, the only question was who. He spat into the fire. 'That's great! So you allow some quack to feel you up?' His assault, so misdirected, elicited only a condescending snort from his wife.

'I might as well say my bit too,' started Giulio. 'I've given it some thought, Dario, and while I appreciate the offer of assistance from the Fascio coffers, I have to decline. Photos of the Duce wouldn't match the sort of décor I'm planning for the Palace.'

'You'll regret it, little brother. I was even going to encourage Zio Joe to take an interest. You're a born loser.'

I saw him only one more time, drunk but smiling, before he left for America. I was alone, working on Giulio's sums, and he was expanding on the celebrities he'd be meeting, none of whose names meant anything to me except that of *Al Capone*, who was *dying to see him*—it must have been meant as a joke, since he laughed at it himself.

Then he was gone, really gone, for the first time ever. The whole tenement seemed to exhale more deeply than it had done in years, loosen its belt, relax.

17

Not that this slackened the search for funds. When the portly Edinburgh Consul deigned to receive me, his sole suggestion was to ask my brother—'him with his hands on the purse strings'. Signor Cavazzoni and a few other well-wishers put up a few pounds, but the trade associations of which they'd been a part, which had helped them set up business in the past, had somehow been absorbed into the Fascio. Giulio took the train to Glasgow to try the Casa d'Italia, but only to receive the same incredulous response: for him it should be easy, with Dario on board, what with his direct link to Rome, now America—everyone knew about Zio Joe, and they winked at mention of the Americano's name. Paola revealed she had been saving, put her pounds in the pot; Emilio offered to take an evening job. Yet it all looked helpless, with only one hundred and fifty pounds collected of the five hundred needed. I blushed when Mr Morton stopped on his way to lunch to ask if the capital was accumulating according to plan.

The LIDU premises were to be sought on the Old Town's dingiest wynd, off the lion's spine of the Royal Mile. The dimly lit squalor became more menacing with each unfamiliar drunk; the office barely visible, half-underground, with only a photograph of the Leaning Tower to announce it. We entered, Giulio and I, a tiny smoke-filled room as dank and uninviting as anything outside, with three rickety chairs and a desk. Carlo had said the Secretary of the League would be present, and after a minute, Carlo himself emerged from a backroom to ask how he could help. When Giulio said he was hoping to talk to the Secretary, Carlo explained that this was what he was doing. Giulio tried in vain to find a comfortably obtuse angle to his interlocutor's penetrating gaze.

'I heard,' Carlo started, 'about your run-in with *manganello*.'

It was Giulio's chance, an easy rope to cling to; being Giulio, he was bound to refuse it. I couldn't comprehend why, even as he sought to create communities, he also had to refuse them. 'It would be convenient,' he said, 'for me to blame the Fascisti now—now that I've left their ranks.'

'Convenient and true!' I added, clutching the rope that my brother had left dangling.

'Who knows,' he added, 'maybe it was an attempt to give us a bad name. You realize, don't you Carlo, why the Fascio has been so successful? Because it was the only place where Italians could really meet . . . meet and talk, somewhere other than the pub or church. Because it made us feel we were not just exiles, brought recognition from home, the trips to Italy.'

'I thought it was because your brother's got most Italians in the city scared witless.'

But Giulio wasn't listening. 'That's why we need somewhere new. And this is what the Ice Palace sets out to be. A place where everyone—nearly everyone—will be welcome, where people can gather and talk, share hopes and memories. No alcohol on the premises so it can open on Sundays without enraging the Temperance Society. Italian mammas can bring their bairns and sit with their hen-friends, take a minute out from chores. Maybe some singing.' Almost imperceptibly, Carlo had begun to rock back and forth in his chair. 'And there'll be someone on the door at all times, built a bit like you, so if anyone starts in on that anti-Semitism that's currently infecting the Fascio, or against any of the other groups . . .'

'Like the Suffragettes?'

'Like the Suffragettes.'

'Like the inverts?'

Did the blank expression on my brother's face mean that he too was retrieving the word's significance? 'As you say. Or if anyone tries to enter wearing a black shirt or starts saying we can't greet each other with *Lei*, or punching their arms in the air, then they'll be out on their ear as fast as you can say *Duce*.'

Carlo's chair ceased to rock. I sensed in him an impulsiveness curbed by years of inner discipline, though it was unclear if he wished to embrace Giulio or clobber him for his years of support for the Edinburgh Fascisti—maybe both? In the event, he did neither. 'The LIDU's not a commercial organization, and with Rome supporting the Fasci and London supporting Rome we get little enough assistance. Every second day we need to repair the windows. Everyone goes in fear of the Chief Extractor.'

'Chief Extractor?' Giulio repeated.

'Don't play the kiddy. Call him what you like, he's your brother.'

'But he may not be chief for long.' I'd been wanting to voice this ever since I'd heard the sinister term. 'McEwen says his gang will soon be taking over, that they'll make Mussolini seem like a softie.'

'Your sister seems to know more than you do. Protection, extortion, blackmail if he's got anything on the person. How do you think he married in a church last year? You think the priest in Leith wanted to welcome a horde of blackshirts? Before the toady Pio caved in and blessed the whole diabolic bunch of them . . . What do you think he's gone to America for? It's not to sell your Papà's statues.' As Giulio was speechless, Carlo could go on, 'If you don't know what your Zio Joe is up to, then it's not my job to educate you. Your brother will make a willing apprentice . . . We can't help you directly, but since you've ambitions for your place . . . Only, don't expect your brother's thanks when he finds out the LIDU's involved.'

All the way home, Giulio was silent. Only on the stair did he turn to me. 'You know,' he said, 'I've been too wrapped up in myself. I forget that other people have secrets too. Must never make that mistake again.'

He was half-way up the first flight by the time I formulated my reply: that what he needed was not to know other people's secrets, but to share his with me. When I caught up with him in the kitchen, his nose was deep in another futile set of figures.

Over the weeks that followed, Paola watched the postman like a cobra, though no letter arrived from America, only the daily missive from Rome in which Valerio made suggestions, well-meaning but unhelpful, for how to solve our financial impasse. Papà retreated into Infant Jesus, in demand again since the Wall Street Crash—another incomprehensible event. Nineteen twenty-nine looked set to end with nothing to show for all our efforts, when Giulio came home and announced that Carlo had passed by Cavazzoni's with over two hundred pounds towards the Palazzo; which, with the forty per cent loan and the hundred already put together, meant only three hundred short. I didn't point out that three hundred might as well be three thousand, given every source had now been tapped.

I didn't recognize the caller who knocked after eight, and who placed a packet in my hand before retreating down the stairs. Inside it, like in a dream, was a fat wad of notes. The letter I scanned before reading it aloud. '*Roma, 27 November. Carissima Lucia Mia.*' I tried to keep the tears from my voice. '*Papà had free tickets for Lucia di Lammermoor, which I can not resist because of the name.*'

Our own Papà broke the spell. 'I know the story now,' he sighed, 'but we hadn't read it when we named you. We just thought Scotland . . . Italy.'

'*Our destiny need not be tragic like that of Lucia and Edgardo.*'

Emilio applauded silently; Paola stared dreamily into the fire.

'*So I watch the flow of money at work. I trust the man who brings you this letter but better say no more, only that what you find here is for you and your brother, in hope it makes possible your wishes. I trust you will not think less of me if I hope to have a place in your future. Write soon. Your fondest Valerio.*'

Everyone was staring at the wad unfurling on the table. One by one I unpeeled the five-pound notes, all used bills, until they counted 350. I expected noise, instead of which there was silence . . . which eventually Papà broke, to say he would write to Valerio that we could certainly not accept his charity.

'Yes indeed,' Giulio agreed.

Followed by more silence.

'You're joking?' Paola jabbed the poker into the fire. 'Or are you all *pazzi*?'

'It's Lucia who will decide,' said Emilio. 'Without any pressure from us. The money is hers, after all, while the obligation would be on us all.'

Pressure? Obligation? When Valerio could have me for free, where was the pressure? If he had kept this money, then I might have become his the sooner, in marriage; but how could we marry when my dearest elder brother could not even get engaged until he had realized his ambition? 'Of course Giulio should accept the money,' I declared. 'It'd be an insult to return it, and what use could I have for it? This time next year, we'll be preparing for the New Year in the Ice Palace, the mirrors shining bright, Giulio in his apron, the customers all smiling.'

'And you,' said my brother, 'will be officially engaged to this *gentiluomo* from Rome.'

18

Treacle toffees, walnut toffees, aniseed balls, jelly babies, liquorice coils, raspberry boilings, jujubes, chocolate hazelnuts, chocolate buttons, dolly mixtures, fudge squares, butterscotch, sugarplums, marshmallows, hazelnut caramels, snowballs, macaroons. And these were just the 'frivolities', as Giulio termed them, distractions from the frozen essentials.

Lists, lists, and more lists. The Palace could not open before sixteen months of lists. I stencilled the sweeties' names onto gleaming glass jars with silver lids that spun off through a single twist of the wrist. Up on their shelves behind the work-top, with the mirrors reflecting them, they would promise return to a childhood of indulgence few customers had in fact known.

But first there were the disused shops to visit: from burnt-out basements where ice-cream would have been an insult to the meths-drinkers on the flagstones; to posh purveyors of lace and linen which had slid into West End bankruptcy (their eerily silent dummies displaying unsold stock). With so many trades going out of business, it should have been easy. But the downward spiral meant that almost anywhere could become a slum where bone-pinching necessity would mean no one would feel right with an ice-cream in hand. The dump that finally spoke to me on Annandale Street had known better times. But pedestrians on Leith Walk might be tempted, it was close to but not in the heart of our Italian district, and it offered a splendid high ceiling and an ornate cornice that Emilio was determined to restore. The walls were blackened, but beneath the grime they were sound, dampness slight, windows stretching almost from floor to ceiling.

Site supplies: cement, taps, pipes, tubing, beading, putty, nails, screws, tacks, plaster, glue, wooden panelling, majolica tiles (Paola insisted they be sent from Naples), marble work-tops, skirting boards.

Later, towards the end of the year, as the structure of the Palace took shape after nights of holding the ladder for our Michelangelo Emilio, helping Papà mix plaster, advising Giulio on the position of a tap— later came the indispensable plumber, joiner, plasterer, electrician (for not a corner of the Palace but would be illumined) who plied their trades with quiet dedication. Then brass drawer handles, rattan-bottomed chairs, wooden folding tables, tin ashtrays, tea-spoons, cut-glass goblets, scoops, ladles, pinafores with *ICE PALACE* embroidered on them, bonnets, napkins with the *IP* monogram, brushes and dustpans, kitchen cloths, beeswax polish, Brasso, even Brilliantine for the boys' hair.

And to supplement every list, the *Yank*.

'Pop's gone to buy some booze,' he threw out, from deep within Papà's armchair 'To celebrate the homecoming.' Gone so many months, he returned unannounced, dressed in what he explained was a *tux* and *trilby*. 'Come sit on my knees, lil sis.'

I had to re-run everything he said. He was expansive, suave, menacing.

'So what's bin cookin?' Even after I gathered this was not to be taken literally, I could find no response; Dario rarely asked questions to which he didn't know the answer, and I presumed he'd already scouted the site. 'Not much action down the Fascio, from what I hear.'

'I'm still attending, with Papà.' I shouldn't sound so apologetic.

He waited until all were assembled in order to regale us with tales of Chicago high life; the clubs, the bars, the jazz bands. Even Emilio sat up and listened, intrigued (as he later told me) less by the tales than by his brother's accent, as he rose from Papà's armchair to explain how mighty the Chicago Italians had grown, how no one would dare treat Zio Joe the way we were treated here. 'Not that they savvy much about Fascismo, however often I told them about *Credere, obbedire, combattere.* The idea you've got a *padrino* commanding from on top, that they comprehend. And they love the idea of con-trolling police and press, that your enemy can be shipped off to some rock in the Mediterranean never to be heard of again.' He unbuttoned his double-breasted pinstripe and loosened his tie. 'But there were three sticking points. *Primo*, with the broads, that the Duce is no looker. "Pug-ugly," they tell me. "But what about his animal magnetism?" I say to them, "and the hundreds of mistresses?" But they've studied the photos and they're not convinced. *Secondo*, the reports about how all the *capi* down in Sicily are being locked away and that the Duce seems serious about sharing power with no one but the Pope, not even with the local bosses who've kept things profitable down there for so long. I tell them you gotta bend with the times, but they tell me there's too many uncles or brothers in the nick.'

During the pause for breath, I realized how glad I was to have him back, despite it all. Family was family.

'Slug us another bottle, Pop.' He drank deeper than before, as if his new-found sophistication had dried him up inside.

'And *terzo*?' said Emilio.

'Gimme a chance. *Terzo*, they can't understand that the Duce's no interested in money. Why's he living in some crummy public building, bragging how riches mean nothing to him? If it were an empty boast, they'd admire him the more. But they hear it's for real, he's really not out to make the biggest fortune since the Medici took up banking. They've got junior henchmen richer than the Duce. I says to them, "For what does he need riches when he owns the whole fucking state!" But they say to me, "What use is that, if you have to share it with millions of peasants!"'

'Language, Dario. Whatever the accent, the word's still got four letters.'

'I regret to have to tell you that the Chicago bunch are a dumb fucking lot, including Zio Joe and Zia Sabrina, for all their cars and cigars.' Even as he said it, he was shedding the American self; within a week he'd be back to his brogue. 'But what about you guys here? Hear you're mixed up with the LIDU, Giulio—you wanna watch your back with crooks like that.'

'We didn't have a choice,' I said. 'We needed the capital.'

'Took a look at the place, coming along nicely. And your Valerio, I hear he's now one of the *famiglia*? Hand in the till one day, ice-scoop the next—that the story? We're gonna be busy, in any case,' he went on. 'There's all these *gruppuscoli* going round claiming to be the true heirs of *Fascismo*. Time to demonstrate to these bastards what the black shirt really means. And the wife'll be busy too. I want the first *figlio* born before summer next year.'

'I can't do it by myself,' Paola challenged.

'Better get to it!' he laughed, heading for the door. '*Andiamo!*'

In the further months required to prepare the Palace for its April opening, he was seen on the site only twice. *Primo*, to announce his disapproval of the 'pig hide colour' chosen for the ceiling. ('It's *terracotta*,' Emilio told him.) *Secondo*—he could not contain himself—to publicize that Paola was pregnant ('I can tell from the shape it's a boy').

The floor was laid, luminescent sea-green cement tiles. Mirrors, panelling and plaster went up. The heavy equipment was fitted into the back-room kitchen, while in front the shelves were installed, the tables, the chairs, the goblets and spoons and saucers and light-shades. In April, just as energies were flagging, Giulio, who spoke of nothing but emulsifiers, batch mixes, basins, ice-picks, measuring glasses and *overrun* (a principle he alone grasped), who let himself be distracted only by the sight of Paola's expanding belly—Giulio announced the sign-writers. His *Palace* claim was vindicated: it gleamed, was modern, sharp, had every latest gadget but also ample space for customers to sit on tall swivel stools at the counter or in the six capacious booths on the rear wall, each of which had a table and crimson-leather benches. There was nowhere like it in Edinburgh; even the Lucases' shop in Musselburgh, or the Zavaronis' in Rothesay, or the Nardinis' in Largs, had nothing better to show.

I was wearing my smartest clothes for the gala-opening photograph, but when I reached the shop, Giulio was on a chair outside by himself, gazing in from the pavement. The sign above read *THE ICE PALACE* in bold green capitals outlined in gold; on the left window, a paler shade traced an italic *Giulio Pezzini*, while on the right, shone *Purveyor of Frozen Fare*.

19

Home late that evening of the gala opening, I let what I had heard roam round my giddy brain.

'What a load of light!'

'Calls itself a palace, Auntie Lena,' I explained before moving on, 'so it could hardly be dingy.'

'And this is my dear wife, Mrs Eunice Morton. She's keen to try the new flavours Mr Pezzini has devised for us.'

I gestured Mr Morton towards the counter and invited him to place his order.

'They high chairs are no very comfy, mind.'

'But they're modern, though, go and admit it.'

'A scoop o that yin wi the bits, please.'

'Stracciatella?' Giulio asked, beaming.

'Go scratch yerself! But sure yous Eye-talians speak an impossible lingo. No bad though, the taste, no bad at all. The crunchy wee chocolate bits. Be back for more of that.'

I was wearing my *ICE PALACE* apron, and Mamma's prized gold earrings with the tourmalines.

'It must be a proud day for you, Dario.'

'We've worked for it, Mr McEwen. Not that we'll be taking custom from your chippy, mind.'

'I'm no worried about that. It's my Ewan what worries me, the company he's keeping. All those fancy ways of dressing up his anger at being born an ugly wee ferret, son of a fish-frier.'

'We do our best to keep him in line, you ken, but ever since he's heard about Germany, it's no been easy. Bunch of nutcases over there, a right tinderbox waiting to ignite.'

It was more than I wanted to hear, on this of all nights.

'Like Aladdin's cave more than like a palace. I never kent how they Italians do it.'

'Support from their Pope, I wouldn't doubt.'

'I'm glad to hear you suggest that, Mrs . . .?'

'Mackay. Oh, I'm sorry there, Minister, I was only jokin.'

'Not at all, Mrs Mackay. Most folks know me as the Bishop, though it's Archbishop more exactly. I like the idea of His Holiness having a personal hand in the matter. Though alas it's not Giulio himself but his dear father and his sister Lucia who invited me, with Giulio's forbearance.'

'Ma man will ne'er forgive me if he hears I've been speaking to a big yin frae the papist church.'

'*Caspita*! Not tasted such good Torrone in the twenty-five years since I left Sorrento.'

'But wait till the winter comes, they'll find it gey hard to keep the place busy then.'

'Nonsense. It'll be a cosy spot to escape from the wains. I hear they'll have a hardman on the door? I hope it's no that Carlo, fair terrifics me he does, Mr Cavazzoni, the size of him.'

'But he's a gentle soul, Miss Sandy. I've heard it'll be that friend of his, Fausto—there's no shortage of unemployed dockers.'

'But he's almost as muckle! And yonder's PC O'Donnell, he'll be keeping an eye on the place.'

Signor Cavazzoni was doubtful. 'Only if Dario tells him to.'

'Aye, I hear there's bad blood twixt the brothers.' I didn't want to hear this, nor what followed: 'And there's that poor soul Paola, fingers worked to the bone and just a month afore she's ready to pop.'

'Heard the one about the Italian tank with only one gear?'

'The sister's stuck on some laddie in Rome. Soon be four year since she's seen him, but he writes her every day.'

'How romantic!' said Auntie Rebecca. 'My man can barely sign his own name. I'm ashamed when we meet Rabbi Daiches, him being so very bookish.'

'Reverse!'

'And what's to be the opening hours, Giulio?'

'Open from noon until as long as anyone's got an appetite. Emilio and Lucia will be helping out, though they've both got their day jobs. Even Papà has said he'll work the till.'

I never saw him coming. 'Hey,' he said, as I stepped backwards. 'I'm no the one about to catapult a rock at you that'll scar you for life!'

'Who invited you?'

'Those were the days though, eh? When you'd sit on that wall in yer gym slip. Over here, Dario, yer sister's giving me the cold shoulder again.'

'She's a tough wee tyke, our Lucia, runs in the family. You ken we stick together, strength in numbers . . . It's no as if we've been swept to power here, the way happened back home.'

'And is about to fuckin happen in Germany.'

'Spare us the Germany shite, Ewan. You cannot compare our Duce with that pathetic Austrian corporal.'

'It's meant to be no politics,' I declared, as I backed behind the counter to serve—the chill cleared the head—and where Giulio was spreading more amazement.

'Are you telling us that these are made of ice and all?'

'Ice sculptures. Artisans back home have been making them for centuries, a lot fancier than the swans you see here. You can put fruit inside, or butter, then serve it up at table. You'd be surprised how long they take to melt. Something for every pocket, down to a bag of ice cubes for a farthing. But excuse me now, it's time for my wee speech.'

Much clinking of spoons on goblets. People on the pavement were straining to hear.

'Ladies and gentlemen,' Giulio started, standing on a stool. '*Signore e signori*, I hope you like what you've found in the Ice Palace. I trust you'll keep coming back, and find new surprises—come to meet your pals too, Italian and Scottish, and to relax.' Loud cheers and applause. 'Those of you fortunate enough to have visited Giolitti's in Rome or La Scimmia in Naples will recognize the sources of my inspiration. Outside we have no beautiful piazza or blazing sun, we cannot stare at the Pantheon or Capri. But something of the piazza lives on in the Palace, I trust, something of Capri in my granita. And something grand,' he concluded, 'grand and pagan, like the Pantheon, in my ambition.'

When spring turned into what was, by Scottish standards, a glorious summer, the Palace duly thrived; even when autumn came, followed by a perishing winter, the customers queued for their favourite flavours. I was seated behind the Angel (as we called the lady of the night whom Giulio had made welcome so long as she was off duty, and who was crocheting a baby's bib, for when she retired and settled down), reading the latest from Maclodio (which included a sickness of Zio Roberto's maid-slave and an infestation of mosquitoes), when Paola's laughter turned into a howl of pain.

In the kitchen, amid the blenders and eggs, her waters broke spectacularly. Only then did it dawn on me that the roles were reversing, that soon I would be *zia*. But first we had to get Paola home—and how? Auntie Rebecca was sent with instructions for the neighbourhood midwife. In the front shop, Giulio was pacing, while Fausto the doorman rolled up his sleeves.

'You're not thinking . . .?' I said. 'She weighs a ton—*they* weigh a ton.'

Fausto asked if he could enter. Swathed in *ICE PALACE* towels, Paola ceased groaning just long enough for Fausto to stoop over her. As if he were picking up only baby—not baby's first home as well—he straightened his knees and turned to squeeze through the door. For the first time since the Palace opening, a *Back Soon* sign went up, as Giulio locked the door. I explained to the inquisitive that Paola's time had come: behind us, when after fifteen minutes we reached the tenement, stretched a train of more than twenty children, awed to silence by the event they were witnessing. I obeyed the midwife's orders during labour, and swooned only after the girlie had taken her first breath. When I came to, the wean was already at the tit, Paola weeping softly, midwife preparing to leave.

'I knew it,' Paloa sobbed. 'I so want a girl. And her father, I was sure it's what he gives me.' It seemed an odd thing to say, given Dario's determination to sire a son. But she had a right to say peculiar things. 'I call her Giulia.'

Peculiar—but not outrageous! 'You can't do that, Paola,' I warned, mopping her brow.

'You see the resemblance?'

I peered, but in newborns all I could ever detect were shrivelled ancient sages. When Dario finally staggered in, after five too many, he picked the baby up, had his doubts, pulled down its swaddling, turned up his nose. 'So what's it called?' he sniffed.

'Assunta,' I blurted out, before Paola could say a word.

'Aye, right. Better be off, then. Got a big speech to prepare for the Fascio.'

'On the importance of the family?'

'On the present chaos in Germany. On the Kraut National Socialist Anton Drexer who's claiming the Duce is a Jew.' It was hard to tell which insult was greater: fathering a girl-child or being told the Duce was a Jew. There were worse insults to come.

He'd spent the following day feeding on his bottle of J&B, as thirstily as Assunta at her mother's breast, the better to burst into the Palace that evening, startling the customers. 'So they told me about the ambulance!' He was leaning over the counter, helping himself to a scoop of Torrone.

Giulio had spent his three afternoon hours off convincing himself the wain was smiling, distinguishing between Italian and Scots, innumerable other precocious feats. As if in twenty-five years of being bated he'd learnt nothing, he asked what Dario was referring to.

'The one offered by the fucking LIDU—that fuckin Fausto!'

'Ah well,' chirped Emilio from behind the till, 'if you'd been around then you could have carried her yourself.' He inspected

Dario's arms and turned up his nose. 'Or maybe not.' The blob of ice-cream hit Emilio full on the face. Rather than brush it off, he extended his tongue and slurped appreciatively.

'You let that ape-man by the door lay hands on my wife? Well? He fucking manhandled her, and you all said nothing?'

'You cannot be serious,' smiled Giulio. 'You've a beautiful wee girl, Papà's first grandchild. You cannot be angry on a day like today.'

'Don't be telling me what I'm supposed to feel! I take orders from the Duce, no from some arsehole like you!'

'Wait for the telegram from Palazzo Chigi,' joked Emilio, 'congratulating you on this victory in the Battle for Babies.' This time it wasn't ice-cream, but a fist that flashed across the counter. Dario was strong, but Emilio was fast: he'd seen it coming, and the fist brushed past his curls.

'Any problem, boss?' asked Fausto, who had emerged from the booth without so much as a glance in Dario's direction.

'And you keep out of family business,' Dario snarled.

'This is my job, *amico mio*.'

'Don't *amico* me, you Neanderthal.' His eyes were yellow from booze and lack of sleep, but they were sufficiently sharp to take in Fausto's bulk, Carlo in the booth behind.

20

An ice-cream vendor, accurate down to miniature *cornetti* and *ICE PALACE* printed on the cart. 'And if you open it . . .' Giulio instructed Emilio. 'Go on!' Inside the cart were two tiny scrolls, tied by silver thread. 'The second one's for you, Lucia.'

Emilio put Papà's magnifying monocle to his eye to decipher the minuscule script. '*To my dearest brother, without whom no Palace. This certificate gives one-year membership of Drumsheugh Baths, starting 1 January 1932.*' He held the monocle on his eye longer than was necessary, to conceal the tear.

I cut the thread on the second scroll, unfurled the pixie paper, put the monocle to my eye. '*To my one and only Sorella. With this ticket you may travel to Rome next summer and finally take Valerio to be your promesso sposo.*'

When I wrote to Valerio that night with the news, I breathed not a word about Papà's second Christmas statue, for I would not have known how to describe, still less name it. Emilio, recovering from his excitement, pointed in disgust.

Papà looked shamefaced. 'Forgive me, children. It visited me in dreams.'

'In nightmares more like!'

He explained how he had been reading in *L'Italia Nostra* about a German admirer of the Duce who had ambitions to spread our Italian example. The creature his reading had produced was compact, dense as granite, stunted, gnarled, infinitely dark, almost spherical yet with lumps that might have been truncated limbs. It was a creature unmistakably misshapen though no one could have said what shape it should properly have taken; unnaturally heavy in the hand, and cold to the touch. Was it some sort of troll? Or wolf? Or wild dog?

'A boar?' Emilio suggested, taking it from me. His hand seemed to burn on contact with its frigid surface.

'It lived underground all its life, only now it has come up. That was my dream.'

I begged Papà not to put it anywhere near the Christmas crib, unable to remove my eyes from it but unable to focus on it either.

'Nobody likes it, then?'

'Like it?' said Emilio. 'But Papà, it's monstrous!'

With something like relief, Papà stowed it at the back of his cupboard, amid the broken Magi and the damaged mandolins. 'Oh well,' he sighed, 'at least now I've made it, maybe I can forget it.'

One week later, Valerio's reply said that Giulio's generosity was the best New Year's present he had ever received. He was counting the days—nine whole months of them . . .

Roma Aeterna

September 25

Dearest Giulio,

So here I am again, after five years away! Everything feels familiar & yet new at the same time. And it's all thanks to you, Valerio agrees. He asks me everything about the Palace & how you run it & insists we speak only English as he says he'll be too embarrassed if he doesn't improve before coming to live in Scotland (which will be in nine months' time, God willing). Though he's an only child, he understands that I couldn't part from my brothers. I do hope you won't object to a service in St Mary's & that Dario will not invite his cronies.

Speaking of such matters, I promised to be your ears & eyes for politics. I've been a dutiful sister. With Valerio's father the Party bigwig, talk is all of two matters. First comes the need for Italy to possess her own empire, as Ancient Rome once did & as we have in Britain. Fertile lands full of cotton & coffee & ores & space for all the *bambini* won in the Battle for Babies; civilization brought to heathens living in a night that sounds even darker than in Scotland (though presumably warmer, as I dared put in!). How can it be fair that in Britain we own half the world, while Italy possesses only a few acres in Libya that are teeming with rebels. Though I must admit I can't work myself into a fury like the Blackshirts are doing about some battle we Italians lost to the Darkies back in 1896!

Second comes Germany. Our Duce has proclaimed that Fascismo is not for export yet this doesn't stop it being a *universal doctrine*. Like Dario but presumably for different reasons, Valerio is dismayed at people saying that Adolf Hitler is the *new Mussolini*. A newspaper called *La Vita Italiana* got VV very upset by claiming Mr Hitler & his gang are right about Jews being a degenerate race. They obviously don't know many Jews like Auntie Rebecca or Valerio's uncle who practise their religion full of dignity.

See, I did my duty! But as you can imagine, mostly my mind has been full not of empires future but of empires past, as day by day we stroll through the Forum, visit the Villa Borghese & marvel at the sculptures. If I were not a worker in a bank (& a Palace!), I'd like to be an archaeologist, sifting through the past with a teaspoon & then recording and reporting on it all.

In a few days, Maclodio. You didn't think my head was so turned that I'd neglect family duties! I hope everyone is well & that the Palace is enjoying an Indian summer.

With love from your most grateful sister

Lucia

My brother seemed to understand me better than I understood myself, yet I prevaricated: no mention of the purpose of those visits to the Forum.

'*Salve*,' I liked to start.

'*Te amo, Luciabus.*'

'Your Latin needs work, sweetest. I like the look of that shade over by Augustus's villa. Have you ever been here with a girl before?' And when he shook his head, I felt almost sorry, for if he had then he might know what came next. Under the fig tree, with its broad sweet-smelling leaves, he complained he couldn't see me. 'Then nobody can see us either. Give me your hand.'

Were those my *cigli*?

'Eyelashes, they're called. Give me your mouth, put it here. Always wondered how it feels, watching Paola and wee Assunta. Don't speak! There's the other side too, don't neglect it, give me plenty to confess to Padre Clemente.' He obeyed my command, claiming it was surely no sin, as soon we would be wed. 'As if after all these years, I can wait another minute. June brides, then high season at the Palace, you in your smartest suit and both of us wishing— don't stop!—that our mammas were there to help give us away.' When he grumbled that he wanted to lay me down, I said, 'But my clothes'll be ruined by those rotting figs. Oh hold me! Tighter! Don't let the world squeeze between us!' He clasped as hard as he could. 'Do you think that Dorothy and Emilio have ever embraced like this, in the shadows of Dean Village behind the swimming baths? His *silkie* as he calls her.' I knew Valerio could barely understand a half of this, but talking steeled my nerve. 'Her *shining star* she calls him. Now here's my hand. Stop a second, let that soldier pass. He didn't spot us?' It should have been obvious what I intended with my hand; still he was surprised. 'But I want you to explode—only not on my skirt. You're not stopping me like last time. Help me rather, show me how.'

'*Così*, then *così*.'

I had to look. 'So you're not?'

'Don't stop. Not what?'

'Not . . . I thought that with your Mamma . . . the Jewish way?'

'*Così e piu veloce*. Papà would not let them.'

I had to look again. 'I want to see it.'

'I'm *timido*. Don't stop!'

'Oh, it leapt! Look at it all on the ground.' Only my hand was preventing his knees from buckling. 'Are you all right?'

'Don't let go of me.'

'Nothing a dab with a handkerchief won't mend. On the ground, like Onan.'

As he returned to himself, he feared he had neglected me.

'Your happiness is my happiness, your pleasure mine. Kiss me again, so winter disappears and we're standing in the warmth of next June.'

Quickly buttoned, he thanked me for saying such beautiful things.

'You make me say beautiful things. Mamma taught us to use every word at our disposal. *Seen and not heard* was for Scottish children. Now let's stop talking, please, put your lips to mine.'

Back at my *pensione*, I could not forget the feel of him in my hand or the sight of his . . . not having a word for it, I named it his *hiccough*.

Every afternoon, when the piazzas asserted their emptiness, we made for the fragrant shadows of the Travertine Hill, or the Pincio, or Tiberius's baths. The moment was arriving when I'd have to invite him inside. Four days more before leaving for Maclodio, after which Naples for the long ride home. Years I'd been waiting for him, all through the summer of serving at the Palace, while I helped feed and change Assunta, listened to Emilio's joy at swimming—a joy topped only by his delight at being in love, topped in turn by his instructor's feelings for him . . . all the time waiting for that part of him which, Paola assured me, would fit me, when the time was right, like my favourite calf-skin gloves—only, I would be the glove and he would be the hand. Never before had I wanted anything with so much of me; his voice, his smile, his gentleness, his patience, his office-worker's fingers, the unruly hairs which escaped through his shirt, the fact that he was Italian and Jewish too, the way he pouted whenever his father lauded some fresh Duce initiative, the smiling faces of the waiters in the trattoria on Via delle Botteghe Oscure, the tang of coffee on his tongue and the musty after-taste of his RSI cigarettes, the details on the Trastevere churches I'd have missed without his guidance, the abundance of his seed, his motherlessness, his inexperience in discovering the parts of me that made me shudder . . .

'Tonight?' I whispered as we passed our favourite elephant on Piazza Minerva. 'I don't care what happens or who finds out. My brother would not blame me. For soon we shall be *sposi*.'

21

The engagement party thrown by Valerio's father had ended amid Fascist salutes from officials and congratulations from colleagues. The obelisk looked preposterous on the elephant's back. For every child on earth, I thought, to still my nerves . . . except of course for Jesus (and in the opinion of certain priests, Mary too). It had taken time and money, he explained, but he had found it. I didn't recognize the posh but poorly lit streets, nor the building with the *portone* on the latch. The stairway up—we didn't dare use the lift—was heavily clad in thick red carpet, leading to an apartment which spread before us with drastically modern furniture that was all chrome tubes and leather. Despite Duce photographs on the wall, I knew it had never been occupied, not in its present pristine state.

'From the decorators at work,' he explained. 'Tomorrow arrives one of our biggest *ministri*. But for this night is ours.'

I wandered its vastness, barely daring to touch the tiger-skin rugs, the black armchairs, the console table. Ignorant of design, I presumed this was . . . *the future* . . . And thought how soon I'd be in the future as well . . . Flats could be renovated, humans could not, despite confession . . . Mamma died young and I might die too, as soon as tomorrow, before I even became *Signora Valentino*. But not before I knew a man. Giulio—I smiled at the thought—might even be proud of me!

Words raced round my head in retaliation at the notion, words for women who did a lot of it, terrible terms like *slattern, slut, trollop,* and *drab; virgin* for those who never had. No word could I find, as I tiptoed into the bedroom with its bed bigger than any I'd ever imagined, for someone like I would soon be, who'd done it only once— or twice if I was lucky and Valerio was able (my notions on this were vague).

Slowly, purposefully, I undressed as Valerio stood there watching, immobilized. Should I try to conceal the defects, put my best light forward? Keep the bottom from protruding while making sure he took a suitable bead on the breasts? I'd overheard enough of men to figure what they liked, added to Paola's loose-tongued advice. I concentrated on gestures, each garment in its proper time. For though he claimed I was his first, if he had indeed known Roman ladies, they surely had been *elegantissime*, even in stockings and smalls. Would he care to help? I asked. When finally he did move, his legs were jelly. 'Now you see me naked—' I hid nothing—'do you still want me for your wife? You may change your mind.' My bravery surprised me. 'It's not too late.'

Fully clad, he put his arms round me and held me so tight I could scarcely breathe. An enormous sigh passed through him turning into a sob, and seconds later a tear fell on my bare left shoulder and snailed down my back. I understood I'd have to undress him, as I did Assunta. Only, Assunta didn't have this extra part, jutting up at me, independent and requiring. I regretted, later, that I hadn't put him in my mouth—to have that memory; but even had the idea occurred to me, I could not have been so bold. Instead, I lay on my back on the gigantic bed, noticing only now that the ceiling was one gigantic mirror. In it I admired his naked torso, his hairless back, his muscular shoulders.

All blandishments had fled. I wanted him to know me, by knowing first every refinement in the *ars amoris* (what could never be expected of a Scotsman but should be in the bloodstream of Tiberius's descendant). He said he would be careful, that I should tell him if it hurt. But pain was not in my plan. I was ready, more than ready, I was willing. The ten days in Rome had been foreplay, with the hours of petting and coaxing. Now the act. I smiled to myself in the ceiling-mirror, put my hand firmly round him and led him to my warmest place. Then I learnt that it didn't have to be either/or: for we could kiss and nip and lick and suck and tickle and cup and even slap and squeeze, *and still be doing it.*

He was inside me, and what little pain was past. 'Go!' he told me. '*Dai tu!*'

For a moment I thought, in English, that he was wishing me dead; rather liked the idea, dying under him, never to awake. And by the time I realized he was urging me in Italian to run my own path down pleasure's gauntlet, I was so far down it that even the thought of the neighbours couldn't stop me.

'*Stai bene?*' he asked. 'Are you here? With me?'

'Where else.' It came to me, of a sudden, that in one year's time we wouldn't need to hide away in someone else's property, that I'd be Valerio's in name as well as in flesh, and that what had just happened was repeatable, not something I had to save up for, not reserved for thoroughbred Scotswomen; something I could go on trying yet never master or comprehend. 'Like a duck to water . . .' My voice sounded as if someone else were speaking. 'Now you.' I pulled up my knees the way I'd seen Paola do on the Fascio floor, feeling him deeper inside me . . . It was such a shame to stop him, then, that I almost let the devil take the consequences.

But 'Aich!'—it was a horrible sensation when he withdrew.

'I cannot more,' he gasped, directing my hands to hold him tighter than ever I'd have dared.

'On my tummy!' I watched his seed fill my navel, felt him shrink in my hand.

The white marble floor of the bathroom looked impossibly wide. I'd never met a bidet with such levers and taps; turned and pulled, they launched a five-foot fountain into the air.

Not once, in fact, but thrice did I sit astride that bidet: Valerio surpassed my ill-defined expectations. By the end, I was aware I was sore. We sat naked in the giant window-alcove and watched the dawn rise over the Capitol. 'We must leave soon. At seven come the men with the final furniture, then the *Ministro* himself.'

After removing every trace, after we'd stepped onto the landing, I read the bronze plaque—*A. STARACE*—that was gleaming there brand new.

22

In Maclodio piazza the *zie* vied with one another, when I alighted from the mule, in extravagance of congratulation, praise of the *promesso sposo*, the beauty, number, and prosperity of our future sons. Even Zio Roberto was present, sporting a battered top hat which signified a rise in rank since Paola's pay-off. But how they had aged in just five years! Now Zia Flavia, in whose bed I slept, was thickened and yellowed, as if claimed by the surrounding hostile land. Zia Antonella queried my fiancé's income and spat upon learning his mother had been Jewish; her wraithlike husband pinched my bottom and exclaimed how lucky was the man who would bed me. Zia Lalla had turned so hairy that I itched to employ my razor. Talk was of malaria, children born with six fingers and webbed toes, men who beat their wives, wives who beat their children, children who beat their goats. When I told them of the Ice Palace I felt as if I were reading from Emilio's poem about Xanadu; so dull and inexorable seemed their lives, the passage of the hours and days, from now to still greater old age and hirsuteness, compared to my own future so imminent and alluring. Reports of Nonno were few, as since her latest attack of gout even Zia Lalla had ceased to visit with olive oil and rusks—a holy man, said some; a lunatic, said others. After the olive groves, I had to fight my way through the briars.

'My dear Lucia,' he started, in his mix of Italian and dialect without the slightest hesitation, as if he'd met me that morning. 'I didn't expect to see you so soon.'

I reminded him of the years that had elapsed since my last visit, and insisted he open the one official letter I'd brought him, which turned out to be a demand for explanation of why he had not joined the Party. He was smiling at me as if I were the crazy one, from a face in which the one clear feature was the eyes, jewels in a coconut shell. His beard stopped somewhere near his ribs, and he was wearing the same trousers as last time, now more holes than stuff, torn off below the knee; nothing on his back except a leather harness from which, he explained, he dangled the birds and rabbits he captured. With no great conviction, given he looked perfectly contented, I asked how he could live this way, and implored him to think of poor worrying Papà, of his grandchildren, of his great-grandchild who would want to meet him some day.

He merely sighed, before fetching from his cave a little bird he had carved for Assunta (how he knew of her birth was a mystery). He was curious about Papà's nightmare statuette, less so about the world and its politics; told me of a comet on the night of San Lorenzo, an olive tree that had burst spontaneously into flames, a litter of wolf-cubs raised by a stray dog, an aeroplane in the sky and his urine turning blue by the light of the full moon.

'And you, Lucia, you will marry soon?' I didn't recall telling him. 'I shall not be sorry to leave this world. But you will have your part to play. Your Mamma loved words, but with words it is hard to shoot straight. You will have to wait. And remember . . .' He went back into his cave and re-emerged with another gift, for me this time: it was a catapult, another, carved out of olive wood harder than steel, and beautiful in a way only Nonno could have fashioned, with my initials, *LP*, burnt into the shaft.

Only now, when he pointed, did I spy the tin can on a branch ten yards off, painted black. 'Listen,' he ordered. 'Let me fill that can with everything unbearable . . .' He closed his eyes. '*Eccola!*'

I squatted, and—just as had always happened in childhood—a perfectly shaped projectile stared me in the face. More than fifteen years since I'd tried: ever since McEwen's forehead, I'd put a check on myself. Each catapult being different, I was sure it would take some shots to find my range. I placed the pebble in its soft leather tab . . . squeezed it between forefinger and thumb . . . lifted the right arm . . . pulled on the rubber with the left . . . took aim . . . closed the eyes. I no longer cared if I hit or missed.

'*Brava!*' went the cheer when the tin can flew up and clattered onto the stony ground. '*Bravissima!*'

I had to reach the village before dark. 'Don't cry,' Nonno told me.

But I could not obey, certain as I was that I would never meet him again.

On the bone-bruising third-class bench of the train heading north, I rehearsed a marriage list—top of which would be sheets. We'd probably have to share the recess at first, my husband and I, but there must needs be some reminder of the giant satin spread of Signor Starace's bed. And if folks made fun of my fancy tastes, then there was one who'd understand, the same who'd surely know that I was returning a changed woman.

He was waiting when, filthy but smiling, I alighted in Waverley Station. Even Dario was there to greet me. The Scots folk rippled away instinctively, tutting at the spectacle of so many kisses and embraces . . . all except one who was watching from the upper concourse . . . until I summoned the nerve to stare back, and found him no longer there. I told myself it must be exhaustion: lots of overcoats looked like that, plenty ginger hair in the land of carrot and neep.

'Big news here too,' Giulio announced. 'But not till you're out of your travelling clothes. More soot on you than a sweep.'

I wheedled it out of him before we even left Princes Street: Emilio engaged to Dorothy; wedding planned for summer.

An obvious question ensued: And if we made it a double?

Awake in the small hours that first night home, still chugging to the rhythm of the tracks, I tried to figure her out, this lass with whom I might share the aisle. She'd been so unimposing at the start of the year, then she was everywhere, indispensable. Twenty-two like myself, barley blonde, slim and sporty, *modern* in a way no Italian could ever be, not even the well-to-do merchants with their gramophones and automobiles. Her father was an inventor who'd made a fortune with devices that included one for trimming the hair that protrudes from gentlemen's nostrils and ears; a man whose letters advocating an enlightened view of the labour movement were regular in *The Scotsman*;

who'd corresponded with names like Aldous Huxley and Bertrand Russell. Her mother was the author of two books on Somaliland, which she'd visited alone on horseback. Dorothy, pale aquatic Dorothy, my brother's swimming instructor, had reacted to such over-stimulating parents by finding another mode in which to excel: not brilliance or daring or endeavour, but *kindness*. Four cats, all strays, three mongrels and a broken-legged squirrel whom the others wished to eat.

Such was the count I made on the one occasion I'd visited their enormous house on Learmonth Crescent—by far the biggest private home I'd ever entered, with a staircase connecting not flats but rooms to other rooms, landings to landings. The parents talked so enthusiastically about Scotland receiving new blood from abroad that I detected a wariness. Dorothy smiled and went on holding Emilio's hand as if to say she didn't give a tinker's cuss if her parents approved or not since this was the man she had chosen . . . 'under-water', as she put it. She might not be a genius like her brother, who was already a Professor of Mathematics at Oxford University, but she had taken a degree at the varsity in some useful subject and then found herself a job with an import-export company, since for all her folks were wealthy, they held that a modern girl must be gainfully employed.

Dario was busy, of course, on the evening we siblings were all invited, but Giulio arrived with Torrone and Cinnamon Sorbet. He refused to be awed by the size of the dining-room, its chandelier and its enormous bow window with the view across to Fife. He led the parents down into Inferno where ice was the apogee of evil, across the East with its spices and ass's milk, through America with its soda fountains and sundaes, to end up here at this table where 'a sacrament of sorts' had just been performed (he knew he risked nothing with Dorothy's devoutly irreligious parents). Not only, he concluded, were ices proving popular in Scotland, he viewed it as his duty to educate his countrymen in what ice had done for civilization, and was open to suggestions as to how best to accomplish this.

A smile crossed Dorothy's father's face: marrying down had just been turned into an occasion for political improvement.

Whenever Dorothy met her fiancé after work, she would chum him down to the Palace, offer assistance, then sit contentedly in a booth so as to regard her man. Or she'd ask me questions about Mamma, Valerio, whether I shared her nervousness at the thought of becoming a bride. In her I could detect none of the confusion or self-stifling I'd detected in myself: living was enough for her, for her manner of living was somehow necessary, like when she cut through the bandage on the squirrel's leg after it was mended and the critter was ready to go free.

We were seated round the fire in our kitchen: I'd needed to wait for a suitable moment to distribute presents. Assunta, amazingly, did not put Nonno's wooden bird in her mouth. She looked at it, tilted her head, then looked at it more narrowly. Only when Dario entered did she toss it on the floor. He was enjoying the enlarged audience. 'Can you credit it, Dot? That popinjay Oswald Bloody Mosley, with his wife some Churchill or other, yes the man with the money and the teeth, he's gone and called his lot the *British Union of Fascists*, as if they'd invented the thing. Bloody outrage, eh Dot?'

Emilio began with a sigh. 'Dorothy's never been a *Dot*. And can you not leave her out of it?'

'If I'm to be one of the family,' Dorothy said, 'then I'd better understand your concerns. I can argue my own opinion once I've formed it.' I asked myself whence the glow on my cheek. Admiration, a little, but mostly just envy: for years—for a decade—I'd been hoping to utter something so confident and cool-headed, so independent and un-Italian. Dorothy explained that her father had known this Mosley fellow years ago, but now had no time for him.

Dario looked deflated. 'Good on you, Emilio, you've finally been teaching the little lady something useful.'

'Not I. Must have learnt it all by herself. A miracle of nature.'

From across the landing, Paola was calling to her husband that his tea was going cold. But he was intent on explaining to Dorothy the natural affinity between Scotland and the Duce's Italy—Scotland, a country that had sent its officers around the world to impose order on the natives, from the Paddies to the Gyps to the Chinks. 'Who's the general of Bloody Bengal if it's no another Scotsman? That John Anderson Lucia's so keen on.' I had time to imagine a kilt made of tiger's pelt, before he went on: 'When he has to sum up *Fascismo*, what does the Duce say? He says, *Life mustn't be taken too lightly*. I mean, what better slogan for the hard-arsed dour-faced dreich-weathered Protestant-guilt-ridden penny-pinching sex-starved crabbit-hearted Scots? He's going to plant pine trees in the Mezzogiorno so's to encourage more Nordic spirit. And look at me now, I've got Hitler and Mosley claiming to be the brand new Duce, bigger and bolder than the original, Adolf with his brownshirts smashing up Berlin.'

Dorothy agreed it was troubling. She had read how Hitler had refused the post of Vice-Chancellor, and judged it only a matter of time before he was on top.

Dario was pacing round the kitchen, forgetting in his disgruntlement that it was a woman he was addressing. 'Right, and here I've got to contend with his acolytes, the likes of McEwen.' He saw me squirming in my chair. 'Aye, the same. He's been brandishing a letter he claims to be from the club-footed water-rat Goering—sorry, Emilio, but he's a lot worse of a cripple than you—which turns out to be Ewan's receipt for his copy of *Mein Kampf*, of which he cannot read a single word, what with him being the pig-swill-ignorant son of a chip-shop owner.'

'I thought he was a friend of yours.' It escaped me, though I was determined to keep my mouth shut unless I could sound at least a quarter as intelligent as Dorothy.

'We're pals, right enough, but it doesn't mean it's acceptable when he goes round saying to forget the Duce for the new world leader, Adolf the Austrian Corporal.'

Paola ignored her husband when she came through to fetch Assunta, whose hand was back round Nonno's wooden bird.

'Not that he'll manage it, mind. Mosley may be a fool who's only interested in licking the aristocratic *culo*, but he's no about to start licking some corporal's *culo* and all.'

'Dario! What will Dorothy's parents say if she reports the language she's hearing here!'

'It's all right, Mr Pezzini. Better he speaks his mind.'

'Please, call me *Papà*, if you want to make an old man happy.'

'Well, Papà, we're used to lively debate in our home. And nobody's in love with Mr or Mrs Mosley.'

23

As the wedding plans hardened, over lunch-hour we brides-to-be would visit the shops, inspecting crockery and linen. Dorothy would not be squeezing into the tenement; her parents had found them a ground-floor flat in Stockbridge—nothing grand, she said, blushing. The dress she'd like to wear, from Jenners Store, cost the equivalent of four months' pay—but no, there'd be no awkwardness, Emilio insisted, when I doubted Scots so well-to-do could be combined with Italians so modest. I was beginning to think *Cinderella*, until Valerio wrote to tell me not to be so *Nordic* . . . It was all within the family, after all. Giulio announced he'd move into the recess, leaving what had been the boys' room to me and my man. I struggled to imagine repeating Signor Starace's bed, let alone further refinements or transports, in the room where my brothers had gone from bed-wetting to spot-squeezing to fighting over who had assassinated the Duce's enemy Senator Matteotti—and the envy doubled of my future sister-in-law.

Envy: not a colour on Dorothy's spectrum; however hard I searched for it, I could not detect the slightest trace, not even for what she did not possess, such as fulsome breasts or curls. I envied her the more . . .

Nor was envy was the worst of it, since my return from Rome: for whenever I left home unaccompanied, on my way to work, from work, approaching the Ice Palace, even if I varied the hour; as if he had access to my innermost ruses, as if he'd modelled himself on one of the doubles of our Edinburgh's Robert Louis . . . there he was across the road or down the steps or round the corner. Only once, in early December, did I succeed in surprising him, sneaking up from behind. With a miniature spyglass, he was scanning the pavement where normally I'd have been passing. I sneered something about bird-spotting, regretting my foolish remark the moment it was out.

'There's only one burd interests me,' he said, unnaturally slowly, turning as if his neck were stiff. From up close, his clothes were shabby beneath his topcoat, which itself was a pin cushion of badges and emblems, among which I recognized an imperial eagle and those broken-elbowed crosses whose name escaped me.

'I'm engaged now, you know, so why don't you leave me alone? Engaged to an Italian who's twice the man you'll ever be.' I hated myself for saying it, wading into his trench.

'Heard all aboot it,' he hissed, his breath vaporizing on contact with the freezing air. His father had refused him entry to the family chippy in his regalia; he looked like he hadn't eaten a square meal in weeks. 'Aye,' he went on, catching my glance, 'yer Dario was right about this much, we have to suffer for our convictions.'

'You can suffer in Inferno for all I care. Don't you understand, I never want to see your face again.'

'But we can't all get what we want, now, can we. *I'll* be seeing *you*, mark my words, when the time is right.'

As I sat trying to catch my breath on the nearby steps, I wondered if everyone possessed one—or all women perhaps: an ill-whelped creature who trod their shadow, occupying the slipstream of doubt that all but saints and Dorothy left behind them. He had always been present, would for ever be, here to eternity.

At the Fascio, my personal creature from the penumbra lit up in the bright glow of dogma, adorned in badges and armbands. I should not have been surprised to hear on Dario's lips that Adolf had some ideas worth considering. In the weeks leading up to Christmas, the tradesmen who advertised their wares and services were heckled from the back of the hall. 'Who needs pipe-cleaners?' cried one of McEwen's crew. 'When you can use yer spaghetti?' Talk was of limiting the Fascio to Italians, until Dario, who laughed off interruptions, pointed out that half of McEwen's gang were in fact Italian and that it was important to win them back from 'the prison-house of fanaticism'.

Though Emilio said he might come for an hour, Dorothy avoided the Christmas party, the Fascio being beyond her parents' pale even for strictly social occasions. Giulio was absent too, but supplied the ice-cream, offering receipts on sales to a charity for jobless Italians. I felt relieved, who didn't wish either of them to witness McEwen and his followers, luridly dressed (if brown can be lurid) with motorcycle boots and riding crops that would have been laughable (given their lack of any sort of steed) had they not been so menacing.

'I want yous all to listen!' As he wore no cap, the brush was fully visible, a carrot yanked screaming from the ground. A dumbstruck carrot.

Dario swore, then shrugged. 'No so easy making speeches, eh, Ewan? Cat got your tongue?'

'Take that statue down from the stage!'

'Give the boy a dobbin to go with his boots!'

Even his own crew were laughing. When finally he shifted on the dais, he looked like an automaton from Chamber Street Museum. His arm rose in salute, though to whom was unclear.

'Duce!' Dario assisted him.

The mouth opened slowly, but the words spilt out so fast they were almost unintelligible. 'I'm warnin yous all . . . goin soft . . . yer Duce too wi his crappy wee army.'

'He's warning us! Pipe down!'

'Shut your gob, Dario!' he countered. 'Just because you've been making a display of yourself ever since the age of two, waving your potty around.'

'Now here's Doctor Freud, one of Adolf's favourites'—he pronounced him A-dolf—'going to sort my head out.'

'He's another yin for the chop—bloody decadent! Soon be purged, I've read it all in the papers.'

'He reads! Ring the bells of St Mary's! A miracle on earth!' It was Emilio.

'Yer days are numbered, you Pezzinis. Once the BUF gets its legs, you'll be trampled underfoot. We'll suck you up and spit out the weaklings.' His face was more beetroot than carrot, fists clenched.

Dario had donned a Christmas paper crown to join him on the dais. He explained—for those of us who hadn't had the honour of meeting Mr Mosley's band of impoverished aristocrats, bankrupt industrialists and wife-swappers—that the BUF was the British Union of so-called Fascists.

McEwen hocked upon the floor. 'And the time will come when you'll see yer march on Rome was a pathetic wee parade compared to . . . And that what starts now will ignite like a . . . fuck!' He stared into space as if space had stolen his metaphor.

'A puddle?' suggested Dario, chortling.

'A damp squib?' tried Signor Borsari, getting into the spirit.

The vein on his temple was set to burst. 'Hitler is the Duce!' he lathered. 'I'm no fuckin finished yet . . . and yous Italians, yous had better all remember that you're here out of *our* generosity.' With that, he waved his arm in the air again and clicked his heels to attention. One of his gang applauded; the rest were silent.

'Thank you, Ewan,' Dario finally said in his poshest Archbishop accent, 'for a most elegant and enlightening speech, from which we ignorant Eye-talians, for whom English is but a second language, after the music of Dante and D'Annunzio, can surely profit greatly.'

Laughter rang again. McEwen's crowd stamped their feet and clinked their glasses, impervious to irony.

'As my old pal rightly implies, in beer-cellars up and down the Black Forest, stout men with pencil moustaches wearing leather nappies and pinnies will be banging their tables just like their representative here.' Few knew who it was Dario was alluding to, never having seen a photograph of Hitler, let alone of his followers. But it didn't lessen the jollity. 'And yes, we'll listen to them, Comrades and fellow-Fascisti. In so far as they speak the voice of reason, we'll converse with and try to teach them. For they have much to learn from our ten glorious years.'

Though it was Giulio who brought home the newspapers, now I purchased my own copy of *The Scotsman*. But where it looked easy under the arms of bankers and insurance clerks, under mine it felt on fire. I had little notion of what I was seeking, but I had to find it fast before it found me. Nothing to do with the freezing weather, of which the paper was full, as Hogmanay came and went. Bundled up in coat, scarf, mitts, I pulled the paper apart over lunchtime in Princes Street Gardens. *Strasser's departure . . . resigns from Nazi Party . . . Industrialists appeased . . . Schleicher's position uncertain.* The names scuttled like ugly unfulfilled promises, unpronounceable, into unexplored corners. I studied Giulio's atlas for clues, but so many countries—of what significance their colours? I enquired at the university about evening classes, aware I had no free evenings. Valerio's letters offered little relief, full of the difficulties of obtaining emigration papers (procedures were stricter now the Duce needed a rise in population). Yes, he'd heard about the turbulence in Germany, feared the worst. But what was *the worst*? I told myself not to panic, that History had always been flowing round us, even if I had neglected it, leaving that to the boys; History might go on ignoring me, even if I could no longer ignore it.

The temperature dipped far below freezing, and customers would linger in the bank imagining adjustments to their accounts rather than brave the icy street. The Palace was full, but only after defrosting near the radiators was anyone in the mood for refreshment.

He, however, wore nothing over his brownshirt, wherever he was loitering. And still he appeared overheated. If I nipped into McVities and lingered with Auntie Sandy, when I snuck out the back he was present two minutes later, sporting a black armband.

'See ye're reading the papers these days. No before time. They call him *Führer* in German, which sounds a damn sight better than Duce.' The way he pronounced it, I heard *Fury*. 'You've still no twigged, have you? Not got it yet, yous Eye-talians. That you've started something, but it's no up to you to stop it just when it gets interesting. You're all responsible, most of all your family. It's us what's the future, the Nordic race. Even Mosley's barely cottoned on yet. The streets'll be fire and blood.' So he *could* string sentences together, if not yet in public.

I quivered, backing away. On my way to the Palace in the evening, I stopped at the family chippy, hoping to appeal to his father, but I'd mentioned only the first syllable of his name before McEwen Senior burst out, 'Dinnae mention that lunatic to me! A disgrace to his mother's memory. I'll batter him and dunk him in the fryer if he so much as sets foot in my shop again.'

As January died, I sought some way of announcing that I'd never had the least interest in politics—all that mattered to me was family and marriage to the man I loved. Giulio advised me to stop appearing at the Fascio. From *The Scotsman* blared the headline, *Germany Holds Its Breath as Hitler Sworn In as Chancellor*. The frost clung to the inside of our windows at dawn. Emilio sought help in planning the reception, to be held at the George Hotel despite our protests that it was surely too grand; the catering, gifts, guest list. My intestines were in revolt: it was all I could do to get through the days, scour *The Scotsman*, serve the granitas, scribble perfunctory answers to Valerio's anxieties about his forthcoming move north. I was on my way to work when the headline brought me up short. Two nights before, on 27 February, the Reichstag building had been set ablaze. Three months previously, it would have meant nothing to me. Now, the Führer stomped through the embers in his long leather coat, breathing triumph. Mr Morton asked if I shouldn't be in bed, I looked that pale.

It was on my way home that it happened, came to pass, only eighty yards from home, with the Reichstag roaring through our heads. For a second, not more, it was almost a relief, after the dread of more than days or months, as the bowels released involuntarily.

'Ye filthy little slut. But if you think a bit shite's gonna put me off . . .'

He had grabbed me from behind, all I could see were his motor-cycle boots. I recognized the yard into which he hustled me, recognized the wall against which he pushed me, bruising ribs and chest—right next to where I'd sat when I fired the shard that scarred him. I screamed; it sounded slight. Something soft—a filthy handkerchief I discovered when finally I extracted it—was stuffed into my open mouth. I stamped on his toes. He released one arm for long enough to put a blade to my throat.

'Next scream,' warned the whisky breath, 'will be yer last. Ye remember this spot? Or would ye rather I said it with the Eye-talian brogue? Zis? Remember zis wall? Ye thought ye'd won the war, but it was only the battle.' He yanked up my skirt with his free hand, tore away the suspenders so the stockings slid down. 'Fuckin disgusting.'

My body flopped like a ragdoll.

'Show a bit o life ye bitch!' His grunts from behind me were coming fast and they gave me something like hope. 'This is what all bitches get who thinks they can marry Jew-boys. Their fuckin days are numbered.'

What I heard gave me strength to seize my single chance. I felt him push, eager to enter where his fingers had probed. Heard him panting harder. And that was when I squirmed, so just as he thrust he missed me.

'Ye fucking bitch! I'll murder ye!'

I felt his splatter on the backs of my thighs, his hands releasing me to wring out the final drops.

'Ye think I'm gonna gee you the satisfaction of taking my hand across your face? So you can run to your brothers and clipe on me?' He sounded altered, now his fluid was spilt. But he could revive. 'So you won't be bringing any wee stormtroopers into the world this time—what a waste.' The knife had disappeared, he was buttoning himself up.

I pulled down my skirt, tried to rise to my feet, tugged the rag from my mouth.

'Wipe yerself on this.' He offered me his shirt-tail.

'I want to go home now.' It was all I could think to say.

'I'll see you home, sure I will. Ye canna be too careful, these dark nights.' He walked beside me as I hobbled into Broughton Street. 'It canna hurt,' he said, 'I barely touched you.' There was fear in his voice; I had to escape before it returned as rage. The entrance to the tenement was in sight. His hand was in the pocket with the knife. 'Ye'll no be telling Dario about this?'

I just kept on walking.

'It'll only cause problems. He can stay Chief Extractor for all I care, but once Mosley gathers his troops, he'll be needing me the more.'

Another few steps.

'He wouldnae believe you in any case. Already warned him you'd try and set me against him.' He stopped, fearful as a child, bent over. He ordered me to remove the scraps of stockings, which he pocketed. 'So?' We were at the entrance to the close. 'When will we be seeing each other next?'

I hadn't put my shoes back on. The stairs were lit, I knew each one like a friend. If he caught me, I could scream. I thought of Zio Roberto and his remarkable bounds.

I leapt. I ran. I climbed faster than I'd ever climbed.

He started to give chase, but on the first floor gave up. From the top landing, I could see the red glow of his cigarette in the dead night air.

25

For once I was glad the toilet was on the landing, where I could lock myself inside before being spotted. I stared in the mirror: I must be somewhere behind that face. The blade had left no mark upon my neck, the brick dust on my jacket brushed off. I took the family towel, wet it, and slowly wiped myself clean. Rinsed the towel, hitched up the skirt, padded the thighs, rinsed again in the basin, padded them again and again and again. Finally, I looked down: there was nothing to be seen. The tears came silent and sobless. This was what he wanted, I was almost good as new. Only Paola's tapping on the door said I could not spend the rest of my life in the toilet. I threw open the door and strode past her. Inside the flat, mercifully, there was only Papà. I climbed into the recess, pulled the curtain behind me.

When I awoke, or stirred from the numbness into which I had sunk, Giulio was watching me, the curtain held back. '*Vieni*,' he said, stretching out his hand.

I resisted only a second, allowing him to ease me from bed, into the kitchen where the others had somehow assembled. 'What you all doing here?' I asked. 'Who's at the Palace?' All present, as for a family *chiacchierata*.

Emilio said not to worry, Fausto was in charge. 'Papà sent a message,' Giulio explained, 'so Emilio and I came up. Now you can tell us what's the matter.' Paola put a hand round my shoulder, where I sat on the kitchen chair wishing for time to think, to know how I felt, what I had become, let disgust subside into something I could speak. I tried to keep the tears from my eyes, but when I looked up, they were streaming down Giulio's instead. 'Something to do with McEwen?' he tried.

For some reason, Dario was wearing his American suit. 'Quit putting ideas in the broad's head.'

'Well?'

I nodded. Cursed myself. I might as well have been five years old.

'He's been nasty to you? Taken advantage?'

'Come on now, Ewan's a bit of a *ruffiano*, his half a brain filled with all this Nazi nonsense. But there's no malice in him. He wouldn't dare.'

Emilio stood up, wobbled. 'You know we've all been busy, and with Dorothy and all I've not been . . . But you're still my only wee sister.'

No one had the words in English, so Paola had to help. '*Non ti ha violentata?*'

Papà, from habit, felt obliged to translate. 'He did not violate my baby? Tell us he did not?'

How to tell them that he had—or almost?

'Just trying his luck, I bet.'

He had threatened me with a blade, thrust his carrot-fingers into me, spilt his filthy seed over my arse. I could not utter a word.

'He ravished you? By force? Do you need to see a doctor? Lucia, look at me. We can pay for that, if you need to see a doctor.'

'No,' I got out. 'I cleaned up.'

'Well in that case . . .' Dario was shaking his head.

'Will you get out of here, Dario?'

'I live here too, you know. It's one of my pals she's slandering.'

'Paola, will you take the wee one next door.' The tone of Giulio's voice was new, efficient and undeviating.

Emilio offered to go and see Mr Morton in the morning, tell him I was sick. 'No!' It was my first real reaction. 'I'm going to work tomorrow.' I didn't know why I was so decisive.

Then Giulio did what no one else had dared and which could have been a disaster: he put his hands under my armpits, raised me up, and clasped me tightly. 'Don't worry,' he whispered, 'little sister mine. You will not be seeing him again for a very long time. We'll take care of it. We may be almost Scottish, but we've not forgotten our southern soul—you can count on it.'

I didn't know what he meant, but it was momentous, his tone as inflexible as the knife against my throat. Paola undressed and inspected me, brewed some infusion that made my head spin, held my hand until I slept.

I awoke in the night to the sound of men's voices trying to speak in whispers. 'I'm sure he didn't mean it,' said Dario. 'Just a wee bit foo.'

'Are you with him or against him?' Emilio, usually so nuanced, put the question.

'You know that *famiglia* comes first with Dario here, soft-hearted soul that I am. What you proposing?'

Did I hear the word *vendetta*? It was Fausto's voice, surely: I already suspected I had special place in his affections, and he had crossed McEwen before; this was his boss in trouble who had taken him from the streets and given him a living. 'What'll you have me do?' I heard him say.

'Find him tonight,' Giulio ordered, 'wherever he's run to ground. Take him somewhere dark but not too dark. Remove one of his *coglioni* with this.' I pictured him handing Fausto the hook-shaped razor-sharp knife that Paola used for opening potato sacks. 'Right or left. Tell him that if any Italian sees him in this city again in the next five years we'll make him eat the second.'

I heard Dario splutter and it sounded as if Emilio might have fainted. But Fausto had been a seaman and had doubtless heard worse.

When next I awoke, I heard him reporting back: the 'surgical intervention', as he called it, had been simple enough; from wherever they were stitching him up, the patient would be going direct to Waverley Station—my brother had given Fausto the necessary to get my attacker out the country.

When I entered the bank the next morning, Mr Morton was changed. Or I looked at him differently; even Mr Morton, of the sweet tooth and kind heart. I knew I had to do something to stop the spread—even Giulio had looked scary over breakfast. I didn't go out at lunchtime, didn't even snack. I sat at my desk and wrote:

Edinburgh

1 March

Still dear to me Valerio,

I write with tears on the page and the heaviest of hearts, to tell you that henceforth you are a free man. I cannot bring you to this country, where my family has stirred up so much trouble and where it is set to get worse. The world does not permit it. Don't ask me to explain. Tell yourself only that I'm not worthy, that you're fortunate to escape me. We Italians have somehow courted disaster, and I'm the one has to pay for it.

My family is indebted to you. I don't make much money, but what little is left over will be saved in order to repay you. You are young and true and handsome and noble, you can still find someone with whom to be happy.

Your ever-loving

Lucia

My ideas of psychology were primitive enough, but some part of me intuited I could not extinguish anger by monopolizing guilt; I just needed to be reassured that I could *do* something, could *initiate*, even if what I was initiating was self-destruction. My ideas were primitive, but just sophisticated enough to prevent me from posting that letter, which I stored in my handbag as if it could protect me from further affront.

Dario was the only one to read my mind that night (unless he had gone through my bag and read my unsent letter), and he offered his special sort of consolation. 'I can see what you're feeling, mind,' he said, 'and I'd say you have a point. Damaged goods and all that.'

I did not have to wait long to learn just how ineffectual was my protection. Two days after the attack, uncannily, echoing not just my
nightmare of powerlessness but even my own expression, came a letter from Valerio. I opened it with a rush of gratitude.

27 February

Carissima,

Now you I rend a free woman. I am betrayed. My boss found the truth
about the money I taked to send to you. Also worse, he finded the other
money I taked to give to the League to Promote Judaic Understanding,
to the Communists hiding, to anyone who tries to stop what happen
here. I am ruined, and there will be no trial, already I am a condemned
man. My father says he will try to 'tirare le file', but I refuse. I confess,
I am proud I finally have acted.

I writing you to tell you what happened to me. For the moment,
Cara, I ask you not to write to me. It will only make the police more
severe that I receive letters from a country strange, and now they watch
everything I do: they have taked my passport, this letter I give to the
waiter at the trattoria you know on Via delle Botteghe Oscure.

You must to live your life without me. If I am lucky I shall survive
but I shall leave never this infernal country again.

Your ever-devoted
Valerio

However often I read it, I could not take it in. In the evening,
when I had recovered enough to read it out to them, my brothers'
reaction was the predictable mix of outrage and satisfaction; only
Dario managed to outdo himself with his 'Great news! So now he'll
be locked up for life at the very least, which means no need to pretend to pay back the money he sent!'

I stood by the downstairs doorway waiting for the postman as
June approached, cursing myself for still wincing from McEwen's
assault, when Valerio was facing so much worse. 'Pink,' I said to
Dorothy, as if trying the words on for size, not the dress, 'rather than
white.'

It was strictly unbelievable, yet it was happening to me. Papà failed to paint the posies he had designed for the reception. Paola, with ruthless maternal instinct, kept Assunta away from the fount of misery I had become. I longed to travel incognito to Rome and salvage Valerio, and when I'd ruled that out as impossible, I longed to become a nun, to run away and turn terrorist in Bengal where riots were happening, or in Ireland—suddenly the whole world seemed in turmoil, how had I not noticed it before? Dorothy shopped without me. No, I did not wish her to postpone her marriage until I recovered or Valerio was freed.

I had to force myself to open the envelope containing his next letter.

2 May

Cara,

I do not know if you will receive never this letter, but I do know that it must to be my last in the case I am caught communicating with the world outside then I shall be lucky to live. I not could stop my father from pulling the cords, and without him I probably would already be died. Instead I am sent to internal exile on an island in the mid of nothing, with no term to my sentence, and for company only the waves and donkeys. I must not to tell you which island, and you must try not to discover, as I know you enough well to think you might come to find me.

Forget me, amore mio, or if you not can forget me then leave me be the man who did at least one thing right in his life, help you and your family. And maybe one day we shall meet again, when the war has ended that will bring this terrible regime to its knees. Live your life and make yourself happy for me, ti prego.

Your Valerio

Ten times each day I re-read Valerio's letter, with every time a new objection rising in my throat. Yet even Giulio agreed that I must obey his order, and not attempt to contact him—where would I have started, in any case.

I soon tired of sympathy. I ate without taste, worked like a machine. Mr Morton approved of my brand new suit, bought by Giulio who insisted I discard everything I'd been wearing on the night I was attacked. For seconds at a time I'd feel normal, then I'd remember Valerio alone on his rock, I'd remember what we'd done, what McEwen did to me, and I'd rush to the toilet where I'd fail to throw up.

I knew I had to inure myself: the less the world had taste for me, the less I would feel the pain. I had to try and think of life as one great big list, an idea that had the unreal lucidity of one of the ice sculptures on which Giulio so prided himself. I could be an ice sculpture too.

Round the Rob Roy pub, McEwen's cronies, leaderless, were drunker daily. What remained of their regalia, what momentarily had linked them to a Germany none had ever visited and of whose present ideals they had only the faintest grasp, grew tattered and then fell off or was removed. 'Walked out on us, the wee bastard,' one of them breathed when I strayed too close. 'Ewan left us in the lurch.'

I went to Papà's cabinet. At the back, where it squatted behind a damaged cherub, it tried to elude my grasp before yielding its knotted coldness to my palm. That night I slept with it by my pillow—the hound that might have been a troll that might have been a boar.

26

As I walked through the doors of the Registry Office in Victoria Street, I was taking it all in, but only to guarantee the fact that deep down I was absent. The service was mercifully short, and when I took up position on the steps with my bag of rice, Dorothy caught my eye and ensured the bouquet flew beyond my reach. When I cried, I hardly knew if I was doing so for the newlyweds or for myself. Walking into the reception room of the George Hotel, I thought I'd chosen the wrong door: this, patently, was a Scot-Scot wedding. Yet here was Papà seated in his new ill-fitting suit at the head of an almighty table, surrounded by strangers; the sea of Italians had evaporated, and present were only family and a few such as Carlo who'd hired black tie for the occasion. While Dorothy's family had turned into Highlanders, their relations now clansmen, their numerous friends with the posh English accents henceforth *lairds* and *mistresses*. I thanked Giulio for having dragged me through the first half of Walter Scott's *Redgauntlet*, as without it I'd have been even more lost.

I had asked my brothers to put it out that I'd decided I was too young to wed, hence no one but Dorothy cast me pitying looks. Her father, in a brogue hitherto undetected, stooped over me to say, 'It'll be a saer fecht indeed, Lucy, if amongst this fine assembly you canna find a joe to help you change your mind.'

For me, being Scottish had always implied being lots of things my family was not. It meant being Protestant with a terror of the Sabbath, meant whispering when the body was mentioned, meant support of the maroon of the Hearts FC, meant marching with drums in orange suits to celebrate some battle won centuries ago in Ireland. Being *really* Scottish meant getting drunk and celebrating this with a fight, or falling in the gutter, or a night in the cell. Or it meant being a Freemason and carrying a wee leather case concealing a pinnie; meant a proud look in the eye, as if the street (even to the poorest and most unemployable man or woman) were a private possession. It meant talking about a distant relative who'd hit the big time in Vancouver or Melbourne. And of course it meant moaning about the English, even more than about the Italians or Irish: the English who'd taken away the Parliament, the crown, the wealth, the language, the dignity. To be Scottish, above all, meant not having to think about it. Yet here, dressed in tartan, affecting unheralded accents and an affection for *usquebah*, were Dorothy's parents and friends, as awkward as novices in brand new habits. If I'd had the heart I would have laughed.

'It's a curious thing,' Giulio remarked, as if he were monitoring from Mars. 'For this lot can't blame the English since most of them went to school down south, or made their fortunes there. And they're too free-thinking to blame the Catholics, publicly at least. So I suppose they have to find other ways of being Scottish.'

It was the first time I'd eaten salmon, let alone venison. On my right was a cousin of Dorothy who was dismayed I'd never played hockey; on my left, an old friend of her father who expected me to sing an aria from the opera of my name. When I admitted I could not, he did so himself, but in such a ludicrous accent that I spluttered into my ice-cream. (Giulio had manufactured a special mould that ensured every dessert plate displayed the Italian flag in Pistachio, Vanilla and Raspberry, surrounded by a saltire of vanilla on dark blue Bramble Parfait.)

Then the speeches. The father spoke of Dorothy's girlhood passion for sports and pets. He turned her love of atlases and gazettes into a prelude to her encounter with the exotic Emilio. She'd soon be fluent in Italian, 'the language of poetry and love'. The Edinburgh establishment needed to open its doors to the hard-working souls from abroad who were raring to inject new life-blood. No one should forget that Mary Queen of Scots was educated in Italian, nor where Bonnie Prince Charlie chose to end his days—nor indeed that Maria of Modena had married Scottish royalty, sealing the link between the allies. (Most of which was news to us Italians, and surprising given that Ted—as he insisted he now be called—had repeatedly declared he was dead set not just against George V but against 'the whole royal shower'.) He was drawing to a close, he said, because he didn't believe in lengthy speeches (his had lasted twenty minutes), but wished to add that if Scotland were going to be the brave, as its famous march claimed, then it had to embrace the fact that all individuals within its borders *and without* were born equal, with an equal right to marry, settle and prosper, as on this splendid and historic occasion.

Through the tinkling of glasses, as the crowd turned its bemused attention to this Italian best man about to address them, I wondered why I had rarely felt less at home. Yet Giulio looked at ease. 'I hope you enjoyed the taste,' he began, 'and also the symbols of your ice-creams. We live in troubled times, and our community, into which Dorothy is now formally welcomed, feels the strain. We rely on our hosts, even those of us born here, for your protection and support.'

Dario was fidgeting: for years he'd been talking of applying for British citizenship, but had failed to take the first step. Next to me, the hockey player mumbled his disappointment at the lack of lewd jokes about the groom.

'My family is pleased to make your acquaintance, and we only wish our dear Mamma were here with us. Now, to conclude, let me ask you to look once again at your pudding plates.' He paused while the guests, flustered, stared at the ice-cream remains. 'That's a symbol too. No pure reds, no Hibernian greens or Midlothian maroons, no whites or blues or blacks. Patterns, pastels, mixes and smudges. It's what we ice-cream makers strive to avoid. Today, on this day of the marriage of Dorothy and Emilio, it's the effect I planned for the hardest.' He said nothing for ten whole seconds, allowing his message to sink in. 'Ladies and gentlemen, *signore e signori*, let us toast the bride and groom, *brindiamo la sposa e lo sposo!*'

Everyone rose to their feet. Emilio shocked the tenor next to me by striding up and kissing his brother on the lips. Then came dances, where it was a relief to see that many of Dorothy's family were almost as unfamiliar with the Gay Gordons and the Eightsome

Reel as us Italians—Dorothy's brother, up from Oxford, being particularly clueless.

When the Scottish jollity appeared to be turning morose amid dirty plates and streamers, Paola took to the centre of the floor and performed a tarantella, looking quite possessed, so people didn't know whether to clap or commiserate. Beppe fetched his accordion and began one of his most plangent brigand songs, while listeners strained to catch every word, as if by straining they might absorb the unfamiliar tongue. Then the guests started to leave, and I began to clear the plates.

'What *are* you doing, Lucia?' said Dorothy, smiling. 'There's staff for that, you know.'

I tried unsuccessfully not to sob as they left in a motor car with tin cans attached, Dorothy at the wheel, en route to honeymoon on the Kyles of Bute.

27

I had seen them aplenty, the Great War produced them in droves: old maids, turning in time into parents to their own parents; eyes of sadness, down-turning. Only Giulio's presence at home was sparing me an awful life of emptiness, with Papà, never the most exciting companion even in his prime.

'You're only twenty-three,' Dorothy reminded me.

I felt sixty-five or more, and I was sure it showed. Almost nightly I would dream of Valerio on his rock: I would fly down (whether in a plane, or like a bird, or even at times in a barrage balloon) and snatch him up to freedom.

'Let me guess,' said Giulio one evening, 'You feel like life is passing you by?' Despite my self-absorption, I had seen how the Palace was prospering, Giulio turning into a man of substance, an eminently eligible bachelor. He still found time to go dancing with Auntie Sandy, and I watched the single women eye him across the counter, calculating their chances. After a particular night where he had taken so much pleasure in bathing and dressing Assunta, I asked him if he wouldn't care to raise a child of his own. From the look on his face, I imagined my fear must be audible.

'Worried you're already on the shelf? Missed your one chance? And to judge from all the newspapers you're reading, I'd guess you probably feel your existence has been overrun by world events?'

I nodded feebly, ashamed at my transparency.

'But look at me, the role of Zio is not so bad. I'm happy at the Palace, have everything—nearly everything—I could ask for.'

'But your own flesh and blood? Would it not be different?'

He took a deep breath, opened his mouth, then seemed to change his mind, and sighed.

'Men have all the power,' I blurted out, wondering where I'd come by such a Dorothy-like notion. 'They can do anything they like.'

'Unnatural creatures they are, right enough.' What followed was as close to a lecture as I'd heard from him since he'd quit the Fascio. 'Never know the bleeding or what it feels to nurse a wain on the tit. Just a shot in the dark, as often as not in the wrong direction. And hoping that nine months later the wee lump bears the imprint, but never quite sure of it, making up for that fact with aught else.'

'So you're saying that all we're good for is bearing brats? We're heifers?'

He hardly paused for breath. 'I'm saying that women, even child-less spinsters, have in them what men can only dream on. We're hopefuls, trying to convince ourselves we've a stake in life. Ice-cream's my way, others, more and more of them, want uniforms and eagle badges and now these swastikas we're seeing on the Mosley mob ever since the press turned against them and their fiasco.' (We'd read that news weeks before: twelve thousand supporters squeezed into the Olympia in London, with banners, flags and jackboots, hecklers beaten to a pulp while the police looked on approvingly.)

'Are you telling me men turn into Nazis for want of a womb?' I was proud to have followed him this far, even if what I said made him chuckle.

'Maybe I should quit giving lectures.' He laughed another few seconds. 'What are those you've been meaning to show me?'

Newspaper headlines: ever since I was attacked I would cut them out, along with their columns if these seemed relevant to our lives. '*Governor of Bengal Escapes Assassination Attempt.*' I pointed to a photo where the Governor in his official robes looked like a cross between Zorro and the Archbishop of Canterbury.

'Your Mr Anderson again?' He read on silently about how at the Spring Meet of the Lebong Racecourse, just as the Governor rose to congratulate the winner, the assassins chanced their hands. The race starter overpowered the first after his shot went wide; the Raja of Barwari tackled the second after his revolver jammed from point-blank range. The Governor himself tripped on a loose carpet and fell headlong. His only comment upon picking himself up— 'And they wonder,' Giulio remarked, 'why Britain has an empire and Italy does not!'—was, '*I have spoken about that piece of carpet before— most undignified.*' Giulio's eyes sped on. 'Ha, I like that! Anderson says he keeps the temperature down in his house by having fans play over blocks of ice.'

Headlines—I presented my brother with another: '*Mussolini Meets Hitler in Venice*'. 'Dario claims it's better the devil you know. I keep thinking that if I stay in with the Fascio, then maybe I'll be able to help Valerio some day.'

'And why,' asked Giulio, 'is the Duce in military dress when Hitler's in a gabardine? And what's with the Duce's fez?'

I handed him yet another:'*Stormtroopers*'. The column went into gruesome detail about the night of retribution that had led to the stormtroopers' ringleader, Ernst Röhm, having '*the pistol to his head*'. Henceforth, the brown would be immersed in a tide of black, as worn by Hitler's '*ultimate instrument of terror, the Waffen SS*'.

Brown in a tide of black. I felt the need to clutch the statue I kept close to my pillow, the only creature with which I was sure I had a complete understanding.

Days passed, months passed, a year or more must have passed, virtually unnoticed by one who had learnt the word 'depression' but would never have dared assume it might apply to an individual as insignificant as herself. Even the death of Zio Joe I learnt about through the newspaper: a shoot-out, said the report, while running potcheen. I pictured him embalmed inside a giant *panettone*, surrounded by his hoods wielding sawn-off shotguns. Finally, a letter did arrive from Zia Sabrina, to say her heart was broken. Dario, laughing, said her heart had been sold off years ago to some bigger *Padrino*; then joked about how there might be an opening for himself.

And the next headline came not in the press but, before it could reach us, from our own joker's mouth:

'*Giorno magnifico!*' he cawed. 'Finally we're at war!' He was in the smartest of his black shirts and full regalia. And what was this? A curved Saracen dagger in his belt and a fez!

I asked, foolishly, where he'd found them, as if he might have purchased them at Woolworth's. They were gifts from Ambassador Count Dino Grandi himself, he said, to inspire for the mission ahead. 'Forget your Burmas, your Bengals, your Hong Kongs, your Zulu-lands. The alphabet begins with *a*, and is followed by *b*. Abyssinia is ours by right.' He looked questioningly towards me. 'What do you think? Was going to use it in my speech tomorrow night.'

'It's *a-b-c* last I heard, not *a-b-γ*.'

'Don't be so damn literal!' he snapped. 'Have you no sense of romance in you, woman? No wonder you're going round for years like a clootie-dumpling, still grieving for that half-caste! He was a thief and a traitor, remember. You cannot lay the blame for the end of your romance on the Duce. In any serious country, he'd have been strung up by the thumbs and left there till the crows picked him clean.'

In asserting Italians' rights, when he delivered his speech at the Fascio, Dario turned more Scottish, as if bitten by a lower-class strain of the bug that had infected Dorothy's family at her wedding. It was all very *weil* for *they* politicians to appeal to the League of Nations, to claim the dignity of the African. For *whit* was the country responsible for slavery? And on *whit* country's empire did the sun *ne'er* set? *Whit* was the country *huddin ontae* its every last possession with an iron will and rifle? That had bled their colonies dry of every last resource, *frae* silk to silver, *frae* rubber to rubies, *frae* tea to tin to teak? (He'd learnt alliteration from Emilio and it came to him even easier than to his younger brother.) The Fleet Street hacks could churn out books about the Duce with titles like *Sawdust Caesar*, but the laugh was on the other face now the alarum had sounded. (His accent was abating as he got into his stride.) War was no crime when in the nation's interest. Raw materials were lacking, the Italian people needed new frontiers, needed *the cauterising flame of war* to restore faith in itself . . . and then, with Abyssinia in the bag and the shame of defeat at the Battle of Adwa finally expunged after forty years, then they'd see if the Austrian Corporal would dare to annex Austria. History would be made in *the sublime conflagration of battle*. As some ancestor had put it: Cry havoc, and let slip the dogs of war! He placed his palm on his oriental dagger as if he might draw it on the instant and remove somebody's ears.

And he hadn't finished yet! For he'd had it on the personal assurance of Ambassador Count Grandi (he briefly doffed his fez) that behind the scenes the politicians, canny ones like Mr Churchill, knew that Italy was in the right, and that as long as the Brenner Pass held firm against Adolf then relations would stay cordial between the Patria and its *primogeniture colony*. He surveyed his audience of thirty compatriots, most of whom were Comrades of the Party, many of whom had fought or lost loved ones in the Great War. 'Next stop Addis Ababa!' he cried, before waving to Beppe to join him on the dais. 'Now, Beppe, give us a round of *Little Black Face*!'

Beppe picked at the creases in his trousers. 'I can't mind the words. The tune's escaped me.'

'Nonsense! Everyone kens the words to *Facetta Nera*!' Dario started straight in on the chorus:

'*Facetta Nera,*
Bell' abissina
Aspetta e spera
Che già l'ora s'avvicina!'

'What's your problem?' he asked, looking round the room. 'Here, for those of you who don't know the Italian . . .' And he followed with a translation on which his brothers had refused to collaborate:

'*Little Black Face*
Darling Abyssinian
Wait and hope
That the hour's already near!
When we shall be
Close to you
We'll give you
Another law and another king!'

For years, I'd barely noticed the vacant lot outside the clubhouse, with its junk that gathered and dispersed according to some inscrutable law of supply and demand. But that night, I lingered in the midst of it. There were rusty stair rods and the innards of an oven, a rotting wooden fence-post and three buckled bicycle wheels.

Under the dim sulphurous light of the street lamps, the objects whispered to one another before moving imperceptibly to solidify into a tank.

28

The latest news, that Nonno had been found long dead in his cave by Zia Lalla, had barely been absorbed from the previous week's post. 'You said it'd be over in weeks, that Haile Selassie was an ignorant dwarf who'd run for cover at the first sound of artillery.' Giulio had been avoiding his brother, but towards Christmas the bad news abroad had generated a rush of orders for Papà's horned talisman (the *cornetto* which fended off the *malocchio*): he was stuck home threading the chains since Papà, in mourning, was slower than ever.

'We've been too soft on the darkies, giving them a sporting chance. But now, with General Badoglio in command, we're in for some fun.' Dario theatrically popped whatever he was holding in his mouth, and when his tongue protruded it was circled in gold. It was Paola's, he said, sliding it off. 'She kens the necessity.' He was expecting questions, but since no one obliged, he explained unprompted about the call for gold to support the war effort; Queen Elena had put her own ring ceremonially in the cauldron, Benedetto Croce too, and Luigi Pirandello his Nobel Prize gold medal.

'Bubble bubble,' I muttered, 'toil and trouble.'

'Do you intend,' said Giulio, 'to shoot the negroes with golden bullets?'

He turned to me. 'A hoarder like you must have something. What about Mamma's jewels? Never did see why you got to inherit them all.'

'You really believe they'd suit you?' said Guilio.

Papà emerged in pyjamas and black armband. 'Don't even think of it, Dario!'

I was still awake when Paola eased back the curtain. 'When I tell him No,' she sobbed, lying down next to me, 'he says he'll have it with or without the finger, and takes my potato knife. I ask him if he knows what it means, that he take away my ring. He tells me he'll cut off more than my finger if I make him wear the horns.'

As the sobs subsided, I tried to think of some consoling thing to say; then couldn't hold back my own tears, at the thought that I didn't even have a wedding ring to sacrifice.

For the Fascio Hogmanay Party decorations were few—'There's a war on,' Dario reminded folk—and Papà sold out of *cornetti*. In a flurry of flapping black, like a giant lost crow, an unknown priest strode in holding a golden censer which he deposited on the meagre pile collected. 'From the Holy Church Herself!' Dario glossed, 'by orders of Papa Pio. Our Sacred Mother makes the sacrifice so few others have yet ventured.'

At the table next to me, Giulio's old pal Ermanno whispered that the priest was probably a Glasgow thug in disguise, the censer nicked from St Ninian's.

'This is easy for none of us,' Dario continued from the dais. 'We're not wealthy, we are far from the fields and forests of Africa where our soldiers are building our empire. Yet we are Italians. We suffer with our compatriots as they civilize the savage. Our hopes fly with them. And this is why . . .' He raised his hand to reveal Paola's ring. 'This is why I too, with my wife and child, am making the sacrifice. For what need have we of gold when honest steel will do.' He dropped the wedding ring onto the pile.

The wise ones had seen it coming and had turned up unadorned. The less prescient were all ears and flicking fingers, dipping into pockets and handbags. Despite Dario's invitation, no one came forward. He lifted the four corners of the scarlet square of velvet on which the gold was lying: the whole of Edinburgh had produced only ounces. He glanced reproachfully in my direction, then gravely left the hall—to the relief of everyone present.

His battered suitcase was open on the kitchen floor when I arrived home, containing a shirt, a tie, his threadbare Chicago suit. When he emerged from across the landing, he had that look I'd detected on men over forty, uniting distraction, self-loathing and disdain; it had arrived on my brother eight years early. He asked about wife and child, but I hadn't the heart to tell him they were avoiding him. 'Did they tell you I'm for the off?' If I didn't look surprised it was only because he was always off somewhere, to some pub or other. 'To fight the darkies. If I leave now, I can be in action by February.'

So he could still impress me. 'What? In Africa? You?'

'They'll ship us there from Italy.'

'But what about your family?'

He turned up his nose. 'The wee thing only has eyes for her Zio Giulio.'

'I refuse to believe you're going to Africa because you're jealous of your own brother. What about all that gold you've been collecting?'

He squinted at me like a laddie who'd just peed his pants. 'It wasn't worth much in any case. But when the Consul finds out, then Ambassador Grandi, there'll be hell to pay. Best I make myself scarce for a while.'

'Can't you tell them you were robbed?' I could hardly believe I was saying it.

'I'm tired of these street corners, *piccolina*. If we can't beat the blacks, then what are we doing claiming to be a civilized nation, let alone an empire? We've got Mosley and his BUF, mad Adolf pronouncing German blood and honour with his Dachau camp full of Gypsies and his Nuremberg Triumph of the Will. They talk about a Stresa Front that's going to stop him going home to Austria and grabbing it for keeps, while they expect us Italians to be the ones to prevent him.' I'd been reading the news assiduously, but could never have assembled it like this. Even explanations seemed to exhaust him. 'I need out.'

I was sure he hadn't even prepared himself a sandwich for the road. Cut him a round of bread and ham, added some shortbread.

'That's my wee sister. That's my Lucia. Always happy families.' He closed the suitcase without adding anything.

It was not fair. Somebody should have been present to see him off on this frozen Hogmanay.

'At least it'll be warmer, down there,' he said, as he headed towards the steps. 'Do you no reckon?'

29

Giulio waited until Dario had left in order to inform me that the LIDU had requested he travel to Italy to deliver false identity cards to dissidents in danger. He could no longer sit on his hands doing nothing; Fausto could run the Palace for ten days; everyone else should be left in the dark.

'Why you?' I pleaded, picturing him crossing the border in a clip-on false-nose-and-glasses. 'We need you here.'

It was only when the first-footers left the kitchen, with their oat-cakes and coal, that Paola announced her own news. For too many years she'd worked the steamie, the Palace, cooked and washed at home. Her husband was gone and she wished him in an African pot, boiled and de-boned. 'I'm sorry, Lucia, I know he's still your brother.'

'Father of your child, after all.'

She laughed dismissively, before recollecting her disgust at the first time she'd tried Mr McEwen's fish and chips. 'The Scots have no clue how to make a *frittata*—the batter cardboard, the fat greasy, the temperatures all wrong. I've been up in Tollcross, down in Leith, they're no better.'

I wondered why I felt defensive, given she was certainly correct.

'So 1936,' she announced, 'is the year that will see the opening of *Paola's Neapolitan Fry*.'

'You're not actually Neapolitan,' I pointed out, my pedantry revealing that Scottish side to me.

'But the food will be.' She brought through drawings of how her shop would look, situated somewhere near the Palace so they could eat their fish supper—not that there'd only be fish, mind—then progress to pudding at the Palace . . .

And so it was that, through the freezing months, we roamed the neighbourhood, questioning shopkeepers, following hunches. Mr Morton, keen to betray no surprise at Giulio's rapid repayment of his debt, agreed to meet Paola—'Unofficially, of course'—over a scoop of Pistachio at the Palace. A loan, as he put it, 'was not unthinkable', and even became 'a distinct possibility' when Paola revealed the depth of her savings.

Far from her disdainful gaze, I scoured the pages of *L'Italia Nostra* for news of her husband. *The greatest colonial war in all history, being waged through a glorious display of Italian aerial superiority.* At Mai Leu, Haile Selassie's counter-attack had been repulsed by *heroic infantrymen and the masterful tactics of General Badoglio.* I tried to square these accounts with what I'd read in *The Scotsman* and *The Times,* where talk was of the barbarity of bombardment of undefended African villages, the poisoning of crops and rivers.

We were seated in Princes Street Gardens, enjoying the evening glow, the distant strains of dance music from the bandstand. Giulio's secret mission to Italy had been postponed, during which time premises had been found on Annandale Street, a lease had been signed, the Abyssinian war was won, and our Duce was hailed as a god, with the Pope's blessing on the arrival of light in darkest Africa. 'Does it not worry you though,' I ventured to ask, 'that we've heard not a word? With all the bombing and dying?'

Paola raised her left hand and waggled her ring finger.

I said, 'It was only a piece of gold.'

'Even Roberto the hog would not have sold my wedding-ring.'

'Bodies piled high, burning in pyres?'

'He's that steeped in alcohol he must burn well. The fires I wonder about are whether to heat the fat with coal or the new-fangled gas.' She didn't miss a beat.

Nor did it take her long to turn the shabby premises into Paola's Neapolitan Fry, just eighty yards from the Palace. Her shop had little of the style or panache of Giulio's vision in ice; a bare functionality with three tables from the flea-market, a fryer (she chose gas), fans and ice-box. But she counted on her fastidiousness with cooking temperatures, her batter recipe, the freshness of her fish, the brand of potato, its cut, its dryness even as it descended into the fat.

'What's making you so nervous, Lucia?' Papà would regularly ask. I tried not to make it obvious, that I was listening for Dario's feet on the stair. I told myself he'd surely not been allowed to fight (though as his passport was Italian, I could find no reason why not); the blacks in the Italian Army had been given the front-line positions and sustained the heaviest losses; in *L'Italia Nostra* the Duce was *The Incarnation of Providential Will* and Abyssinia was *The Promised Land, the Jewel in the Duce's Crown.*

Giulio counted on bad weather and slow trade for his absence. The forged documents he had to deliver he nicknamed his *recipes*, and he instructed me in a code designed to defeat any snoopers who might interfere with his mail. Everyone was in the kitchen, discussing his departure, scheduled for the morrow, when I heard the footsteps I'd been expecting these past seven months.

I intercepted him on the first-floor landing—which showed how slowly he was climbing. Then thought I was mistaken: the face belonged to a man who could have been Dario's father . . . only, *he* was upstairs.

'Lucia?' The voice was a whistle, as if he were trying to inhale even as he squeezed out the name.

'Oh my God, Dario! What's happened to you?' I felt the tears falling. 'Why in God's name did you never write?' I shouldn't be berating him, but it helped disguise the shock.

'You know me . . .' Between each snatch he had to catch his breath. 'Never a big writer . . . you ken . . . and no grand . . . stories . . . to tell you.'

I knew I shouldn't: 'But your hair? What's happened to it?' Jet black when he left; now grey, what remained of it.

'Have you no seen . . . photos of the Duce? His hair . . . gone white and all . . . Thought I'd follow . . . *la moda.*' His laugh lasted long enough to register as intention, before yielding to a hacking cough. A redness protruded from his filthy collar. When I explained that it was not the right moment, that he should come back tomorrow when Giulio was gone, I expected him to object. The way he nodded, turned tail like a chastised dog, made me want to call him back.

'Where are you going to stay? Have you had your tea?' He was already in retreat, his neck, from behind, even redder than the throat. 'They'll be glad to see you at the Fascio!' I tossed out my lie as he reached the bottom step.

Back in the kitchen, Giulio asked me where I'd disappeared to. I told him I'd heard an animal in pain; I tried never to lie to Giulio, least of all when he was about to take leave of us.

Rome, 27 October

Clever little Lucia,

The fact that you're reading this means you've remembered our secret and unbreakable code! I collected the 'ice-cream recipes' from a house in Soho belonging to one DA (head of the LIDU). He introduced me to many interesting people who are hopeful of change. He spends his time warning of the dangers of Spain, and of Italy being pushed into welcoming Nazi arms. In Rome I find that either DA is a prophet or he already knew that Galeazzo Ciano (you recall Benito's son-in-law, married to the daughter Dario so fancied?) was with Hitler in Bavaria, devising who knows what. Soldiers are leaving for Spain who barely know where that country is, let alone who's fighting or why.

You never asked me to enquire after Valerio, whose father I was determined to meet, but I am guessing you would like to know. He refused to tell me where he has been sent to exile, and his paternal care was mixed with bitterness at what Valerio had done to betray his father's cause—his father's cause and faith! Yes, in the weeks before he was sent to exile, Valerio was seeking to become Jewish! The father, disgusted, told me his son would never be allowed to go free.

To cheer myself up, Giolitti's, where Signor G remembered me from so many years ago. He gave me a seat by the window and served me new flavours, some old ones too. Pistachio which doesn't die on the palate but lingers and changes as it fades. Greek isles, Persian temples, Ali Baba and the gods of Odysseus! Blood Orange from fruits picked where the Etruscans grew them centuries ago, that combination of sweet and tart, the very apogee of sorbetto. Fig-and-Pine-Kernel where the figs have been so macerated that the seeds have turned soft, and the pine kernels have been lightly toasted. We gelatauri need our poet laureate too: Help us, Emilio!

Signor G saw me inspecting a photograph of Mussolini that hangs above the bar. He reminded me that in four days' time he'll be making a big speech in Milan, telling us all what to think. I couldn't say if Signor G was being ironic or not. These days everyone is careful what they say.

Whoof! It's tiring writing in this code.

Your loving

Banana Split

It took Dario eight days to return, and I didn't dare ask him where he had spent the interim. I was watching for him from the window, then counted the time he took to climb the three flights . . . nearly as many minutes. I urged him to remove his shirt for inspection. Normally, he'd have blustered; now, dumb obedience. His chest was speckled with red blotches, but this was only prelude to the back. I tried to stifle my gasp.

'Not too *bello*?'

As if its fire might spread, I had to dare myself to approach. 'Is it sore?' A ridiculous question, given his entire back was one furious scab. 'How long have you had it?'

'The day in March . . . when the Duce's sons . . . mistook us for the *negri* . . . dropped their gas . . . Only two of us thirty . . . survived.' Air issued as from a bellows. 'And the wain?' he asked. 'The wife . . .? How . . .? What they saying . . . of their soldier?'

'You don't still have Paola's wedding ring?'

'Could buy her another . . . Still the same Lucia . . .? Always hoping . . . to keep us . . . all straight?'

'Another identical?'

'Something like . . . once I get some cash.'

I should stop clutching at straws. 'You put your shirt back on. Don't let Assunta see you like that, she'll have nightmares.'

'And the Fascio . . .? Still *in avanti*?'

'Been busy with other things this year.' Should I tell him? 'Paola's starting a chippy—or rather, she's about to handsel her Neapolitan Fry.'

'Fuck that!' He made to rise, but the pain changed his mind. 'No wife of mine . . . wasting her hands . . . fat and batter.'

'You think working in the steamie saves her hands?'

'Steamie's all women . . . Chippy's with . . . any codger . . . off the street.'

'And the colony?' I asked. 'They're saying it's not so huge, in *The Scotsman*.'

'Fuckin shit-mirage . . . Crappy villages . . . worse than Maclodio . . . dung . . . mules . . . dysentery . . . mosquitoes size of vampire bats . . . vampire bats size of crows . . . snakes and rabid dogs Heat . . . like you never . . . imagined . . . Move a mile . . . from the outpost . . . and have your head cut off . . . by some darkie *pazzo* . . . who thinks Selassie . . . is god incarnate.'

I wanted to encourage him. 'But *L'Italia Nostra* says the war is over at least.'

'Over! In Addis . . . Ababa maybe . . . Elsewhere . . . wilderness . . . Kill twenty of them . . . makes no difference . . . Not that your average . . . Italian soldier deserves . . . better than a spear up his *culo*.' His breathing was improving, phrases lengthening, the more he talked. 'Treacherous ill-disciplined . . . sack of spaghetti-guzzlers.' I'd never seen him reluctant when it came to pasta, and figured he might be hungry. But no: 'Kills the appetite . . . the skin thing . . . Only way to make a decent army . . . out of Italians would be a bit of Prussian discipline . . . Duce's right on this much . . . You wouldn't see the Luftwaffe . . . bombing its own men.'

I couldn't help myself. 'You remember McEwen? The way he felt about the Germans?'

But maybe his ears were scorched inside their curlicues? 'Speaking of treachery . . . where's my dear brothers? Emilio still failing to father . . . a *bambino*? And Giulio, away is he? Not on a honeymoon . . . I don't suppose?' The urge to laugh was so intense, it defied his cough for a full five seconds.

'Mighty secretive our Giulio, so I couldn't tell you where he's gone exactly.'

'Ye wee witch,' he smiled, his eyes closing. Within two minutes, he was asleep in Papà's armchair, his mouth open and his eyelids twitching. He woke only when his wife and daughter ran up the stairs. 'Suppose I'd better . . . go through then?' If he'd been facing a line of Abyssinian rebels, his question could hardly have been posed more timorously.

When I popped my head round their door the next morning, he was asleep on a rug on the kitchen floor in front of the range.

30

Naples

Cara,

All 'recipes' safely delivered. And I got to listen to the Duce's big Milan speech, relayed on radio megaphones in Piazza del Plebiscito. Here everyone has watched endless Duce newsreels, and they know a thing or two about theatre . . .

The first performer could have been the Duce's younger brother. Then a second the Duce's twin. Even a woman had him down pat, and by the end I must have seen a dozen Duces miming the speech, each more convincing than the last. There was black and there was white; there was good and there was evil . . . and so long as the speech continued, there could be no confusing the two. Almost as uproarious as Pulcinello routing the Saracens. Who needs the Teatro San Carlo (which was looming as a backdrop) when every emotion was here! Only once did these piazza orators lose their stride and fall off their pantomime horses. The 'entente', said the Duce, between Italy and Germany was no longer a 'diaframma'. 'Cosa?' they asked, as if betrayed by their prompter. They barely recovered in time to attempt: 'but more like an axis round which every European state motivated by a wish for peace can revolve'.

'An axis? An axis?' The mimics raised their palms in disbelief. The groups looked round to one another and made that Neapolitan gesture with the thumb under the chin that accompanies the word 'Manaccia!'

The 'axis' word (or 'asse' more precisely) spread through the piazza like rumour of plague. Between Italy and Germany? Between the Duce and his parody? Several Duces were so disconcerted they strode off in high dudgeon. I tuned in to the remainder as they regrouped. 'We've only just got rid of the Austrians, and now they want them back again!'

'At least the Hapsburgs were aristocrats, but now it's a plebeian who can't even grow a decent moustache.'

Ensued an impromptu competition: the Duce who did the best Hitler would win a granita from a nearby caffè. Six tried, all of whom had obviously studied the newsreels and two of whom even had some German. Ghastly looks and arms flung out in salute. The surging tone with much goose-stepping and frothing at the mouth—frothing literally! And every second phrase about how 'der Jude' are 'ein Parasi'. The Hitler who won the day didn't look the least like Adolf when he returned to his workaday self. None of them had the heart to follow what remained of Mussolini's speech, but drifted off to vent their indignation at this new 'axis'.

I needed a tiramisu after that, so you can imagine where I headed.

Tomorrow Maclodio. Then home—I feel the Palace calling.

Your very own

White Lady

The shop was ready, down to the sign for Paola's Neapolitan Fry. Dario was debarred, 'looking like some dragon, to give the customers the willies'. Yet though windows were gleaming, frying vats polished, vinegar dispensers full, the contract settled with the fishmonger by which Paola promised to take some of the less usual types off his hands (less usual than the haddock, hake or cod that Scots folk could countenance), she would not consider opening until Giulio had returned.

There was no chance to warn him, hence the look on his face when he saw the back was unrehearsed. For coolness, Dario had removed his shirt, the window wide despite the season. Giulio dropped his suitcase and opened his arms fraternally, before memory returned with a blunt appraisal of just desserts.

'What's up wi you . . .? Never seen . . . a burn before?' Dario was almost enjoying his brother's discomfort.

'Gas?'

'Aye, so? Want to massacre . . . a few thousand darkies . . . you got to spread it around a bit.' The forced chuckle was even less successful than the genuine variety. 'Lucia tells me . . . you been over . . . in the *patria* . . . collecting recipes! That'll . . . be right . . .'

The opening proved modest, but aunties showed up, with Rebecca looking as young as ever, Sandy accompanied by her taciturn new husband, his mandibles like a pike's, chewing their way through what must have been half a stone of King Edward's, cut and fried until crisp—'braw', his accolade. Mr McEwen came by, bearing a silver-plated salt cellar, and he even dared sample Paola's fried home-grown zucchini ('marrow', he called it). The batter was crunchy, not granular; the fish and vegetables moist without being sodden.

I slid the final cod into a *Scotsman* poke and hid it in my shopping bag for Dario, who had barely ventured down the stairs since his return. He ate it cold, wordlessly, staring into space. Elaborating on what he had told me, I pictured him seated on an Abyssinian mud-mound, gazing across a savannah of corpses, the faint whiff of yperite, shells exploding in the distance.

Only at the Fascio did I detect the brother of old, asking me to take notes on the speech he insisted he didn't need to prepare. He wore a high-collared black shirt and neckerchief to cover the worst of the damage, sported a cross-shaped medal on his breast; spoke of victory in Addis Ababa, the Imperial Eagle flying over Haile Selassie's palace, the raw materials flowing in to the fatherland, even the smiles on the nigger children as they tasted macaroni for the first time. He didn't wince once, and though he wheezed, he completed whole sentences without gasping.

'And what of the reports we've been hearing, Dario,' asked Signor Borsari from the floor, 'about gas being used?'

Dario nodded knowingly. 'Exaggeration, the usual British envy. Remember who wanted to gas the Arabs a decade ago? Winston Churchill. Propaganda.'

'What's propaganda?' somebody muttered.

'About the gas.'

'No, what does *propaganda* mean?'

Dario was incisive: 'It's lies told by enough powerful people to make them sound true.'

'And now?' somebody else asked from the floor. 'What about this *diaphragm* we're hearing about?'

'It's not a diaphragm,' came the correction from Ermanno, 'it's an *axis*. Means we're to trim our moustaches to a slug crawling up the lip.'

For a moment, my brother's pain was forgotten, amidst the heckles and heat of debate; transfigured by talk of men in uniforms whom he'd never met, he waited for the hubbub to settle. 'It may not be Rome I've returned from . . .' He pointed to the medal on his chest as if it had just been pinned there by some grateful superior. 'But I have it from the source . . . Germany's nothing . . . The BUF— yes, Mosley's lot—may still be shouting about the Nordic race . . .' He held back a coughing fit. 'But their membership's declining fast. If the Duce ever did finance them . . . then he's surely thought better of it . . . This new Axis, you don't want to be taking that too literally. Maybe Ciano, who was jammy enough to marry the gorgeous Duce daughter Edda . . . maybe he got a bit carried away with the German *wurtzels* and *frauleins* . . . Went too far . . . But let me ask you: what is Ciano's abiding passion—other than women, food and fast cars?' He gave his audience time to realize that their Foreign Minister's *abiding passion* was obscure to them. 'Golf! Yes, golf, child of our Royal and Ancient . . . That's what Ciano dreams of . . . as he struts round Bavaria with Adolf . . . While the Duce?' This time, his pause was for breath—each inhalation an act of will. 'Don't imagine the admiration . . . the Austrian feels for him has turned his head. He loathes the runt, publicly calls him a *psicopatico degenerato*, suspects he's a Jew.' He waited for the guffaws to subside. 'The Duce's only hoping that finally . . . the world will see he means business.'

I wondered if, in his Abyssinian hut, my brother had sought inspiration for just such a speech.

'After the snubs and sanctions . . . after the hot air about Spain and the posturing of Anthony Eden . . . the Abyssinian Empire will be recognized, mark my word. For it is with us . . .' Revolving his arm in an inclusive gesture gave time for another shallow in-breath. 'With *us British* the Duce wants to ally himself. Both Chamberlains understand, Neville and Austen, even Winston Churchill . . .' His body was slowly but inexorably folding, as the lungs shrank. 'Soon we'll see concord . . . between our two great countries . . . whose separation . . . has caused us such . . . pain in the past . . . two years . . .' He had to close soon. 'Italia and Britain . . . together . . . empire with empire . . . future linked . . . to fu . . . ture!'

The applause was louder than any heard that year. As it faded, he had barely the strength to make it back to his seat.

31

Two months later, he seemed about to be proved right, in the signing of a pact between the two countries—my two countries. Decio Anzani might write to Giulio from London to say that this so-called *Gentlemen's Agreement* could not last, but it was enough to make me wonder if one day I might feel whole again.

Before bed, if no one was about, I'd inspect myself naked in the mirror, searching for signs of ageing: a sag in the breasts? The start of a stoop? I was twenty-six years old, but I felt I'd lived three life-times already. It was years since I'd let a man really look at me; met a glance with a glance, a stare with a stare. Did I somehow imagine I was going to rescue Valerio by turning *morbid* (the word I'd over-heard Papà use of me to Emilio)? Or was I merely keeping pace with the world, with Spain, China, Germany—my head would explode if I tried (and I did try) to fathom just the tenth of it, and where would that leave Giulio, who seemed no closer to settling down or leaving home, or Assunta, who needed to be tucked in at night when her Mamma stayed late to cater for the crew in search of something solid to soak up the booze (which usually ended up, quarter-digested, on the pavement minutes later)? Frequently now, I heard the word *war*, used not about the victory two decades before, not about Spain or the campaign in Africa, but *war* that might include us, require us—and not just Dario. (I had failed to persuade him to get naturalized; he displayed his Italian passport as if it were a second medal to pin to his chest.)

'I'm trying, honestly,' I pleaded to Emilio when he came in car-rying a newspaper, in September. 'I'm trying to keep up with what's happening in the world.' I asked Giulio to read from Decio's LIDU dispatches. I listened to Dario at the Fascio. I felt the tension between my brothers when the town of Guernica was invoked.

Her father was concerned, Dorothy said, about how Eden was refusing to recognize the empire in Abyssinia, so pushing Mussolini into Hitler's arms. She was pointing to a photograph of the Duce in Emilio's *Scotsman*. 'Eight hundred thousand Germans turned out for him, and he even harangued them in their own language. Hitler's all for absorbing Austria and the Sudetenland, and the Duce's not about to stop him.' I wanted to ask her the source of her calm. 'In Berlin's Olympic stadium, no less.'

'Can you imagine,' Emilio asked, 'what's going to happen to us if Hitler starts expanding and the Duce joins in?'

'Us?' I asked, as if the word were new to me. I felt a wave of relief . . . followed by shame: soon I'd not be the only one isolated and unable to connect—we'd all be isolated together. 'But none of *us* will have to fight, surely.'

Emilio patted his bad leg. 'Drive an ambulance, if they'll have me. Dorothy's been giving me lessons.'

'I mean, for Italy?'

'Are you joking?'

I wished to reply that he must be the joker. For I was picturing him, my little cripple, racing an ambulance down Queensferry Road like the Flying Mantuan Tazio Nuvolari in his Maserati, under bombs raining down as they had on Addis Ababa . . . as they had on Guernica . . .

When the reverie faded, there was no one joking, only seriousness once more before me, in the form of another article in *The Scotsman*, stating that our representative, the one Dario claimed as a personal friend, would be visiting the North.

'To calm our nerves,' sneered Emilio, 'according to our dear brother.'

Who was of course the one to open the door of the Ambassador's Bentley when it glided to a halt. His arm went up in salute to a— given his name—disappointingly diminutive figure, who shook the hand of the Consul, then gazed at the crowd as if he'd expected kilts and claymores. He barely glanced at Dario before staring, dismayed, at the midden of the vacant lot. Instinctively, he picked out the journalists, whom he addressed in a sensuous voice heavy with humour and vintage wine, his accent self-consciously thick.

'This pile of broken stoves and beds outside our noble Fascio.' He pointed, nodding meditatively. 'Let me ask you reporters, of what it is the symbol?' He waited for a response he knew would not come. 'Of what awaits us all if we do not affirm and strengthen the ties which bind our country to that of our hosts—ruin and perdition.' He turned at last to Dario, who was regaled in every accessory he owned (and some he did not), ignoring the cruel contrast this cut with his own top hat and tails. 'An excellent idea, Comrade, to set up this debris as a reminder.' He held the Chief Extractor's hand long enough for the photographer to startle the crowd with flashbulbs.

If Ambassador Count Grandi was disappointed at what he found inside, he was sufficiently the diplomat not to show it. A rare visit from the Archbishop signalled the importance of the occasion, and the two men seemed uncertain whose honour should be greater. 'And who is this *bella ragazza*?' the Count asked the Consul, when I strayed too close.

'This is the sister of our Fascist Chief, Lucia Pezzini, one of the most devoted servants of the Party.'

My eyebrows raised involuntarily—but so did the Ambassador's. After taking my hand in his, which was the softest I'd felt since Mr Morton's, under his breath he whispered, conspiratorially: 'The Party, I divine, is not your main concern, Signorina. Like me, it is Italia that moves your heart?'

For one speechless moment, I saw myself in a tiara, sweeping through the London Embassy in the sort of gown that Jenners never put in their Stocktaking Sale. I tried imagining I was Dorothy, for confidence. 'Indeed, Your Excellency, I'm worried for my family and country—countries.'

He nodded.

'And I don't hate the Jews.' I wanted to say more, but did not dare to mention Valerio—'the criminal', as Dario called him.

He tried to hide his surprise. 'You're a wise girl. I trust that you will, then, enjoy my speech.' He turned back to the Archbishop, who was hovering over his shoulder like some exotic bird.

And I did. For he spoke an Italian the likes of which I'd never heard, as if he'd swallowed volumes whole, of poetry and history. He didn't consult his notes as he praised the Fascio's efforts to represent the community, to glorify Italy, and recalled the links—of character, interest, ambition—that made Great Britain the natural ally of the *Patria*—Prime Minister Chamberlain understood it, and so did the Duce. Yes—his soft white hands rose above his head—it was right to worry about the Axis with Germany. But our *Capo* (he turned to Dario) had surely explained the strategy. For who (he lowered his voice) could take seriously a country which sent as its ambassador a man whose name was *Rib-ben-trop*? He pronounced it as if naming a child's wooden marionette.

Dario would have been the first to his feet in applause, if only he had sat down. Clapping lasted until hands hurt, as if we hoped we might be heard as far afield as Whitehall . . . as far away as Rome.

'He's not the worst of them, Count Grandi,' Giulio conceded when I showed him my hands, still red, later that evening. 'Even Decio admits that.'

I was vexed it was all he could find to say, of the man who had judged me a *bella ragazza*. 'What's so big about Decio all of a sudden? Can we not make up our own minds?'

He felt my irritation. 'You're right, of course. Maybe it's because I had such a wonderful time in London. Down there, everything seemed possible again.'

'Everything?' I could sense there was more to say, and not about the LIDU's defence of human rights.

'After Edinburgh, I mean, where everyone knows everyone and I've got to mind my step.' I waited for him to expand, but he shook his head, rather, as if to dispel the memory. 'And Decio's right, you know, times are getting harder. One hundred and seventy dissenters imprisoned in Italy this year, sentenced to nine hundred and ninety-four years of hard labour.'

A sudden panic seized me. 'I've the picture behind my bed, of the Duce patting my shoulder.'

'If we're judged, we'll all be judged together.'

'I'm also Dario's sister.'

'You may need to take a distance, *cara*. There may be no more socializing at the Fascio.'

'Enough politics—always politics! Don't you ever grow tired of us, Giulio? Is that what you're trying to say? Need to cut loose? Of Papà and me and the rest of us?'

The pathos in his smile made me want to slap him. 'We have the Palace, and it's thriving. We have Assunta. Come over here, you, looking so peely-wally.' He reached over and placed me, lump that I was, on his knees. 'It's you who should be getting out and about, not me. Don't object! You know what I mean.'

I laid my head on his chest, absorbing the sweet Palace odour.

'Look,' he finally said, when I'd almost drifted off. 'Here's your favourite from your Bengal-terrorist period.' Alongside *The Scotsman* photographs of the first snowfall in Glenshee and the Duke and Duchess of Sutherland visiting Holyrood Palace was one of the returning dignitary riding the type of enormous perambulator favoured by royalty. *Governor of Bengal Sir John Anderson Saying Good-bye*. Next to it was another: *Sir John Anderson Arriving in Waverley Station after Seven Years in India*. To say he looked *inexpressive* would be an understatement: a floor-board, a poker, the blackened door to the kitchen range were more expressive.

'His last act,' Giulio remarked after reading, 'before he left Bengal, was to pardon the two young Indians who tried to assassinate him. Seems a likeable sort.'

32

Something must have been happening to me, between Sir John's return and 11 March when Hitler marched into Austria and my life changed. As ever, events, when they did come, came not singly.

'Hardly a shot fired in anger,' Giulio reported. 'All eyes on Italy, but there'll be no retaliation.'

The evening being a quiet one, I could drift at the till. I pictured a Stormtrooper dressed in brown, up to his knees in snow on an Austrian mountainside, staring across the border through binoculars . . . at a Blackshirt planted amongst olive trees and poplars, staring back . . . an imperial eagle flying overhead, seeking for prey . . . and just as I was shuddering, that was when I saw him—someone other, quite other than the objects of my fears, talking to Giulio, ordering an ice. Or not ordering an ice, just chatting, a smile on his face. I'd never seen him before, no doubting that. Something he said to Giulio made my brother forget Austria for a second, and laugh. I thought of Christ, though the priests said there was no record of his laughing. (Padre Clemente had been hard pushed to conceal his boredom recently, and through the grille and his long grey beard I could feel him willing me to go out and commit some sins worth confessing.)

What flavour was he choosing? Chocolate-and-Cinnamon with a dab of Bramble Ripple.

I could taste the place where the ices would meet and the buds would attempt to discern: this sweet, that tart; this Eastern, that Scottish . . . Only in the end to accept that there was a single taste, or that any taste was a blend of many. My mind seemed almost to be functioning again—it was alarming.

'Lucia!' Giulio called over, before informing the newcomer— 'It's on the house.'

'Not at all.' Whoever-he-was had his fingers in his purse, removing the farthings one by one and placing them on the saucer before me.

I uttered not a word until he had counted out six. Then, quietly, 'I can't disobey my brother,' adding a look of sisterly submission. It was all over so fast (as I'd heard robbery witnesses report) that I wanted to play it over. A crowd came in with their orders, keeping me busy at the till. I didn't even spot his departure.

But that night as I undressed there was an unfamiliar sensitivity to the left breast—or *on it*? I had a cancer like Mamma and would die without so much as learning his name, this gentleman with the jaunty smile and the delicate fingers. A similar sensation in the right breast. Double cancer would be unlucky, even by my standards. The draft was chilly, but something must be happening for each molecule of air to be present, as if the breasts were weather-vanes. Weather-*cocks*? The word flared my nostrils . . . oh, the trickiness of language, despite Mamma's insistence on precision.

The tears, unaccompanied by sobs, coursed down my cheeks, until I feared I'd be desiccated by morning. I was walking through an invisible wall on the far side of which was my pillow. I slid a hand under, to where it lay in the cavity dug by its own weight. I clasped the nightmare statuette, returned it to the depths of Papà's cabinet.

It was well after midnight when Giulio pulled back my curtain. 'I thought you might be awake,' he said, an unfamiliar twinkle in his eye.

'Good business today?' I asked, determined not to be the first to mention his pal.

'Good business every day, come rain or shine. It has dawned on the Edinburgh public that Wall's Vanilla is not the final word in flavour. Nobody baulks at Pistachio.'

'Or Cinnamon mixed with Bramble Ripple?' But he was not taking the bait. 'Or Paola's zucchini balls, or seeing fish with their heads still on.' If I couldn't tell my brother that something was happening to me, whom could I tell? Yet the words would not out.

'All we need is for the politicians here to acknowledge the so-called empire in Abyssinia.'

'I wish the politicians would all disappear. I'm sick of reading about them. I wish we were in Nonno's cave, just the two of us—

just a few of us . . .' I was glad he couldn't see the colour I had turned. 'You want the politicians to bless Dario's back and all that went into the burning of it?'

'It's called *realpolitik*. The lesser of two evils.'

'What about no evils?'

'We can't all be like you,' he joked. 'Most of us are *macchiati*, full of twists and turns and dark patches.'

I wished I could stop smiling—even my toes were smiling. When finally I slept, I dreamt I was behind my desk at the bank, but the walls were purple and soft. Stuck to them were ten-pound notes which everyone was invited to remove. I went to the lavatory, but it was full of athletes from the Berlin Olympic Games. I recognized and congratulated Jesse Owens. 'Nobody,' he told me, 'knows to run fast enough. Except . . .' The bathroom door was closing. 'Except perhaps your brother.' 'Which brother?' I tried to ask him. 'Which brother?' But the door was too heavy to reopen, and I couldn't tarry as I had to tell Mr Morton how much it would cost to save Auntie Rebecca's synagogue . . .

I expected to be tired next morning, but had energy to note down my dream, shave my legs, put on new Lisle stockings, and arrive at the bank with five minutes to spare. The walls weren't purple—not *bramble-coloured*, as it occurred to me upon entering, alongside Mr Morton, his *Scotsman* under his arm. *Anschluss* had made the stock market tremble, but as owner of not a single stock or share, why should I care. I only stopped smiling when, arriving home that evening, I forced myself to face the letter that was waiting for me. He had not written to me in more than five years.

> Roma
> 1 March 1938

Dear Lucia,

You surprised I write again one letter more? Ultimate time. Me pleases to imagine you think still me your friend. You are Italian, you must know what occurs here. The shame, the vergogna, beasts from Inferno. My proper father one of them, we us see never more.

Two weeks ago I escape from my rock in the sea. Yesterday with ceremony I make me circumcise (remember not pleases you the word). Today I walk with difficulty, but Mamma smiles within me. From now I may properly call me Jew. I not know what will succeed with Hitler on the frontier. We can die, but first some shall fight.

Remember me. Per sempre tuo

Valerio

I crossed and uncrossed my legs . . . then crossed them again. The blood, at his age, the cutting, the mutilation of the only male member I'd voluntarily known; scalpels and scar tissue, if scalpel was what they used—for a moment I pictured a pair of secateurs.

Even if I had had an address, how could I reply? What should I send? Condolences? Congratulations? When my thoughts escaped towards him, I found myself embarrassed to be picturing his unfortunate foreskin: was it given him to keep, as the dentist had given me my abscessed molar?

33

'Been shaving your legs more carefully, I see. Trying something with the straggly locks? What's in the air I should know about?' He patted his pockets. 'Some big-timer at the bank, let us hope, with plenty lucre and cracked ice to lavish on ma wee sis.' The thought of gain was turning him American. 'You know what they call a mobster's bomb over there? An *Italian football*. No bad, eh?' His shirt was off in the kitchen, revealing that the pus was clearing. 'Only keep away from the Eyeties, I say. Once you're seen them in battle you want to change your nationality—even the jigaboos ken better how to perish. We'd see the darkies not complaining with their arms cut off at the shoulder and their stomachs hanging out.'

Not even his comment on my hair could upset me today. For more than twenty years, Dario's tormenting had worked. Now, abruptly, it did not. More curious still, my brother appeared unperturbed at this loss of authority. Just a matter of time, I told myself, it was *just a matter of time* . . . I didn't even have to complete the phrase.

And I was right. I was behind the till—he smiled to me from the entrance, the evening sun beneath the clouds drawing an ochre stripe. With his back to the customers, preparing a bag of boilings, Giulio failed to notice him as he snuck into a booth, gesturing me to shush. Now he was here, I was content to ignore him. My hands were in the till, paddling silver sixpences, when I glanced towards the booth.

'Hazelnut and Torrone, please!' I was looking towards him when he called it, so I didn't spot the look on my brother's face when he heard who was ordering from the booth. But I caught the chuckle. He was English, surely, from the accent, and posh, probably, though it was hard to tell with the English since at first they all sounded posh, by comparison.

'Jings almighty! Come over here if you're wanting to be served, you loafer!' Normally, Giulio would have carried the goblet himself. 'Serve him a Hazelnut,' he ordered, 'with a dab of Vanilla on top.'

I executed the order, then passed my brother the goblet.

'I can't be getting mixed up with riff-raff like that. You take it over, Lucia, ask him what he's doing with the newspaper when he's barely learnt how to read yet.'

I put one foot in front of the other as if I were on stilts; if the hips swayed as a result, that was unavoidable. In any case he'd presumably notice I was barely touching the ground.

'Very pretty too,' he remarked, as I laid down his ice-cream, hoping he was referring to more than that. 'You must be Giulio's sister, of whom he's told me so much?'

I attempted an impersonation of indifference that I suspected looked merely imbecilic (as if I were uncertain whether indeed I was his sister). He rose to his feet as best he could inside the booth, outstretched his hand. Soft I had already divined, but now I'd find the rest. Warm? Dry? Clammy? Cold?

'I'm Harold Moore, friends call me Harry.'

Soft, dry, and neither hot nor cold—temperate hands. I released his before he could release mine. 'Lucia,' I said, pronouncing it the English way. 'Friends call me Lucia, with a *ch*.'

He smiled. 'Not Lucy, then?'

'Do I look like a Lucy?'

'I couldn't see you fainting if a Highland cow was running at you, if that's what you mean. Or obeying your father's every word to the letter.'

He was testing me. 'But you could see me waiting for years because my true love's gone abroad? Or losing my wits because he comes back five minutes late and finds me married to another man?'

He'd sat down again. 'It's always been my favourite opera.'

I wondered about his *always*: he couldn't be much older than me, younger-looking than Giulio. 'I've never been to an opera.' I tried to sound neither deprived nor defiant. 'My parents didn't know the story when they named me. But Giulio gave me Sir Walter, and I managed the libretto by myself.'

His eyebrows rose appreciatively. 'I imagine you Italians to be singing arias day in day out.'

'What you two gossiping about over there?' Behind his counter, Giulio looked more handsome than I'd seen in a long time, his moustache neatly trimmed.

'I can't believe it,' said Harry, his spoon heaped with Hazelnut. 'You've never taken your sister to the opera? You the successful businessman? No Rossini? No Verdi? Should be ashamed of yourself, it's downright unpatriotic. No Caruso!'

Giulio flipped a glass in the air and only just caught it. 'I'm no my sister's keeper! In any case, when do I have time for gallivanting? All very well for you men of leisure. Why don't *you* take her, if you're so keen on Caruso and Co.'

He suppressed a startled look. 'Perhaps I shall!'

I resisted the temptation to curtsy. 'If I'm free and can find the time. And so long as it's Italian.' That wasn't bad. 'Speak the language yourself, do you?'

'Your brother's taught me a few words. I can get by in French.'

'Known him long, have you?'

He didn't care for this, to judge from the shrug. 'Your brother's better on dates.'

I was needed behind the till. But how to reach it without either flaunting myself or retreating? In *Woman's Weekly* I'd read that the art of seduction begins with the rear view—something to do with the apes. I managed a couple of steps backwards, but this would quickly prove ridiculous. I turned, crossed the floor not the least apishly, and ensconced myself behind the banana tree of the till. For the following half hour it was a relief to be busy with the usual customers, the usual flavours. Paola sent along her potato-peeling lad for a Strawberry cone in reward for working overtime. (Chippies from all over town would come by, openly or incognito, to discover the secret of her success; jokes were flying, that Annandale Street would soon be renamed *Via Pezzini*.) He smiled to me, this *Harry*, left an over-generous tip before leaving. The evening was a busy one, I had to wait until Giulio served the day's final scoop of Stracciatella.

'A long way for him to come,' I said, trying to bring it out casually though my chest was beating like an Orange-man's drum.

'I met him in London, has his suits tailored by Decio. Transferred by his company, junior manager in one of the big insurance firms, Standard Life I think. That'll be two pence, please, to my sister here.' To himself, as I took the cash, he muttered, 'Ironic name, when you think of it, *Standard* Life.'

'A tidy coincidence, his being sent up here?'

'I told him he'd enjoy it. Works on George Street, not far from your bank. Plays golf like our great Foreign Minister Ciano. Has even been to Italy—Chianti of course. I said I'd invite him over for Paola's pasta some Sunday when we've got an hour off. It's going to be important to know a few folk in positions.'

'Don't frighten me, Giulio. Have you thought how, soon . . .?' My mind had been echoing the fact ever since I'd first seen Harry. 'Soon it'll be five years since McEwen received his marching orders?'

'I hadn't forgotten. I'm in touch with his dad. He'll warn me if ever he sees him. Should have made the banishment permanent. But you never expect time to pass so quickly. Pictured us both in bath-chairs by now, being pushed round the Botanical Gardens.'

At Jenners—and it wasn't even sales time—Assunta helped me choose a new skirt and blouse, affordable copies of what the tall slender ladies sported in the drawings in the fashion section of Friday's *Scotsman*. I bought a fresh safety razor and a minuscule bottle of Je Reviens perfume which I chose as much for its name as for its scent. With the quantity of strolling I was doing up and down George Street (I was hoping it looked casual), I'd soon be needing new shoes. Auntie Sandy, who bumped into me on her way home from McVities, asked me whom I was intending to ambush, 'accidentally on purpose'. If Giulio hadn't mentioned a hole-in-one, scored at the Braids course, then I might have thought he'd been sacked or recalled to London. The mention was a meagre crumb before a bitter main course.

A tap at the Palace window meant family; I had a déjà vu that even the thought of Harry could not disperse. Dario was drunk, but as Fausto had just left for the night, he could fall, more than step, over the threshold. His brother left him sprawled on the floor as he explained to me that the papers in Dario's hand were what the LIDU had translated and sent to the press—not that they'd get printed, since they might upset the so-called 'Easter Agreement' between our two countries. 'Number four,' Giulio read, having taken the papers from his brother, 'from what the Rome authorities are calling *The Defence of the Race*. Want to hear it?' He didn't give me time to say No. '*The present Italian population is mostly Aryan in origin and civilization.* You hear that? Not Mediterranean or a mix, not even Roman—now we're Aryan.' He pointed to the spread-eagled brother. 'Aryan, clearly. Number six: *Henceforth there exists a pure Italian Race. This ancient purity of blood is the Italian nation's greatest title to nobility.* Forget Cicero, the Renaissance, D'Annunzio and Marconi, forget even Augustus, it's our blood that makes us great!' I had rarely seen my brother so disgusted. He took the pointed clip on which he hung the orders, and before I could prevent him, jabbed it into the ball of his thumb. A quick deep red bulbed out. 'You see it there? Eh, Dario, the purity?'

I wrapped his thumb in my handkerchief. Men and their wounds. No surprise to hear another knock at the window. 'What you do to yourself?' said Emilio.

'My purity needed out.'

'You have the text there?' He passed no comment on the brother on the floor. 'Read us the worst.'

'Wake up, Dario,' I tried, as Giulio repeated what I'd already heard. When I applied a damp cold cloth to his forehead, he sat up with a grunt, staring as if cornered by Abyssinians. Then, focusing, he laughed.

'Statute number nine: *The Jews do not belong to the Italian race.*
Number Ten: *The physical and psychological characteristics of the Italian
must not be changed in any way whatsoever.*'

'Hah!' crowed Dario. 'Try telling that to the soldiers who were
shoving it up every *nera* in Addis Ababa!'

This silenced all, even him who had uttered it. I attempted not
to picture it: ten thousand McEwens with no Giulio to restrain
them. Tried to think instead of Auntie Rebecca, who hardly ever
mentioned her parents' Lithuania, though the term *pogrom* hovered
round her, rumours of houses burnt, synagogues razed to the ground.

'What about La Sarfatti,' Dario resumed, 'she's Jewish, and is still
the Duce's tart, last I heard. In any case have they no enough brains
already, without taking over our universities? It'll do them no harm
to try some manual labour for a change, instead of filling people's
minds with their Marx and Lenin.'

Emilio finally turned to what was rising from the Palace floor.
'If that's all you have to say, then why don't you go home and puke
up over yourself there. Leave us in peace.' I could hardly believe it
was happening . . . again. All my life . . .

'Oh, who's the tough one now! He's going to don flippers and
swim off to save some Jews!' Slowly, he was dragging himself to his
feet.

Giulio hardly listened. 'Next the Romanies, then the mentally
defective.'

'And the inverts, don't forget them!' Dario hooted at his own
contribution.

'Get out!' Giulio ordered.

'Don't scare me, *piccolo*! The roaring of the African lion is douce
by comparison!'

Emilio leant over and put his hand against his brother's chest.

'Take your hand away, or this will turn ugly.' Dario's arm flashed
out faster than should have been possible for one so drunk. He held
Emilio by the throat, squeezing gently. 'Like I said, a bit of respect
for your elders and betters.'

'If Mamma were alive,' I hollered, 'she'd be ashamed of you both!'

Emilio was choking, I would have to do something. But then he lashed out with his left arm, dislodging his brother's grip enough to let him land a heavy slap on Dario's back. The scream that followed was hardly human.

'You'll live to regret this!' Dario stammered with the shock, aiming for the exit. As he lurched through the door, he almost knocked over Harry, who must have seen the Palace light and thought to come in for an ice-cream nightcap.

34

'Your brother?' he said, unused to seeing a grown man whimper.

As Harry ordered his ice, we tried to become Pezzinis: a respectable, almost prospering Italo-Scottish family; not squabbling bairns, not fanatics or sadists. We managed to talk like civilized adults, even reminisced like old folks. I had to work next day, but so did the three men beside me, who tacitly agreed to ignore the clock. Harry said he didn't understand how we could ever feel like under-dogs when we were 'all so articulate'. Giulio explained about Mamma and her insistence on words. Harry spoke of his apprehen-sions in moving to Scotland and his dread of the *Sassenach* label . . . He'd never considered his accent; where he'd been educated, every-one spoke alike, even the occasional West Indian . . . Most boys played cricket, rugby, fives, but he'd discovered golf and was happiest on the fairways. Had never forgiven his parents for sending him off to boarding-school . . . They rarely met . . . One day he'd inherit their estate in Buckinghamshire. When it was finally admitted that clocks did exist, the one on the wall accused us with *2.15*. I wished we could all go on living in one enormous booth. Instead of which, Emilio went his way and Harry accompanied us only as far as the turning to his Northumberland Street flat.

'You quite like him, no?'

I had told myself: Next time Giulio gives you a chance, seize it. 'He's your chum, so of course I like him.' I cursed my craven self.

'Look around you, *cara*. Is it no a magical thing? Everyone in bed, and here we're out enjoying ourselves. We're not decrepit yet. It's all going to work out grand. He's a timid soul behind the laddie chucked into a boarding school too young.'

'I don't know . . .'

'You heard him saying he'd take you for a round of golf. I don't imagine he says that to just anyone.'

'When you were at the toilet, I asked him what he'd do if there was a war. He knows nothing about the Sudetenland, doesn't seem interested in what's going on in the world. All he said was that he had four years of cadet training at his school, so he'd be made a junior officer and be gunned down in the opening campaign.'

'You'd better hurry up then and accept that offer.' Though he was trying to joke, there was an unmistakable gravity to Giulio's tone.

I tried to do as my brother advised, and was waiting so intently for the invitation to be formalized that I paid little heed to Chamberlain's speech about 'peace in our time'. What need had I of History, I told myself, when I had Harry—not that I actually had him yet, except on my mind (and between my mind's legs).

People round me sensed the thaw. Mr Morton proposed tea at McVities. Beppe suggested a drink in a quiet corner of the one pub into which a woman could venture, where he spoke with regret of how he'd never more be singing at the Fascio. Dorothy invited me to her parents' home, where Ted expressed outrage about the night when Viennese shops and synagogues were ransacked.

I had to wait until Christmas for its gift of an invitation.

'Think of the woods as big hitters but risky, the irons as lifters but a little more secure. What would you choose for this tee shot? Two hundred and fifty yards?'

It meant as much to me as ballistics, but I liked the sound of the words. *Risky . . . big hitter . . . lifter.* By dint of wishing, I had forestalled the forecast snow. I'd put on and taken off every combination of underclothes and over-layers my limited wardrobe would afford, seeking a balance between fear of frostbite and looking like a woman. I liked the appearance of this skinny club, tall and assertive.

'But that's a putter, my dear! You won't drive far with a putter!' He pulled the single wood from the borrowed bag of six lady's clubs, set the ball on its tiny wooden peg which he had trouble banging into the frozen ground. Few others were sufficiently foolhardy to try their luck amongst the gorse and whins on the Braids, though an occasional rabbit played sentinel, having forgotten to hibernate. 'Now remember what I said on the last tee. Practice swing first, keep your eye on the ball, bend the knees. You don't need to hit it to the moon.'

I tugged off my mittens: the moon was exactly where I wished to aim. How many hopeless swipes would I have to take before he completed what he'd started three hundred and sixty-two yards back, on the first tee, where he almost put his arms around me so as to direct my grip and wield? I ignored every one of his *six golden rules*, stopping short only at gripping the club by its wooden-mallet end.

'No, no, that's not what I told you! Remember the golden rules. The feet. The hands, interlocked; the heels, light.' With his own club he stood opposite.

'But you're back to front,' I objected. Would he cotton on before I had to be carted to the Infirmary to have my fingers unfrozen from the club?

'Well, if you don't mind too much, there's only one real way of doing this.' He moved into position. 'Though it's just as well your brother's not here to witness it.'

I was smiling, undetected. 'I don't think you know my brother as well as you think you do.'

He responded by moving my hands together—his own clad in their special chamois leather—and pushing his knees into the backs of mine, which were pliant now. He swung the club with all four arms attached. 'Again!' This time it avoided the turf and picked up some velocity. He stepped back. 'Now alone!'

I tried to prevent these words from spreading significance through the crystalline air, swung as hard as I could, almost fell over on what he'd taught me to call the *follow-through*. The ball smiled up at me cheekily.

'Keep your eye on it.'

I slowed down the *back-swing*: time to show what I was made of. And when the ball skited off in almost the right direct, I pulled a critical face, all lips and nose, to signify it could have been better.

'Bravo!' he cheered. 'Thirty yards at least.'

'Brav-*a*,' I corrected him. 'Unless this rig-out has made you forget something.'

'Brava,' he repeated, taking his own swing. Then, as we watched his ball sail off towards the flag, he added, 'It's not something one easily forgets.'

Bunkers, caddies, wedges, niblicks, hooks, the rough, the deep rough . . . My head was spinning by the time, as the light was extinguished with that particular melancholy of winter afternoons in the north, I was led to what was named *the nineteenth hole*. 'I'm afraid the fair sex are not allowed inside the clubhouse,' he explained. 'But we can take a hot toddy out here on the veranda, if you don't think you'll freeze.' Leaning on the balcony as the sun, so briefly, offered its horizontal last. 'Some splendid strokes you managed today.'

Strokes. With the warm sherry going straight to my head, I wished he meant something different. 'You'll be coming back for a bite, I hope? I'm sure it's what Giulio expected.'

'So Giulio's the boss?'

Handicap. I hadn't grasped the golfing sense, but was wondering if his being Giulio's pal was quite the advantage I'd imagined. 'We're all the boss, seeing that the real boss, Mamma, passed away. Or maybe my niece Assunta is *capo*? Or Zia Sabrina who runs guns and booze and has shoot-outs with Chicago cops.' I was racing; should be home before I fell over or did something rash. '*Wops* and *dagos*, that's what we're called over there. Here it's usually *tarries* or *spics*. *Niblicks* and *tarries* and *wedges* . . .' I placed my empty glass on the veranda post and signalled to him to approach. Gingerly, quizzically, he did so. 'Say it,' I ordered him.

'Say what?'

'Tarrie. Dago. Wop. If I've learnt all these golf terms, you can learn too.'

'But they're insults.'

'Not if *you* said them, they wouldn't be. No more than *niblick*, which sounds pretty scabrous if you ask me.' If he'd been wearing a tie, I'd have pulled it.

'If you insist, then.' He was smiling. 'Wop! Eh . . . Tarrie!'

'Rather feeble.'

He cleared his throat. 'Wop!' He was warming to it. 'Dago!'

'Everything all right here?' We both jumped and stared. 'No problem here, miss, I trust?' The groundsman had poked his head round the clubhouse door.

'Everything fine here, sir.' I stifled my giggle. 'Fine and nibbly.'

35

The ride home to Broughton Street was one of my first in a taxi cab, so silent and felted compared to the bus that the pedestrians barely seemed real. At the top of the tenement stair, the odours of Christmas cooking, the warmth from the fires of both flats, the jingle of voices and laughter . . . it was all I'd ever hoped for, all that was appropriate for an Italian *famiglia*.

Giulio sparkled, Dorothy took Harry's hands with a directness I'd never have dared, pressing their cold against her cheek. By the window, Beppe was chanting in dialect. From across the landing, Paola carried our largest dish, laden with *timballo*. With a carving knife, she cut through the outer crust to reveal amber jewels within precious veins of ore, aromas wafting from Maclodio of drying hay, over-ripe tomatoes, oregano in the afternoon air, farmyard chickens, a sulphurous hint of egg-yolk.

'Look!' Beppe's nose was glued to the window. Soft, fat flakes were drifting downwards, taking their time. Golf would no longer be possible. But there could be walks in galoshes and chilblained toes before the fire.

Even Dario couldn't spoil the evening, though he refused to approach Emilio or sit at table to eat, chopping at his plate mechanically as if he had bully beef before him, not a testimony to southern groves and hilltops. Once main course was over, he took out his pack of cards and amazed Assunta with tricks learnt in Abyssinia. Auntie Rebecca called by, carrying tiny wrapped posies of sugarplums. There was a place for her at table. 'I won't be gone long,' Giulio announced.

Ten minutes later, he was back. 'With the heat in here,' he said, 'we're going to have to be quick.' He laid the tray before us. Everyone was watching, including some children who had followed him up the stair, their knees trembling with excitement beneath their hand-me-down short trousers. '*Eccola!*' He whisked off the muslin cover.

'A tower!' gasped the malnourished five-year-old from the first floor.

'A rocket!'

'It's a lighthouse,' asserted Assunta, with the authority of her eight years' standing.

The sea was emerald. Only when sampled did it reveal itself as Pistachio laced with something darker, some liqueur or *amaro* which evoked the threat of shipwreck. On top of that lay a rock at least two feet in diameter in the darkest of bitter cacaos, with flecks of vanilla foam, sprigs of sugar-icing seaweed. And on the rock, sculpted so every stone was visible, tapering towards the candle on top, was the column of a lighthouse. It looked grey at first, then a sandstone suggesting Hazelnut. And the details: sea birds on perches, a deep-sea swordfish, the lighthouse-man behind his glass, setting flame to candle—Papà's handiwork, surely, confirmed by his contented smile.

Even in the time it took to admire, the stones had started to sweat. A bird fell out of its window, the door-handle slid towards the rock. 'Turn down the lights!' Giulio ordered. Only the fire disturbed the dark, until, with a flicker, a bulb shone from the summit, shedding enough light for Giulio to serve. 'Stone, sea or rock?' he asked the children.

The malnourished wee neighbour was far too shy to respond.

'And we'll try and catch one of those sugar fishes too,' he said, 'as you look like you could use it.'

'May I have the gull?' asked Assunta.

'Gull supper it is, with a spoonful of sea thrown in. And you, Paola?'

'Anything's fine for me.'

By dint of chipping, the lighthouse was subsiding fast. 'Lucia?'

Harry was at my shoulder. 'Stone, please, if it's the Hazelnut I think it is. And the man, I'd like to have the man, when the moment is right.' Only when the words were out did I realize what I'd said, trying to claw it back with, 'I recognized Papà's crafts . . . man . . . ship.' But words were betraying me: *the man* was inches away.

'Emilio, no need to ask you. Sea and more sea? I thought of having a sugar Emilio swimming round the rock and a Dorothy mermaid . . . A little of everything, Dorothy?' He served with professional dexterity. 'And you, Dario?'

'Foundation rock, given that's what I'm required to be for the family.'

'Chocolate rock it is. And you, Auntie Rebecca?'

'A little Vanilla from round the top where the light is.'

'And you, Harry?'

'Give me . . .' He hesitated. 'Give me the same as your sister.'

'Hazelnut it is, but without the man this time.' My brother pulled a wry face before serving himself.

Only once he was seated, after second helpings for all the children, nothing left of his construction but a multicoloured puddle, did Paola ask, 'Why a lighthouse, Giulio? It can't have been easy.'

'You know I've always loved Robert Louis.'

'Jekyll and Hyde,' said Dario, 'very appropriate.'

'All those marvellous self-contained worlds of his. A lighthouse must be like a separate universe. I remembered how his family used to build them.'

'But it's not just that though, is it?'

'It takes a few years' practice to erect a vertical statue in ice-cream . . .'

'Spare us accounts of the erection,' Dario muttered, causing Harry to giggle.

'A lighthouse seemed appropriate this Christmas. We're going to need to see clearly in the darkness ahead. And to do that we'll need the love Mamma taught us and the respect Papà has always shown us.'

A year ago, it might have sounded sickly, Hazelnut rock and sentiment. Now, it was even easier to hear—and eat—than it was easy for Giulio to serve . . . and say.

First to leave were the children, sent off to dreamland, their faces flushed with sugar and cream. A year for them was an unthinkable eternity, but Giulio's lighthouse would revisit their thoughts and chatter for months to come. Then left Auntie Rebecca, Paola, Dario. Papà retired to pray. Dorothy, snoozing by the fire, woke with a start and thanked Giulio for his 'excellent little speech'. From the window she could be seen helping Emilio find his balance in the snow, already over their ankles.

'You want to kip down here?' Giulio asked the remaining guest. And when he looked at my brother doubtfully—'We can pull out Nonno's camp bed.'

'The thought of my freezing flat is none too appealing, I must admit, and my hobgoblin landlady.'

Get him out of here! I wanted to shout. And Stay! Stay! Be here for breakfast!

'Let me find you a rug,' Giulio said. 'Put your feet up, make yourself at home.'

Finally I had to withdraw to my recess. 'I hope you sleep well there,' I stammered. 'Mind and stoke the fire before you nod off.'

In bed, I tried to calm myself by listing his qualities, beyond being handsome, a good pal of Giulio, having sweet breath, holding a respectable job, not being given to drinking himself to oblivion, possessing delicate hands, showing interest in everything to do with the family, having visited Italy and picked up a few words, and being the right age . . . When I awoke in the night, surprised I'd fallen asleep so quickly, I was still working on my list. Surely I was imagining the whispers, then a chuckle. But when I inched back the curtain, there they were, the camp bed unmade, gossiping before the fire like two ancient wifies—and surely not about politics. I could add this to the list: his lack of interest in the big bad world, as well as his distance from the classic Scottish male for whom the growling of *Aye* and *Right hen* constituted a major concession.

By 6.30 I was awake, dressed, make-up sparingly applied. Giulio was gone to prepare the ices for his Boxing Day customers. I pulled back the curtain, hoping—but he was already up.

He turned and laughed, Giulio's razor in his hand, his braces about his knees. 'Ended up sleeping in your father's armchair,' he explained.

'What do you like for breakfast?'

'Whatever you're having. Just the usual.' My usual was a boiled egg and soldiers, but he didn't need to know that—yet. Into the skillet I dropped a hearty slice of lard, and to that, melted and hot, added four rashers of bacon, three pancakes and a chunk of square sausage, a tattie scone for good measure.

Once he'd downed it all, we left the close together (from behind the lace curtains, neighbours' tongues would be wagging, I hoped). 'Four and a half,' I counted, the half having had its carrot removed and its sides damaged. 'Which do you prefer?'

'I like that small smiling one with a twig for an arm.'

'He's my favourite too. Let's award him the prize.' I removed the chips of coal from its eye-sockets and wedged in two halfpenny coins. 'Here's hoping the bairn who built it reaps the reward.'

'That's a nice thought.'

'You fill me with nice thoughts.' The day seemed unlimited, as it must have done to the child who'd built the snowman. Soon our ways would part, since he could hardly go to work in his golfing out-fit. If he invited me home, I'd accept—but I trusted he could not read my thoughts. I was no *hussy*, though men were taught to think that of women who wanted what they wanted. 'Are you fond of chil-dren yourself?' I asked, since he'd been silenced by my last remark.

'You know, despite how miserable my parents made my own childhood, I'd be happy to give it a go.'

I liked it when he blushed. So much so that I wanted to call him back and embarrass him some more.

By four o'clock, I figured he'd be calling it a day, heading home before the freezing snow turned Howe Street into a ski slope. Not that I'd mind if he broke a leg, since he'd require no end of assistance, would need to be changed and fed; later, like Emilio, he'd require a shoulder on which to lean.

When I finally did get down to typing, the errors obliged me to start over again. Yet my desk was easy compared to the Palace, where I kept seeing him in his favourite booth—notwithstanding the diminutive Glaswegian with the bulbous nose who bore mercifully slim resemblance. What would he be doing now? Where eating? Drinking? 'No Harry tonight?' I remarked to Giulio, not even bothering to sound casual.

He gave the Italian '*Boh!*'—face raised and lower lip protruding, to indicate he had no clue.

Home was even worse, the full force of the invasion. On my bed, he was in the kitchen. By the fire, he was by the sink, shaving, taking his time on the bacon, as if the day belonged to him. He didn't sprinkle his salt but created a little pyramid on the edge of his plate, into which he nudged his tattie scone.

Finally came company, Giulio's face flushed from his tramp through the snow. 'You'll see,' he told me. 'Nineteen thirty-nine is going to be your big year.'

'And for you?'

'A big year for me is when I see Assunta growing up happy, when I see you smiling the way I've done recently.'

'Don't exaggerate.' The last thing I needed was someone else believing that my feelings were all that existed.

'No exaggeration. You don't know how it spreads from you, through the whole house . . . your mood.'

I'd never thought of myself as having *moods*, still less that these might have been infecting the family. 'Why didn't you say?'

'Would that have helped?'

I wished to tell him how he could now help me and my mood. But he knew it, knew that I knew it, and maybe was already doing so behind the scenes, in the rooms where only men met. I wished to ask him to forgive me, but knew he'd done so already; even knew, maddeningly, that nothing I would ever do could outreach that (determinedly un-Christian) forgiveness.

36

The year would open, I realized now, with Harry in my arms. Only on the dance floor, admittedly, but the way he led my inexperienced steps made me think of what Auntie Sandy had once reported about the delights of dancing; this, added to the three gin-and-tonics, the smoke and singing in the Café Royal, made me cheer when the bells finally rang. When Giulio appeared, we took hold of one another and circled slowly in a ring. Only in the freezing night air did I remember I'd been drinking. I longed to tell Harry to finish the night with me, start the year with me. But Giulio was waiting, ungloved hands clamped under his armpits, as Harry led me by the arm towards the close. 'It'll be warm by the fire,' he said, 'if you care to come up?'

'I've an aunt who's visiting in the morning, motoring up to some castle in the Highlands.' The idea that he had an aunt was a shock; I'd imagined him a waif we could nurture and coddle.

Giulio lit a cigarette and handed it, after an initial puff. 'I'll be up in a minute,' he told me.

And if I refused? asked the gin inside of me, as I climbed the steps. Why should men get to stand and smoke together? What had they to discuss that was so pressing? The ember of their shared Capstan was visible from where I leant over the banister on the top landing. I pretended to be reading the newspaper when my brother at last stepped in and warmed his hands by the fire. It felt like years since anyone but Papà had stroked my hair.

'It's daft, you know, to think you're too old.'

'Did I tell Harry that? It must have been the alcohol talking. In any case what's he doing cliping to you?' My tone was like the lemon rind at the bottom of my gin glass.

'He's shy, you know. Needs some coaxing. All that public-school upbringing means he likes a bit of bossing. Bear that in mind.'

'Are brothers not supposed to care for their sisters' honour?'

'Strange times, Lucia,' he said, with a frown, 'and set to become stranger. Your honour's safe inside of you.' The frown gave way to a smile. 'I'll take pleasure over honour any day.'

I doubted if Dario would agree with him, where their sister was concerned. After the *Easter Agreement*, the *Gentlemen's Agreement*, the *Munich Agreement*, he was determined to convince the unconcerned Harry that there was going to be a permanent pact between our two countries. He used a supper from the Neapolitan Fry to illustrate, his newspaper poke representing Europe, his chips the German armies, his fish the Italian boot—'Not that I'd eat fish from a boot, mind. Is that no right, Assunta?' His daughter was hiding under my bed in the recess. 'Harry, you should come down the Fascio with Lucia and me.' It was months since I'd been, and I was not the only truant. 'You'd soon get the picture.'

'Baden-Powell neckerchiefs?' Harry asked 'Black leather and salutes?'

'Harry's busy,' I said. 'He's booked to take me down the pitch-and-putt at Inverleith Park.'

'It's dark in the evenings.'

'He's got luminous balls.' It was bound to go wrong whenever I tried inventing.

'*Mamma mia*! Luminous balls! How can I argue with that!' He was still guffawing, and Europe was lying greasily on the table, the German armies consumed and Italy reduced to its Apennine fish-bone spine, when he left minutes later.

'What's so funny?' asked Assunta, creeping from her lair.

Harry cocked his head. 'Would you really like to try pitch-and-putt?'

For lack of *luminous balls*, we ended up ten-pin bowling in a smoke-filled hall in Murrayfield. Harry tried to conceal his irritation when on my opening throws I hit an occasional skittle, while his ball slithered into the gutter. 'I think I prefer golf,' I said. 'The men in the next lane keep staring.' Their glances at my bottom were cursory, but I hoped to take Harry's mind off his poor performance and back to what mattered.

'Or we could try skating?' he suggested, to the accompaniment of sniggers from the neighbouring lane when I achieved what they declared was a *strike*. 'It's just next door.'

On the eerie echoing expanse of the ice-rink, I was a limpet affixed to its unstable boulder. The regulars, whose arabesques turned into leaps and spins, might have been cherubs for all their manoeuvres seemed plausible to those of us for whom the simplest forward motion promised twisted ankles or worse. 'Giulio would be happy though,' I got out, between nervous gasps. 'What's wrong? Did I say something wrong?'

He'd never sounded so English as when he asked, 'Why should he be happy?'

'That we're slithering round on his element. What did you think I meant?' When he failed to answer, I ignored the pinching of the hired boots on my ankles to push harder. 'He's not one of those old-fashioned brothers, you know, who'd have your head off were I lucky enough to find you'd taken a shine to me.' Was this coaxing? Was I doing as commanded?

He juddered to a stop. 'You're full of surprises today.' With blue lips, he kissed my forehead lightly, and when I raised my lips for more, said, 'I'm starving. Let's go to Paola's for some nosh.'

My instant smile belied my disappointment. But as we untied our skates, I did wonder why, with Harry, there were always things to do, be done. Comparisons might be odious, but—had it been like that with Valerio? I recalled strolling through streets to nowhere in particular, clocks smiling down from their towers . . . coins tossed hopefully into fountains . . . the air about my legs. Hadn't Valerio needed some coaxing too? And of course he had been helped by heat, that lengthening of limb; while here it was colder outside the rink than in, the thickest of stockings could hardly keep the veins from showing; that anyone could remove underclothes in a country like ours was a miracle.

'Did you catch the news?' Paola asked, serving up her fried zucchini with an angry tomato *sugo* she reserved for Italians (and the very rare Indian) amongst her clientele. Despite the vapours of frying and the hours she'd spent behind the counter, she still looked glamorous, unflustered—only her hands showed the cost.

'No news please,' I pleaded. News was like things to do, get through, and tomorrow there'd be more, probably worse.

'These fritters are mighty tasty,' said Harry, 'and the sauce is . . . unusual.'

'*Peperoncino*. Will purify your innards. Speaking of purity,' Paola said, battering another haddock and ignoring my embargo on news, 'the Pio—Pius to you, Harry—is dead. Our *Papa*, your Pope. The one who freed me from Roberto the hog. Maybe,' she went on with her customary pragmatism, as I was trying to take it in, 'maybe those cardinals will choose someone who says *damn you* to the politicals. They won't see me or Assunta on our knees in St Mary's if they're licking the feet of Adolf and Benito.' In an access of irritation, she slapped the haddock as if it were alive and wriggling, then cursed. 'At least we'll be seeing the Archbishop in his raiment.' She turned to me with a knowing wink, mouthed the word *coaxing*. 'Blast it!' she exclaimed. 'Run out of chips, and the boy's off this evening. Could I ask you, Harry, to prepare a few tatties? Man's work this is.'

He summoned an obedient smile. 'Not tried it before, but I'm sure I'll soon get the hang of it.'

She pointed to the alcove at the rear of the shop, with its tap and bowl, then hesitated before selecting her sharpest knife. 'Don't waste too much peeling. Go over and help him, Lucia, move out of my way here. Let me serve these starving folks.'

I refrained from pointing out that there was no one else in the shop. Pulled up a stool next to Harry, who was staring at the half-dozen underwater King Edwards as if they were piranhas, not potatoes. 'Never had to cook much for yourself, then?'

'Is the posh education,' Paola answered for him. 'Don't teach them anything useful, as a matter of principle.'

'But Dorothy's dad Ted,' I said, quite as if we'd rehearsed this routine, 'is often the cook. And not just the standard Mrs Beeton.'

'But he is a *uomo moderno*, not like Harry here who expects the woman to stick in the kitchen. Let me show you.' Two steps, and Paola had his hands in her grip, while the water turned murky from potato clay. 'Take the knife *così* . . . Here, Lucia will show you.'

'I'd like to be a *uomo moderno* too.' He whittled his first potato as if sharpening a stick.

'You'll waste too much,' I warned him, directing his hands with mine. 'Cut towards the thumb, not away from it, unless you want a single chip from each potato.'

'Even Dario, who thinks he's such a lady killer, when it comes to it, is timid as a kiddie. *Moderno* or *antico*, you men expect us to do all the work in that domain too.' It was the first time she'd mentioned her husband in over a year, measure of her match-maker's earnestness. 'The laddie who works for me—you'll not put him out of a job, peeling at that pace!'

'Trying my best, Paola, but not being helped by having to defend our masculine honour.' He grimaced. 'Not quite mastered my technique yet.'

'There's a woman looks after you? Cleans and cooks and laundry?'

'I'm a working man, Paola, no time for housework. She does for me twice a week.'

'How many rooms she cleans?'

'I've a drawing room, a bathroom and a bedroom. I don't have guests, hardly know anyone except your fine family.' The knife was cutting perilously close to his thumb, but when I thought to warn him, Paola's frown instructed me to leave well—leave *ill* alone.

'Is no life that, all space and nobody to fill it. What about the Battle for Babies? You would not say *No* to me now, would you,

Harry? Always ready to please?' Paola's expression showed she was willing to go further.

'You're right, you know. I went to a head doctor in Hampstead who told me it was because I felt I'd never pleased my parents and I imagined this was why they'd sent me off to boarding school.' With two potatoes to go, he was turning reckless. Paola watched his hands like a billiard player who knows the opponent's break must end. 'Ah bugger it! If you'll excuse my language.' The water turned crimson in seconds.

'Run the tap, and let's see. Are you for fainting? You're white as a sole's belly.'

'Cannot stand the sight of blood!'

'In that case,' Paola said, 'you'd better get him home, Lucia.' She was an experienced border collie, urging its sheep towards the fold. 'Needs some dressing.' From a drawer she removed a shoe-box with a red cross taped to it. 'If the patient feels a need to scream, put this between the teeth.'

When we reached 42 Northumberland Street, he asked me to feel in his pocket for his key, so as not to bloody his jacket. As I did so, he remembered—'Oh god, Mrs Richards! Let's hope the nosy old witch isn't spying on us! The landlady who lives upstairs. She'd have a fit if she saw a beautiful young woman accompanying me.'

His key unlocked the front door, but no key was required to open the door into his ground-floor flat, leading off the spacious hallway straight into what he called his 'drawing room'. Never having been inside the home of a *bachelor*, I felt a list come over me: bachelor neatness, bachelor hideous porcelain milkmaid (presumably Mrs Richards'), bachelor floral curtains and thick pile carpet, bachelor lack of plants and photographs—everything spookily unlived-in.

'Does it hurt very much?' He shook his head unconvincingly. 'Iodine, then.' I sat him on the couch and opened Paola's box. Men in pain—I'd seen my share of them, each with his stock of tolerance and denial. I didn't wish to hurt him, but was curious to gauge his reaction. 'We don't need the cork between the teeth, do we?' With the teat-pipette I squeezed out a drop of the dark brown liquid, which darted under the flap of skin on his thumb. He puffed out his cheeks. 'You can squeeze, or swear if you like. *Porcomiseria*! *Madonna*! *Caspita*! *Cavallo*!' By the time I'd run out of expletives, he was laughing. I folded the gauze over his wound.

With something of the same delicacy, he applied his lips to mine. He tasted of tobacco and fright. I lifted his damaged left hand and laid it on my cheek.

'Are you sure this is wise?' he asked, inches from my ear.

'Is *wise* the most important thing?' I loosened his tie. Not having visited the rest of his flat, I didn't know where to steer him. My throat was full of certainties that I needed him to deny: that he did not find me beautiful, despite what he'd said, still less desirable, still less irresistible.

'I just think we should go slowly,' he said, with my shoulders uncovered and his jacket off.

The carpet on which he should have laid me, with its floral pattern, looked very uninviting all of a sudden. 'We've all the time in the world.' I was proud of my words. 'And this way we won't be offending Pio's holy ghost.' I inspected my watch, trying to ignore the longing to have him deep inside me. Men, I thought, offending Pio's ghost worse than our bodies might have done—men, I thought naively, were spared this cross to bear.

37

Days of circling, smiles, fingertips touching to the sound of Cardinal Pacelli's name; at St Mary's the priests went in awe of his austerity, his piety, his single minded devotion, whispered of his languages, his prodigious memory and scholarship. Giulio said, from the moment he was elected, that this man—this *man*, not *Cardinal* or *Papa*—was nobody he could ever trust. 'Even less than the rest, this so-called *Pius*.' He spoke of Pacelli's time in Germany, confusing his tale in the telling; unless I was the one confused, who cared only what Harry might think of the family fascination with this *Romanissimo* of popes. The wireless was playing in the sacristy, and for as long as I could escape the bank, I listened to the breathless commentary of the BBC reporters describing the sight of forty thousand heads bowed before His Eminence. Would Harry mind that mine bowed with the rest of them?

My route to the Palace was lined by imaginary pilgrims, so I barely noticed him at first, when I turned into Annandale Street. His coat was long, in black cashmere with a crimson rose in its buttonhole. Shirt, tie, patent-leather shoes. He was pretending not to have seen me. Then—so he really hadn't spotted me—he turned, and we were only three feet apart.

'Well hello there, darlin'!' He lifted his fedora to reveal hair that had mellowed almost to auburn. His accent too had softened. 'Was wondering when I'd bump into you, Lucia.' He reached out. 'Will you no at least shake hands with me, let bygones be bygones?'

With the spirit of Pius inside of me, it should have been possible —everyone made mistakes. 'Ewan McEwen,' I forced, unable to take his hand. The scar screamed from his forehead.

'You see?' He gestured to the coat. 'A bit of time away was just what I needed. Not doing badly for myself now.'

'I'm not interested.' Pius was shrivelling. 'I don't want to see you. Please keep away from me and my family.'

The old familiar scorn was settling in the lines round his mouth. 'I'm right sorry to hear that, Lucia.'

He hadn't forgotten how to pronounce me. 'And stop saying my name.'

'My feelings for you . . .'

'Feelings! You speak of *feelings*?'·

'They have not changed. Met loads of lassies in the meantime but none of them matches you. I hoped you might have learnt some Christian forgiveness.'

'I thought politics was your religion.' He'd transformed himself from whippet into greyhound, yet not a single muscle twitched. I could not avoid thinking that here, before me, was the last man to have touched me . . . *there*.

'You think I'd back a loser?' The sneer had returned to his voice. 'No scrap of paper waved by Chamberlain's going to stop them now. Yer Duce must be missin the limelight though?'

It was exactly what I had to avoid, a conversation, as between consenting adults, members of the same species. 'It's Pacelli who's centre-stage, in case you hadn't noticed, not your Führer.'

'The two get along like a house on fire.'

I was losing this. 'Your dad must be pleased to see you.' It was low, but I could sink lower.

One eye registered hurt, the other was vacant. 'Surprised his fingers have no turned into chips by now, his face into a flounder. Waste of a life. I've developed a taste for German cuisine.' He pronounced it *kooseen*. 'I can see you've no forgotten me, mind. Gives me hope.'

I ordered my legs to move . . . which was when I saw him, Harry, coming round the corner in his plus-fours, his clubs slung casually over his shoulder. The meeting was what I most dreaded. Only, as he approached, what I most wanted as well, that this creature witness who, despite him, I had become.

'Who's this ponce? What's he think he's smiling at?'

'Harry!' I gasped. He clasped my hand, turning to the man in the coat. 'Let's go!' My muscles moving freely again.

Harry raised his shoulders in apology, a dumb-show of being dragged on a lead. 'Not one of your best friends, then?'

'Ewan McEwen. Please avoid him. He was nasty to me all through my youth. Disappeared for years, but now he's back.'

Most Palace customers seemed barely to notice when, days later, the Nazis moved into Bohemia, took Prague; or when, one week following, the Duce sent his troops into Albania, forcing out King Zog. How I envied them their insouciance. Pius hailed it as a triumph when General Franco captured Madrid. Clients queued for Mr Morton, anxious about their savings. Giulio told the few who enquired, over a free scoop, that in any case Albania was not worth the occupying, made Edinburgh slums look like Valhalla, Highland crofts like Eden. Dario claimed Chamberlain was right and that Churchill, even if he had once been the Duce's great supporter, was henceforth a dolt: nothing on the Continent merited a fight. Papà, for whom the three flights up to the flat had become a mountain, said he hoped he wouldn't live to see the day—he'd rather join Mamma, who was expecting him.

In the booth behind where I was seated with Harry, Carlo and Fausto were bemoaning their lack of passports: their Italian ones had expired years before, and they'd been too ashamed of their *patria* to request replacements. I had to try something new, or the tension would devour me. 'Would you like me to read to you? I could read from the *Vita Nuova*—that's *New Life* to you. It's a poem, a love poem, by Dante.'

'Will I understand it? You know, despite the opera, I'm rather prosaic.'

'Picture six hundred years back, with me dressed in one of those beautiful robes with girdle and coronet.'

'You look good for a six-hundred-year-old.'

'And you look like a wee boy who's not trusting he can be happy.'

Heavy sighs. 'It's true though. I'm not very used to the idea of happiness. I wasn't cut out to be a rebel, yet somehow I became one—even living up here is seen by my family as an act of rebellion.'

I held a spoonful of melting Pistachio to his mouth, spoke softly so as not to be overheard. 'You know, Harry, you shouldn't be so nervous. I'm not so very fragile. I've had some experience.' Now I'd started, I almost felt like telling him about Signor Starace's mirrored ceiling—relief writ large on his every feature. 'I'm aware that maidens are meant to be a treat for men, Italian men especially, but it struck me you're not that kind?'

'I can't imagine how you'd guess such a thing, or how we're having such a frank conversation. Is it because of the awful news abroad?' He shook his head as if to break a spell. 'I've never wished to be a teacher, except at golf, and I've never wished to *own* anyone either. Does that sound awfully *moderno*?'

'Dario would have liked to own Paola. You've seen how that worked out.'

'So . . .' He took a deep breath. 'What if you came back for a nightcap?'

'I've got to take over at the till soon. But I could pop round after closing. If you'd like. Giulio's always saying he's no need of me for clearing up.'

'I'll be expecting you, then.' All of a sudden decisive, he gave me a wink, got up and bade my brother a slow farewell.

'So you're sure you don't need me?' The last customer had left, and I had counted the bills and coins.

'What's needed is for you to enjoy yourself. Especially now.'

As I pulled on my coat, I didn't dare ask which bit of bad news he was referring to. Northumberland Street felt antique and austere, with my heels clicking and scarcely a pedestrian in sight. Other people had walked here, their legs heavy with yearning and their feet light. I was not wearing finest lace, but nor was I wearing ragged old cotton; in significant spots I had dabbed Je Reviens (hoping it prove true). Even my own parents had done it, not just once. Even *I* had done it, a night of it, though it was hard to remember—not *it*, that was easy, but the *me* who'd been part of it. Harry had warned that Mrs Richards, his landlady, was a prime nosy parker who had to be avoided. I tapped on his bay window and heard the front door open. 'Shhh . . .' he whispered. 'Come in. Take your clothes off.'

I had obviously misheard him—he must have said, 'Take your coat off.' Yet with my coat off, he still looked expectant. After passing through the entrance he shared with his landlady, then leading me through his door, he explained that Mrs Richards didn't believe in locks for her lodgers. 'Please,' he said, his voice gravelly. 'Go on, Lucia, do show me.'

It was not what I expected. Was it what I wanted? Oh, anything rather than another night alone in bed with my blood stagnating. Maybe it was usual in a man, to want to watch—what did I know. 'You'll have to unbutton me at the back.' He went at it with the fingers of a choirboy. When I'd removed the lambswool blouse, my arms looked unnaturally long in his mirror. The skirt fell of its own accord. I had never felt so naked, and yet I still had on my slip, under skirt, brassiere and stockings. 'Wouldn't you care to join me?' It sounded as if I were enquiring if he'd care for one lump or two. I sought the term to describe the look on Harry's face, as he permitted me to undress him. After reaching for the obvious—surprise? delight? curiosity?—it came to me: *relief*. His skin was almost shiny, surprisingly olive-coloured with tiny blonde hairs on his chest and shins; his bones were prominent and his muscles pronounced (I found myself with the word *thoroughbred* in my head). I imagined squeezing every part of him. He wanted me, I hoped; he was relieved that he wanted me, I knew. 'Put your arms around me,' he requested. 'I've anticipated this for a very long time.'

Nervous though I was of breaking the fragile spell, I could not resist asking, 'How on earth did you expect me to know?'

His head flopped forward like a chastised child's. 'I don't— you might have noticed—have a very high self-esteem. I know, I know, I come from privilege, but that cuts both ways, given I've done nothing to deserve it. Sailed through Cambridge, barely opening a book. Gilbert and Sullivan at the Opera Society. A job in insurance because my uncle knows a chap who knows a chap.' I feared it turning into a life story, which at any moment but this I'd have welcomed. 'Are you sure?' he muttered, as I pushed him back onto the couch and knelt between his knees. I had failed to once before. He'd understand, presumably, if I could not reply—rude to speak with your mouth full (as Mamma used to say) . . . Shouldn't be thinking of Mamma in such a moment, should be concentrating on this new—oft-imagined but not exactly simple . . .

'Careful!' he gasped. 'Oh no!' But I was not about to let him push me away, not after so long a wait. I didn't want to be admired like some Roman statue in imperfect marble, wanted to feel him jump inside, letting go of all that past and future. Most of him ended on the carpet. 'Don't worry,' he eventually said, before he noticed I was shivering. 'But you're freezing here, how inconsiderate of me.'

'It's not for cold I'm shaking. It's for you, for me, for what I feel for you.' The words leapt out of me; in all my rehearsals not these ones. 'Don't be so considerate with me, Harry, don't be so damn English even if you are English. I'm happy making you happy.'

'Come with me, then.' He led me, finally, to his bedroom.

'The lair!' Even Signor Starace might have gasped. Where the rest of his flat was drab, unlived-in, tired floral wallpapers and china ornaments, here, suddenly, were colours and patterns, textures too.

'I feared you might find it alarming. It's the only place I spend time in when I'm alone. I've tried to make it fit the cut of my dreams.' Over the walls was stretched some sort of silk; I'd seen similar at Dorothy's parents', but here an unidentifiable shade of grey. The floor was covered in a sea-blue rug, the quilt on the bed embossed with two enormous sail-boats which seemed to flutter as I moved round them, a trick of light perhaps, which was rising and falling . . . a bronze electric wall fixture in the shape of a Chinese Mandarin held a bulb in his hand over which a pyramidal hat revolved, casting shadows and patches. The two chairs, of chrome and leather, looked as if they might be upside down. 'They're Bauhaus,' he explained.

I heard *bough-house*, dogs barking. 'Do you realize it's Saturday, 29 April, I'm twenty-nine years old, the year 1939? There has to be significance to so many nines?' As he had no reply, I asked, 'Can I dive under the sails?'

When he climbed in after, finally he was naked too. Everything about him was firm, and when he lay on top I felt through to his bones. French letters were in a drawer beside his bed; I tried not to notice if the box was already opened. 'Tell me what to do,' I said.

'Be yourself.'

'That's no fun. I'm myself too much of the time. I'd rather be . . . Marlene Dietrich.'

'If I can be a sailor on the China Seas, then you can be Marlene Dietrich. Are you sure I'm not hurting you?' After some minutes he was ready to be led to where he seemed unable to navigate alone.

'Why should you hurt me? It's made for this.'

When at last he was there, I put my hands round his buttocks and pulled. I would not let go until he'd seen that I had . . . Then I did . . . then he did . . . then I laughed, which turned out to be unwise, as the convulsion squeezed him out and he had to make a quick grab so as not to leave the rubber inside.

Through the night, he told me of his longing, for our family and all it represented. I told him of the disputes, the fights, the night when Giulio was beaten. He said it all only showed we mattered to each other; if he'd never known the violence, nor had he known the warmth—always a stranger, to his parents, his schoolmates, his social class. Only when he met Giulio, and through him our family . . . me . . . had he started, for the first time, to feel he might belong.

I wanted him to be harsh with me, but he was gentle when he caressed my tummy, so gentle and tender that I wished him gentler still. The sails rose and fell. Towards dawn, Harry also rose, and entered me again, taking the pain, his solitude, my wasted years, and compacting them into seconds. All would die some day, and who was to say if heaven really did exist. But because of that—not despite it—we were making love this morning: me, making *love*.

38

When I reached home after my night with Harry, I ached pleasurably all over. Even the dawn altercation with Mrs Richards on Harry's doorstep, during which she called me 'a painted Jezebel', was not enough to disturb my delight. When Assunta reported over breakfast that she hadn't found her *zia* when she'd sought comfort in the night, the scowl she received from Zio Giulio was so unfamiliar that it brought her to tears.

'You look well today,' he said.

The kitchen was calling for a spring clean, the sun peeking in. 'But what if war really comes?' It bolted out of me. 'Or if Papà objects? Or the priests? What if he's only curious?'

My brother rose from his bacon and eggs. 'You're just beginning, and here you're worried about endings? You're worse than me!'

I leant my tiredness into him. 'You're the one forever saying that the peace may not last.'

'Folks'll still be needing insurance companies, banks, ice-creams. Emilio's an insider now, with his job at the Scottish Office. Papà's fifty-nine years old. Dario's the only one without a British passport, and with the wounds on his back, nobody can expect much of him.'

I wanted to tell him how it felt, how *I* felt, but it would have been the hardest thing to relate, even if a sister were permitted such words. A man inside of you . . . just a part of him, but as if all of . . .

As I walked to work, I felt heartstrings stretching, like Angelo Siciliano with his chest expanders (Charles Atlas to non-Italians). Ease and invitation, moments into minutes, minutes into ticker tape unfurling in the air from the upper storey of the bank, reading HAPPY LUCIA HAPPY HARRY HAPPY GIULIO HAPPY ASSUNTA . . . Mamma would be happy too, even proud of me beneath the crosses she'd be drawing in air. I listed the reasons for gratitude: for making me and for making me *me*; for giving whatever it was that had allowed me to resurface—it wasn't Harry alone who had dragged me back to the land of the living; for making me willing to risk; for gifting me a body I could enjoy; for making a brother who'd rather bless her lover's head than remove it. I thanked her. Then—unheralded—I forgave her.

It was so surprising that I had to ask myself what on earth there was to forgive. Mamma, of all people . . . I forgave her, yes, for leaving me so young; forgave her for dying.

He hadn't actually said he loved me, it occurred to me over lunch, but then I hadn't told him I loved him either. What did it matter? The evening no longer hung like a fisherman's lead on the end of an afternoon line. It could bring anything: work at the Palace, but the night might end anywhere (except at Harry's flat, now that Mrs Richards had debarred me). He hadn't proposed, but he had said that now he'd entered our family he never wished to leave it.

'Could I see you in my office?' requested Mr Morton. 'In five minutes?'

This time, the Directors' portraits practically smiled at me.

'First, I'd like you to convey to Mrs Paola my congratulations at the speed with which she is acquitting her loan. Admirable industriousness.'

'She's always been a rare worker, Mr Morton sir.' I waited. His smile seemed uncomfortably fixed. 'Was there a second thing?'

He moved jerkily, like someone caught napping. 'Ah yes . . . I just wanted you to know that whatever happens, whichever way the political wind blows, you will always have my personal support at the bank. The question of you . . . of your background is of no significance so far as this branch of the Royal is concerned.'

I tried to conceal my panic. 'Very kind of you, sir.' I wouldn't admit that the contrary had not occurred to me. 'As it happens, both myself and the two younger of my brothers were born here in Edinburgh and hold British passports.'

It was his turn to hide—relief in his case. 'Capital! Capital! Then we shan't mention it again.'

Now, when I'd spot McEwen before the Rob Roy or stotting along the paths of Princes Street Gardens, his black coat discarded in the warm spring weather, I felt only a flicker of the long-suppressed rage. The apple trees had blossomed early, offering inviting evening shadows where I imagined informing Harry of how often I had reached the peak of pleasure in the past twenty-four hours. I suspected I shouldn't count, that it was certainly un-ladylike to be in the least arithmetical, yet surprise at my capacity required it. I had to be discreet about it as we had not yet reconnoitred our own secret spots. And to add to constraints, Papà got to asking, and Dario overheard.

'What's this? Home at midnight. We canna be having this.' Presuming he was joking, I merely smiled. 'I thought that worthless brother of ours was meant to keep an eye on you.'

'What business is it of yours?' asked Papà from his armchair.

'It's my business. *Primo*, because I'm the oldest brother. *Secondo*, because it matters how the local rabble judge us, now there's going to be trouble. And *terzo*, while I'm at it . . .' He had to search for his *terzo*. 'Because no sister of mine is going to get herself knocked up by some Sassenach, however *bravo* he is at golf.'

'I thought that your pal Ciano said golf is an honourable game.'

'Golf, she says! At two in the morning! More of your luminous balls, *vero*? My eye's out for you, Lucia, won't let you disgrace us, now of all times.'

The idea was horrid, of his eye upon me when Harry was leading me down some darkened wynd. 'It's not me who has to worry,' I said. 'I'm Scottish, mind? You're the one's who's not British. I haven't been bombing the blacks in Africa. And I'm not the Fascio's *Chief Extractor*.'

If I'd told him I was a member of the secret police, he could not have looked more alarmed. 'Who the fuck told you that?' And when I shrugged—'You better no go repeating it.'

'Well that all depends now. I haven't told Harry yet, for example. Though if I'm to be home straight after closing, then I'll need to explain who's *enforcing* the curfew.'

'Listen, *cara*, there was a time when tougher tactics were called for. But these days are gone. We're going to have to call a pause at the Fascio. Now's no the moment to be spreading gossip.'

'What's an extractor?' asked Papà.

'You neither, Papà. I'm no telling you how to lead your lives, just concerned about your well-being. I'm away up Registry House, sort out this nationality nonsense.'

Impediments spurred inventiveness; where once he was hesitant, now he was urging. With summer almost upon us, we could disrobe without turning tartan. I'd never indulged myself in a more pleasurable list.

(1) Kisses in the Palace kitchen, whither the Angel watched us retreat, a professionally approving lift to the eyebrows over her Cinnamon ice.

(2) As the weather improved, on the lawn of Princes Street Gardens. Harry had found a missing railing on the Mound, and carried a towel in his knapsack, against grass-stains. I couldn't help thinking of the Forum, the figs, the heat of that first finding; then, of all the poor souls who'd never had anyone, boys and men seeking some part of themselves, shards of some greater whole, like the Castle Rock towering above, relic of its self-destructive eruption, now a seat for soldiers.

(3) Inside David Hume's mausoleum. Harry pointed to the lintel above the doorway of the sawn-off cylinder on Calton Hill, where carved in sandstone were the thinker's name and dates. I could recall only fragments of what Giulio had once told me . . . something about billiard balls. The sequel came back in a succession of ideas that made me giggle: how one day a ball decides not to bounce the usual way . . . From within the darkness we could see without being seen. All that mattered was the present sensation—hadn't Mr Hume said something similar?

(4) In Central Library, amidst the stacks. With the *Scots Thesaurus* (Chambers, 1925) in an obscure corner of Reference, I pointed to myself while indicating *racer, nickname for a loose woman*, and *quine . . . a mistress, concubine*. Many unknown words from counties never visited, like Banff and Caithness. But *Hochmagandy* I recognized, preferring it to the biblical-sounding *fornication*.

And, just as I was running out of sites, Harry led me to (5), down Clarence Street to Henderson Row; the main entrance being locked to the imitation-Greek temple, he fiddled with the latch on the side gate. We clung to the shadows, past the four Doric columns, past the school library, beyond a giant bell which I imagined summoning masters to punish us interlopers.

'In here!' Harry pushed me into an entrance-way, and when the grey chipped door on 22C wouldn't open, he borrowed a kirby-grip and applied it to the lock. 'One of the few useful things public school taught me. My own looked much the same, with six pillars rather than four.'

The lock turned, the door opened, he pulled me inside. I felt almost nauseous, who had rarely done anything so illicit: if he were caught, he'd receive a reprimand from some other posh sort; I'd be locked away for life. 'What on earth is this?' he asked, raising the lid on the master's lectern.

I'd expected something grander than the chalk dust and rows of desks. 'It's called a *tawse*. Dario used to feel it across his arse.'

Harry laughed, handing me the long strip of leather divided down the middle. He leant over the nearest desk. 'Please Ma'am, don't beat me too hard!' I took a playful swing, then had to check I hadn't scarred him.

(6) was discovered ten days after Giulio had foretold that war was inevitable, now the Germans were secure to the east. I interrupted breakfast to lean out of the kitchen window: four men were shifting an enormous corrugated-iron hen-house. 'Let's hope they're never needed!' called up one of the workmen as he began digging.

Dario, up early for once, appeared out of the close and handed the workman an envelope. The air was enormous, August light and warmth, puff-balls floating past the window, the back yard lushly green, swallows cutting by, the neighbours' washing almost dry on the line.

'No bad, *vero*?' He passed through the kitchen with a purposefulness not seen in months. 'They'll soon be bedded down.' Perhaps it was the expression that planted the idea: who ever heard of bedding for hens. 'Ken what they are? They're Anderson shelters.'

I'd heard about them, picturing something less rustic. 'Same Anderson? The Scotsman from Bengal?'

He could never admit to ignorance. 'It won't be Bengal you're worrying about when the bombs start dropping.'

'I thought they were reserved for posh folks with private gardens.'

My brother tapped his nose. 'You think your Dario would leave the family unprotected?'

Home from the bank that afternoon, the shelters were sunk in the lawn, turfs on the roofs, as if the Picts had returned. Children were pacing round them, scared to touch. Rather than let Harry lead me up the stair that night, after the Palace closed, I lured him through the close into the back yard.

'What's with the mound?' he asked, as I opened the door and pulled him inside. *Bedded down* indeed! 'So this is an Anderson?'

'And this . . .' I took his hand and placed it where I was ready for him. 'This is a Pezzini.'

The following day, when the Nazis invaded Poland, I had only to remember what he'd told me in the shelter: for he had told me that he loved me, had said he'd never leave me.

Two days later, I clung to his words. For the British parts of me were at war.

39

It was scant consolation that the following week proved Giulio right:
crises were profitable. By evening, the ices were blotches of colour
in their basins, and the sweetie-jars emptied as grown men and
women lined their pockets with Aniseed Balls and Hazelnut Toffees.
On his rare moments off, he listened to the wireless in the Palace
kitchen. 'The Muss is going to stay out,' he insisted. 'Not so big a
fool as to repeat the mistakes of the war that left him wounded. Let
him call it *non-belligerency* if it suits him.' The same Duce whose every
decision had been condemned for a decade would now demonstrate
judgement, circumspection, a sense of fair play.

'Dammit,' said Harry, 'I haven't even taken you to the opera yet.'
When the Germans captured Warsaw, he said, with a wink, that it
was all just 'foreplay': worse, far worse, was coming.

Emboldened, yet not bold enough to risk Fausto on the door,
McEwen stared through the Palace window twice a day, his motor-
cycle boots pacing to a military gait.

St Mary's was jam-packed for once, and Archbishop Smith delivered the sermon in person, recalling that national duty began at
home, with family and friends. It had to be demonstrated what civilized democracy could mean. What it did *not* mean was suspicion
of one's neighbour. 'Not if this neighbour is Czech,' he iterated. 'Not
if this neighbour is Austrian.' His arms went out in cadence. 'And
especially not if this neighbour is German. We are fortunate, as we
face the dark uncertainty, that we have faith.' (I could not but wonder
if in the depths of enemy territory some Munich or Berlin archbishop was saying the same.) 'And that our men of state have learnt
from the past. In his inaugural speech, our new Home Secretary Mr
Anderson—an Edinburgh man—has spoken of the need for calm

and a liberal internment policy. We must pray for our servicemen risking their lives in defence of the realm. We must open our hearts to Christ.'

My heart had never been more open, and when I forgave those who had trespassed against me I almost—almost—managed to include McEwen. Arriving was a war that would spare nobody, with weapons bigger, faster, heavier than ever before. Papà held my hand as he sang; Paola's knuckles were talons on the back of the chair; Assunta was trembling like one of those breeds of miniature dog, though for once it was warm. I wished Harry were here, compact with the city's Catholics.

'Will you be coming down the Fry with your man?' Paola asked me as we left the cathedral—my wishes shared, apparently. 'Remember the trick with the potato knife?'

I felt a sudden pang. 'Do you think I'm daft, Paola? That I should wait? Be cautious?'

'Come down later.' Her encouraging pat was more of a slap. 'It's not your doubts I'm interested in. Wails of *bambini* I'm expecting to hear.'

Her own *bambino* was cutting chips, when finally we reached Paola's shop that afternoon. Harry pulled a sherbet from his pocket, for which Assunta thanked him shyly. She'd grown into a pretty girl, with Pezzini traits pleasingly confused by Paola's complexion and liquorice-dark hair. She didn't guzzle her gift but deposited it in her satchel where she stored her rag-dolls and whichever book Giulio was reading to her. 'Would you like a shot at the chips?' she asked.

Harry laughed. 'I still bear the scar!'

'In that case,' said Paola, 'you can make yourself useful by explaining to the wee one about the English that we're fighting alongside, you being the only one she's ever met.'

To judge from Harry's face, even peeling might be preferable. Yet he went at it didactically, explaining about 1707 and the act uniting the two countries' parliaments, sounding distinctly like Giulio as he reached back to James VI and I, leaping forward to the different legal systems, churches, universities. 'And English folk are special in another way. For we believe . . . yes, we believe we are the centre of the world.'

'Funny,' said Paola, 'it's what we Italians think about the Scots.'

'I've seen that too, men in the pubs proclaiming how Scotland built the empire, how they'll win the next football World Cup, directors at work who pretend the entire insurance system grew out of Scotsmen's heads, how only Scots could have had the genius to make fortunes from others' vulnerability.' It was the longest speech I'd ever heard Harry make (Assunta must have been instructed to feign interest), and he'd only paused for breath: 'Scotsmen stake their claim, but Englishmen don't need to because they themselves are the centre. With the width of their bottoms, the way they look at darkies, how they draw their maps.' He looked around, suddenly self-conscious. 'If that makes any sense?'

'And now we're all in it together,' I said. 'All fighting the same war.'

'You should speak out more often,' said Paola, gauging the temperature on her frying fat. 'You don't want to be cramped by they Pezzini boys. Love the sound of their own voices, all three of them.' It was a shock to hear that anything could be true of all three *Pezzini boys*. 'Only be careful, now, not to sound unpatriotic.'

'What? Up here? They'd probably award me the St Andrew's Cross for abusing the English, or make me chief of some clan.'

'Anyway,' said Assunta, 'Harry's not English any more, he's one of us. And soon I'll have a wee cousin to play dollies with.'

Paolo's discomposure was pure Maclodio puppet theatre. 'What are you saying, child! They're not even engaged!'

Harry was laughing, nodding knowingly and laughing. 'Enough! *Basta*, as you say! I admit I've been a bit slow, when times are moving fast. Assunta is right.' From the pocket that had produced the sherbet he removed a box. 'I had thought somewhere more romantic . . .' On an azure velvet pad sat a ruby-and-diamond ring. Two customers held their order. 'Unless I should have asked Lucia's father first? I don't know how you Italians do things.'

Paola shook her head; her daughter shook her head.

'Won't you pick it up, my dear?'

I preferred to stretch the fingers of my left hand in the air. He took the ring and held it close to my eye: inscribed in tiny italics were the words *Alla mia sola Lucia.* 'I admit,' he said, 'I needed some help with the wording. And now I have to ask you . . .' He sounded as if he were about to speak Shakespearean; I half-expected him to call me *thee.*

'Yes?' Paola prompted.

'If you'll marry me?'

'The date?' Paola asked.

'Soon!' replied Assunta.

'There's my own family to tell,' said Harry, screwing up his face. 'How about . . . next summer?'

I threw my arms around him, as the customers—four of them by now—put hands together in silent applause.

The haddock, when Paola retrieved it, was charred.

In the evening, when he laid me across a desk in the Edinburgh Academy's 22C, I figured, with what common sense remained to me, that just because he was my official *fidanzato* (Papà approved, of course, Emilio and Dorothy were delighted, Giulio put on an amused impersonation of surprise) it did not mean my pleasure need be still more intense—though it was, and was again.

40

The fourth of September had yielded no Italian response to Britain's declaration of war, but this, said Dario, was hardly surprising: even the *Man of Destiny* (as his biographer had named him) needed time to deliberate. 'Anyway, he'd never be that stupid.'

I told him how McEwen had sidled close to me, whispering of how glad he was that we were 'all on the same side now'.

'Ignorant *porco*. He's praying the Duce will side with the Nazis. Knows nothing about Ciano and Grandi and their love of us British. How could the Duce cast his lot in with the Krauts? We'll soon have the Nazis beat, then the Duce at the winners' table, and this time there'll be no repeating the treachery of Versailles.'

Fifth of September, nothing, sixth, seventh, eighth, ninth—right through that first sermon preaching neighbourliness and into the next Sunday; the Archbishop voiced relief, given half his congregation was Italian. I so urgently wished to believe, to dispel the shadow over the congratulations I was receiving. But into the unreality of this not-yet-quite-war, events insisted on protruding their thorns. At the end of September, flattened against the window of the Palace, a map.

'Poland,' said Giulio.

The hands holding the map were visible, though the face was mercifully concealed . . . but only for a moment, before a gleeful McEwen tore Poland up and tossed the scraps in the air.

Mid-October, the *Royal Oak* was sunk by Captain Günther Prien, and the fact that his U-boat struck in what was a Scottish safe port, at Scapa Flow, rendered even crueller the death of over eight hundred sailors. We were reading about it on the way back to our respective offices, after lunch together at McVities. 'The counting of corpses,' said Harry. 'I'm afraid that's what war is all about. Men turned into numbers. Boys who've never known each other proving that nobody has a right to grow old. Not that I'm any different. I'd like to press a button and make all those damn Krauts disappear.'

'You think it would be better if women ran the show?'

He gave it some thought. 'Might be crueller. But more personal too?'

We were talking, sharing, in a way I'd never done with anyone except Giulio—not even with Valerio had I been able to say so much. 'I wish we could write to each other too,' I said, thinking aloud.

'Oh you Pezzinis, you're so dashed literary. What chance a poor semi-literate Cambridge graduate?'

Before I could reply, we both had our noses in the sky. Coming from the north, unlike anything previously heard, as if they had our names on them and would pursue us to our most private places . . . thundering up from the Forth at hypnotic speed came three gigantic aeroplanes, pursued like crows by mobbing sparrows—only here the sparrows were screaming too, with propellers.

'Spitfires!' Harry glowed. 'It's bad,' he followed coolly, as if noting an irregularity in an invoice. 'There should have been a siren.'

I covered my head as two German giants flew over, at no great height, their identifications clearly visible.

'Prang the blighters!' Harry cried, in a way that made me glad to be a woman—a woman walking out with a man. It lasted only seconds, long enough for me to cross myself twice. Then the planes veered east.

The next night, as we squeezed through the gap in the railings, Harry held a torch. The city was half-hearted in its attempt to respect the blackout, and automobile headlights cut like cinema projectors through the darkness. 'Look.' He unfolded *The Scotsman* on which I would shortly lie, illuminating the report of how Rosyth, across the Forth, had been the bombers' target; one of the JU-88s had been brought down near Port Seton, a few miles from the capital.

'*The first enemy aircraft destroyed by Fighter Command.*' He read it as if he had flown the Spitfire himself.

3 November

Dear Harry,

How could we marry without ever having written to each other? Only now, having started, I feel shy! I who am so brazen when you take me to the Edinburgh Academy . . .

So, what would I like to tell you?

I'd like to tell you how enchanted I was when you encouraged our boys in the Spitfires. I saw you wanted to be up there with them—not that I'd ever permit that!

I want to tell you how proud I am at McVities when I see the looks on Auntie Rebecca & Auntie Sandy. (You find it quaint that I call them *auntie*, while I pity your lack of aunties.) And speaking of *zie*, I look forward to taking you to Maclodio. It's nothing like the Tuscany you know, yet you'll eke out its charm & understand us better, our occasional heartlessness as well as our more tender side. I'll only be sad you won't meet Nonno.

I'd like you to know what happened that first time I saw you, how you took me from where I was locked & returned me to the world. And to words—including the ones you're reading now. You say this is no great merit on your part. But the merit is in being who you are.

I so like it when you let yourself think out loud, and want to hear you more and more. I want us to hang our blackout curtains together & if the bombs have to fall then I want us to share our fear as well. When I wear your ring, then all my cares dissolve.

Enough for a first shot? With lots & lots of love from

Your

Lucia

I had to wait for a reply: long enough for the War Office to declare there would be no mass internment of Germans; long enough for a bomb to fail to assassinate the Führer in a Munich beer hall (and for McEwen to chant 'Indestructible!' outside the Palace). I resisted thinking how replies had arrived faster from Rome, until finally came the much-awaited post.

29 November 1939

Dearest Lucia,

I am sorry to have been so slow to reply, but I have not wanted to offer lame excuses. I have only ever written letters to my parents, and those in order to disappoint them again (as when I chose Downing College over Pater's Magdalene or refused to go to Sandhurst). It was topping to learn of the expedition to the family seat in Maclodio. If only old Musso keeps his nose out of other people's business. As for your high estimate of me, maybe after you read what a poor hand I am at letters you will think again . . .?

I know you like a list so here goes. I dream of our playing on week ends and my teaching you the pleasure of hitting the ball squarely, of introducing you to my little sister and watching her fail to wrong-foot you in some ridiculous rule learnt from her latest guide to etiquette, and even to my parents despite their snobbish ways. And if none of that sounds much fun I also dream of such simple pleasures as watching you dress for dinner in the frock I shall have bought you, learning Italian as you order me to open my mouth wider to pronounce Al-lo-ra and even the punishments I shall receive with the tawse! Big family parties with lots of Italian fare and ice-cream and you feeding the little one—little ones!—with Assunta nodding approvingly and myself bearing no resemblance to the cold and forbidding figure I knew as a father, rather a real and caring person with foibles and weaknesses you have helped me to accept. And all the joyous things we shall do to make these 'wee yins' but which I would not dare commit to paper in case it falls into hands other than your own.

I can not pretend I am without worries. Your brothers tease me for being so poor in politics, yet everyone feels the darkness gathering. If the Duce is not sensible? If Hitler is not satisfied with his ill-gotten gains? If Stalin wants more than just his share of Poland? It is a very poor show that our lives may be in the hands of this triumvirate of hotheads (NB my Roman-sounding word!) next to whom Mr Chamberlain appears downright weedy and Mr Roosevelt indifferent. Let us never need to part except to go to work in the morning.

Your loving

Harry

PS. How did I do?

41

I'd never felt the absence of the Fascio so strongly as at Christmas, when even with the family swelled by Dorothy and Harry I felt marooned on an Italian atoll in an ocean of Scots. Where was Beppe? Where Signor Baldini and Ermanno and the wives with their births and baptisms and recipes and which new priest was prettiest? For nearly six months L'Italia Nostra had ceased circulation, its editors having packed up shop and retreated to Milan. It was as if every Italian in the neighbourhood, over the course of the year, had withdrawn: lips so tightened they looked almost Scottish; glances over the shoulder as if two might be a crowd and more than two a riot.

'Rabbits,' said Dario, referring not to Christmas lunch but to our community. 'Feart of their own shadows. We Italians should be speaking out now, especially now, to let the authorities know we've always been loyal to the British constitution.'

'Wouldn't swear to it,' Harry demurred. 'But from what I remember of my Tudor history, we don't actually have a constitution.'

'Constitution or no constitution, we're loyal to king and country.' Dario was evidently rattled. 'You'll be wanting to get the wedding over, Harry, in case you're called up?'

'We'll do it in our own time,' I said, 'thank you, Dario.'

He puffed up his cheeks and exhaled in a muted 'Porco!' Nodded theatrically, Duce-fashion. 'Now we see who'll be wearing the pantaloni! OK with you, Harry, having the wife make the decisions?'

Harry smiled. 'Uomo moderno. It's one of your dear wife's favourite expressions.' Wrong-footed, Dario darkened further at the sound of Dorothy's laughter.

'Hoping for snow?' I asked Giulio, who was staring out of the window.

'Hoping,' he said, 'just hoping.'

'As well you might,' said Dario, 'with rationing starting in a week.'

'Will it affect the Palace?' asked Dorothy.

'It might in the end,' said Giulio. 'But my suppliers are loyal.'

'And what they can't supply by the book . . .' Dario was beaming. 'Aye, but wait till the eggs and pistachios run short. Then we'll see who comes crying to big brother!'

'We'd better all prepare for the worst,' said Giulio. 'And hope the worst won't happen.'

I tried to do just that, even if it meant pretending to read newspapers from cover to cover, listening to the wireless in the Palace kitchen each spare minute, repeating the scraps that might have a bearing. Daily missives from Decio, endless talk with Carlo about how to bring the LIDU's activities to the attention of the authorities—and who exactly were these *authorities*? Emilio suggested contacting our local MP, placing an advertisement in *The Scotsman* pledging Italian allegiance to the nation, asking Dorothy's father to write to Bertrand Russell or George Orwell, mounting a petition to be signed by former Fascio members stating that the organization had only ever been a glorified social club and the trips to Rome just a chance to visit relatives. When he was turned down for ambulance duty, he wrote a poem of protest and sent it to *The Times Literary Supplement*, whose editor replied, doubting *the virulence of sentiment* as well as *the awkward use of terza-rima*. The danger was not for those of us born here, of course. The danger was for newcomers such as Carlo and Fausto who'd arrived since the Great War, for Italian standing in the city; for dignity, pride, prospects. Harry, grimacing, reported that his superior at work had asked if he was truly intending to 'marry a foreigner', and if he was sure it was wise 'from a career point of view'. A roster had been compiled of every citizen of foreign extraction, but enquiry at St Andrew's House yielded the assurance that it was only to prevent the muddle that had occurred in 1914. I knew I ought to remove the photograph of the Duce from above my bed, though to do so would be to admit that dressing up in gym slip and brandishing a bow and arrow were more than good clean fun.

Blackout had failed to dent the appetite for fried fish, to which Paola added onion rings, vegetable balls, fried pizza dough and different shapes of chip, not just the lardy chunks, like cobble-stones, served up elsewhere. She'd cut a fish-shaped hole in her blackout curtain, and through this clients would peer as if at some fairground peep show. After minutes in the queue, I felt the breath on my neck. 'Hey darlin, looks like we'll be together again soon.' The voice was so close, I didn't dare turn round. Something pricked my left hand, and when I glanced down I was holding a tie-pin in the form of a swastika—the shape had become so familiar to me that I even knew which way to turn it so its elbows pointed in the right directions. I refused to give him the satisfaction of seeing me wipe off the bead of blood.

'Pricked again, eh?'

Harry's eye turned from the peep-hole, and his hand reached instinctively out. 'I don't believe we've had the pleasure?'

'Nae pleasure for me.' He sounded more doggedly Scots than ever. He was wearing the black overcoat which once had looked smart, his arms held stiffly by his sides. 'It's beyond yer type to gee me any pleasure at all. Though no beyond the wee missus here.' There was whisky on his breath fit to overpower the shop vents.

'The problem being, my good sir, that I don't believe Lucia is inclined to give you anything, except permission to scarper.' As if on skates, Harry had slid between me and McEwen.

'And who's tae say she'll have the choice. When her Duce makes his move and the world comes tumblin doon around her ears.'

'We've heard all about you, Ewan, more than enough of your views.'

'But you heard o Dachau? Or Mauthausen?' His German sounded German. 'Cos that'll be the place for your type o Sassenach ponce. Ye'll be breaking rocks and growin thinner by the day. What you think I was up to during ma years away? Seen it all wi ma own two eyes.'

'I believe I said enough.' Harry had released my arm.

'Don't you fuckin tell me what to do!' His carrot skin had hardened to sea-urchin.

What happened next went so fast, I only understood it after. Harry leant his weight on his right leg, then released two punches, a left then a right, which flashed past McEwen's temples—barely grazing him—before he had time to blink, let alone raise a drunken defence. The fists, almost as quickly, returned to Harry's pockets, as he emitted a gentle laugh. 'Sassenach ponce perhaps, but Southern Schools Middleweight Champion none the less. You'll be a Schmeling supporter, I suppose. Me, I put my money on Joe Lewis.' With which he turned, re-linked his arm to mine, to lead me into Paola's shop.

'Boxing?' said Dario, later. 'Never seen him down the gym. Just as well as I couldn't be massacring my future brother-in-law.'

'Papà,' said Assunta, 'Harry wants me to play golf with him and Zia.'

'Golf!' She had a way of saying precisely what would irritate him.

'He says your big hero is a golfing man.' It was too much for Papà: his own daughter citing Harry on Ciano, the playboy of his dreams who had bagged Edda Mussolini. He slammed the door behind him.

'Is it true?' I asked my niece, 'Did Harry really say that?'

She had a guilty look. 'But I wanted to ask you something secret.' There was no trace of Italian in her accent. 'Two thingummies.' Since Harry had entered my life, I'd seen less of her, except at Mass. What could be so secret? 'Is it right it was you who called me *Assunta*?'

I knew better than to ask who had told her, past master as she already was at *she says he says*. 'It was your Mamma and me together. You seemed such a godsend and we were more religious in those days.'

'So it's not for something nasty Mamma did?'

'Is that your second thingummy?' I didn't like the sound of it: who could have told her anything so compromising?

'No. Can I borrow your catapult?'

I was too shocked to heed my own wisdom. 'Who says I own a catapult? Who's been telling you tales?' I could think of only one person, though I told myself not to panic. Assunta squirmed by the fire, tying and untying her shoes.

'I heard it's really strong and dangerous.'

'Who told you?' The higher the volume, the less likely I was to learn. 'Was it Harry? Giulio? Somebody else?'

'Are you angry with me? Please, Zia Lucia, show me how to work it.'

My childhood catapult was stored beside the model which bore my initials on its wooden handle. I told myself I ought to be glad to keep a family tradition alive—maybe one day I'd teach my own daughter. 'Here it is,' I said, 'The very one I used when I was your age. But it really is dangerous.'

'I want dangerous.'

'But we're here to protect you.'

'Not against the Germans. Against the Germans we all have to be brave, I heard it on the wireless.'

Something told me I should press harder, but my niece's little hands were feeling the shaft and fingering the leather tab. The missile would find me . . . And there it was, on the mantelpiece, a pebble holding down my newspaper clippings.

'Come to the open window.' I hadn't fired a single shot since that final occasion with Nonno. 'See the Anderson shelter? Well, imagine there's someone down there we don't like, he doesn't have to be a German as they'll never get this far. Picture him? Here goes . . .' The shaft in my right hand, pebble snug in the left, the back yard flat as a stage set . . . until perspective abruptly returned. I stretched my arms, pulled back, took aim.

'Ahh! Shit!' I tried to remember to breathe through the pain as
I figured out that the rubber had snapped. Assunta was wailing, her
arms round my waist. 'Look! Is it still there?'

'It's mighty red.'

I let myself slump to the floor, now I knew I'd not go blind.
Even laughed. 'So that's the first lesson, check your equipment.'

'It's angry,' said Assunta, 'for being neglected so long.'

At work, the black eye drew titters and stares. 'Strange ways, these
Italians,' a clerk whispered. 'Not so different from Scotsmen,' came
the response.

The eye was still smarting when, on 9 April, Mr Morton summoned his staff, after closing the doors to customers. Carrying a
metal ruler and a clipboard, he more than ever resembled his office
portraits. Like schoolchildren awaiting a scolding, we tried to find
our balance in the echoing marble of the bank's central hall. 'An era
has come to a close,' he began, 'and another is commencing. Today,
as I just learnt from Central Office, Denmark and Norway were
invaded by the Nazis. None of us should presume that this conquest,
if it occurs, will satisfy Nazi ambitions. Our customers will expect
the worst, and your job will be to calm their nerves in coming days
and weeks. Even the smallest saver is an investor, whose investment
is better protected by the Royal Bank than by a mattress or hat box.'
The longer he talked, the more military he sounded. 'To your posts,'
he ordered, clicking heels together. 'And may God be with all of us
who fight for justice and democracy!' He almost had to stoop to
pass through the doorway, so tall had he grown. A round of applause
followed him in.

The following day, as predicted, queues formed for withdrawal,
with counsel proffered which featured the name 'Winston' and the
reassuring resonance of 'First Lord of the Admiralty'. Narvik had
brought victory, so the Germans were not invincible; ships sunk on
both sides, planes downed. When Winston's plans foundered and
retreat from Norway became imminent, Harry joked to me, 'What
if we organized for you to assassinate Adolf with your catapult?' I

sat up and stared. 'Yes,' he said, 'I've seen Assunta trying it, the one with your initials. She's got a lot to learn.'

I told myself not to be alarmed, stay rational. 'If I could fill a pebble with all our fear and hatred, all Adolf's done to those poor Poles.' I tried not to think of Valerio. 'Squeeze into it every poor Norwegian. Launch it at his forehead . . .'

'Or at the Duce?'

Was he testing me? Was Harry-of-the-very-English-name testing Lucia-whom-Donizetti-stole-from-Sir-Walter? 'Hang on a moment,' I told him, pulling back the curtain onto my recess that I always kept closed when he was visiting. 'Take a look at this.' I unhooked the photograph, framed and under glass.

'But you look so adorable! So edible in your little gymslip!' For a moment, I was almost jealous of the girl on the photo. 'Not the Duce, then. No one who can dream up such uniforms.'

Now I was jealous of my uniform. 'I should hide it, just in case, don't you think?'

'Hide it with me! I'll hang it in my bedroom.'

'Fine,' I said, replacing it on its hook, wondering why I felt anything but fine. 'I'll give it to you soon enough.'

42

War could not, simply could not, go so badly so fast. Despite his bold pronouncements, power slipped from Mr Chamberlain's hands. I tried to draw some comfort from the fact that the new Prime Minister had until so recently been Mussolini's admirer; and a little more from the local lad, Sir John, who was at his side. Harry's hopes for the Maginot Line evaporated in days, not months, as the German tanks drove through the Ardennes, and the Low Countries fell. But as the French government withdrew from Paris and the Expeditionary Force was cornered, cut off, forced to retreat to the coast, all I could do was scrutinize Giulio's face for signs of reassurance, as he attempted to sustain a smile for customers. For as long as the Duce had not pronounced, we'd be waiting. It was like watching a storm break over Fife, when the south wind reminded us that our own rain would have a different source . . .

Until the waiting—*our* waiting—was over.

'Read it!' Dario ordered. 'Forget the fucking translation, what does the Englishman care what the Duce says.'

Giulio was in such a funk that he obeyed him, before catching himself and continuing in English for Harry and Dorothy. Even as he spelt out the news whose consequences could not be calculated, I could not help noting how my brother had advanced—my brainy brother—since the opening of the Fascio when he'd stumbled to find equivalents for the Consul's pomposity. He'd received the briefing one hour earlier, from Carlo who'd received it from Decio. For the first time since Assunta's birth, he had closed the Palace early, sent Fausto through the early-evening sunlight to fetch the family for its gravest *chiacchierata*. Had *this* Scotsman been told? Had *that* Scotsman heard the wireless? No need to ask the Italians, for as if by telepathy all knew the news; all were thinking that this 10 June was the day when they'd declared war on themselves.

'Let them punish me,' Papà groaned, 'if they must punish someone. I'm the one responsible.'

'Listen,' said Giulio unnecessarily—the Palace felt cold, despite the warmth of the evening—'Here's what Muss said. *An hour struck with destiny is in the skies of our Patria. A declaration of war has been sent to the ambassadors of Great Britain and France. We are joining a field of battle against plutocratic and reactionary democracies.*' Never had I seen this look on my brother's face. 'More rubbish about revolution and the struggle of the poor. Then *This is the battle for fertile young peoples against the sterile ones who are destined to decline.*'

'He's got a point there,' said Dario, as if commenting on the football scores.

'Then, *Let us salute the Führer with our shouts, leader of our great German ally.*'

'I know someone who'll be crowing,' remarked Dario, almost enviously.

'*Italia has stood up a third time, strong, proud, and united as never before.* What were the first two times, dammit?'

'Spare us the rest,' said Emilio. 'In any case we're British. Some of us have never even been to Italy.'

'They can't be planning reprisals,' said Dorothy. 'Ours, as the Duce reminds us, is a *democracy.*'

'Even the wives of the Germans,' Fausto put in, who normally would speak only when spoken to.

'And the first two times?' I needed to know, for some reason.

'Obvious,' said Dario. '*Primo*, the Glorious March on Rome, *secondo*, the victory in Abyssinia.'

'Shouldn't we be doing something?' Harry asked. 'I don't know, offering your services—our services. There's supposed to be some Civil Defence Force.'

'It's our Scotsman Mr Anderson,' I said, 'who's in charge of it.'

'As he will be,' Giulio added, 'of any one of us judged to be an *enemy alien.*'

We'd heard the words applied to Austrians, Germans, Czechs. This was the first time the words' long finger pointed at us. 'But Lord Rothermere,' I said inconsequentially, 'is the Duce's greatest fan. Support from him, surely, and his *Daily Mail*?'

'Surely,' Harry agreed.

Giulio stubbed out the cigarette that he never normally permitted himself in the Palace. '*The order of the day is a definite word, for all of us an imperative.*'

'Let me guess,' sighed Emilio.

'*Vincere*! At which, says the report, the crowd cheered ecstatically on the piazza.' Every one of Giulio's words was a gobbet of rage.

'Please,' groaned Emilio. 'Is that it? No more!'

When we left the Palace, near midnight, no one cared to disperse. We crossed the street and stared into the shop, inspecting it more closely than since the day of the gala opening. Wordlessly, we went our several ways.

If Giulio slept, in Papà's armchair, it can only have been during the half hour I permitted myself to nod off. Dawn surprised us both, rising so early, and we had to go to work, just like yesterday. Mr Morton smiled from the entrance to the bank, and if with more determination than joy, this was normal: the nation was alone against the foe—since yesterday more alone than ever. No one quite believed that valour and the small ships alone had averted catastrophe at Dunkirk, and many said Adolf was about to drive his bargain, the price of which throbbed through the head when the head was not fighting on the beaches and never surrendering.

I broke early for lunch and headed straight back down to the Palace. On the way, my newsagent refused to sell me a *Daily Mail*, saying it was a 'bloody disgrace what's written there about yous Eyeties'. I told myself there was nothing sinister about the stillness behind the brightly polished glass. Giulio looked up from his counter. 'Quiet today,' I said, for want of better.

'Lunchtime,' he mumbled.

'Better tell me.'

He dipped a spoon in Vanilla, and when he raised it to his mouth, I was reminded of how I would receive the host. 'Carlo telephoned Decio. The arrests have begun.'

'But not of British citizens?'

'Not yet. People on the Fascio lists. Men. I don't imagine Dario ever removed me or Emilio, despite our requests. He's probably busy trying to get himself onto Bastianini's roster.'

'Slow down,' I pleaded, putting my hand on his. Bastianini had replaced Count Grandi as Ambassador, this much I knew.

'The Ambassador's gathering the big-wig Italians he wants repatriated, in some exchange deal. A ship awaits them in the Clyde, so he must have seen it coming.'

'And Decio?' This distant figure was no longer just the person to whom I indirectly owed Harry; he was a source of information that offered the fragile chance of staying one step ahead.

'He's not been back to Italy for over thirty years. Been fighting the Fascists for almost as long. He was heading to his Labour Party Office to pledge his support.'

When the door opened, it was the Angel, up early by her standards. She didn't head for her usual booth, but took one of the stools at the counter, where Giulio placed a Cinnamon ice before her. 'How long you been running the Palace, Giulio?'

'Nine years. What's on your mind?'

'It's made a difference, you ken. Wanted to tell you . . . in case. For those of us, Scots folk included, who didn't have a place to feel comfy.'

'Kind of you to say so.' Giulio wiped imaginary crumbs from the spotless marble counter. 'Why *in case*?'

'I heard the men-folk gabbing last night after the pubs were out and the news went around. Put a pint of beer in a Scotsman's gut and if he's no ready to take on Adolf single-handed, he's right for a bit of local bother.' His eyes appealed to her to reveal all she knew. 'And Paola's Fry down the road . . . Such a braw fish she fries, and all.'

'I'll go by to see Paola,' I said as I left. 'But I'll be back down at five, with Harry.' I didn't like what the Angel said as I was leaving:

'If you run into your other brother . . .?'

'Emilio?'

'He'll no be much use. The other yin, the big yin.' She knew his name, of course, but wished to avoid any hint of intimacy. 'You should tell him to get down here.'

I nodded to Giulio, who nodded stiffly back. As I forced my legs down Annandale Street, I told myself that I did not know, only feared, that by the end of this day much would be altered. What could happen, after all? Giulio would be fine, Harry would be here—he was not going anywhere except, when we met after work, into my arms.

I thought I'd be entering Paola's Neapolitan Fry, but instead walked into Maclodio. Paola had shed her Edinburgh veneer and was back on her hillside choosing which sheep to slaughter first. She always kept her hair tied up at work, now it was loose. The knife in her hand was much longer than required by potatoes; the eyes on the fish she'd gutted looked grateful to have been dealt with decisively. Echoes were audible of Beppe's songs of blood, treachery, eternal feud.

'Mustn't show them we're nervous,' she said. I dared not ask who exactly *them* referred to. 'You did right to give Assunta your weapon. She feels stronger with it.'

It was my chance to ask the question I'd failed to finish with my niece. 'I didn't give her the catapult, she must have taken it herself. You've never seen her . . . talking to anyone strange?' Paola looked me hard in the eye, then spat into her sink. 'I'll come back down after work. With Harry.'

For want of sheep, Paola returned to potatoes. 'Don't you try to help Dario,' she warned. 'They'll need him in Abyssinia.' With her thumb, she was unconsciously stroking the finger which once her ring encircled. 'Or in the Alps to kick poor France in the kidney.'

43

Outside McVities for my five o'clock appointment, it was rare for Harry to make me wait. But if there were jitters with savings, then a rush for insurance was probable. After twenty minutes, a young man I recognized, one of Harry's staff, came to say that my fiancé had been detained, that he'd meet me later at the Ice Palace.

My frustration dissipated by the pleasure of *fiancé*, I cut down Hanover Street and along to York Place. Two neighbours failed to hail me with their usual 'How you doin, hen?'—gazes turned towards the cobblestones. The closer I came to Annandale Street, the more anxious I became. Boys from other parts of town were roving in shirtsleeves, sharing conniving glances. Mr Taylor from downstairs was haranguing one of them, waving his arms, until he was pushed and almost fell. When he saw me, he signalled to keep moving. My stomach was in spasm by the time I reached the Palace. The *CLOSED* sign was up, door locked, blinds down as if someone had died. I banged on the door as if I were being chased, and when I looked behind me, there was indeed a cluster, one or two customers I recognized in the maroon of the Hearts. So used was I to dreading one particular figure, I almost thought I was imagining them . . . until the door opened abruptly and Fausto stared at them too. He pulled me inside.

'*Scusami, signorina*, but I don't like what I see.'

I turned to Giulio behind the counter . . . but no Giulio, only Fausto, alone, stripped down from his usual smart jacket to singlet, braces, knuckles—cracking. 'But where is everyone? I can't believe Giulio's deserted the Palace at a time like this.'

Fausto beckoned towards the booth he usually shared with Carlo. Outside, the sun was blazing: on a bright June afternoon, there should be another six hours of customers queuing. 'You will understand.' Fausto sat opposite me. 'At four o'clock, Carlo comes round. None of the men are at work.'

I stared back at him. 'You're at work.'

'This is no work. This is home. Carlo tells Giulio that many are already taken by police. Every man between eighteen and sixty.'

'But Giulio's British!'

Fausto released the two words I dreaded: '*Il Fascio.*' I wished to object that Giulio . . . that Emilio . . . that 1924 was not . . . But if Fausto was no policeman, still less was he Mr Anderson who had set his force upon us. 'Carlo is here just a minute, but Giulio is wondering what to do when Dario arrives. He has a tip-off from PC O'Donnell that they come for your family at eight this evening, starting here, then going to your home. Dario says, or go into hiding or be taken.'

I must have been silent for over a minute as I slammed this information against my brain. 'Giulio must hide! And Emilio!'

'Emilio is with his wife at home. He says for him no running. He doesn't fear a few nights in a cell. Says the father-in-law will help.'

Emilio's reaction calmed me long enough for embarrassment. 'But what about you, Fausto? No passport . . .?' My voice was rising again. 'What about you?'

'I'll no be leaving here.' He shook his heavy head. 'Not *volontariamente.* This is more to me than belongings.' His right arm pointed round the room.

'But what shall we do? Who'll run the Palace?' As if in answer, there was a rattle at the window. When we raised the blinds, two groups of men were on the opposite pavement, six or seven in each. 'Let's offer them ice-cream. What can they have against us? Half of them are customers.' Fausto went to unlock the door. 'Wait a second! Where are the police?'

'You think police will help? They're too busy uprounding us.' Fausto opened the door and stood before the windows; even his broad shoulders could not span them. 'What you wanting, lads?' he shouted. 'After some ice-cream?' Addressed directly, the men were shifty, as if unsure of why they were present. 'What flavours you like?'

'Raspberry!' somebody exclaimed, before receiving a kick from one of his companions.

'Don't be shouting at us, you fucking tarrie!'

'Fucking wop tarrie traitor!' came from the second group.

'What we do to you?' Fausto threw out. 'We hate the Mussolini much more than you do. Why you think we leave Italy?'

'They Pezzini boys are the ones what started that club!' The voice belonged to one of the Mosley gang.

'Those days are long gone. Is Giulio the boss here. He works to stop the Duce. Look.' Fausto signalled. 'Here's his sister. She knows how you feel, it breaks her heart, how Italy goes making war. All we do here is give pleasure.'

I was turning my head from one group to the other, nodding in between, as if by the intensity of my stare I could stop what had to happen next.

'We bring out the basins and you help yourselves. How's it sound?' From the way they looked to one another, weighing, shrugging, it sounded good enough—a bumper punnet in exchange for an imagined injury. Then:

'Sounds like a fuckin insult, that's how it sounds!' Head to toe in black, he was suddenly between the two groups; first time I'd seen a true smile on his face since before the assault. 'They ought to be congratulated, boys,' he laughed, 'for finally makin up their minds.' He was pacing between the groups, uniting them by an invisible thread. 'So now they've thrown their lot in with Adolf. But only once the Nazis have gone and done the hard bit. And they'd win us off wi sweeties! With ice-creams!'

I looked down the street for support, but there were only heads, poking out from tenement windows: couldn't afford the pictures, but hoping for an early-evening show.

'But do we need their invitation, lads? Do we need their dirty Duce to be tellin us what to do? When we can help ourselves?'

A cry went up, like the roar from Easter Road stadium. In his hand was a missile. As he advanced across the street, Fausto moved towards him. The two groups converged, then someone grabbed my arm, dragging me aside; to protect me, Fausto would have to leave the Palace window unguarded. 'Just yous move oot the way now, tarrie-boy, and no harm'll come to the little *signorina*—or should I say *signora?*'

'Aught happen to her, you're a dead man.'

He paused to register. 'Gently, boys, gently.' I was being frog-marched across the road.

'You have to kill me anyway,' Fausto spat.

'That'll no be necessary. The cops'll be doing it for us. Winston's order, you ken?' The brick was above his head.

The noise that followed, of plate glass shattering, was what he'd been craving all his life; he would have willed us build the Palace in order to hear it.

Treacle toffees, aniseed balls, jelly babies, jujubes—all the jars containing them. Then the ice-creams, the counter stools, the *ICE PALACE* aprons, the wireless, the cash till, the tables, goblets con-fectioner's cones: stock still, I could hardly even register as the Palace was emptied. First, having climbed through the window frame, they went at it with the quiet efficiency of experienced removers. Work-ing on movables, they formed a line, passing objects from hand to hand. At the end of the line, a cart. I knew I should leave, it could only turn worse. 'Go!' I told Fausto. 'There's nothing you can do.'

'Go where? What's left?'

As the last of the movables turned into immovables, I had no answer to offer. Marble sinks, brass taps, wall mirrors, Neapolitan majolica tiles, cement floor tiles, glass cabinets, blenders . . . The cart was overflowing, but the men were frustrated at how reluctantly tiles and marble were yielding to fingers and knives.

'That's it, boys. We've all that's worth the takin.' He picked up a length of heavy copper piping. 'Yous lads are mostly too wee to mind their Duce's speciality when he was your age. Canna put a name to it, something like *magello*. To you and me a *cudgel*.' Which he pro-ceeded to bring down on what remained of the glass cabinets.

Seizing whatever could serve as a club, his followers did their best to imitate, mustering force as they threw themselves into the task, impervious to ricochets, even hurling plates at Emilio's cornice. They squealed and shrieked as they clubbed. What took sixteen months to create took fifteen minutes to destroy. 'And now,' he shouted, when the muscles were weary, 'a little bonfire?'

'Leave it at that, boss,' said an Irish voice. 'Don't need the firemen messed up in this.'

Fausto pulled on my arm to lead me away.

'Be seeing each other soon, Lucia! Once the men-folk are all locked away inside!'

He had ceased to scare me, but I was so nauseous that I had to pause. 'My photograph!' I whispered, remembering. 'They'll find it . . . we'll be ruined.'

Fausto kept pace with me as far as Broughton Street. Then, to a solemn '*Arrivederci*', we embraced for the one and only time.

'Where is he?' I snapped, before I was through the door.

But Papà had sunk so deep into his armchair that he might have been down a pothole. 'Should have died with Mamma. Rather than this disgrace. My own sons . . . hunted like animals.'

'And Paola?' I asked, ashamed to have forgotten her. 'And Assunta? Papà, speak to me!'

'Or taken her with me when your Nonno left, we could have hidden in his cave. Forty years I live here . . .'

I checked what Giulio had taken: some clothes, spare shoes . . . so he wasn't intending to sit around and be captured. 'I can't believe it,' I moaned to Papà, 'that our own Mr Anderson, who pardoned those assassins and thought up the shelters . . .' I climbed into my recess, pulled the back off the frame within which was my photograph, rolled it into a tube. 'Where will he hide?' I asked.

'He's gone, gone, *è partito*.'

'I know he's gone, Papà, but he can't have gone far. He'll want me to go to him. Harry can help.'

'Harry!' he repeated, lucid for an instant. 'Yes, Harry.'

44

I did no more than nod to the other Italian women—the mothers, sisters, daughters—who were wringing hands and shedding tears on the street. The windows were smashed on Signor Baldini's shop, the Italian drinks store gutted, and it was still only 7 p.m. I tried not to imagine what the cover of night might bring, thanked the June sun which would barely have time to set. I needed to find my brother before he went to ground for however long it would take to sort out the misunderstanding—for that was what it had to be, a misunderstanding: I'd read Sir John on civilians' rights in *The Scotsman*; Carlo had cited habeas corpus, and I'd explained the Latin. For a second, it occurred to me that Giulio might have taken sanctuary in the Royal Park at Holyrood where in olden times the law could not venture. Then, at the junction of Broughton Street and York Place, wondering where to start, I suddenly knew how to find him, ran the sixty yards, dashed up the steps of St Mary's—in his moment of need he'd have remembered the faith Mamma always wished for him. One of the more athletic priests was minding the door. Inside were thirty, maybe fifty women, most on their knees, several clawing at the hem of the Archbishop's robe, pleading for his assistance. As soon as I saw them, I knew I'd not find Giulio . . . though here was Ermanno, and over in the shadows of the transept was Beppe. He shook his head as I approached.

'What has the Archbishop said?' I asked him.

'We can stay here for now, he'll do what he can. But the round-up is going on all over the country.' Beppe was tapping his forehead. 'If I'm going to be locked up, better be with the other men. What more can they do to us? Just needed to catch my breath. They gave my neighbour no time to pack, dragged him off screaming and kicking.'

'They won't hold you long, Beppe.'

'I never once sang "Giovinezza". Not once.'

'Nor "Little Black Face".' The very name made me quake. Little Wop Face now.

The saints were smiling down; a special evening prayer service was announced. My lungs were set to explode when I surged back out into the evening sunlight. I cursed my fancy for obscuring what was perfectly obvious: Harry's junior had said my fiancé had been detained, and Giulio had gone up to meet him, counting on his pal for a hideaway. I dashed up to George Street, incredulous at young couples strolling, clerks on benches enjoying the warmth as they leafed through the sports pages of the *Evening News*. The undeviating straightness of George Street seemed an insult, the lack of apocalyptic aeroplanes in the sky. The massive doors of Standard Life were shut, but I rang the bell and after a minute appeared a janitor.

'I'm looking for Mr Harold Moore.' I had never called him *Harold* before, it only added to the alarm.

'There's nobody here now, ma'am, except the cleaners.'

It occurred to me that if Harry were harbouring Giulio, then he'd not be broadcasting the fact. 'Could you take a look and check? Tell him it's his fiancée.' He looked doubtful, but decades of obedience obliged him to nod and withdraw.

'Crivens, Lucia, is that you?' At last one other person, not Italian, whose face reflected my feelings.

'Auntie Rebecca . . .' I accepted her embrace. 'What on earth are we going to do? They destroyed the Palace.'

'I was just on my way to see you all.'

'There's no *us all*. Only me and Papà left.'

'And it's happening elsewhere. All the Austrians and Germans, including the women and the ones who escaped here.'

'I'm sorry, ma'am,' said the janitor, reappearing. 'It's as I said. Mr Moore left over an hour ago.'

'Where can he be? When I need him most?'

'You tried his home?' asked Auntie Rebecca.

'What an idiot! I'm that scared of his landlady.' No time to explain how his home was just a place to which he reluctantly retired after pleasure, to be spied on by a resentful ogre. But if Harry could sneak my brother past that scrutiny, then they'd be secure for a while.

'And Paola? Has her shop survived?'

'I don't know, I haven't had time. It's all happened so fast.'

Of course the witch was leaving, exactly as I needed not to happen, just as I arrived at number 42, crocodile-skin handbag over her arm, the seams on her stockings not quite straight. 'What can I do for you?' said Mrs Richards (with stress on the *you*).

I thought of pushing past her, thought of punching her—what did I care, if Harry was inside. 'I'm here to see Harry. Is he in?'

'I believe I heard him arrive.'

I tried to conceal my relief. 'I won't be staying long.'

'Indeed you will not!'

'I am his fiancée!'

Disapproval dripped off her nose as she held the front door open. 'I shall be back in one hour.' It was clear she was going out for the evening. 'I imagine, with what your countrymen have been up to, you'll have business of your own to attend to.' She would have liked to add her handbag to the cudgels against the Palace.

But what did it matter, Harry was here, and with any luck he had Giulio hidden with him. I tapped lightly on his door, and when there was no reply, I turned the handle softly. I stepped inside, knowing I ought not to feel like a burglar. The hideous porcelain milkmaid, the couch before which I'd kneeled to take him in my mouth . . .

Now I was worried about giving him a fright, as I tried to walk naturally through the room towards his hall. The bathroom door was open, but nobody inside. From the bedroom came noises. I didn't stop to ask myself what they might mean. Gently, I pushed his bedroom door and stepped inside. And here was Harry all right, with his shirt still on but his trousers off, pushing face down on his bed.

Yes, Harry with his shirt on but his trousers off . . . muttering, 'Oh you beauty . . . oh you beauty . . .'

Beneath him, a noise not so very different from the noise I made myself, coming from a body almost concealed by the quilted sails into which it was being pressed. The mandarin lamp, its shade revolving. Odd, I thought, that a woman would permit herself such hairy legs in a moment like this.

Then observation stopped. Everything stopped. I knew there had to be some mistake, but was ignorant where to find it. Controlling his panting long enough to speak, my brother's face looked up at me. 'Oh my god, Lucia.' It can only have lasted seconds, my standing there. But I knew it would last for ever.

Harry held his hands over his eyes as he wriggled free, as if what he could not see could not be seen. As I retreated out of the bedroom, I told myself I must have known such things were possible, between men.

45

Thoughts, as I wandered the streets, were either so numerous that they blotted one another out, or so few that my head felt like a baby's rattle which had lost half its dried peas. My feet kept moving for fear that, if they stopped, I'd have to admit that what I had stumbled upon was real. I did not understand why I was still carrying the photograph of the Duce, yet I could not abandon it. Faces approached and several spoke, but I did not slow or respond.

Then a face refused to let this face past. 'Evening there, Miss Pezzini.' However I responded, it was not with words. 'Can see you're upset.' The face peered harder. 'You recognize me? PC O'Donnell?'

Did I recognize him? I repeated the question to myself.

'We've got Emilio. But the other one—not Dario, the other one, he's not at your home and he's not at the Palace—what remains of it.'

The Palace . . . what remains of it.

'He wouldnae be wanting to leave his wee brother all alone in the cell, now would he? Better it be me who takes him in than one of my heavy-handed Proddy colleagues.'

'Forty-two Northumberland Street, ground-floor flat.'

'What? That's where I'll find him?'

I could still take it back. In a clearing through the fog, I saw that. But I nodded instead. 'He's with a pal of his there.' I passed him the photograph of the Duce. 'You'll be wanting to take me in too.'

'I wouldn't be showing that round,' he advised, rolling it back up and returning it to me. 'We're not after the women. Don't you be worrying, I'll look after the brothers.' The wail of black marias was audible in the distance. 'And you take care of yourself, a night like this.'

However long I walked, it was not long enough, while the sun declined but refused to set. Then, without my noticing, it was almost dark, as dark as it would go so close to midsummer. I was on Leith Walk, not far from Paola's Fry. I remembered, from another life, feeling anxious, even guilty, not to have checked how she was faring. Turned automatically into Annandale Street. Outside the ransacked remains of the Palace, a few folk stood staring. I crossed to the other side of the street and kept my head down. The noise level was rising as I rounded the bend to where I could discern Paola's voice. 'Come here then! You want to try me?' I quickened my pace. 'Come on, what you waiting for?' Through the twilight, I could make out a group of maybe half a dozen men.

'You fucking tarries!' one of them shouted.

'You gone off my fish, then? Thought you liked my onion fritters.'

'How the fuck she recognize me?'

Paola was in front of her shop with her apron off, her hair unruly, and in her hand was the axe she used for splitting kindling.

'Where's Ewan?' asked another voice. A third man held a stone and made as if to throw it . . . but Paola did not flinch.

'My men are all gone,' she shouted. 'And I don't care if I go too. But I'm taking one of you with me, I swear you!'

'Sounds like she's in earnest.' There was fear mixed in to the mocking tone.

'Arms like cables wi guttin all they fish.'

'Call Ewan, get him to do it if he's that keen.'

'Always did like her chips.' They failed to see me approach, jumped when they saw the blankness on my face. I stood next to Paola as the gang retreated to the far pavement.

'Come inside a second,' she commanded. Then withdrew like a bull-fighter, never taking her eyes off the street, not even when inside the shop, on which the blackout curtain was ripped. 'I can stop them,' she breathed.

'It's all gone.' My voice was hollow as a ghost's. 'I betrayed my brother to the police.'

'Quit your havering. Giulio and Emilio had decided to turn themselves in. Here, take this.' She handed over the most lethal of her gutting knives, short but razor sharp. 'Pull yourself together.'

'Where's Assunta?'

'I sent her home, but she didn't want to go. I know she's out there somewhere. She saw the Palace. You've got to find her. Do that for me, do it for Giulio.'

I had just enough sense left to think it was an odd thing to say. 'I'll do it for us all. For myself.' I slipped the knife inside the rolled-up photograph.

'Be careful,' Paola ordered, as we left the shop and she re-assumed her guard in front of the window.

I was almost home when I spotted my niece, back turned at the entrance to a tenement close. From her left hand the catapult was dangling, while her whole body shook with her attempt to escape the fingers clasping her right wrist. Though the body attached to her was in shadow, I knew whose fingers they were . . . and what I had to do. It was almost a relief to stop thinking about myself, what had been my life, my hope. He had always been there, with his loathing. Had I tried hard enough to fathom it? Understood anything at all? Too late for that now.

'He called me over here,' stammered Assunta through the tears, as she turned and saw me. 'But I can take care of myself.'

'Away you run home,' I said. 'Your Mamma sent me to tell you that you're to go and look after Nonno. You're a big girl now the men-folk are gone, and big girls have responsibilities.' Still the hand did not release.

'Me?' she asked, ageing five years in five seconds.

'You, *cara*. Away and make him some tea. I'll have a word with this man here, it's really me he's wanting to see.'

Finally, the hand let go, allowing Assunta to back away slowly. 'It's no the first time he's speaking to me.' Then she took to her heels.

I admitted to myself my error: of course I should have probed, should have doubted, should have known. But if not for so much else, for this there was time. 'So where will it be, eh, Ewan?'

'Wherever you like it, darlin. I've been waitin long enough.'

'Would you rather call me *Fraulein*?'

He was laughing as I led him through the darkened close to the tenement's back yard. I would have liked to take him to our favourite brick wall, but that might give him time to think.

'Lovely lassie,' he grunted, 'that Assunta'   and his breath, for once, released no alcohol.

I smiled, glad of that: I wanted him to know what was happening.

'But this is a fair exchange.'

'Lovely she is, Ewan.' We faced each other. I measured the distance between us. 'And lovely she will remain.'

46

For forty-eight hours straight I hunted, passing from police station to police station, to prison, to Scottish Office, back to prison, back to police station. When I told Mr Morton what had happened to the Palace, he ordered me to take a week off work, found it hard to hold back his tears. 'I am ashamed of my compatriots, Miss Pezzini. Humbled and ashamed. Thank the Good Lord your sister-in-law stood up for herself, saved one of the properties.'

PC O'Donnell confirmed, when he saw the state I was in, that first he'd taken the two of them to the station on Saunders Street. Harry had not objected, and had even (claimed the PC) addressed him in Italian. After 'the Sassenach' was released, he didn't know where my brothers had been shifted, along with hundreds of other men, women too, Germans and Austrians, moved, as he put it 'in a giant game of tiddlywinks'. I believed him: what did he have to gain by lying to me? Dorothy, meanwhile, was pursuing her own dead ends, cursing her father for not pulling sufficiently important strings.

The short man who delivered the matchbox wore a cloth cap and smelt of camphor; inside the box, a coded note. When I put half a crown in his outstretched palm, he said, 'Another yin and I'll tell you where he is.' When I paid him, he told me, 'Both the spics are in Donaldson School for the Deaf, though nobody kens for how much longer.'

I forced myself to read:

I know what I've done is unforgivable, but please let me talk to you. Your more-than-ever Giulio

Now I understood where to go, I couldn't get myself out of the house. Papà had taken to bed, the armchair not sufficing for the supine state he craved. Paola had found time to pay for joiners to board up what remained of the Palace. It was she who laid out the *Evening News* where McEwen's death was announced—not front-page headlines, but it had made page four. *Edinburgh Man Murdered.* The subtitle drew ghoulish grins from her: *Political Assassination or Gangland Slaying?* The text was riddled with inaccuracies and speculation: the gashes were a sign he'd been interrogated . . . the crime had happened in the early morning . . . he had bled to death slowly . . . the Swastika pin I had fixed to his cheek was indication that a rival cell within the Fifth Column had eliminated him, a clue confirmed by the copies of *Mein Kampf*, the Nazi tracts and posters, which the police had unearthed in his squalid digs. His father was quoted as saying his son 'had reaped what he had sown'.

Paola kissed the blade of her knife as she lifted it from the kitchen range where, after scrupulous rinsing, I had left it. '*Brava!*' her sole comment.

A thousand questions, insistent as fleas, were assailing me, beginning with 'Paola, did you know . . .?' I was lucid enough to admit to myself that I was humiliated even more by my ignorance than by what I had witnessed between brother and lover; lucid enough, just, to wonder whether *ignorance* was quite the right term surely I had known, if I had just been frank enough with myself. Instead of questions, I took pen and paper, hesitating only because I had never written to a Knight before.

6 Broughton Street
Edinburgh
14 June 1940

Dear Sir John,
Forgive my writing to you when you must be a very busy man, but desperate straits urge desperate measures.

I tried to imagine what Giulio would have written next—the Giulio I knew. I was almost sure he would not waste words on regret that the Germans were about to march into Paris, but would move straight to the point.

I have followed your glorious career with great interest & admiration, from Edinburgh to Bengal & back. That is how I am sure you will help me. For my two dear brothers have been taken from me & imprisoned, for no crime that can be named. Both, though of Italian extraction, are born-and-bred British. One of them, Emilio, has never set foot in Italy. While the other,

The pen refused to trace his name. I squeezed out every loop and curl, like when learning shorthand:

Giulio, has been working for the downfall of Mussolini through the Italian League for the Rights of Man (the LIDU), as its leader Decio Anzani will testify. On the night of the 11th, Giulio's pride & joy, his ice-cream parlour, was ransacked by local mobs filled with envy & indiscriminate rage.

Indiscriminate was inaccurate, but the contrary led down a path I could not travel.

Our Prime Minister says *We shall never surrender*, but is it not already a surrender to treat our own folk like this? I beg you to give the order to release these two honest & upright *Scottish* citizens who might have been your very own neighbours had you stayed up here in the north.
Yours in hope
Lucia Pezzini

I made a neat copy and slid it into an envelope. The men were gone to whom I'd have turned for an address. The best I could come up with was *The Home Office, Westminster, London*. Once the stamp was licked, I finally felt ready for duty.

Whenever I'd passed Donaldson School on the bus, I had marvelled at its fairy-tale towers and its barracks-like bulk. Now, I wondered how they'd presumed to lodge the handicapped in a building designed by an over-imaginative witch. Its towers implied dungeons, its giant façade looked like anthracite, the hundreds of yards of its railings were interlaced with barbed wire, sandbags abounding.

'Can I help you, miss?' asked the soldier by the sentry box, while the barrier rose to permit vans to pass.

I read his stripes and hoped to impress him. 'Thank you, corporal. My brothers are inside. I'd like to visit them.'

'Germans, are they?'

'Italian.'

'Which means they're in detention, for what their Duce done.'

'I understand that, corporal, but I need to see them.'

'You heard of Quisling, miss? And the Fifth Column?'

'For pity's sake, my brothers are as Scottish as you are. I only want to speak to them.'

Finally, after checking my handbag for weaponry, he let me advance; so I could repeat the plea to four more soldiers and two Home Office officials, until I told the final one that he should imprison me too if that was the only way I'd get to see my brothers.

'No rallies permitted in detention,' this official pronounced. 'You may see only one individual. For five minutes. With a soldier present.'

After all my efforts, I almost chose Emilio, just because it would be easier. Then I pictured his look of disappointment when he found only me, not his wife. Tomorrow, Dorothy could succour him.

'And please note, this is an exception we're making, since it appears your brothers do hold some claim to British nationality.'

The stale room into which I was shown appeared to announce that the deaf should also be blind, since the windows were set high in the wall, and the paintwork was the saddest shade of grey.

'Nae touchin!' warned the guard, as Giulio, unshaven and exhausted, rushed towards me. 'Sit across frae each other at this desk here.' I was unable to look my brother in the eye. During the long minute of silence, I wanted to scream, slap him, hug him. 'You've only four left, so yous better make it snappy.'

He reached out for my hand. '*Sai, cara, che non sono io—*'

'Quit that foreign stuff! Another word and you're back in yer cell.'

'Not me, but you, your loveliness . . . Just a lapse, out of sympathy, a left-over from his public-school days . . . the wedding . . . everything as planned.'

If I could have produced the saliva, I might have spat at him. 'Am I the only one you didn't tell?'

He seemed about to speak, but only shrugged. So chastened, he found nothing more to say, his mouth opening and shutting like a drowning fish. It reminded me—

'Paola saved her Fry.' I wanted the next to hurt. 'But we lost the Palace to vandals.'

'McEwen?'

'One more minute.'

'And Emilio?' I asked.

'He's with me. Too angry to think clearly.'

'Tell him I'll bring Dorothy tomorrow.'

'And *soldi*, lots of *soldi*.' Giulio eyed the guard. 'Then maybe we can talk, Lucia.' The guard consulted his watch.

'Call me Judas,' I said. 'I cliped you to the police, led O'Donnell to you.'

'You did me a favour. I was waiting for him. You think I'd leave Emilio alone? And Carlo and Fausto and Decio? Hide like a rat behind the wainscot?' He shook his head. 'You saved me a tearful parting from Assunta, the shame of the police pulling me down the stairs.'

I so wanted to believe him.

'That's it, over. Maybe next time, miss,' said the guard from out the side of his mouth, 'I could give yous two a bit more . . . eh . . . *privacy?*' He gave a wink and rubbed his fingers together. 'If you ken what I mean?'

Like many Sicilians, Padre Clemente, in his eighties and in need of an oxygen inhaler, was easier with violence than with milder transgressions of the flesh. Hence it was not for fear, still less for shame that I neglected to confess to him. Not for shame but for lack of shame. Apart from relief at Assunta having been spared, I felt no more about McEwen than I would have felt about a cockroach crushed in the Palace kitchen—probably I understood the cockroach better. Still I stopped in at St Mary's to pray.

The next day, our pockets filled with cash, Dorothy and I were at the Donaldson School gates. 'They're gone,' we were told. 'Been transferred.' We pleaded with the guard to tell us where. But either he did not know or he was too well trained to divulge.

47

Through June, I sent daily letters to Sir John, pleading for his help. Then, after nearly three weeks, a letter finally arrived—but not from him.

Somewhere in the Midlands

16 June

Dearest Sister Mine,

I know how you'll be fretting, but please do not worry. Here I am with Emilio, and though the camp—some disused mill—is squalid, we are both surviving well.

Please please please forgive me. For what happened before they arrested me, for everything I've kept from you. I shan't ask you to forgive me what I am, rather to know me at last . . . I've cadged pen and paper from a sympathetic guard, who in exchange for cigarettes promises to smuggle out and post my letters. They haven't told us what they intend to do with us 'enemy aliens', yet they can't keep us fenced in here for ever, with no beds or blankets or sanitation, no heating, food that's barely edible (except by the rats, which are everywhere).

Emilio is brimming with bitterness and rage; his leg hurts keenly after nights on the concrete warehouse floor. But I'm not writing to complain. I feel no anger, unless at myself. And alongside my shame— dare I admit it?—an excitement at how it's going to be different when we're released and home again: no more subterfuge, no more deception. It surely won't be long before the authorities realize they're repeating the very mistake committed at the outbreak of the Great War, locking up indiscriminately just because of a foreign-sounding name. Apologies will follow, we'll read them round the kitchen table with Papà. And despite what they're saying (Nazis in the camp loudest of all), we're going to win this war—believe me. Sanity will return to Italy once the Duce is defeated. Then we'll take that trip together to Maclodio and rejoice at how far our family has travelled since Nonno set out forty years ago.

Love,

Your Giulio

I did not share the letter with Harry, though he visited us daily. This little act of cruelty seemed to permit me, though he did not dare try to touch me, to pass him my hand. I listened to his explanations, his avowals of devotion, his tears of remorse, listened patiently with an unintentionally immobile smile on my face. What did I feel? When I asked myself this question, the response came back that my feelings were hardly the point, that my personal melodrama was not going to count for much in the reckoning that was about to happen. I asked myself again: what *exactly* did I feel, when indeed there was room for feeling round the edges of that image of him dismounting my brother?

Yet whenever anger began to pulse, my heart was overwhelmed by the single simple longing for my brothers to be home again.

Wharfe Mills

21 June 1940

Cara,

What strikes me every day is the look of panic in the eyes of so many of these young guards: they wish to believe they are doing right, but for that they need us to be enemies of the realm, when we are former neighbours and drinking partners. They feign amazement that we speak English as well as they do and they tacitly urge us to pronounce some anti-British sentiment. Of course there are those here, a minority, who are ready to oblige them. I tell myself that all will be well, but in the middle of the night, listening to the rats scurry, there are moments of doubt . . .

They fill our time here with futile duties, but of course I think of little but of how to write to you.

If you were still to care enough about me to ask me why I am the way I am, I'd have as much trouble answering as if you were to ask me 'Why ice?' I was born that way I presume, as I was born to be an ice-man. Not that I love to be cold, on the contrary, except in the mouth, where the chill captures flavours—those frozen taste-bombs on which I have dreamt. Maybe I could have joined the professions as Mamma hoped, but in ice I could be not just professional, in ice I could be unique, make and remake myself every single day. It's hard to explain. Maybe something happened to me on that first trip to Italy, with Mamma fading and my first taste of what ice could offer. Did I some-how imagine that if I could reach perfection in my trade and import the tastes to Scotland then I could bring her back to life? Oh do not underestimate the curse of a mother's love! Or the weight of a sister's— all you expected of your faltering brother . . .

You asked me in the prison if you were the only one in the dark. I can't tell you who knew as I never discussed it at home, but my broth-ers surely, Papà perhaps, and yourself—yes, yourself too—I presumed, at least some part of you that you never sought to test. When you've lived as I have lived—please understand this—you prefer not to know what others know, you try to exist as if there were nothing in you worth knowing . . . But of course McEwen, most certainly. It was me he loathed most of all, having sniffed me out while we were still young-sters. I sensed that strength lay in numbers. Newcomers as we were to the country, we needed to group together to defeat such hatefulness. You carried your catapult; for a time I wore my black shirt. I was only 18 years old when we started the club, half a lifetime ago, but I realized already that the lot of the happily married man was not to be mine.

Do you remember, from around the same time, your stealthy moves with Auntie Sandy? How I loved to dance with her! I need you to know that I have always adored the touch, the company, the words, of a woman—and not just Mamma. Sandy sensed it of course, and yet I never felt she judged me; told me she'd seen more than enough fine specimens of Scottish manhood, and the damage wreaked.

I so longed to tell you about Daniele—you remember him, from my one sponsored trip to Rome? We happened to be in the same compartment on the train from London, but even had we not been we would have found each other out. He told me of his parents' hope, that by joining the London Fascio he would be turned into a true-blooded Italian. Once he had courted a girl, when he was sixteen, but a single kiss had been enough to convince him to desist. I can still see his pout as he recounted that. We corresponded until the TB laid him low, chaste letters for fear of being over-read. Our Dante consigns us to the seventh circle of Inferno, but then he also allows some of us (for reasons I've never properly grasped) to escape to the upper reaches of Purgatorio . . . so there's hope! Sometimes I think my reading has exerted a bad influence, all that R. L. Stevenson encouraging day-dreams and a double life. When I think of how things might have been different, I of course begin with myself: how I should have been more trusting, less occult. Forever fear of the judgement, the disgust, the rejection.

Emilio has just heard a rumour that we're soon to be freed and returned home. Someone else has said that Winston Churchill has got it in for us Italians and refuses to listen to the pleas for moderation coming from your Scotsman John Anderson. Who knows what's really the case.

I do hope you and Papà and Dorothy are not worrying too much, there's really no need to as Emilio and I are mostly just impatient, longing to be home with you all again. You can then punish me as much as you would like.

Love,

Your Giulio

PS. Don't forget that our parents had never seen the opera when they named you after it. Nothing need be tragic!

Every evening Harry would devote to those few left of us, to Paola, Assunta, Papà, and myself, laden with gifts for which he must have paid a wicked sum on the black market that was springing up round the edges of rationing; as tearful as the rest of us, as speechless at what had happened. Dorothy was incredulous that Giulio had found a way to write but Emilio had not. I refused to read to any of them from my brother's letters.

Wharfe Mills, 26 June

Dear Lucia,

Latest rumour—how caged men love rumours!—is that we're to be sent to labour in the mines. There's a tiny part of me will be sorry to leave this squalid site, on account of the people I've met here, the things I'm learning from the exiled Polish thinkers, Czech professors, Italian engineers, German musicians . . .

I understood of course when you visited me in prison at the School for the Deaf that you expected me to say more about Harry. I often tried to tell you about the time I had in London on the way from delivery of my 'recipes'—only a few days there, but like an oasis on a long desert march. I never needed to tell Decio about my proclivities: though a family man himself, he seems to have a feel for these things (perhaps, with being a tailor by trade, all those inside-leg measurements?). He made a point of introducing me to several of his particular friends from the LIDU, and among them, almost for the first time, I felt I could be myself. What, you ask me, does that mean? I mean not having to pretend, or pretend to pretend . . . many things. It was on the second night out with this Soho crowd that I met Harry, at a bar, he was one of Decio's customers and was wearing one of his suits.

The following morning, both of us woozy from too many whiskies and cigars, Harry explained to me that our being there together was only a cast back to his boarding-school days and that I should expect nothing more of him. He informed me of his discontent at work and his need of a change. I can't tell you for certain when I had the idea that he might be someone you would like. But if I encouraged him to think of moving north when his insurance company announced an opening, I can say—is this something to be ashamed of or proud?—it was you, not myself, I had in my mind. If only you knew how much I worried for you after you were attacked and Valerio was exiled, how I wanted you to stretch your wings, to remember you are young and beautiful and worthy of love, that life is short and brutal and vanishing faster than thought itself . . .

Those weeks and months we all spent together at the Palace were the happiest I have known since Mamma died. Whatever my mistakes,

I will not let the memory of them be dimmed. The love that dare not speak its name? But I'm speaking! And if only you knew how little real love there has been.

Emilio longs for his Dorothy but refuses to write from such anger. I can't help wondering every second minute how Assunta will have changed—three whole weeks without seeing her. I know you'll be taking good care of everyone, and you shouldn't worry about money as there's plenty in the bank. (Mr Morton will make it simple.) We've heard of letters in the press objecting to the way we Italians have been treated, and I'm sure your Sir John is doing his best to mollify Sir Winston.

It was not Harry's fault, all the blame is mine. I thought of myself as practically a brother-in-law already. But I was so panicked and desperate, so childishly selfish, felt so emptied of everything I've ever owned, so utterly dispossessed. I shall not offer any more excuses, but I begged him, begged him, before I was sent away . . . He took pity on me, that's all. You say you betrayed me to the police. The betrayal was only mine. And there's a force of forgiveness in you; not by chance were you named Lucia, full of light as you have been and will be. Turn your light upon the man you love and who loves you in return. Forgive him his past and, if you can bring yourself, forgive me my future.

Your Giulio

PS. There is one more thing I have kept from you—but no longer. My only excuse this time is that it was not for my sake but for hers that I kept the secret . . . I want you to know that not long after she married, Paola came to believe Dario to be infertile, despite all his bluster about siring a son. When she turned to me, I thought she must be kidding. She begged me to make an exception, just this once (for she had guessed the way I am within days of her arrival in our home). I could not help thinking that I was being offered a chance, a chance to stay on the side of life, to feel a love so often denied to my kind. Not only had I never been with a woman, I had never even properly—or improperly—imagined it. I warned her success was far from assured. But Paola was persistent, she found a way to urge me . . . Assunta, nine months later, was the result. If Dario were ever to find out, it would not just be my head that would roll, not just his wife's, but Assunta's too—or so we feared. Often, when I bathed the baby, when I read to the child, when I cared for the wee thing's grazes, I thought you had twigged. I can keep it from you no longer, not least because I need to ask you to watch out for her, watch over her closer than ever, for who knows what will be released upon the children of us Italians.

On the last day of the month, a man in a bowler hat appeared at the bank. He invited me to McVities, where Auntie Rebecca wrung my hands and Auntie Sandy—she'd lost her looks quite suddenly, and her ankles had thickened—barely seemed to recognize me through her sighs. The gentleman explained that his mission could not be committed to paper, nor indeed could he confide to me his name. But he did wish me to know that Sir John had received my letters and read them with compassion. If there were something he could do he would do it, but the pressure on him from the press, from on high, was intense. He asked me to remember how alone the country stood, with its back to the wall, how for all the talk of how this would be 'their finest hour', the battle in the air had not yet been joined, still less won, and that invasion remained more probable than not.

Then, as suddenly as he had appeared, he disappeared, leaving behind him an absurdly large ten-pound bank note for the two cups of tea we had failed to drink.

Dorothy lodged complaints, petitioned MPs, devoted every minute of every day to trying to contact her husband, hardly permitting herself to sleep. Until, on the seventh of July, arrived the telegram that we read aloud together:

Pezzini, Giulio, missing, presumed drowned, subsequent to sinking of The Arandora Star.

48

Thenceforth I could attempt to sleep only with the feel of Papà's figurine of the boar—I liberated it from its cabinet the night of the telegram—in my hand. I do not know how I spent my days, into what sort of blackness I had sunk or for how long.

When I recovered sufficiently to pretend to adult conversation, I pleaded with Harry that it might turn out to be an error. But Harry shook his head: he had read of the sinking of *The Arandora Star* in *The Scotsman*, during the days I was unconscious with grief. He spoke to us of injustice, of the shame of his government's treatment of our family. He said he would always be present for us. And even if I knew this could not be true—as he had often told me, he was officer material—I let him hold and try to comfort me. Through my misery throbbed a determination not to let yet another man disappear from my life.

In the weeks that followed, he explained the Battle of Britain to us and how its outcome meant that invasion might not happen, spoke of his hope for American intervention. He asked if I would marry him before he was posted, and I was surely summoning the courage to do just that, as Giulio had urged me, when his orders came through.

Then, before I could post the banns, before I could vent my rage, before we had time to do more than utter private promises, Harry was gone, posted to Burma. When he wrote from the Far East, he was awkward, wary to put anything in writing about what had happened between us, knowing he could not ignore it. Even if I had had a return address, I knew that nothing I—a woman, a nobody—could say would have the slightest bearing on events.

Two months after he had left, the letters ceased.

It was from Birkenhead that, shortly before Christmas, there arrived a typewritten envelope with, inside, a letter in the code which Giulio had used when he worked for the LIDU. It took me minutes to decipher it.

Isle of Man

15 December

Dearest Lucia,

I know I should have written before now. When you read what I am enclosing you will understand why I have not. Even this letter I have had to convey by means best left unspoken. I don't know what to say to you, can't think better than to send you what I have been able to write since it happened.

I should have died along with him. Somehow I did not.

Emilio

To my brother's letter was attached a document in his hand, written in our code in the margins of pages torn from a French-language textbook.

. . . The darkness underwater, the shock of impact running through my body, from feet to skull, so at first I fear I've hit a rafter. But no, it's water all right, I can feel it on the face as I sink . . . and sink . . . till the lungs feel fit to burst . . . before I start to resurface with the life-jacket still wedged between my legs. A desperate breath before lungs implode. Carlo? And Giulio? They must be somewhere here, we all jumped together—but first clear my eyes of the oil.

'All right?' Carlo shouts.

Before I can answer, a wave breaks over me, blackening the skin not already mired. The sea, which from up above on deck looked flat-calm, is troubled and moving. 'Hold on to your life-jacket, Giulio! Don't pull it on yet! Let me help you. We've got to get some distance. Look!'

Then a head bobs past us with the neck below it snapped: a face—thank god—I do not know. The ship's hull looms above us. I hold my brother under the armpits, while my legs flap like a frog's, to drag us through the spawn of corpses, canvas, canisters from on deck.

'Kick!' I order him. 'Use your legs, Giulio!' Is fifty yards enough? 'Giulio!' I lose my grip on him, and he's upended by another wave, re-emerges soused in black, into which he opens his eyes in desperation. 'Quick, pull on the life-jacket!' This time the wave assists us by somehow dragging it over his head. He tries to tie it beneath his legs but cannot reach the straps. Carlo has dis-appeared from view; so little is visible from the surface. 'We've got to head for that lifeboat. Oh no! There she goes!'

A long hand reaches up from the ocean bed, to drag the liner downwards . . . downwards . . . A few seconds more, and no drag is required, the hull torn by the torpedo has drunk enough for today.

'Help me, Emilio, help me!'

This is not how it is meant to end, with his mouth full of engine grease, the Germans on the lifeboat flapping oars at us, screaming at him to grab hold.

But he can't, because his hands have lost sensation, his legs now immo-bile. I have to shout at him to move away as they're more likely to brain him than save him. My own hands are frozen, can't clutch him any longer. He rises on the swell, then it breaks over him again.

'Move away, Emilio!' he shouts. 'Save yourself! Think of Dorothy! Think of the bairns you'll have! Do it for me! You can still get into one of those lifeboats!'

Overhead, the buzz of a reconnaissance plane, there'll be help coming soon . . . if we can only stay alive. I'm peering through the blackness but my other senses are dimming. They say a drowning man sees his whole life pass before him, but all I see is other lives failing, as they sink and fail to resurface.

The next wave parts us further. I refuse to be saved without my brother. Then a wooden beam just misses me, carried by a wave, and crashes full on his face, fifteen feet from me. His head is down, and I cannot reach him . . . Cannot swim, only float, cannot see, barely breathe, cannot cannot . . .

After I decoded and read to myself what Emilio had written, I felt an urgent need to ask Paola for permission to tell Assunta who her father really was.

Paola said: 'Would you give her a father only to take him away? Dario is hopeless but at least he's alive.'

I mouthed some objection, but I could not deny it. For with PC O'Donnell's help, he had evaded the June round-up. He hid out in the cellar of Joe the boxing coach, emerging at night to roam the blacked-out streets in search of food. With that instinct of his, he reckoned if he could just lie low, the police would soon have more pressing matters on their hands. Whichever way the war went, he could only win in the long run, he figured: either, as seemed likely, the Axis would be victorious, in which case he could reap the rewards of nearly twenty years at the Fascio's head, move upwards, present himself for mayor—the sky was the limit (and then he'd see if his wife refused to speak to him!). Or the Brits would muddle through, with the Yanks' assistance, and he could re-emerge from underground with the martyr's air at what he'd been made to endure for the fact of being foreign. The chief thing was to stay out of the authorities' clutches until hysteria died down.

The first I saw of him after the sinking, he was hiding in the loft of some petty thief in Leith. He only nodded when he heard of his brother's death. I'd visit him once a week, climbing through the trap-door. He knew of the Italian invasion of Egypt before I did, though he never requested newspapers, just cigarettes and pin-ups. He'd hung a hammock, and with his paraffin lamp and his smokes he seemed almost contented.

49

It was nearly a year before I heard from Emilio again. At the bank I wore black, where Mr Morton went on muttering to me of the shame he felt at his compatriots' behaviour. I admitted to him, when he asked, that I did not expect Harry ever to return from the East. When an envelope finally did arrive, the stamp bore the King's head, postmark London. Again the announcement was short.

Dorothy finally evinced what I thought her incapable of, envy —envy for any announcement at all (she had received from her husband not a single word since the day he was taken).

Then:

Isle of Man
November 1941

Dear Lucia,

They will not let us write freely, and without that freedom what use is there in writing at all. But I think I have found a way of getting one more document out. Let me bring you all up to date.

Your Emilio

I could hardly bear to crack the code which this time was filling the spaces between the lines on an instruction manual for two-stroke engines. Crack it I did.

When the Canadian seaman pulled me out of the water, six hours after we'd plunged into it, I was no longer swimming, just able to keep my blackened face up, my arms attached to a plank from the liner's ballroom floor. 'I had him,' was all I could say, 'I had him.' I tried to resist, determined not to come alone.

On the deck of the SS St Laurent I passed out; then was dragged back into consciousness hours later by the pain in my leg and hip. Lamentation was all I could hear, from men basted in oil; then the agonies of those who would never reach land, their broken limbs and collapsing lungs, the shrieks for loved ones lost, the taste of salt and grease and fear and relief . . . and fear again. And already—I could hear it—of guilt.

Despite what I knew in my heart, I dragged myself round the deck on all fours, pulling back the blankets from the corpses, exchanging grim nods and hand-clasps with those amongst the survivors whom I recognized. I closed the eyelids on Fausto, whose leg had been severed above the knee. Decio was amongst the dead: hundreds of bodies stretched out, the medics flitting wordlessly among them. No trace of The Arandora Star's Captain Moulton, who must have gone down on his bridge. And here too was Carlo, helping the doctors carry the critical below decks, distributing rations, coaxing coughers to regurgitate. I had only to catch his eye for him to know what I was asking: the big man shook his head.

Land was in sight when next I came to consciousness. One day, I thought, it would be explained to me where they had been taking us, along with fifteen hundred others. 'Born and bred'—the phrase raced round my head—I'd been 'born and bred' in Scotland, as had my brother. At the word 'brother', I cursed myself for forgetting him for two whole minutes, and threw up again over the deck.

On the quayside there was confusion on the locals' faces as they discovered here were Krauts—the worst—and bastard wop Eye-talians . . . but speaking English, most of them, not in any sort of uniform, and some with accents close to their own.

'Over here if you're Italian!' The soldiers on the portside were youngsters, scared by what they'd heard on the wireless or read in The Daily Mail.

I was on a stretcher, shivering uncontrollably despite the summer sun. A nurse lifted my blanket, saw the leg, and directed the stretcher-bearers towards the line for hospital cases. On my way to hospital, I saw warships under construction at Greenock and Port Glasgow, fifty miles from home. My heart rose for an instant, only to fall the heavier when I remembered. I passed out again. When I came round, a nurse was swabbing the oil from my limbs with a pungent green jelly. She smiled at me and asked if I was 'one o they Italians'. She told me I'd better make the most of my bad leg, tarry in hospital till the rumpus died down. Four days later, after screaming and flailing whenever the surgeon palpated, I asked the friendly nurse why she'd helped me.

'I always enjoyed an ice, doon the pier,' she explained. 'They Di Rollos who made the ice-creams, thems were a right friendly family. Dinna deserve what's befallen them.'

For more than five weeks, with coughing, play-acting and indulgence of the friendly nurse, I malingered in hospital on Clydeside, before being loaded onto a train heading south, no explanations given. They pinioned my arms to frog-march me on board. Talk was of Ireland, India, Bermuda, the Falkland Islands. I sat up on deck and waited for the torpedo which did not come. The journey turned out to be short. After disembarking, we were herded—Italians, Germans, Czechs—into what looked like a toy village, enclosed in barbed wire. I was shown where I would sleep, and only now did I learn we were on the Isle of Man.

For three months I lay speechless on my back, not responding to orders, participating in none of the camp's activities. I produced a psoriasis so severe that my body became one open sore (worthy of Dario's Abyssinian back). The doctors spoke of an allergy to the oil, but I waved them away. Dorothy's letters lay unopened by my bunk. Spitfires flew overhead, which the men would watch silently, uncertain when to cheer: their loyalty to the British airmen seemed an insult to family and friends who had drowned; while from the Nazi section of the camp the cheer went up as a Junkers or Messerschmitt roared past. Other Edinburgh Italians who'd lost loved ones tried to tend to me. Doctors predicted a fatal peritonitis.

Then I awoke one morning—I was sleeping long, hard, dreamlessly, waking tireder than the night before—to find a slip of paper on my naked chest, stuck to my sores, obliging me to peel it off. I screwed it into a ball. For hours I stifled the noise in my head that sounded like engines cranking up on a distant airfield, or typewriters being struck in a neighbouring office. That night I spoke for the first time, asking to be transferred to the hospital—a request denied since my malady was judged non-infectious and of no known cure. I surged towards sleep, but sleep had now deserted me. In the darkest hour of night I scrabbled on the floor beneath my bunk to where the scrap *was lying. The pleasure I felt made me nauseous, as I read the lines by torchlight:*

> Now that my ladder's gone
> I must lie down where all the ladders start
> In the foul rag and bone shop of the heart.

I'd never seen them before, knew I'd never forget them. Never meant the future—I didn't like that. When finally I slept, dreams were of ice and Vaseline. When I awoke, my skin was cooler for the first time. A second slip of paper was affixed to my chest. I was in a fairy story, cursing the fairy.

> What happens to the living when they die!
> Death is not understood by death: nor you, nor I.

That afternoon, I propped myself up in my bunk, looked in the mirror. The second slip could be Auden, though it was new to me. But the first? Then the third?

> Slowly the poison the whole blood stream fills.
> It is not the effort nor the failure tires.
> > The waste remains, the waste remains and kills.

I took my first shave in over three months, revealing the crevices and scabs that would take longer to heal. Scraps of paper were everywhere but I was determined not to read them. Until, written near the mirror where I shaved . . . I was caught off guard . . . and the tears began to flow which would not stop until they had rinsed the shaving soap from my face.

> If her horny feet protrude, they come
> > To show how cold she is, and dumb.
> > Let the lamp affix its beam.
> > The only emperor is the emperor of ice-cream.

The final two lines went round and round my head until they chased out every thought: my brother's epitaph was being written, by one who'd never known him.

I imagined the verse-fairy would be hard to find. But it was as easy as asking. He was a thick-set Jew from Berlin called Isaac Rosenstein who had lived some twenty-five years in London; he had edited a poetry magazine in his free time, when not selling leather goods. He'd been informed by someone that I was a poet and he was in search of associates for his Poetry Group. W. B. Yeats, I learnt, for the first; I was right with Auden for the second; the third, 'Missing Dates', by William Empson, had been published first in Rosenstein's magazine; about 'The Emperor of Ice-Cream' he asked me to write my own poem by way of a response. This I tried—am trying still—to do.

I was back in the world, despite it all.

50

To understand more of what had happened, I needed to wait until later, until after the war was over; even then, despite enquiries, I never did find out exactly where Harry had finally starved to death.

Only belatedly did it emerge that 'Collar the lot!' had been Churchill's exclamation, in cabinet, when referring to the British Italians, after Mussolini's declaration of war on 10 June. What Giulio had heard, about the failure of the efforts of John Anderson to resist mass internment, turned out to be true. Though François Lafitte, when he wrote his book *The Internment of Enemy Aliens*, was ignorant of the efforts of Sir John, perhaps he was right to address his Home Secretary directly, to judge at least from the results his book produced: Churchill's war cabinet studied it, and within months relaxed their policies in accordance with most of Lafitte's recommendations. The Isle of Man was seen as a safe alternative to deportation of the 'enemy aliens'. Of course, no apology emerged from Lord Rothermere, proprietor of *The Daily Mail*, who right through 1938 had been bosom pals with Mussolini, but who, when his buddy declared war, had turned against the Italian community with the vindictiveness of disappointed love, printing column after column about *Traitor Wops* and *Quisling Eyeties*.

Through the 1930s *The Arandora Star* had been the most luxurious liner belonging to the Blue Star Line, host to such celebrities as Noel Coward and the Queen of Holland, equipped with every conceivable comfort and convenience as she cruised with her three hundred and fifty first-class passengers between Tenerife, Cape Town, Majorca, Panama, Lisbon, Madeira, Buenos Aires, Rio. Not long after war was declared, she was refitted and repainted as a troop ship.

In June 1940 Kapitänleutnant Günther Prien was already one of the most famous of U-boat captains, having sunk the aircraft carrier *Royal Oak* in Scapa Flow the year before. He was returning home, with one torpedo left on board U-47. Hence the temptation at 6.29 a.m. when he spotted the liner on the radar and surfaced to inspect: two guns fore and aft, no markings to suggest a hospital ship or anything other than an Allied supply vessel; her zigzag course a sure indication that she was a legitimate target and expecting trouble. The chance of hitting her at three hundred yards no more than fifty per cent—but what was there to lose.

When the torpedo met its target, his officers gathered round to congratulate their captain. Periscope down after confirming the broadside. In his log Prien wrote: *Ship stops. Enemy remains stationary. Slight list to starboard. Some boats in water—others being lowered.* Another fifteen thousand tonnes in his swift-mounting record. 'Set a course for Hamburg,' he is reputed to have declared. 'Tomorrow champagne on the Reeperbahn!'

When she was hit by the torpedo, *The Arandora Star* was transporting more than twelve hundred enemy aliens to Canada, one of the few countries that had expressed a willingness to receive them and set them to work. Mayday came through in Morse from Captain Moulton's bridge: *Torpedoed 175 miles off Bloody Foreland. Engines wrecked. Many persons dead. Ship sinking.*

Dario's glee at Allied defeats turned to disgust when America entered the war and Stalingrad turned the tide. By the time Italian surrender was announced, in September '43, he said he was ready to wring the Duce's neck. After Badoglio was named Prime Minister by the King, PC O'Donnell advised him he could re-emerge in daylight so long as he kept out of trouble. For someone who'd been so long in hiding, he looked insultingly fit and well fed, and as he walked round the flat again—the two flats—he expanded into the space left vacant by the brothers.

'*Allora*, Papà,' he'd ask, 'glad to have me back?'

'Just pipe down, Dario, show some respect.'

'Respect?' He rubbed his hands across his cheeks. 'The ice-man's been dead three years, and the other one's having a ball in his holiday camp, being entertained at us tax-payers' expense. Going round with a glum face is no about to bring them back.'

When the Allies landed in Salerno and the fighting turned tough on the Italian peninsula, he found he had to say that 'as an Italian' he'd 'always despised the Germans'. The Fascio clubhouse had been vandalized, but Papà ordered a new door, and no one seemed to notice that rent was not being paid. Dario proposed re-opening it as a Centro dei Partigiani; until, after two hours of holding forth in the Rob Roy, he despaired of explaining to Scotsmen that there was more to Italy than the Duce, that the country was at civil war, partisans daily laying down their lives. As soon as the Italian stigma lifted, he'd sign up for duty himself, he said, and help liberate Maclodio, which was languishing just miles behind the Gothic Line. He'd march into the village wearing British uniform—and then he'd see what Zio Roberto was made of, with his shepherd's crook against a tommy-gun!

Indeed, once Dario had started on his fantasy-liberating, there was no stopping him: right through '44, as he read of the reports, starting with Rome in June and working northward, it was one city after another he was freeing, the *ragazze* greeting him with bouquets of flowers and open legs. Strutting round the kitchen with a broom for a rifle, then ducking beneath the table for shelter, he imagined himself on the Piazza della Signoria in Florence, taking sniper fire behind a Michelangelo statue. He used the rope of the clothes-pulley to demonstrate how he'd have helped secure the knot on the noose thrown over the neck of the Bologna *podestà*. Then flung open the kitchen door, in lieu of the doors on the church at Marzabotto in which hundreds of villagers were incinerated. To cap it all, in '45, he hoisted a rolled-up rug across his shoulder to explain to me how he'd have snatched the Duce as he attempted escape into Switzerland, dragging him back to Milan. 'Not that I would have shot him, mind, or strung him up. It's the moment for forgiveness, *vero?*'

When in May the last German troops surrendered in Italy, he decided that he'd be ideal as Maclodio's first post-war mayor. But when he failed to find a sponsor among the few Italians who still spoke to him, the idea passed from his head, as would every idea for his life's remainder. He was drinking more and more, and as Paola kept his money tight, his beverage became harder. He'd be dragging himself up the stairs in the morning as Assunta left for school.

When Emilio finally returned from internment, all Dario could find to say was, 'You could have done something to save him, couldn't you!' He couldn't see a future in Edinburgh, he confided to me, when Paola finally threw him out on his ear.

Emilio refused to utter another word to his brother. 'I'm done with him,' he said, despite my pleading. He was impatient to get on, he explained, after so many lost years, after taking in so much at what he called 'the University'—the classes set up by the internees on the Isle of Man had been given by some of Europe's finest intellectuals and artists. He learnt enough there to get him into Edinburgh's more conventional university, with Dorothy's parents assisting (racked by guilt as they were at what their country had done to their son-in-law). By '52 he had his first real job, as a lecturer in Italian (Dante and Montale his specialisms). Later still, he was one of Sussex University's founding fathers, along with the historian Asa Briggs and the literature professor David Daiches (whose father had been Edinburgh's Lithuanian rabbi, so respected by Auntie Rebecca).

Dario had only one more moment of notoriety, when Anne Frank's *Diary* made a splash, and he managed to get himself onto the front page of *The Glasgow Herald*, dressed in a vest. The saga accompanying the photographs was of persecution, attempts to save his brothers from *The Arandora Star*, survival by sustaining himself on rats and rainwater (the photos had been shot one week earlier in a loft so cramped he'd have needed to be a contortionist to inhabit it).

Occasionally he would turn up from Glasgow to cadge money, and the two of us would end up in the Rob Roy together. Then he was too broke, or too sick, or too confused to remember me even for a loan. When his body was laid next to Papà's, a pair of Glaswegians showed up in Celtic scarves expecting me to discharge my brother's debts. Carlo was present, still muscular; he said he'd come for old times' sake, though I read on his brow the wish to confirm that Dario was truly six feet under.

After the ceremony, Dorothy recounted the occasion in 1937— she'd never mentioned it before, for fear of provoking further sibling strife—not long after his return from Africa, when Dario had turned up at her door, invited himself in, and proposed over tea that he help her start a family where his brother was proving remiss. When she threatened him with a scalding teapot, he told her to have a heart, even the Angel was shunning him, now she'd seen the state of his back. Carlo recollected how Fausto would survey my oldest brother in the Palace, ever ready to pounce at his boss's signal; he still missed his friends, not a day went by that he didn't think of them all . . . of Giulio . . . of Decio . . . Everlastingly, Carlo blamed himself for not having saved Fausto from the waves: as had happened to many, his life-jacket had knocked him unconscious when he jumped from the ship, leaving him unable to avoid the falling debris that tore through his leg.

Perhaps it had been the guilt that made Carlo susceptible to snap, later, on the journey to Australia. For, like all those who could walk or whose injuries were light, when he was lifted from the ocean and ferried to safety in Greenock, he was then put on the first train South, back to Liverpool. One week later, along with two hundred other Italians, many screaming with fear and hallucinating from their recent experience on *The Arandora Star*, he was frog-marched onto the SS *Dunera*. The ship narrowly escaped German torpedoes off the Scottish coast, then again near Cape Town. Captain Scott, in charge of the enemy aliens, was so systematically brutal that he was later court-marshalled for misconduct. But not before Carlo, choosing his moment shortly before arrival in Australia, hit him with the full force of his massive fists: three months in solitary, before being delivered to a work farm for the next four years.

When finally he'd made it back to Scotland, in 1947, it was just in time for the christening of his namesake, Carlo, which name Emilio had chosen to give to his first-born, after the man who'd helped save him.

51

On the very first holiday I took from my job as a secretary at the Edinburgh Italian Consulate—despite Mr Morton's civilities, when the war was over I never wanted to work for the British again—I journeyed to find him, knowing I would not. The Consul advised me to travel by aeroplane, but what I needed was to *see*; from our Scottish outpost, we'd witnessed so little except on newsreels.

The train ride to Rome seemed as eternal as the city—damaged—did not. On Piazza Minerva, the elephant still supported its obelisk, taller than I remembered. The *vicolo* where once I'd offered myself was home to a family living under rubble and broken doors. If I wandered, my feet would certainly lead me, past shoeless starving *scugnizzi* and whores. The *portiere* required only a few lire to permit me to climb to what had been the private lodging of Party Secretary Starace, the man responsible for many of the most grotesque Fascist shenanigans and displays, for trying to convince the populace to wear togas, for publicly announcing on one occasion in Mantua that any woman who wished to see how hard he worked, 'even in bed', could try him out backstage. As I started to climb, the *portiere* reminded me—as if I could forget—how the *palazzo*'s Lothario had ended his days. When I rang the doorbell, an elderly gent with an ebony cane seemed to find it normal that I should inspect the flat, from which every piece of furniture had been removed. I asked to see the bedroom, and we had to be careful crossing the planks which traversed the beams where the parquet had been looted.

'I lost my virginity here,' I explained, unbidden, looking up at what remained of the mirrored ceiling, just a few stubborn shards.

'But he's dead!' explained the old man in a Venetian accent. 'You cannot punish him more. I helped raise him onto the scaffold on Piezetta Loreto, alongside the Duce, with my own bare hands.'

The journey to Maclodio was slower than ever. The Duce's twenty-year reign had left few traces. But two days of Allied advances against the Germans in November '43 had altered almost everything. Scarcely a building in the village but its windows were blasted out or its roof torched or its walls pitted with bullet holes. Caution as well as recognition on the faces of those who came to see the visitor arrive on her mule. If there existed a Third Republic, of which I was in some distant way a representative, then no one had told the folks here, who lived in fear of the Duce's supernatural return, or worse, of the GIs with their Moroccan Goumiers from whose brutal attentions few of the women—not even hirsute Zia Lalla—had escaped. Zia Flavia explained how she had hid in Nonno's cave, but that this had not made things easier, as the women who had been raped regarded those who had escaped with suspicion. 'Children born with skin too dark, who knows how many more infants of whom we shall learn nothing, children of violence who ended in violence.'

Here, among the sufferers, I might have felt at home—doubly at home after what had happened in Scotland. Instead, I felt adrift, alone, unable to comfort my aunts or myself. Zia Antonella had taken refuge in the crypt but the *musulmani* had found her there. Judging her too old, they'd been content to humiliate her by stripping her naked then dressing her in the priest's best vestment. No one thanked me for Papà's gifts; questions were sparse about life abroad. Zio Roberto, more wizened than ever, received me outside his house. 'They took everything,' he said, 'slaughtered fourteen sheep, nineteen goats, and the few I saved were stolen one week later by the Partisans, the same who crucified the Mayor in the piazza.'

Back in Rome, by the end of the second day, I felt prepared to approach. I guessed his papà, if he had remained loyal to the Party, would have gone to ground to escape reprisals. The family's neighbours gave me tips, claiming to know nothing of the son—the *pagano*, as one crone put it, who had 'betrayed the faith'.

In an almost lightless room in Trastevere I found the father, though I had to be patient as he had not dressed in months. In the single café still open I offered him grappa and a raw egg. The former he sipped like a bird, the latter he downed *colpo secco*. It was unclear which was killing him fastest, loneliness, age, or starvation. He told me, strength returning, he had rarely seen his son after he had escaped from his exile on the island of Lipari and made it back to Rome—his only son, stolen by the Jews and their thirst for sacrifice.

'He was a brave man, my Valerio. When he escaped he could have gone into hiding, but he came back to Rome. He somehow avoided the massacre of the Ardeatine Caves, where more than three hundred were executed. Even after the Nazis occupied the city, he would not go under cover.'

'Was he brave?' I asked. 'Or was he desperate?' All questions seemed permitted; nothing could shock, after what had been witnessed. 'How did he look?'

His father thought for a second. 'Jewish. He looked Jewish. He and his tribe were waiting in vain for Pius to speak out. In October many of them were taken, thrown onto trains for the north. In June the next year, one thousand more. The laws passed in January took away their final rights. When the explosion killed the SS guards in Via Rosella, everyone knew reprisals would be heavy, and they hid themselves in their burrows. Not Valerio. Still he was not taken. But then, one morning, two days before the Nazi retreat, he was gone.'

In the buildings round us were men—and women—who had denounced the Jews, for spite or profit or what they believed they had done to Christ; others who had protected them at risk to their own lives.

'You wish to know what happened next to my son? From here, on the cattle truck, he was moved to Fossoli, by Carpi, in Emilia.' Carpi meant nothing to me—yet; we had heard of the Camps, the deportations, but not that the route to extermination had its staging post in a nondescript town near Modena. 'Barbed wire, guards, rifles, dogs. No longer Italy, this was the Reich. Several have returned who came to know him there, where he lasted for nearly one month. They say he even won some respect from the guards. In August his name was on the list. He knew there would be no train back. Beyond that we have no details.'

At the British Embassy, after queuing for hours, I was allowed access to a telephone that functioned. Papà had refused to have one in our flat, but Dorothy had installed one to celebrate Emilio's return from internment. I needed to talk to my brother, needed to listen.

'Come home, Lucia,' he insisted. 'You're wasting your time there. There's nothing you can do for the aunts in Maclodio, nothing you can do for Valerio. You need to be thinking of the future, not the past.'

'The future?' I sobbed.

His voice, so faint, only reminded me of distances. 'Come home now.'

Then the line went dead.

'Time is on my side, yes it is. Ti-i-i-i-me is on my side.' The song was blaring from the open window of a parked car while I sat at my favourite of the Italian cafés on Broughton Street. The driver had dashed inside to purchase a *panini* (which appears to have become a singular noun these days) filled with grilled aubergine, buffalo mozzarella, mortadella and a drizzle of Modenese balsamic vinegar —in a single sandwich, more fresh produce from the homeland that I would eat in a year, his age. I was tired, less from the walk than from the discipline I had imposed upon myself: not just to *make my report*, as Emilio had ordered me to do in the royal box at the Albert Hall eighteen months before, but to avoid the wisdom of hindsight while writing, to eschew the knowing backward-forward glance.

To stretch my legs I had paced a few times round *The Manuscript of Monte Cassino*, the Paolozzi sculpture of a giant foot recently plonked in front of St Mary's Cathedral. Then I'd made it down Leith Walk to Valvona and Crolla, the oldest Italian grocer in the capital, remembering, while the shop-assistant weighed my *parmigiano*, the Crolla grandfather who had died on my brothers' ship.

To the accompaniment of that blaring song about time, I emptied from my shopping bag my companions of recent months: the Penguin Special by Lafitte, John Wheeler-Bennett's biography of Sir John Anderson, Nonno's catapult. Heaviest of all, so I hoisted it only as high as the seat next to mine, Papà's figurine of the boar: it has been with me ever since the drowning, has sat patiently on my desk, staring at me through lidless eyes as I wrote. Last from my bag I lifted the parcel I'd received earlier that week from James Thin's bookshop. I had a good notion of what I'd find in Terri Colpi's *The Italian Factor: The Italian Community in Great Britain*, having been interviewed by the author years before. I skimmed through the chapter headings until I reached Appendix 3. Here was the document I'd been trying for years to extract from Home Office files: a list of all four hundred and forty-six Italians *missing, presumed drowned, from The Arandora Star.*

My cappuccino went cold as I read the list. (It was only when I had climbed the three flights of stairs back home that I realized: I had returned the books to my shopping-bag, the catapult, but had left behind on the café chair Papà's nightmarish statuette of the boar.) Here they were again, aged not a day since last I met them in black shirts or tweed. The Crolla brothers of course, Alfonso *and* Donato (whom Emilio would invoke to persuade me our family could have suffered worse). Then here was *Alfonso Paolozzi,* the famous sculptor's father.

Just before number 320: *Giulio Pezzini.*

Though before I started writing I had been embarrassed by my performance at Emilio's memorial service, now I am glad I did not hold back in front of the two hundred who attended, crammed into the non-denominational 'Meeting House' at Sussex University where, for the final years of his career, my brother had been Distinguished Professor of Italian and Poetry.

Dorothy and their son Carlo had to support my arms as I rose to the lectern. I had chosen to recite 'All Saints', written in the Isle of Man internment camp in '42 and published in Emilio's first collection in '47.

Its opening was easy enough for me:

The first wave surprised us both,
My brother and me, with unholy oil
Blacker than evil, voluptuous trove—
The thick world-blood sucked by human toil
To tankers, liners, Englishmen's engines;
For surface smiled benignly from towering deck.

What followed was harder to utter:

The second tossed us together like apples
Dunked in a barrel for tutti i santi.

Three said I could save him if I grappled
With life-jacket, silenced his ranting,
Avoided the oars of German Herren;
For Moulton's mayday had left the wreck.

By the next stanza, my voice was cracking:

The fourth made him splutter, cold as precious
Ice. He screamed, 'Save yourself! For me! For the wife!
For future bairns!' Five distrained us.
Six, on a beam, took his teeth, almost life,
If life be allowed to us un-Scots-Protestant;
For they'd dragged us from our homes by the neck.

After a pause to take the deepest of breaths, the final verse I had to force out through rekindled fury and resentment, through my awful dawning awareness that I alone was left now: I alone, to tell of my brothers—of that brother, *that* brother, the Emperor of Ice-Cream:

The seventh snatched him from me, overturned,
Submerged, straightened, aliened, apple-cored.
I sharked round his sinking, I screamed
At him to float: 'Live, Giulio!' I roared,
But no echo to the Dago—no 'Eccolo!'
For I nothing; he gone, he morto, he dreck.